H

SNOWBOUND
Together

Four fabulous brand-new stories by

LINDSAY McKENNA
CARA SUMMERS
LAURA MARIE ALTOM
ANNE STUART

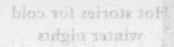

SNOWBOUND
Together

LINDSAY McKENNA
CARA SUMMERS
LAURA MARIE ALTOM
ANNE STUART

M&B™ and M&B™ with the Rose Device
are trademarks of the publisher.
Harlequin Mills & Boon Limited, Eton House,
18-24 Paradise Road, Richmond, Surrey TW9 1SR

SNOWBOUND TOGETHER © Harlequin Books S.A. 2010

A Healing Spirit © Lindsay McKenna 2008
Aunt Delia's Legacy © Carolyn Hanlon 2008
Caught by Surprise © Laura Marie Altom 2008
Star Light, Star Bright © Anne Kristine Stuart Ohlrogge 2004

ISBN: 978 0 263 87700 7

009-0110

Harlequin Mills & Boon policy is to use papers that are
natural, renewable and recyclable products and made from
wood grown in sustainable forests. The logging and
manufacturing processes conform to the legal environmental
regulations of the country of origin.

Printed and bound in Spain
by Litografia Rosés S.A., Barcelona

CONTENTS

A Healing Spirit

LINDSAY McKENNA

Lindsay McKenna is part Eastern Cherokee and has walked the path of her ancestors through her father's training. She is now infusing her books with her many years of experiences in hopes that readers will discover a newfound awe for the magic that is around us in our everyday reality. Her intent is to bring readers compassion and "heart" through her storytelling, for she believes the greatest healer of them all is love.

To the Verde Valley Medical Center staff,
Cottonwood, Arizona, and Dr Barbara Braun
and the Cottonwood floor nurses, who took
such good care of my mother while she
was in the hospital.
Thank you.

CHAPTER ONE

"DIVE LEFT! Dive left!" Corporal Chet Beltran screamed into his microphone.

Marine Corps Captain Tahcha Grant, pilot of the mighty CH-53E Super Stallion, instantly took evasive action. Her aircraft, the largest military helicopter operating in Afghanistan, groaned and shuddered as she gripped the collective tighter, working the rudders. Dammit!

The stress of the unexpected maneuver caused the huge engines to shrill. Out of the corner of her eye, Tahcha saw the missile, a bright yellow light emanating from the barren brown desert below. Her heart rate soared. Her mouth went dry. It felt as if she were going to burst apart from the sudden adrenaline pouring through her body.

"It's a surface-to-air missile!" the crew chief yelled, his voice cracking with terror. "It's comin' right at us!"

Tahcha wheeled the large, unwieldy helicopter to the left, knowing there wasn't much chance of outwitting the missile. Her team was in the mountainous region near the Pakistan border, flying a special ops mission. They had flown under cover of darkness from their air base out on the plains. Hedge-hopping over the peaks of the high mountains, they would sink into the valleys and fly nap-of-the-earth maneuvers to avoid being seen by any Taliban, who lived to shoot down a helo. It was a dangerous business.

With night-vision goggles, a pilot could see through the darkness and fly close to the earth. The only problem was Taliban soldiers watching for such maneuvers, who could nail them with SA-7s—Soviet-made shoulder-launched, heat-seeking missiles. The Taliban's favorite targets were slow-moving helos coming in for a landing, hovering while they unloaded cargo or personnel, and taking off again.

Cursing to herself, Tahcha feverishly worked the controls. Her copilot, Lieutenant Jed Reynolds, grunted. "It's locked on to us!"

With only five hundred feet of clearance from the ground, Tahcha was hemmed in. Dawn was a lurid red band accentuating the jagged mountain peaks on the horizon. Above it she could still see glittering stars. Everything slowed to single frames, as if she were watching a movie unfold. Only it wasn't a movie. It was real life—her life, and the lives of the people on board, for whom she was responsible.

Aware of her heart thudding in her breast, Tahcha felt her breath jam in her lungs. She swung the Super Stallion in a hard left turn. The six blades thumped violently above them to compensate for the unexpected escape strategy. Through the earphones in her helmet, she heard Chet, who was manning one of the side door machine guns, gasping for air.

Sweat popped out on her upper lip. Her mouth became a tight, grim line. Tahcha felt the pull of gravity against the straps of her harness. The light was bad. She'd already pushed the night-vision goggles to the top of her helmet.

Her team had almost reached their objective: a mountain-top forward base, where ten Marines were going to be off-loaded, along with a month's worth of supplies and ammunition. And the ten Marines who had manned the base for thirty days would be brought on board and returned to their unit. Right now, the added weight of the ammunition made her aircraft a helluva lot less maneuverable than she'd like.

Tahcha glanced in horror toward the missile still streaking toward them. Her gaze leaped back to the green glowing instrument panel, then to the deep, gaping canyon below. The air was cool in the high mountains, which hadn't yet unleashed the nasty winds frequently stirred up during the heat of the day. Mind racing, Tahcha saw that there was a mountain peak less than half a mile away. And it was much higher in altitude than their current flight path.

She didn't have the power or distance needed to climb up and over it; the SA-7 would take them out. The heat-seeking missile would lock on to the engines of the Super Stallion; and if it hit them, they were dead. The information scrolled through Tahcha's brain as she continued the tight turn. There was hardly any room to maneuver!

She gripped the controls even harder with her gloved hands. Her entire being was focused on finding a way to avoid getting hit. The heavy vibration of the big chopper, usually comforting to her, raced through her like a jittery warning. She felt beaten up and bruised by the reaction of her bird to the demanding, nearly impossible turn. Teeth clenched, Tahcha watched the canyon floor race up to meet them.

She had been coaxing her stalwart helo toward the base,

now less than a mile away. Tahcha knew they were always most vulnerable to the enemy when landing. Sure enough, a Taliban soldier been waiting patiently among the boulders. And now he had her.

"Evade! Evade!" Beltran shrieked. "It's locked on us! Go left! Dive! Dive!"

Impossible! Tahcha heard Chet's scream. Heard the desperation and terror in his strained Kentucky drawl. She, too, could see the bright light streaking directly toward them. The SA-7 had fixed on to the Super Stallion's heat signature. There was so little room to escape! She took the helicopter down, down, down, flying between two peaks into the canyon beyond.

Suddenly, Tahcha heard her grandmother Willow's ancient, reedy voice in her head, saying, *"It is a good day to die."* Shaken, Tahcha realized her Lakota heritage was leaking into her military world, her reality for the past ten years.

Born on the Rosebud Reservation in South Dakota, Tahcha was one of the few Sioux women to fly, much less serve as a Marine Corps helicopter pilot. Twenty-nine now, she loved flying and was fiercely patriotic. Everyone she knew considered her a warrior. And her grandmother's fateful words were the ones a warrior spoke as she woke up to meet the challenges of a coming day. Warriors realized that every breath could be their last, and that they should value each moment. Whether they lived or died was up to the Great Spirit.

Oddly enough, Tahcha wasn't afraid of dying herself. But she wanted the men on board to survive. She wrestled the behemoth in a tight U-turn to avoid having the blades strike and shatter against the rock cliffs of the canyon. Rage and fear raced through her as she fought to shake the missile off their tail.

Through the sound system in her helmet she heard Jed, her copilot, calling their air base, which they had left hours earlier. He was giving their location and informing them of the attack, his voice wobbly with fright. "Red Rook One to Blue Beach. Mayday! Mayday! We have been fired upon from the ground. We are one mile from Base Bravo. Over…"

The Super Stallion hurtled through the canyon. Tahcha ordered her copilot to push the throttles to full power. The bird strained as she forced it to make a slight, climbing turn to the right. Sometimes an SA-7 could be fooled by a tight, quick turn. Losing track of its target, it would fly on, straight ahead, eventually fizzling out and dropping to earth. Would it this time?

Tahcha couldn't look. All her concentration, her life, her breath, were focused on the rugged walls of the canyon looming up in front of the cockpit Plexiglas. Every muscle in her body screamed with tension. Her fingers ached from gripping the controls so tightly.

"Oh, God…" Reynolds gasped.

"No!" The shriek came from Chet Beltran, who was at the window and could see just how close they were to the canyon walls.

Grunting, Tahcha used every bit of her strength to wheel the Super Stallion up and out of the narrow confines. If one blade touched those rocks, they were dead.

And if she couldn't shake off the missile, it was game over.

Suddenly, every color in front of Tahcha's eyes became luminous, intense. She was aware of perspiration leaking down her armpits and tickling her ribs. Her breathing sounded like bellows rasping in her ears. The *thunk, thunk, thunk* of the chopper blades trying desperately to avoid the oncoming cliff wall drummed through her. Beltran gave a shriek, half fear, half anger. Out of the corner of her eye, Tahcha saw Reynolds raise his hands in front of his face while she fought to pull the Sea Stallion out of danger.

By some miracle, they missed the rocks and climbed out of the canyon. She couldn't see the missile. "Where is it? Where is it?" she yelled, working to bring the helicopter to a rocky slope about half a mile from the base. They were about a hundred feet above the ground.

"It's turned! It's turned back toward us!" Beltran screamed. "Oh, God, we're gonna be hit!"

His words echoed in her ears as she worked the controls to bring the helicopter down. If they got hit, they might have a chance of surviving, close to earth. There was nothing else Tahcha could do. A sense of futility, desperation and sorrow filled her.

Just as the ground raced up to meet them, Tahcha saw something so odd she couldn't believe her eyes. Out of the lurid dawn sky in front of her cockpit Plexiglas flew a huge white owl—a snowy owl. She could see the bird's big, yellow eyes as it soared directly toward her. Its wingspan was impressive, for it was one of the largest owls in North America....

Her mind shorted out as she focused on trying to land the Super Stallion. If the men could only leap out and run to safety before the missile struck...

Tahcha felt the projectile hit the upper engine of the aircraft, causing a sickening, shuddering jolt throughout the helicopter. An explosion followed, an eruption of heat and fire. The screams of her crew pummeled her ears as the helo fell from the sky. As it struck the earth, she saw the white owl fly toward her and enfold her in its mighty wings.

GASPING AND CHOKING, Tahcha jerked up into a sitting position. Sweat drench her as she tried to disconnect from the nightmare. Every breath was an explosive gasp, and she automatically reached for her throat. Opening her eyes, she dazedly realized that she was sitting in a narrow bunk bed, in a small, cold room. Those strangled sounds she heard were her own—sounds of desperation. Of grief. Of rage.

Her eyes burned with tears. Her long black hair slid across her hunched, shaking shoulders. She was dressed in a gray cotton T-shirt beneath the pile of blankets that now pooled around her waist.

Fighting the cries that echoed through her mind, Tahcha gulped and climbed out of bed. Where was she? Weaving unsteadily, she pressed her hand against the pine wall. The coolness of the wooden floor beneath her feet helped her orient herself. Looking toward the small window, the faded blue curtains, she saw that it was dark outside.

Feeling dizzy, she slumped against the wall. The rough surface prickled her skin through the sweaty T-shirt she wore. As soon as she felt the sensation, she remembered where she was.

Pressing her hands to her face, she struggled to escape the terror of reliving the crash on that mountaintop in Afghanistan. Her fingers grew wet with tears, the strands of hair tangled damply around them. Tahcha automatically tried to keep her sobbing silent so as not to awaken her ninety-year-old grandmother. Wapohpah—Gram or Willow—was a light sleeper.

Desperately trying to pull herself together, Tahcha pushed away from the wall. She concentrated on the coolness of the floor and slowly looked around in the bright glow of the night-light. On a wall hook hung an old pink chenille robe. Tahcha grabbed it and pulled on it, attempting to blot out the odors of burning aircraft fuel, the screams of the men trapped in the rear of the helicopter, the terror that still thrummed through every particle of her being.

Sobbing and hiccuping, she pressed her fist against her parted lips. *Quiet!* She had to be quiet! Grandmother Willow's bedroom was just across the hall. Tahcha had lost count of how many times she'd awakened her since coming to live with her on the Rosebud Lakota Reservation. She purposely kept her door closed because of her nightly dreams.

She sniffled and pulled tissues from a box on the pine dresser near the door. After blowing her nose, she raised her arm and wiped her face with the sleeve of her robe. Desperation drove her out the door. The only way to escape these nightmares was to get up and do something. Anything! Driven down the darkened hall, Tahcha saw that her grandmother's bedroom door was closed. She hoped she hadn't awakened the elder once again. The cabin was small with two bedrooms and one bathroom

As Tahcha wove unsteadily toward the kitchen, and the potbellied wood stove, she saw a glow of light ahead. She glanced at her watch. It was barely 5:00 a.m.

Tahcha halted in the doorway. Dressed in her old green Pendleton wool robe, Grandmother Willow sat at the small wooden table, her swollen arthritic hands wrapped around a white ceramic mug.

"Oh, I didn't mean to—"

"You didn't," the old woman said. "Come, I've made sage tea for you. It will help. Sit with me."

Just hearing her grandmother's husky voice instantly soothed some of Tahcha's roiling emotions. She stumbled to the table.

It was warm in the kitchen. She realized belatedly that her grandmother must have gotten up earlier to stir the coals left in the cast-iron stove, and build up the fire. Usually, the log cabin was freezing on a January winter morning until one of them awoke and stoked the fire.

Grateful, Tahcha sat down. She pushed her hair behind her shoulders and, ashamed of her tears, wiped her cheeks again. Finally, she stole a look at the old woman. Gram Willow's large brown eyes were surrounded with wrinkles, but glowed with kindness.

"T-thank you for the tea." Tahcha grasped her mug with shaking fingers, relishing its warmth. She lifted the cup and inhaled the sage's fragrance, then started sipping it. Drinking the healing infusion finally started bringing her back to the present, and out of the horror of the past.

She sat for many minutes listening to the fire crackle and pop in the stove. The soothing house sounds helped further dissolve the nightmare.

"Sacred sage always helps those who are ailing," Gram Willow murmured as she sipped from her own cup. "The spirits of this plant are powerful, and they love us. They want to see us get well."

Tahcha set the cup down in front of her, but didn't let go of it. It was an anchor to the here and now, serving to keep her mind off the horrifying past. Away from her shame. "I love this tea, Gram. I remember my mom making it for me when I was sick, sad or hurt." Tahcha managed a wobbly, grateful smile. "I really missed having it after we left the res. But Dad had to go where the money was. He wanted a better life for me."

Grandmother Willow nodded, "They did what they felt was right, Tahcha. You were young when they moved away, but I know it was hard for you. You lost your friends, the home where you were born, and perhaps worst of all, the ways of our people. You went into the white man's world. I missed you so much when you went out to the West Coast. In all those years afterward, I saw your family only once. Money was hard to come by and your dad and mom both worked. They were saving for your college education, so I understood why you couldn't make it back here."

She laid her work-worn hand across Tahcha's and gazed at her. The love shining in those aged, watery eyes made Tahcha feel less torn up internally. She squeezed her grandmother's hand gently in response. "I didn't want to move.

I remember crying the day day we left. I didn't understand what was happening."

"I know. I cried, too. I saw your face and felt your heart. You lost your world when you left. But you're back." She gave Tahcha a tender smile. "You've come home, as it should be. And you live with me. I'm grateful, because you are such a gift to my heart, *Tagoza,* Granddaughter."

Tahcha squeezed her eyes shut. She couldn't bear the love shimmering in her grandmother's gaze. "I came home ashamed, Grandmother. Defeated. I lost twelve men's lives! After the crash, the death of the men I was supposed to protect, I couldn't function anymore. I—I just couldn't fly. I was afraid to climb back into a helicopter. I embarrassed my people. Our nation is made up of honorable warriors. We aren't supposed to be afraid. But I was a coward. I called it quits. I left the Marine Corps and stopped flying. And I came crawling home to your doorstep like a beaten dog."

"Shh, stop being so hard on yourself, Tahcha! The Great Spirit brings many situations our way. All he asks is that we try to work through them. We don't have to be victorious. We're allowed to fail. But listen to me." Her grandmother's voice became firmer. "You may have failed, but not for lack of trying. I would call you a coward if you had run. But you did not. I would say you failed if you hadn't tried to avoid that missile that hit your helicopter. But you did everything you could. It simply was not enough. I thank the Great Spirit for saving your life. You could have died, too."

Miserably, Tahcha whispered, "On most days, Grandma,

I *want* to die. I don't know why I survived. I don't want to live. To live is to remember those twelve men. So many children without their fathers, wives without their husbands...."

"You need help, Tahcha. You came back home to heal."

Nodding, she glanced at her grandmother's kind face. "Y-yes. I guess some part of me wants to heal, but I don't know how. Almost every night I have horrible nightmares about the crash. If I drive into town to get you groceries, a sound, a smell, will send me back to that day on the mountain."

"I know, I know," Gram Willow said soothingly, patting Tahcha's damp cheek. "But you were saved. By a spirit owl, from what you've told me. That white owl is important, don't you think?"

Tahcha hung her head. "I—I don't know. I can't explain it. I felt as if it was protecting me from getting killed. It's silly, but that's what it felt like the moment it curled its wings around me."

"And you were the only one to survive that crash," Grandmother Willow stated with finality. She was silent for a long moment, then added, "Take heart, my beautiful *tagoza,* there is help."

"Where?"

"There is a medicine man in training here on our res. I happen to know that his main spirit guide is a white owl." She raised her steel-gray eyebrows as she pinned Tahcha with her gaze.

"Really?" Tahcha sat up, feeling a glimmer of hope.

"Yes. I am sure that this man can help you, heal you. Will

you go see him today? He lives twenty miles from here, up in the hills to the north."

"Truly? He has a white owl for his guide?" Tahcha's mind raced. She knew medicine men and women could heal a person's spirit. And her spirit was badly damaged by the experience of the crash.

Grandmother Willow nodded. "Yes, Tahcha, he does."

"That's great. I'll go see him. What's his name?"

Willow gripped Tahcha's hand and stared deeply into her teary eyes. "Keehonsheca."

Shock bolted through Tahcha and she reared back. "What?"

"You heard me. Keehonsheca. Storm Black Horse. He's no stranger to you. As young children, you were playmates. And when you reached your teens, you fell in love— remember? He left the reservation, too, but came back home a few years ago, after serving in the military. Home to study the ways of healing medicine, because he's descended from a line of well-respected medicine men and women. I know you lost touch with him when you left the res. But I believe Storm can help you now, Tahcha. And I believe the white spirit owl you saw was Storm protecting you. He always did, even when you were children."

Tahcha squeezed her eyes shut once more. She felt as if a was tornado whirling within her. Pressing her hand against her wildly beating heart, she whispered, "Oh no, Grandmother, I couldn't go see him. I couldn't…."

CHAPTER TWO

TAHCHA WASN'T SURE which was worse, living through her horrifying post-traumatic stress disorder flashbacks or having to face Storm Black Horse. She was ashamed at how low she had sunk, and didn't want Storm to see her in this condition. Storm had always been so perfect in her eyes. And she was anything but perfect; a mere shadow of her former self, the girl he'd fallen in love with so long ago. Showing up at his door fragmented, deeply wounded on so many levels, brought up a terrible fear in her. Storm wouldn't recognize her.

Tahcha drove slowly across the res. The asphalt road, plowed and salted, was a black ribbon across the white landscape, where a thick blanket of snow sparkled like diamonds in the early afternoon sunlight. Yellow-brown grass and bare-limbed bushes stuck up through the snow. The sky was pale blue, streaked with high cirrus clouds that reminded Tahcha of a horse's mane flowing in the wind. Homes she passed had smoke pouring from their chimneys because of the freezing temperature.

She nervously shifted her grip on the steering wheel of her Toyota Corolla. The pavement was clear and dry, so there was no concern about sliding on black ice. To her right, she saw tall, sturdy fence posts. Shaggy, dark brown shapes appeared behind them—a herd of buffalo. A good feeling moved through her. Buffalo and Native Americans were synonymous. She was glad to see them once again.

Since coming to live with her grandmother in December, Tahcha hadn't been out and about on the reservation very much. She'd stuck to the small cabin, helping her grandmother with chopping wood, cleaning and cooking, and sometimes buying groceries. Those things helped her feel more emotionally stable. She was so grateful to Gram Willow for sharing her cabin until Tahcha could somehow get past the nightmares.

Her thoughts swung back to Storm Black Horse. Their families had lived a mile apart, here on the res. Being the same age, she and Storm had grown up together, and in grade school, had become inseparable. There had been an almost magical connection between them. When they'd reached their teens, Tahcha had fallen in love with black-haired, brown-eyed Storm Black Horse, and he had loved her just as fiercely. That last year on the res had been the happiest of her life.

Sighing, Tahcha touched her aviator sunglasses. As a child, she didn't know what love was, only that she'd looked forward to seeing Storm daily at school or when their families visited one another. And then, at puberty, he'd become the center of her world....

Their idyll shattered when they were both fifteen, and their families moved off the reservation. Frowning, Tahcha remembered the awful pain of having to tell Storm the news. They'd stood beneath the trees behind the football field and she'd cried. Storm had told her that his family was moving, too. Tahcha had gasped, thrown her arms around him and sobbed.

"Teenagers," she muttered now, shaking her head. She had another ten miles to go before reaching the dirt road leading to Storm's ranch. Gram Willow's directions were on the passenger seat, but Tahcha had already memorized them.

She couldn't help recalling the time when she and Storm had parted. His parents had moved off the reservation in order to find more lucrative work, but had headed to the East Coast, to New Jersey, where his father hoped to find a job in the shipyards. Her family had moved west, to California, where her father had a job as a master carpenter waiting for him.

"What a time that was," she muttered to herself. She and Storm had cried in each other's arms. Storm had pressed desperate kisses on her wet cheeks and lips as they'd said goodbye to one another. Tahcha had never heard from him again. She didn't get an address, since Storm had had no idea where they would end up living. And her family didn't, either. And so their connection—and their hearts— had been broken....

Tahcha shrugged her shoulders to loosen them. Why was she so afraid of seeing Storm? She didn't have a clear answer, only fears that he'd be disappointed in her. She let a blue pickup pass her. She was driving slowly, on purpose. Her feelings were in utter turmoil.

Once again she found her mind drifting back, this time to when she was seven. Storm had saved her from drowning at a school picnic on the last day of school at a favorite swimming pond. Tahcha had made the mistake of gorging herself, and jumping into the water shortly after. She'd gotten stomach cramps and started to sink, and Storm had dived in to rescue her. Tahcha recalled how she'd thought of him as a hero. Her hero. From that moment on, she'd trusted him with her life. Could she now, or was that connection gone? Unsure, she wiped her upper lip in a nervous gesture.

After Storm, she never thought she'd get attached to another man. After college in California, she'd focused on her career. She'd been a member of ROTC and decided she wanted to become a pilot in the Marine Corps. Her father and grandfather had both been in the Corps and she wanted to follow in their footsteps.

Loving to fly, Tahcha had applied for the program shortly after graduating from officer's training, and had gotten in. By the time she was twenty-four years old, she was on her way to Afghanistan for the first of two tours, as a copilot on a CH-47 helicopter. And it was there that she'd met Dan Collins.

Grimacing, Tahcha watched the speedometer as another car passed her. Only five miles to the turnoff to Storm's home.

Her engagement, Tahcha knew, had been a mistake. And she realized something else: Dan looked a lot like Storm. Her ex-fiancé had black hair and dancing brown eyes, and was tall and lean just like Storm had been as a teenager. Rubbing her brow, Tahcha wondered if she had unconsciously seen something of Storm in Dan, and hadn't made the connection. Could her love for Storm have lasted this long without her noticing? It was no wonder she'd been attracted to Dan, and no surprise that their engagement had fallen apart.

Dan had been a lieutenant, like herself, and he, too, flew as a copilot on the CH-47s stationed at Bagram Air Base. But his love of drinking had driven a wedge into their friendship. In truth, he was a closet alcoholic, and Tahcha wasn't about to marry someone like that. She'd always been aware that most Native Americans had trouble handling alcohol because they lacked the enzyme to break it down. She'd shunned alcoholic beverages as a result.

As she slowed the car approaching Storm's road, her heart rate soared. Tahcha felt fear and hope intertwine. Gripping the wheel, she made the turn and inched up the deeply rutted road among the snow-covered hills. After the engagement ended, Tahcha hadn't bothered looking for a love life. Why was that? She was eligible. Moderately attractive. Her youthful connection with Storm had been with her all along, probably. That might explain why she'd never really been drawn to another man as she had to Storm. Tahcha longed to speak to Gram Willow about her thoughts, but that couldn't happen until later today. Right now, she had a date with destiny, or at least the past.

The road twisted among the hills like a lazy snake. At the end of the road, Tahcha saw a large white ranch house, its dark green roof the same color as the trim. Power poles brought electricity to his home. Not all homes on the res had electricity but his did. Near it was a corral, where two horses were eating hay, and a small red barn. The bucolic scene sent a soothing wave through her raw emotions. Gray smoke was drifting out of the redbrick chimney, she noticed. A muddy black Toyota Tundra pickup stood outside a two-car garage next to the house.

There was a large graveled parking area in front, which made Tahcha think many people must come for Storm's healing. Another clue was the deeply rutted road. For whatever reason, that made Tahcha feel good.

The Storm of her youth had been a kind boy with dancing, cinnamon-colored eyes, and long black hair that swung around his face. He'd been very thin as a child, but supple and strong. Tahcha wondered what he looked like now. How had life treated him?

As she pulled into the parking area, Tahcha felt herself becoming anxious and frightened. She turned off the engine, slowly removed her sunglasses and put them away. Did she have the courage to get out of this car, go up to that door and knock? Gram Willow had called Storm this morning and made the appointment for her. Would he remember their connection? Tahcha gripped the door handle and opened it.

The brisk, cold air hit her. From the seat she picked up two wands of sacred sage wrapped in red yarn. One never visited a medicine person without bringing a gift of respect and honor. She felt a sense of familiarity now, following the protocol. Tahcha had missed being involved in such traditions. Her parents had tried to instill their values and beliefs in her as she grew up in the white man's world, but they had been so busy. Tahcha had missed going to a weekly sweat lodge especially, a ceremony ensuring cleanliness of spirit, mind, heart and body.

Holding the sage now made her feel more stable as she made her way across the patches of snow on the pebbled driveway.

It was time.

As she raised her hand to knock on the door, she decided she had never felt so scared. Not even when her Sea Stallion had been struck by that missile. Gulping, she knocked.

Gram Willow's words came back to her: *A warrior is not fearless. She reacts or acts despite her fear. That is true courage.* Right now, Tahcha felt anything but courageous. She was little more than a lump of jelly inside, and her knees felt weak to boot. Some warrior she was.

The door opened.

"Tahcha?" Storm Black Horse's deep, calming voice flowed over her.

Tahcha stared up at the man who stood there. Well over six feet tall, he seemed like a pillar of strength. Her gaze was instantly drawn to his composed features, and to his mesmerizing, cinnamon-colored eyes.

Though he was twenty-nine years of age, his face already had life experiences written upon it. There were crow's-feet at the corners of his eyes. Slash marks on either side of his mouth told Tahcha he'd experienced a lot of pain. Faint lines ran horizontally across his broad brow. He wore a dark blue cowboy shirt, the sleeves rolled up to expose muscular forearms and work-worn hands. His jeans emphasized narrow hips and long, powerful legs. His black hair glinted as it fell across his broad shoulders and halfway down his chest.

More than anything, his warm strength struck Tahcha.

"Storm?" It was all she could manage. Her heart was racing and heat flooded her face. Even though her skin had a coppery tone like his, she was sure he noticed her blushing. How mortifying.

"I was surprised when Gram Willow called me," he said in that deep, mellow voice.

Tahcha could only stare up at him. Her childhood friend had changed so much, maturing into a very handsome man. She opened her mouth and then closed it, at a loss for words.

Tension hung palpably between them. Could he help her? Would their past interfere with the present? More importantly, was he angry at her for disappearing from his life? A million thoughts careened through her in that split second as she watched him intently.

A bolt of lightning coursed through Storm. He couldn't speak. The past deluged him as he held Tahcha's gaze. A barrage of emotions—loss, grief, sadness and anger—slammed through him. And then a bitter sweetness followed. He felt poleaxed by her sudden and unexpected reappearance in his life. How should he handle this?

"Come on in," he managed to murmur.

Relief jagged through Tahcha. She handed Storm the sage wands. "These are for you...."

The moment their fingers touched, electrical shocks raced up her hand and arm. She quickly jerked away. Rubbing her clammy palm down her thigh, she stepped past him through the door.

She scanned the interior of the house. The hall was clean, the reddish-gold cedar floor shining. A sense of peace in the house struck Tahcha as she turned and waited for Storm. He was staring at her as if she were an alien who'd just landed on his doorstep. Well, hadn't she?

His mind whirling, Storm struggled for something to say. A thousand questions begged to be asked. Gruffly, he said, "Follow me. We'll go to the kitchen. I've got some sage tea brewing. We can talk in there."

Tahcha nodded, still tongue-tied. Storm moved with the grace of his family's totem animal, the horse. He was whipcord lean and radiated a sense of calm and confidence she longed to have.

She hung her coat and scarf on a wall hook in the hall. She removed her boots and put them on a designated area of the rug. Padding on her sock feet, she quickly caught up with Storm.

He opened the door to the kitchen and she stepped in. The room, large and airy, was painted a pale yellow. The curtains at the window were something a man would choose, Tahcha thought—a boring dark brown. The rectangular table, made from the wood of the sacred cottonwood tree, was surrounded by four straight-backed chairs. The kitchen counter was clean and bare; he'd recently washed a few dishes and left them to dry on the drain board. The whole space was simple, spare and clean.

"Thanks for seeing me on such short notice, Storm," she said, her voice still strained. If only that tension would ebb. But it hurt to be here with Storm, and Tahcha felt like a blubbering teenager all over again. Rolling her shoulders to try to ease her nerves, she started to reach for a chair, but he pulled it out for her.

"Today is my day to visit elders. I chop wood for them, to make sure they have heat and don't freeze in this weather," he told her, trying to keep the gruffness out of his tone. "I've got a couple of hours before I have to go do that. When did you get back to the res?" He walked to the stove and took the copper kettle off the fire.

Scooting her chair up to the table, Tahcha continued to absorb the homey feeling in the kitchen. "Uh, early December." She wondered if Storm was married. She'd seen no wedding band on his long, well-shaped hand. Children? The house seemed too quiet. Tahcha was dying to find out what had happened to Storm during the years since she'd last seen him. It took everything she had not to ask, since posing such personal questions was considered rude in their culture. If he wanted to volunteer information, he would.

Humiliation once again swept through her. Knotting and unknotting her hands beneath the table, Tahcha felt like a worm crawling back into Storm's life. She just didn't know how he would react to her after all these years.

He poured tea into two dark blue mugs and placed the tea kettle back on the stove. "What brought you home?"

Words stuck in her throat as she tried to answer. Storm brought the mugs over and set one in front of her. He pointed to the jar of honey between them and provided her with a spoon. When he settled down opposite her, Tahcha nervously opened the honey jar. "I—well, it's a long story."

Storm nodded and waited until she was done adding the sweetener to her sage tea. "And that's why you're here?" he guessed, picking up the jar and digging his spoon into the dark gold clover honey. Feelings writhed like a knot of snakes in his gut. She was incredibly beautiful now. Even more so than when she was a teen. Storm swallowed hard and scowled.

Giving a jerky nod, Tahcha sipped her hot tea. Her hands gripped the mug after she'd set it down. She couldn't look into his narrowed, searching eyes. "This is hard, Storm. I'm so scared…."

"Life is scary," he agreed. How he wanted to reach out and grasp Tahcha's hands. She had no idea how hard he was fighting himself. Fourteen years had passed since he'd last seen her, with no contact. No communication. Just the aching heart of a teenage boy who had pined away for his love for so many years.

And finally, bitterly, Storm had given up on ever finding her again. But now Tahcha was here. Sitting opposite him at his kitchen table. He reeled internally at her sudden presence. But she was here to see him as a medicine man, not as someone who had once spent every waking moment with her, at school or with their families.

Tahcha managed to look over at Storm when he wryly said those words. "I…guess I never thought of life as scary until recently. Now, I'm scared all the time, and I can't handle it." She whispered brokenly, "I know I've shamed myself, and I feel so guilty, Storm. I didn't know where to go or who to turn to. I came back here an emotional basket case after resigning from the Marine Corps. All the doctors wanted to do was put me on tranquilizers and talk about what happened. None of that was helping. It just made it worse."

Eyes narrowing, he said, "Marine Corps? I heard from Gram Willow that you had gone into the military after I came back here. I didn't know which service. You went into the military?" That blew him away. For years after their separation, Storm had dreamed of Tahcha being his wife, happy to cook meals, to carry his children and to live a wonderful, useful life with him on the res. That showed him how distorted his dreams had been. He hadn't thought Tahcha would ever choose something so harsh and challenging as a military career. How wrong he'd been.

"When we moved away, Storm, my family settled in San Diego. My dad got a job as a civilian carpenter at the Marine Corps boot camp base located near the airport. He'd been in the Corps when he was younger, and so had my grandpa." Tahcha gave Storm a strained look. "My family moved off the res to give me a better education. I went to university in San Diego and majored in Aeronautical Engineering. Along the way, I entered ROTC. My parents wanted me to follow what felt right to me. I liked the military because it was disciplined and organized. More than anything, I appreciated how everyone worked together as a team. I really needed that feeling back in my life."

"I see…." Storm took a sip of his sage tea and nearly burned his tongue. His gut knotted even more, though he tried to breathe deeply.

Tahcha saw turmoil in Storm's cinnamon eyes. She couldn't guess what was behind his expression. But she understood that in order for a medicine person to decide how to heal a patient, he or she needed to know everything. The whole truth, not parts of it. "I loved to fly. When I flew

I was happy. It felt like I was back on the res. Since leaving my birthplace, it's been as though a part of me was missing, and flying filled that emptiness."

"Your spirit always resides where you were born," Storm muttered. "No matter how far away you go, home is home."

Nodding, she sipped her tea again and said, "I'm finding that out right now. Just being here, I no longer feel homesick. I love the smell of wrapped sage when I walk into my gram's house. I love tasting this tea. It makes me feel alive again." She ran her fingers around the rim of her cup.

Just that graceful, fleeting gesture made Storm's lower body twist into a hot, fiery tangle. Caught by surprise, he ruthlessly squelched the sensation. Hadn't he learned that women were nothing but pain and trouble? His hellish three-year marriage to Belinda Evans should have reminded him even if his foolish body didn't. Forcing himself to concentrate, Storm said, "I remember when you were a little girl, you used to throw out your arms and run around the playground, pretending you were an eagle flying. Do you recall that?"

Tahcha gave him a sad smile. "I did, didn't I? I'd forgotten."

"You loved hawks and eagles. You were pretty good at imitating their whistles, too."

Giving him a long look, Tahcha said, "I thought you'd forgotten about me...us.... It's been so long, Storm." Her heart did a funny flip-flop at the look in his eyes. As children, Tahcha always knew when Storm was happy because his eyes glinted with gold. Now all she could see was warmth mingled with surprise in his gaze.

Storm gripped his mug with both hands and stared into it. "I guess I haven't. When you left, I was pretty heartbroken. And I stayed that way for a long time." His voice hardened and he stared over at her. "A lot of time has gone by. And things are different."

The steeliness of his tone should have been a warning. But Tahcha reached out and slid her fingers across the back of his hand, which had many small, pink scars. His fingers were long and beautifully formed, reminding her more of an artist than anything else. Yet as her fingertips grazed his warm, taut flesh, Tahcha sensed the quiet power and strength that lay beneath his coppery skin. Withdrawing her hand, she felt the heat of a blush rush into her face once more. Maybe it was because Storm's head snapped up, that burning look back in his eyes.

"I'm sorry. I shouldn't have done that." Tahcha tried to smile, but failed. "We used to touch so much as kids. Remember? We were always holding hands. You'd hug me sometimes. And I'd chase you around when we played outside, catch you and hug you back."

"I'd forgotten, Tahcha." Storm hadn't, much to his consternation, but he was damned if she was going to know the truth. The look in her shining dark eyes had always reminded him of the moon casting silvery rays across a quiet pond at night. Storm saw the pain there now, noted how some of the light was gone. As a medicine person, he understood that whatever had happened to her had wounded her spirit. It made him groan inwardly, feeling as if an invisible knife had scored his own heart. He couldn't stand to see the pain and suffering that Tahcha was carrying. He had to know what had happened to her.

His voice a low growl, he said, "Tell me what happened, Tahcha. Why *are* you here?"

CHAPTER THREE

IT TOOK EVERY LAST SHRED of Storm's willpower to sit there for an hour and listen to Tahcha's story. Time seemed to stand still, and in his heart, he felt the pain she had experienced in the crash and its aftermath.

"There's one last thing you need to know, Storm," she whispered, her voice raw.

"What?" What else could she possibly tell him? What Tahcha had gone through, the guilt she carried, was heart wrenching.

"When the crash happened, I knew I was going to die." One corner of her mouth hitched upward for a moment. Giving him a long, searching look, she related, "I saw a beautiful white owl flying directly at me as my helo crashed to the ground—a snowy owl. The missile had already struck us. The cabin was filled with fire and smoke, and I felt I was going to die. But then, as the Plexiglas exploded around me, this white owl came out of nowhere, swooped down and enclosed me in its wings. And then I lost consciousness.

"I awoke later at the mountain base, with the Marines taking care of me. I had severe burns on my neck and arms, and my right shoulder was dislocated. They told me I was the only one to survive. They said they didn't know how I had, because the fire was so bad they couldn't get close to the burning helo. The sergeant who rescued me said I was lying unconscious, halfway out of the shattered cockpit. He told me that the weirdest thing happened. When he and his men were trying to get close enough to help us, a wind suddenly came up and pushed the fire back. They were able to drag me, and the body of my copilot, Jed Reynolds, out of there. And the wind stopped as soon as they got us clear of the wreckage."

Storm looked at her in surprise. "A white owl?"

"I saw it, Storm. As real as you and me." Tahcha noticed the turbulence in his narrowed eyes and the grim set of his well-shaped mouth. She tried not to look at Storm's mouth too often, but it was impossible at this moment. And for no reason, she wanted to kiss him. Of all things! In the middle of relating one of the worst experiences in her life, something inside her urged her to kiss this man. Tahcha pushed the feeling away, deciding it must be due to their childhood past.

Storm was watching her in silence.

Shifting in the chair, Tahcha said, "Gram Willow told me you have a white owl spirit that you work with as a medicine man. That's why she called you. She said you were the one who could help me heal." Tahcha watched as Storm studied the empty mug between his hands. Swallowing hard, she whispered, "Well, will you? Will you help me with a ceremony, Storm? I can't sleep. When I do manage to doze off for an hour or two, I have this ongoing repeat of the crash. I—I can't get rid of the dream. I'm haunted, and I don't want to live…."

Tahcha's last words chilled Storm. He lifted his head and gazed into her soft, dark brown eyes that swam with unshed tears. Tahcha was fighting not to cry, but her full lower lip trembled. Repressing every desire to reach out, touch her and hold her, he said gruffly, "You've lost part of your spirit, Tahcha. This can happen when a person suffers some shocking tragedy, as you have."

Tahcha was unable to read his expression, but he sounded grim. Why would he be? Mind spinning, she felt too vulnerable and desperate to try to figure out why. "Is there a ceremony for this?"

"Yes, there is." He got to his feet, the chair scraping noisily on the linoleum. He walked to the sink, rinsed his cup and set it on the counter. As he looked out the window toward the snow-covered hills, he said, "A doctoring sweat lodge is what is needed, Tahcha. I'll try to call back your spirit." He turned and rested his hip against the counter. Tahcha seemed so broken and exhausted. He could barely hold her gaze, which suddenly shone with hope.

"Thank you, Storm. You have no idea how this helps me, just knowing there's something we can try."

Her words rankled, more than they should have. Tahcha wasn't the first to say that to him; many of his patients did. They came to him in pain, wanting relief from their suffering. As a medicine man, he couldn't guarantee an outcome, for the spirits dictated that. Storm wanted a positive outcome for her. "Look, we'll do the sweat, but the Great Spirit decides what will be done, Tahcha. All I am is a go-between for you and Wakan Tonka. I'm not sure you can be healed."

"I—I understand. But I do need help. I've nowhere else to turn." She rallied beneath his upbeat words and she saw confidence radiating from Storm.

And how Storm wanted to give her some support! He was frozen against the counter, his body screaming at him to walk over to her, lift her out of that chair and hold her close. He couldn't do that. A medicine person never crossed that line with a patient. Tahcha was here for help and healing. She wasn't here to renew an old relationship with him.

Disgruntled with himself over his unexpected reaction to her, Storm moved away from the counter. He walked around the warm kitchen, his arms crossed on his chest. Finally, he turned and stared at Tahcha. "I was in the Marine Corps myself, from age eighteen to twenty-one. I was a grunt. A rifleman. I was sent over to Afghanistan after boot camp. So I understand your experience. I did my share of riding in CH-53s. They'd drop us in the white mountains to search the Tora Bora caves and we'd hunt down Taliban. Helos and the pilots who flew them were always a target."

Tahcha looked at him in surprise, then abruptly relaxed in the chair. "I didn't know that, Storm! But I'm glad you were there. I mean, because you know what it was like over there…." Her voice wavered momentarily. Fighting back tears yet again, she was aware of a joy thrumming through her. She hadn't expected Storm to have been in the Marine Corps, not to mention having served in Afghanistan. Similar experiences connected people emotionally. Being in the military was always a strong link.

Storm nodded. "Funny how our lives ran parallel. I would

never have thought you'd go into the Corps much less become a helicopter pilot." His frosty tone warmed a little. "You always wanted to fly when you were a little kid. Even then—"

He stopped abruptly. Remembering the past only brought up an old ache and yearning Storm had squashed as a teenager. He thought he'd gotten Tahcha out of his system, removed from his heart. Apparently not. And it caused him great consternation.

How the hell was he going to keep the distance he needed as a medicine man, to work effectively for her? To create a doctoring ceremony to call back her spirit? Storm wasn't sure. In an attempt at self-control, he savagely reminded himself he'd already been married and it had turned ugly. A relationship wasn't in his future after that terrible, traumatic experience.

"Come on," he coaxed, heading for the kitchen door. "I've got to visit some elders. You feel like chopping wood with me? It will give them fuel for their fires for the next couple of days."

"Why...sure. That's what I do for Gram Willow." Tahcha smiled and held up her hands. "Look, I've even got calluses."

The look of hope burning in Tahcha's wide, lovely eyes was enough to make Storm weak in the knees. "Maybe some fresh air and sunshine and a little hard work will make you feel better until I can get the doctoring sweat lodge ready for you."

Scooting the chair away from the table, Tahcha stood up. "Sure, physical work helps me. It stabilizes me, Storm. I'm not proud to admit this…but I'm a mess. I know that. Chopping wood feels good. It grounds me."

"Okay, let's get going." Storm waited while she washed out her cup. Great Spirit help him, but her every movement was so fluid, so graceful. Watching her sent a burning ache through his body. The word *tahcha* in Lakota meant deer. Just like the animal she was named for, Tahcha was so slender and lithe. Sucking in a sharp breath, Storm turned away and opened the door. He couldn't have Tahcha. Not like that. Not ever.

It was up to him to fight his carnal desire. She was entrusting herself to him as a medicine man. And his selfish urge to walk over, take her into his arms and carry her to his bedroom was folly at best. Storm refused to break that promise to her by surrendering to his physical needs.

"A GOOD AFTERNOON'S WORK," Tahcha said as they drove back to Storm's house at sunset. She looked over and gave him a weary smile. His profile was set. He seemed unhappy, and she couldn't understand why. Maybe because of the white owl event? Tahcha didn't know and was afraid to ask. In her state of sleep deprivation she often misinterpreted people's facial expressions, voice inflections or decisions. She wasn't in a good space, but today, her heart was filled with hope.

"Yes, six elders' homes will stay warm now." Storm looked at the clouds in the darkening sky, which were edged with pink and gold. "Your help made it easier. We got a lot more supplied with firewood than if I was working alone." Tahcha had labored hard alongside him. He was pleased to see she was a worker bee who took responsibility seriously. But then, she had the discipline of the military behind her, where once you started a job, you finished it. Storm didn't want to admit how light and happy he'd felt with her at his side. It was just like old times....

"We were always a team," Tahcha murmured, watching the highway. Two pickup trucks ahead of them had their headlights on. The daylight was almost gone. Ordinarily, she would fear the night, but right now, she didn't. Glancing at Storm's stoic profile, she laughed briefly. "You know, when we were kids, we worked like we did today. Funny how some things never change, isn't it?"

Her musing left him feeling ragged inside. Tightening his hands on the steering wheel, Storm muttered, "Yeah, but that was the past, Tahcha. A lot of things *have* changed since we used to help our parents carry in wood for the stove." Their homes had been only a mile apart, an easy walking distance. Storm vividly recalled how, come autumn, their families would chop up fallen trees, gather the limbs and put them in their pickup trucks, then take them home to be cut into firewood for their stoves.

Storm remembered those times more often than he cared to admit. Their families had been close, and as children and teens he and Tahcha had always worked and played together. Today, Storm realized, had been a mistake on his part. He shouldn't have invited her along. He should have told her to go home. But he hadn't. He had given in to a secret desire to have her near him for just a little while.

Tahcha heard the warning in Storm's low, husky voice. *That was the past.* Yes, it had been. Compressing her lips, she said, "You're right, things have changed." And then she brightened and smiled wistfully. "You have no idea how often I've replayed our time together, especially since the crash. It gave me peace for just a little bit, Storm."

Her words enflamed his heart and touched his spirit. "Your parents named you after an animal that's completely vulnerable except for being able to run from its enemies." He glanced at her once more. Her black hair was in mild disarray around her oval face, but she looked lovely. "I just never figured you for the military."

Giving a short laugh, Tahcha met and held his searching gaze until he focused again on driving. "What? Deer people are too soft? Too vulnerable for hard military life?"

Shrugging, Storm said, "I don't know. I guess, growing up without you, I had all kinds of fantasies about you. How you were, what was going on, what you were doing…"

"What did you think?" she asked softly.

Tahcha saw his lower lip thin for a moment. Dying to talk to him as a man, a person, as her best friend from childhood, she wondered if she'd overstepped her bounds. He was a medicine man, and to inquire about such private things was considered rude. Was that why his mouth tightened for a moment?

He didn't say, *I used to have dreams about you after we left the res, and we went east and your family went west.* Storm didn't tell her he'd cried himself to sleep one night after they'd been torn apart. His grief over their separation was just too much to bear. "I wondered about your schooling. I know your parents left the res to find better-paying jobs. They wanted the best for you. They knew education was important. I wondered what school you were in and what topics you were taking. You always loved reading and language. I thought maybe you'd become a schoolteacher." *Or a wonderful wife to a man who loved you to pieces and felt like the luckiest man alive.* Those words stuck like a rock in his throat.

"Funny thing, Storm," Tahcha said quietly, "that was one of the things I thought about becoming. A teacher. You weren't wrong."

"You're a natural teacher, Tahcha. You always have been. I guess I always saw you in class teaching little kids, having fun, laughing and helping them."

Tahcha sighed. "I'm not surprised you picked up on that, since you knew me so well. You and I were together since we could walk."

"But when our families left the res and went to different coasts, we didn't stay in touch."

"No," Tahcha murmured. "But then, we're Indians. We usually don't pick up the phone to chat, or write. It's not our way."

"I know. I guess our parents thought it was the end of a cycle, and that was the reason they didn't try to stay in touch. Money was hard to come by, and they probably figured it would be hard to travel the width of the U.S. to visit one another."

"No argument there," she acknowledged.

The evening was beginning to chase away the last traces of sunset. Tahcha felt such peace being in the cab of the truck with Storm. That same wonderful sensation of closeness she'd known in their youth gently enveloped her once more.

"I wanted to stay in touch with you, Storm, but life was so tough. We were struggling just to survive out in San Diego. I realized there was no money left over for much of anything. We didn't have a telephone until I was eighteen. We just couldn't afford it. We called Gram then to stay in touch. My mom told me that she missed the res and your parents more than anyone, apart from Gram. One day I walked in on her and caught her crying, and I felt so terrible. I'd been homesick for the res myself for so long. And for you..." Tahcha stole a quick look at Storm. His mouth was a thin line, as if he, too, was holding in emotion.

He waved his hand. "We know that lack of education hurts us as a people, as a nation. But back then—" he glanced at her again "—none was available to us."

"A sad state of affairs," Tahcha agreed. "So what happened to *you,* Storm? You said you went into the Marines at age eighteen."

"I went in because my father broke his back. He was working as a ship welder when he fell off some scaffolding, and the rest is history. He was paralyzed from the neck down. All the money my folks were saving for my college education was used up on his medical bills. He died when I was seventeen."

"Oh, Storm, I'm so sorry...." Without thinking, Tahcha reached out and placed her hand on his broad shoulder.

His shoulder was burning like fire. The ache in his lower body built. Grimly, Storm focused on his driving and tried to ignore Tahcha's concerned voice and soft, fleeting touch. How badly he wanted her to touch him. All over.

"My mother died when I was eighteen," he continued.

"The doctor said it was a heart attack, but I knew better. She died of a broken heart. When my dad died, the spark of life went out of my mom's eyes. I knew even then that she didn't want to live, but she tried, because she wanted to help me. She took on two jobs to make ends meet. Shortly after I graduated from high school, she had a massive heart attack. After I buried her, I went into the Marine Corps because they promised me an education after three years. I wanted to fulfill my parents' dream for me by getting that college degree."

Shaking her head, Tahcha whispered, "All this tragedy, Storm. I'm so sorry. I didn't know."

He shrugged. "That's how life goes. We never know what the Great Spirit has in store for us from one day to the next. All we can do is react and then try to move on."

"My parents died in a car crash on the interstate just after I finished flight school," Tahcha admitted after a long silence. She stared down at her clasped hands.

Storm glanced at her, his heart squeezing with anguish. "I'm sorry…." And he was. Gram told him when he'd come back to the res many years ago. Again the desire to stop the truck, put his arms around Tahcha, nearly overwhelmed him. Two things stopped him. The first was his ethical code as a medicine man dealing with a patient. The second was his messy divorce from Belinda. He couldn't get into another relationship. Not even with Tahcha.

Slowing the truck, Storm turned left onto the dirt road leading to his home. The headlights slashed through the darkness, revealing deep, muddy ruts. With every bump, the beams would flash across the snowy roadsides. At one point a white hare with black-tipped ears bounded in front of them. It quickly leaped up the slope of a hill and disappeared into the night.

When they arrived at the house, Storm shut off the engine. Still fighting the desire to embrace Tahcha, he quickly exited the truck. She unbuckled her seat belt and slowly followed.

"Come tomorrow afternoon at 1:00 p.m.," he told her. "I'll conduct a doctoring sweat for you, Tahcha. We'll call back your spirit—the part that's still trapped in that crash."

She saw his deeply shadowed features, his eyes burning with a light she couldn't define. "Thanks, Storm."

"Bring a cotton shift and several towels. You'll need them inside the sweat lodge."

All business. Tahcha felt rebuffed by his sudden gruff demeanor, but thought she understood it. To talk of the loss of their parents stirred up a lot of old grief and opened old wounds in them both. "I'll be here."

Grudgingly, Storm said, "I have to go feed the animals. I'll see you tomorrow afternoon." He turned away and headed toward the barn. Storm wanted to invite Tahcha to stay. He was longing for more conversation with her, to find out what else had happened to her. Did she have a relationship? Was she married? Divorced? Did she have kids? He was desperate to ask those questions, but it would have been out of place, given her need for healing. Although Gram had been in touch with Tahcha's parents before they died, she heard no more from Tahcha. Gram had told him about her family when he'd come home. The elder was sad because from then on, Tahcha never contacted her. Gram figured it was because of her grief. The only thing she knew was that Tahcha was slated to go into the military after she graduated from college.

No, he reminded himself, he had to focus solely on his role as a medicine person, to be a catalyst for her healing. Only the Great Spirit knew what would be in store for them tomorrow.

Storm heard Tahcha starting up her car, and without a glance back or a wave, he trudged to the barn. His two horses nickered and trotted to the corner of the corral to greet him. They knew he would throw them some hay for the long night.

As he pulled the door open, Storm's listened for Tahcha's vehicle. Her headlights shot across the corral when she turned the car around and headed down the drive. He felt her absence instantly, and took a deep breath. In helping her heal, he would have to stay on his guard.

Growling unhappily to himself, Storm stepped into the barn, flipped on a light and got the horses several flakes of hay, plus a ration of oats. How the hell was he going to sleep tonight, when the woman of his dreams had unexpectedly reentered his life? And why hadn't Gram told him of her arrival? Storm knew that Gram was a revered wise woman. If she hadn't told him, there must have been a reason. Did Gram have a premonition Tahcha would be coming home? Did she see that Storm would play a central role in her recovery? At some point, Storm would visit the elder and ask. Sometimes, he realized, being surprised was a catalyst for growth and perhaps that was why Gram had not informed him of Tahcha arriving a month ago.

He tossed the hay out to his horses and felt the winter wind sting his cheeks. Storm cursed silently. The last thing he'd expected was for Tahcha to show up on the res. He'd given up any dreams that included her. Standing beside the corral, resting his hands on the top rung of the pine pole fence, he watched as his horses eagerly attacked the hay. Somehow, he had to get a handle on his escaping emotions, his red-hot desire for Tahcha. He wanted her, in all ways, wanted to love her until she fainted from bliss. Wanted to see her in his bed when he awakened, to share the first cup of morning coffee with her, to talk with her....

Groaning, Storm whispered savagely, "You stupid son of a bitch. Remember your bad marriage."

CHAPTER FOUR

"ARE YOU READY?" Storm smiled at Tahcha as he stood at the opening of the sweat lodge and pulled aside the buffalo hide covering the entrance to the circular structure.

Tahcha slipped off her shoes. "Yes, I'm ready." Her voice sounded firm and calm. Maybe a good night's sleep had given her strength. The afternoon was cloudy, an icy breeze making it feel even colder. Storm's fire tender and apprentice, Paul Wahachonkah, was checking on the stones that had been placed in the roaring fire hours earlier.

Storm was bare chested, a bird claw necklace around his thick neck. He nodded at her and asked, "You remember the ceremony?"

Tahcha grinned and pressed her two thick beach towels to her chest. "Oh yes." Getting down on her knees, she pushed the two rolled-up towels into the lodge, to the left of the door. Earlier, she'd brought her contribution for the ceremony: a hundred fifty small bags of tobacco all strung together. The colorful red cotton pouches always reminded Tahcha of a series of lights for a Christmas tree. A person wanting a healing had to sit quietly and pray over each tiny bag as he or she filled it with sacred tobacco, then wrapped it with red string and tied it on the main cord. The bundles would carry the prayers of the person to the spirits who would visit during the sweat lodge ceremony. Storm's assistant had already hung Tahcha's up inside the lodge.

She moved forward on her hands and knees, pulling up the skirt of her cotton shirt so it didn't get in the way. *"Mitakuye oyasin,"* she whispered, which meant, "All my relations." It was a reminder and an acknowledgement that humans were not at the top of the pecking order, but rather, a part of a greater whole that the Great Spirit, or Wakan Tonka, had created.

Crawling inside, she made herself comfortable and adjusted the shift across her knees. She noticed a pleasant musky odor from to the buffalo robes draped across the willow frame of the sweat lodge. Symbolically, the lodge helped two-leggeds not only to connect with Mother Earth, but to honor all the spirits who inhabited the four directions. Together, they could help heal a person.

Nostalgic memories, sweet and haunting, swept through Tahcha. Since her return to the res, she hadn't attended a sweat. Oh, she'd wanted to, but she'd been too wounded to drag herself to one. But this was different. She knew the sweat lodge leader, and only the two of them would be inside. Excitement and dread washed through Tahcha as she pulled one towel across her shoulders and laid the second in her lap. Sometimes the water poured on red-hot rocks created a burning steam. The towels and shift would protect her from the intensity of the heat, but still allow her to surrender herself to the spirits.

Within moments, Storm had knelt down, whispered the ancient greeting and then crawled in. He moved left, avoiding her drawn-up legs, and circling the open fire pit in the center. In a sweat, everyone moved in a clockwise direction to where they would sit.

Tahcha loved sweat lodges. She'd grown up going to the weekly healing ceremonies Storm's father, a revered medicine man, had conducted. A sweat lodge was designed for maintenance of one's spirit. Her people believed that when the spirit was well, a two-legged would not be sick. It was only when the spirit was damaged that physical, mental or emotional ailments appeared.

A doctoring sweat was a special ceremony, unlike the normal sweats Tahcha had attended before. She was curious about the differences, but didn't want to ask. Storm would be directing everything within the lodge after the flap went down. She understood that his prayers, which would be sung in a precise order, were designed to invite the appropriate spirits into the lodge. Tahcha hoped the powerful and invisible beings would take pity upon her and bring back her own lost soul.

Storm settled in. Outside the lodge, on a small hill opposite the opening, the sacred pipe was set up on two forked sticks. Below it was a buffalo skull, filled with dried sage to honor the spirit of the animal, as well as the pipe itself. His fire tender, Paul, would soon bring the first of four rounds of rocks, glowing red from being in the fire. Storm forced himself to keep his mind solely on the business at hand.

He hadn't slept well last night, preoccupied as he was by Tahcha walking unexpectedly back into his life. Glancing over at her in the dim light filtering into the lodge, he liked the fact that she'd braided her hair and placed small, fuzzy eagle feathers at the end of each strand. Gram Willow must have helped her and Storm felt grateful that the elder was there for Tahcha.

The light blue shift Tahcha wore was many sizes too big for her. Storm figured Gram Willow had loaned her one of her "sweat dresses" for the ceremony. He sensed the elder's care and support had helped Tahcha look so vibrant today. Yesterday, she'd appeared pale and washed out after confiding the details of her trauma. Tahcha would need all her reserve strength now. There was nothing easy about a doctoring sweat.

As Storm arranged his drum, his beater and a towel to wipe his face from time to time, Paul set a wooden bucket filled with water in the entrance.

"Thanks," Storm called out. He placed the pail, with its bundle of sage tied to the handle, beside him. Next, Paul passed Storm the pipe; their most sacred ceremonial tool. Storm clasped the red pipestone head in his hand, the wooden stem pointing outward. Getting to his knees, he called out to the fire keeper, "Bring in the stones."

Tahcha was far enough away from the entrance to avoid the heated stone when Paul arrived. He rested the pitchfork on the ground and slid it forward. Storm quickly touched the red, glowing rock it held with the stem of the pipe, and murmured, *"Hau kola,"* which meant, "Welcome friend." With skilled precision, Paul dropped the stone into the fire pit. Tahcha saw Storm lean forward and sprinkle it with a mixture of sacred herbs. The scent of cedar and juniper wafted into the air, and she inhaled the healing fragrance into her lungs.

As the rocks were brought in one by one, Tahcha felt the heat build within the small enclosure. The lodge was about thirty feet in circumference, resembling half a globe set flat on the earth. Buffalo hides covering the willow structure would hold in the heat and steam. The robes also made the lodge pitch-black once the flap was closed. Tahcha looked forward to that moment.

After all the stones had arrived, Storm reached over and handed her two sprigs of dried sage.

"Put one behind each ear. If you don't, the spirits won't visit you."

When their fingers touched, Tahcha felt a frisson flow up her arm. She took the small springs and nestled them behind her ears, while Storm handed Paul the pipe to be placed outside the lodge. He then asked him to drop the flap. The ceremony was to begin.

The darkness was complete. The heat was stifling, but welcoming to Tahcha. She heard Storm moving around, but she couldn't see him.

"The fourth round," Storm told her, "is the doctoring round. I'm going to hand you a *wotai* stone. It contains a very powerful spirit. Hold on to it and ask it for help. When we're done, and the flap is opened for a final time, you can give it back to me."

"Okay," Tahcha whispered. She felt a jolt of fear, along with a building anticipation. Being in the lodge again made her feel incredibly safe and nurtured. The dark space symbolized the womb of *Maka Ina*, Mother Earth. Those within were her children, come to pray and ask her for help and healing energy.

The moment Storm plunged his wooden dipper into the sage-blessed water and then threw it on the heated rocks, steam billowed through the darkness. Tahcha was mesmerized by the spitting, glowing rocks. She saw human and animal faces in them, and when the water hit them, some cracked open, all hissing like riled rattlesnakes. The steam shot upward, then rolled down the inner walls. She could feel the heat despite the towel protecting her shoulders.

And then the drum began to beat, and Storm sang in a deep bass tone. Closing her eyes, Tahcha felt a sense of joy flow through her.

She had been raised taking part in her people's ancient ceremonies, and this was another part of coming home for her. The fact that Storm, the first love of her life, was here, conducting the sweat, nearly overwhelmed her emotionally. Tears flooded her closed eyes, and she bowed her head.

The thrumming of the drum vibrated through the lodge. She felt each thump of the beater on the thick elk hide. A tingling sensation began at the base of her spine and whirled upward through her like a tornado in the darkness. The song beseeched the spirits of the four directions to come into the lodge and help her.

Tahcha allowed the dizziness to calm her, knowing from long experience that the spirits were arriving. She could feel their powerful presence although she saw nothing with her eyes. Sweat rolled down her face, and she wiped it away with the edge of her towel. While the sweat cleansed her physical body, the fire would burn up the dark energy keeping her out of balance and harmony. The songs,

Storm's medicine and unique power, would hold all of the incoming energy so that she could call back her spirit.

After the first round, which consisted of several songs, Storm stopped and asked Paul to open the flap. Icy-cold air flowed in and refreshed Tahcha. She breathed in the cooling drafts as Paul passed in another load of rocks, for the second round. In the light from the doorway, she looked over at Storm. His face was glistening with sweat, his black hair loose and damp against his shoulders and corded neck. It was his eyes, and the faraway look in them, that told Tahcha he was elsewhere, the land of the spirits. Sweat lodge leaders were a fulcrum point between people and the Great Spirit.

Tahcha studied his deeply shadowed features. His face was like carved rock and spoke of incredible strength, and yet she saw great kindness there. Her heart lurched in response, but she knew her feelings for him weren't the focus right now. She managed a smile of gratitude, then bowed her head and closed her eyes once more.

The second round began, the darkness once again complete. The heat was even more intense as Storm threw several ladles of sage-scented water upon the sacred stones. When he began to drum and sing, Tahcha felt the spinning sensation begin once more. She surrendered to the intensifying power. In moments, she felt as if she were flying.

Tahcha lost the sense of sitting on the cool earth, forgot the burning heat and humidity curling around her. Instead, a screen in her mind burst open and she found herself flying in the Super Stallion again. Her gasp of shock was swallowed up by the beating of the drum and Storm's deep voice. Unlike her nightmares before, this dream was real. Tahcha felt the vibration of the helo around her. She smelled her fear-filled sweat.

Swallowing a cry of terror, she realized what was about to happen. She was reliving every torturous detail of the crash. As Storm's voice faded, she became aware of the mountains in Afghanistan, of flying toward the secret base.

When the second round ended, Tahcha was disoriented. Storm and she both spoke prayers one after another. He then said nothing, but he passed her a ladle filled with cool water. She drank, and then buried her face in her hands, her elbows planted on her knees. The vision would not go away, nor did she fight it. Within moments, the flap went down for the third round.

The moment Storm started to beat the drum again and sing another song, Tahcha was catapulted back into her helicopter. She heard Kentucky-born Chet Beltran cry out as the missile was fired at them. Her heart plummeting, Tahcha saw the ten Marines sitting in the rear of her helo, fear etched on their faces as they clung to the web seats. These were the men she'd lost, the deaths she felt responsible for.

It was too much! Tahcha sobbed, her hands pressed hard against her sweaty face. But she wouldn't erase the men's faces from her mind. When Beltran's visage, and that of her copilot and friend, Jed Reynolds, appeared in her mind, Tahcha's heart burst with grief and pain. They were all being wrenched and jostled as she wrestled with the Super Stallion, trying to escape the missile. Even worse than seeing them, she was privy to each Marine's thoughts and feelings. Tahcha heard some of them praying. Others were thinking of their wives, of their children. None of them wanted to die.

The flap came up, signaling the end of the third round. Storm looked over at Tahcha. When he was in this state, he was clairvoyant. In the grayness of the lodge, he saw her terror and shock. She was hunched over, her head in her hands, soft gasps coming from her lips. The man in him wanted to reach out and comfort her, but he needed to guide her further.

The spirits had brought her back to the scene of her trauma, making her privy to new details from the crash. It was done so that she could reclaim her spirit, Storm knew. Still, he yearned to touch her, to try to protect her from the event. Yet he mustn't. That urge had to be put on hold.

Storm asked for the pipe to be passed in again. Sensing that Tahcha was locked within the vision, Storm smoked the pipe, mentally said the prayers, then handed the empty pipe back to Paul, who would reverently replace it on the forked sticks.

Once he pulled out of his *wotai* stone, Storm leaned over and gently placed it in Tahcha's hand.

"Remember," he rasped, "hold on to the *wotai*. Ask it to bring your spirit back to you. Do you understand?"

Tahcha barely nodded, unable to speak. But the galvanizing touch of Storm's fingers stabilized her. For a moment, it partially brought her back to the present.

As she curled her fingers around the stone, Tahcha was vaguely aware of the last set of heated rocks being passed into the lodge, the flap closing and the drumbeat vibrating once more. Then Storm's voice catapulted her back into her vision.

Tahcha was wrestling with the Super Stallion, but this time, she was also floating above it as an observer. She watched everyone on board, even herself. She saw the Taliban soldier who had sat for hours, waiting and watching. His face was young and determined. She received his thoughts, felt his hatred of Americans and his zeal to drive them out of his country. And then she saw the Marines on the mountaintop base, watching in helpless horror as her helicopter was struck by the missile.

The eruption blinded her for a moment. From the burning, exploding wreckage, she saw twelve spirits leave the site, those of the men who'd been killed in the crash. She moved over to them, crying out how sorry she was that she couldn't save them, and how she was unable to forgive herself.

And then something strange occurred. As Tahcha hovered above the wreckage, a huge white owl came flying toward them—the spirit owl. It was much larger now, its wings covering nearly one quarter of the sky before, swooping low, it embraced them all.

Tahcha heard the owl's voice. "I ask that each of you give her a message," it ordered the men.

Thick black smoke rose, and Tahcha felt the heat from the burning helicopter. Sobbing now in earnest, she saw each Marine line up and stand before her.

The first one, a sergeant, approached her. "It wasn't your fault. I forgive you," he said.

The second Marine came up to her. "This was out of your hands. You did what you could. I know that. It's all right."

Tahcha heard a message from each man, and none of

them blamed her. Each one released her from guilt. By the time they'd finished, she was weeping openly. To each man, she was able to say she was sorry, and to ask for his forgiveness. They gave it to her without hesitation.

At the end of their farewell, the white owl took them to a tunnel of glowing white-gold light. Tahcha watched each man's spirit rise and gradually disappear. The owl then flew back to her.

"Turn and look down, Tahcha. Look at yourself."

Tahcha dreaded doing so, but forced herself to look at her unconscious body extending out of the shattered cockpit, arms splayed. The blood leaked from beneath her helmet and across her face. The Marines from the base were running toward her as the fire threatened to burn her alive. At that moment, the white owl flew in and flapped its mighty wings.

Instantly, the flames were pushed back, enough for the men to rescue her from the wreckage. When the owl stopped flapping, the fire leaped forward instantly and enveloped the cockpit.

Amazed, Tahcha stared at the owl. "You did that. You saved me."

"I did, but look at what is left in the wreckage."

Turning, Tahcha saw what looked like a glossy piece of film negative, a silhouette of her unconscious body. "What's that?" she asked in wonder.

"Your shadow. Everyone has a shadow that gives them strength and purpose in life. You must go down there and retrieve it. If you have the courage to do that, I will help you bring it back to yourself. Without your shadow, you will lose the will to live, Tahcha. You will slowly die over time. Your shadow is your desire to walk the path you've chosen in this lifetime. Do you want it back?"

"Yes," she told the owl. "I want to live. I don't want to die. Why did it leave me?"

"Because you took the responsibility for twelve men's lives when it was not yours to carry. Only Wakan Tonka can do that. You must forgive yourself fully, first. No human can give life or death. Such sacred moments are in greater hands than ours. We are but a grain of sand moving with the tide in the ocean of mystery that surrounds us. If you can feel forgiveness in your heart, in your spirit, then your shadow will return easily to you. If you cannot, it will remain locked up in the time when you lost it."

The white owl perched before her, staring intently at her. She looked deeply into its glowing yellow eyes and large black pupils. There was such love radiating from the spirit bird that she felt she might have enough energy to retrieve her shadow, or at least try. As she moved down toward the wreckage below, Tahcha drew a deep, ragged breath.

Leaning forward, she placed trembling fingers on the outline of her head. The thin, flexible material felt as if it were indeed a piece of camera film, and as she tightened her fingertips over it, she made another discovery. Her shadow was a dark brown color, resembling the soil of Mother Earth.

Each Marine's words rang in her mind again, a litany of forgiveness toward her. None of them blamed her for what had happened; she'd done everything she could. And now, as Tahcha straightened, her elusive shadow pliable in her hands, the white owl's words came back to her: *Forgive yourself.*

Tahcha saw the helicopter burning, the roiling black column of smoke streaming into the dawn sky, the mountains brown and barren. As she watched, a new sense of purpose began to tingle through her. The odd, heated sensation continued, as if the shadow was infusing her with life and erasing her depression. A surge of heat spread quickly up her arms, into her head and then flushed through her entire body in what seemed a millisecond.

And then she heard the snap of the white owl opening its wings. Out of the corner of her eye, she saw the huge bird flying toward her. Once more she was embraced by its mighty wings, and then she lost consciousness.

CHAPTER FIVE

TAHCHA FOUND HERSELF lying facedown on the floor of the sweat lodge, her sweaty cheek pressed against the earth. Slowly, she regained consciousness. She inhaled the wonderful scent of the living soil, and it brought her back to the present.

In her right hand, she was still clutching the *wotai* stone, and her palm felt as if it were on fire. Storm's strong, deep voice carried through the dark space, the drum sending healing reverberations throughout her body.

After managing to sit up, Tahcha wiped the dirt from her cheek and sat cross-legged once more. Something had happened. Something powerful. She still felt as if she were fading in and out in some strange way. Honing in on the drumming, Tahcha began to feel more "here" in her body than entrapped within her vision. She recognized the song Storm was chanting as the last one for sweat, and a sense of gratitude swept through her. She'd made it through.

Tahcha gently held the *wotai* stone in her hands. Surprisingly, the heat left the stone, and she became aware of a cooling energy sweeping up into her arms, the soothing sensations flowing through her body. Closing her eyes, she humbly accepted the gift.

Tahcha knew that when the flap came up, Storm would talk with her. He had told her it was customary to sit in the warmth of the lodge after the ceremony was concluded, so a patient could share what he or she had experienced.

But how was Tahcha going to put all that had happened to her into words?

STORM LISTENED INTENTLY as Tahcha related her entire experience of the doctoring ceremony. The winter light was weaker now, the sun low on the horizon. Outside, Paul was cleaning up and allowing the fire to burn out.

Tahcha gazed at Storm across the space. His broad, deep chest glistened with sweat; his hair, dark and thick, hung around his sharply chiseled features. She found refuge in his large, inquisitive eyes, and realized he was still in that magical space. More than anything, she wanted to crawl the four feet between them and throw her arms around him. They'd gone through so much together in mere moments. Her desire for him was both sharp and startling. And yet it wasn't appropriate to act on it in the sacred space of the sweat lodge. That would defile the very reasons they were sitting here, and she would never do that.

"How do you feel?" Storm asked. He shifted at last, placing his drum, the beater and the pail of water outside the lodge door for Paul to remove.

"Better, I think. More whole." She pressed her palm against her abdomen, finding the cotton dress soaked with sweat. "I don't feel as…torn up."

"When you think of the crash now, what's your reaction?"

"I feel as if it had less of an impact on me. I'm not as emotionally shredded by it. I can't explain it." Tahcha searched his face for a sign that he understood.

How easy it was to absorb Storm into her heart, her soul suddenly. Even after so much time apart.

Storm nodded. "When your shadow returns, you won't have such painful reactions to that event. Within a week, you should start feeling freed from the trauma. The nightmares should go away, and that will be your biggest proof that your shadow has returned fully to you."

"I'm so grateful." Tahcha's voice broke and tears began to trickle down her cheeks. "I'll never be able to thank you enough for what you've just done. I realize it was a combination of you, the spirits, your *wotai* stone and the Great Mystery who made it happen. Thank you for giving me back my life, Storm."

Her halting words, filled with such gratitude, nearly broke Storm's last wall of defense. The bright look of hope in Tahcha's eyes shook him. She was wide open and excruciatingly vulnerable because of the ceremony, he knew.

"Let's crawl out of here. Paul has a blanket for each of us. We'll wrap up in them, walk to my house, and you can take a shower and get into dry clothes. We'll talk more after that."

"Sounds great, Storm." With tears blinding her, it was all Tahcha could say. She wanted Storm to embrace her, hold her. She felt like a little girl once more, and that he was her protector, someone who cared for her and loved her.

Love. Tahcha admitted that she'd never stopped loving Storm Black Horse, and that scared her. Clearly, Storm wanted to keep their relationship professional. His tone was clipped and businesslike. At the same time, how could she stop loving him?

The question plagued her as they made their way back to his home.

"THE SAGE TEA TASTES so good," Tahcha said as they sat at the kitchen table. Night was falling. The evening sky was pink along the horizon, the dark blue cape of night silently skimming across the land. It was one of her favorite times of day.

"It always does after a sweat lodge." Storm's mouth hitched upward. "It's a good way to rehydrate. We lose a lot of water during a sweat." How easy it would be to gaze like a lovesick puppy at Tahcha right now! But he stopped himself. Storm could see the new light shining in her dark eyes. She'd unplaited her hair, washed it. The thick strands hung drying in blue-black sheets around her shoulders. The dark pink sweater she had on emphasized her beauty. She never wore makeup and Storm was glad. Tahcha was naturally beautiful, in a way that kept him constantly yearning.

"I called Gram earlier, while you were in the shower," she said. "I told her what happened."

"I'll bet she's happy."

"Very." Tahcha gave him a perplexed look. "I still don't feel right, Storm. There's so much energy moving around inside me. It's hard to explain." She cocked her head and studied him. "Is this normal?"

"Yes, it is."

"I'm glad. I didn't know a person could lose a part of their spirit."

"When shocking events occur, it happens. The worse the shock, the more you lose." Storm sipped his honey-laced sage tea, appreciating the warmth swirling between them. Since the sweat lodge, he had a difficult time keeping Tahcha at bay, but he tried. His resolve never to marry, never to get involved with another woman hardened within him.

Tahcha shook her head. "I can't imagine how people go around trying to survive after something like that. I wasn't doing a very good job of it, that's for sure. How do they do it without a medicine person like yourself helping them reclaim that lost part of themselves?"

He wrapped his hands around the mug. "They don't. Their lives are shortened because they are not whole. And often when they sense the loss, they turn to addictions like food, cigarettes, alcohol or drugs. The loss drives them to fill the void, the emptiness, with something—anything. It can be so mentally and emotionally painful."

"I feel so sorry for those who don't know help is out there." Tahcha smiled. "I'm glad to be home, Storm. Was it your white owl who guided me back to my shadow? I noticed that, when you were conducting the sweat, you wore a necklace of claws around your neck. Are they snowy owl talons?"

He nodded and smiled back. "Yes, they are. My father worked with this owl spirit, and before he died, wanted me to have the necklace. He wore it whenever he performed ceremonies, and now I'm carrying on the tradition." Storm's expression softened even more. "I always feel my dad's spirit near when I wear them. It's comforting. My white owl spirit was helping you, as it does everyone who enters a lodge I'm conducting."

"I understand that medicine people sometimes hand down their ceremonial items to the next generation. That's a wonderful thing, Storm. Your dad was a very kind man. I'm sorry he died so early in your life."

Tahcha searched Storm's eyes and saw remnants of pain there. "Thank you," she said again. "And thanks to your spirit guide. I'm so grateful." She reached out and gripped his hand. For her, it felt like when they were young, touching and talking about everything.

The moment her fingers slid across his, Tahcha saw Storm's gaze grow heated. She read something new there, something incredible and yet scary. She realized he wanted her.

Shaken, she eased her hand away, and that look disappeared abruptly from his eyes. "I, uh…" A feeling of unworthiness crept through her. All along, Tahcha had thought Storm didn't like her anymore, much less love her. Was she right in what she saw, or just confused?

"It's okay, Tahcha." Storm's hand burned fiercely in the wake of her grazing touch. Her fingers were long and beautifully sculpted. How he'd ached for just this moment. His heart was crashing like a drum in his chest, so loudly he wondered if she could hear it. Every pulsing beat reverberated through him, shaking him to his soul.

With the confusion on her face and the blush on her cheeks, Tahcha had never looked so beautiful or so desirable. Wrestling inwardly, Storm tried not to read anything romantic into her gesture. He didn't want to hurt Tachcha. They had been talking intimately for the first time in years. He vividly recalled times they'd chatted endlessly in their youth. They'd always been able to communicate easily, revealing their deepest darkest secrets, their fears and dreams to one another.

As a child, Storm couldn't stand the thought of being separated from Tahcha when she left him after walking home from school. And how he'd anticipated seeing her the next morning. That joy, that yearning, that sense of oneness with Tahcha didn't diminish in their teen years. If anything, it had deepened, broadened and become even more meaningful to him. Now, he was getting a taste of that relationship once again, and a spiral of joy catapulted through him.

Pulling in a ragged breath, he said quietly, "You need to go home now, Tahcha. After a ceremony like this, you have to rest. Sleep. Take care of yourself."

She smiled. "You're right. I am feeling pretty whipped right now."

"You okay driving home in the dark, or do you want me to take you over to Gram Willow's?"

"I can drive. Thanks for offering, though." Tahcha got up and placed the empty mug on the kitchen counter. If she was honest, she'd have to admit she was afraid of herself, of her emotions toward Storm. They weren't patient-medicine man feelings. No, they were her feelings, as a woman, needing him, the man at the table who looked sad and lost in thought. Storm's black brows were drawn down, his hands wrapped around the mug, his mouth pursed.

Really, she was too overwhelmed to sort out all her emotions. As much as she wanted to stay with him, it was best for her to go home.

Turning, she asked, "Do you want me to check in with you in a couple of days? Let you know how I'm doing?" Tahcha picked up her purse and car keys from the counter.

Storm got up. "Just call me." The words *please stay with me* nearly slipped from his mouth. But he couldn't do that to her. Tahcha was too vulnerable during this crucial state of change. That wouldn't be fair to her. Or to him.

Storm followed her out to the hall, where he helped her on with her sheepskin coat. As he opened the door, Tahcha stood inches away from him. Gazing down at her upturned face, her dark eyes now filled with life, he managed a strained smile. "You're going to be fine, Tahcha. I feel it here, in my heart." He touched his chest in emphasis. "There's no need to come back to see me."

Shaken, Tahcha pushed open the screen door and stepped out onto the salted concrete steps, where the bitter wind revived her. "Having you believe in me is all I need, Storm," she quavered. She swallowed hard, pulled on her gloves and waved goodbye to him. As she carefully made her way down the steps, the snow began to fall, white flakes twirling around her in a joyous, silent dance. The porch light shone just brightly enough for her to get to her parked car.

Tahcha couldn't afford to look back. If she did, she'd run back and throw herself into Storm's arms. He'd made it plain things between them were finished, once and for all. With a shaky breath, she climbed into her Corolla and started the engine.

Only then did Tahcha look up. Storm's tall, proud form was backlit by the lamp in the hallway. He appeared so strong and solid. So stable in her shattered world, which now would heal. Lifting her hand, she waved again and backed out of his driveway.

The last thing Tahcha wanted to do was love him. The last thing… He'd made it clear that this was goodbye. Once more, Tahcha realized, she was leaving him, and so repeating a pattern in her history. Tears burned in her eyes and she fought them down. The past was exactly that: in the past.

CHAPTER SIX

STORM WAS SHOVELING SNOW from last night's blizzard, which had dumped a foot of white stuff. His horses leaped playfully around in the corral as he hefted one shovelful after another. He had to clear the area so they could get to their water tank and hay rack. The gunmetal-gray sky still looked threatening, but the worst of the late-January storm was over. A grater had come earlier and plowed his road so he could get out to the main road.

Even though his body was here, in the corral, his mind was centered on Tahcha. And so was his heart. It had been three weeks since the sweat lodge ceremony. And except for her phone call two days after it, he'd heard nothing from her.

Frowning, Storm savagely pushed the snow away from around the large aluminum water tank. He removed his deerskin glove, balled his fist and broke the layer of ice on top so the horses could get water. After wiping his hand on his jeans, he tugged the glove back on.

How desperately he wanted to hear Tahcha's voice. How was she doing? Was she still living with Gram Willow? Was she even on the res? Storm had stopped counting how many times he'd walked to the wall phone in the kitchen, aching to call her, and then stopped himself.

Well, he had no one to blame but himself for the way things had turned out. From the outset he'd made it clear to Tahcha that his relationship with her was professional. Never mind the longing looks she'd given him.

Wiping his sweaty brow, his breath turning white in the frosty air, Storm stepped out of the way to allow his two horses, a paint and a palomino gelding, to get to the hay. Then he gazed around his homestead. The hills were covered with clean, glistening snow. Everything was so quiet, so peaceful. Only the raucous cawing of a crow disturbed the silence. As he looked critically at the corral, Storm noticed some of the wire had come loose during the harsh weather. It would have to be repaired today so the horses wouldn't accidentally cut themselves.

And then something magical occurred. As Storm stood there, nearly knee deep in snow, his shovel in hand, he saw a white bird flying toward him. To his surprise, it came to land on one of the graying fence posts not more than a hundred feet from where he stood. It was a large snowy owl. His spirit guide! The bird had white feathers, speckled with brown. When it lifted its smooth, round head and fixed its large, piercing eyes on him, Storm felt an undeniable kinship with the magnificent raptor.

The bird symbolized his chief guide, who helped him in all ceremonies he conducted on behalf of others. It wasn't that rare to see snowy owls in South Dakota during winter, because the birds sometimes migrated south from the tundra, when lemming and vole populations dwindled. In spring, they would fly back to the arctic, their breeding and nesting ground. Storm enjoyed watching the bird fluff its plumage and preen. He eyed the owl's thickly feathered legs, its large yellow claws gripping the top of the post, anchoring it against the wind.

This was a sign, Storm knew.

What message do you bring me, Brother? he asked the owl telepathically. Storm often had dreams in which his spirit guide would come to him, give him messages and information about his patients. This morning, he felt the owl had appeared for another reason and that the message was personal.

As he waited, his ears caught another sound—of a car engine coming down the snow-covered road. Who could it be? It was barely past dawn, around 7:00 a.m. Storm looked in the direction of the noise, and felt his heart contract. It was Tahcha's Toyota Corolla coming over the rise, making its way cautiously toward his house.

Tahcha! Tightening his grip on the shovel, Storm watched the owl fluff its feathers vigorously once more. Then it turned its head nearly halfway around and looked at the approaching car. Finally, it looked back at Storm.

Storm got it. The instant he made the connection, the snowy owl opened its wings and flew off toward a stand of gray-limbed cottonwoods in the distance.

Wiping his mouth, Storm suddenly felt weak and shaky inside. And scared. For so long, he'd been without a woman. His marriage had burned and scarred him. And yet as he shut the gate and went to meet Tahcha, he realized he'd been stuck in the past. He'd let the past become his present.

How Storm looked forward to seeing Tahcha! And yet

part of him worried. Was she here because she wasn't well? His mind spun with questions until he reminded himself that she could have called him if something was wrong. So why was she here, unannounced? He never thought he'd see her again because he'd made it clear to her after the sweat she was free to move on without him in her life.

His heart soared when she emerged from the Toyota, dressed in a sheepskin jacket, white turtleneck sweater and blue jeans. She was beautiful, with her hair loose and wind-tossed. How natural and free she looked. As she came closer, Storm could see that her dark-brown eyes were clear, filled with life and shining with happiness.

"Hi, Storm," Tahcha called. She pulled out a basket with foil wrapped over the top of it. "I thought you might like a little breakfast. Gram Willow made some of her famous cinnamon rolls, and I wanted to share them with you." Tahcha held it out to him.

Absorbing her warm, sunny smile, Storm halted a few feet from her. "Why, thanks." He took the gift. "This is a surprise."

"A good one, I hope?" Tahcha looked past him to the horses eating contentedly in the corral.

Storm nodded almost helplessly. "How are you?"

Tahcha retrieved her deerskin purse from the car and slid the strap over her shoulder. "Unbelievably well, Storm. No more nightmares. I'm sleeping through the night. I wake up feeling…human again. I still grieve for my friends, for the men who lost their lives in the crash, but it doesn't haunt me like it did before." She gave him a look of gratitude and squeezed his arm. "I wanted an excuse to come over here and see you."

Her softly spoken words touched him to his core, and the firm touch of her gloved hand sent wild tingles through his body. "I'm glad. Come on in."

Trudging through the snow toward the cleared sidewalk leading up to Storm's home, Tahcha said, "I wanted to catch you up on everything."

Storm's fears began to dissolve. Tahcha's voice was like thick honey, soothing whatever misgivings he had. At the top of the steps, he opened the door and stood aside so she could enter. In no time, they had shucked off their boots and gloves, hung their jackets on the hall hooks and made it to the warmth of the kitchen.

"I'll make coffee," Storm told her. He pointed to the cabinet next to the sink. "Dishes are in there, and the silverware drawer is below the counter."

"Roger that." Tahcha went to work setting the table.

Enjoying their unspoken connection, the harmony swirling between them, Storm made a pot of coffee and got down some mugs. He had a helluva time keeping his gaze off Tahcha as she flitted like a happy butterfly around the kitchen. Just watching her move with that deerlike grace sent a keen longing through him.

"Gram thought it would be good idea for me to drop in for a visit," Tahcha confided as she folded the yellow paper napkins and placed them beneath each fork. "And I've been wanting to see you. I hope you don't mind. I know you're a busy guy."

Storm glanced toward Tahcha. "I don't mind. I was wondering how you were doing. I…just didn't get time to pick up the phone and call." Well, that wasn't exactly the truth.

It had taken him until today to realize how imprisoned he was in his own past.

"Hey, I understand. Gram is so proud of you. She says that you're a very popular medicine person here on the res. Just like your dad. Gram thinks you walk in his footsteps, and your fame will do nothing but spread as you get older."

Nodding, Storm poured the coffee and brought the mugs to the table. Tahcha removed the foil from the basket and deposited a large, fresh cinnamon roll on each plate. As they sat down, he was struck by the easy warmth between them. He was grateful for their strong connection. Their knees brushed beneath the table when he shifted position, and Storm hungrily absorbed the brief contact.

Tahcha cut her roll into small pieces. "It's nice to share this time with you, Storm." She gave him a shy glance. "There's so much I've wanted to say, ever since I found out you were here on the res." Picking up her coffee cup, she took a quick sip. "But if you want the truth, I was afraid, too. A real coward." Her mouth quirked at that admission. "I needed time between your doctoring sweat lodge and today to come to terms with myself and…us."

His heart banged violently in his chest, and he stopped eating the roll. He wasn't tasting it, anyway. Instead, he was totally focused on Tahcha. Her hair, black and silky, moved each time she made the slightest gesture. Every time she lifted her hand there was a natural fluidity to the movement, and he couldn't stop thinking about her palms skimming across his body, exploring him, loving him as he would love her in return.

As a lovesick teen, he'd given Tahcha one last hot,

hungry kiss the day she'd moved away. It had been a heart-wrenching kiss goodbye. Now, Storm wanted more. Much more.

"What did you want to tell me?" he asked finally. Though his appetite was gone, he forced himself to finish the roll. He was almost afraid to hear what Tahcha had to say, and tried to steel himself. Was she leaving the res? Going back to the Marine Corps? Did she have a civilian job flying helicopters for some company in another state? He couldn't begin to imagine her leaving him again.

As he searched Tahcha's features, he saw pink creeping across her high cheekbones, and he let himself hope.

"This is so tough, Storm," Tahcha admitted softly. "It's taken me weeks to gather up the courage to drive over here and see you."

"Is it that awful?" His words came out sounding strangled.

After pushing her plate to one side, Tahcha rested her elbows on the table, clasping her hands in front of her. She eyed him wryly. "I don't know where to begin."

Storm moved his own plate aside and gave her a gentle look. "Just tell me what's in your heart, Tahcha. We never needed fancy speeches between us."

"You're right." She gave him a warm glance. "You make things easy for me, Storm. Coming home has forced me to look at everything in my life. I almost died last year. That was a wake-up call. And it brought me back here, where I was born. I hated leaving the res when I was young, but later, when I'd grown up a little, I understood why my parents left. They sacrificed everything for me, Storm. Everything…" Tahcha saw the serious expression on his face melt with each admission.

"Yes, they did," Storm quietly agreed. "And my parents did the same for me. We know what it's like to be here and then have to leave." The turmoil in Tahcha's eyes echoed his words. They both knew the trauma of being torn apart. "Our spirits reside on the res no matter where we go in the world, and we're happiest here because we were born here."

"Yeah," Tahcha murmured, "there's no place like home, is there?" Taking a deep breath, she said, "And until I got some maturity, Storm, I never realized the sacrifice my parents had made for me. They left their way of life to go into a foreign world." Her voice grew husky with feeling. "When you performed that doctoring sweat for me, I realized how important it was for me to sweat weekly, like I used to when I was a kid. To be one with Mother Earth and all the spirits who come into the lodge. It helped make me well again, Storm." She pressed her hand against her throat to halt the tears that came with her words.

"I understand that," he said. "I need it, too." Storm cleared his throat. "After getting out of the Marine Corps, I came home." Seeing the tears glimmering in Tahcha's eyes tore at him. Storm felt her pain and wanted to assuage it. "Home is what my spirit needed," he added.

"I was so separated from the land and of my birth, and my people, that I didn't know it until the crash occurred." Shaking her head, Tahcha said, "I don't know why I closed myself off like that. It was a stupid choice."

"That's not true, Tahcha. We all have to walk different paths in life. Choices have to be made. We do the best we can."

"Yeah." She snorted softly. "But some choices are better than others."

His mouth quirked. "We're human, Tahcha. We aren't perfect and we'll screw things up again. That's guaranteed." How terribly human he was in this moment, wanting her more than he wanted to breathe.

Tahcha placed her hands flat on the table. She had one last confession, and she hoped Storm would be happy about it. "You're right. I realize all that now. But I'm home, Storm." Tahcha became deadly serious, her voice husky. "I'm home to stay. That's what I wanted to tell you. I've signed up for classes at the local college. I've decided to get my teaching certificate. I want to educate the kids here on the res. I want to work with the first and second graders."

Stunned, he sat back, digesting her words. As he saw the resolve in her features, Storm felt a rush of emotions work through him. "You're here to stay." It wasn't a question.

Tahcha nodded. She saw a glint in his eyes, a bit of gold sunlight that told her he was happy about her decision. Dragging in a deep, steadying breath, she forged ahead. "Storm, I—I don't know about your past. Gram says you were divorced. That you have no children. But I don't know if you have a special woman in your life right now…and I need to know."

Storm frowned. He could see the uncertainty in Tahcha's eyes, hear the emotion she was trying to hide from him. "Gram Willow was right. I'm divorced, no kids. It's a good thing considering how things went. When I was in Afghanistan, a friend on my patrol stepped on a land mine, which killed him and wounded me. Broke my ankle, and there was a lot of damage to my right foot. I was sent stateside to Walter Reed Hospital for five surgeries, and then I had to learn how to walk all over again. In rehab, I met Belinda Evans, a Navy nurse. I fell in love with her...or so I thought."

Storm shrugged. "She looked a lot like you, with black hair and brown eyes. She had a lot of your spunk, but she wasn't Indian. We got married the day I left rehab. It took three years for our marriage to fall apart. I couldn't stand the rage and abuse she handed out. I guess my parents' marriage was my guide. Ours was sick in comparison. I finally divorced her, but it was messy and ugly."

"I'm so sorry," Tahcha whispered, feeling his anguish. "Gram never told me the details."

"I never told anyone until now," Storm muttered. "I was too ashamed. At work, she was an angel. People loved her. And she helped a lot of us returning vets. But at home, well, it was a different story. Angel by day, abusive at night. I couldn't handle it. And I wasn't going to lower myself and fight like that. My parents had their moments, and yes, they got angry and shouted at one another sometimes. But I also saw them deal with whatever came up. Belinda didn't. And after three years, I'd had enough."

"I don't blame you," Tahcha said quietly. "So, you came home?"

"Yeah, isn't it funny? You and I both came back to the res to lick our wounds and heal. The land where we're born can turn our sickness back into health if we allow it."

"Gram said that as soon as you got home you went into

training to follow in your dad's footsteps and become a medicine man. And your uncle died and left you this ranch."

"Gram Willow had a lot to do with that. She shepherded me through the process. My uncle had just passed on and in his will he'd left me this place. It was synchronistic. She told me who to train with." Storm smiled. "Gram has been a spiritual guide for me, and listened when I had no one else to talk to."

"She's doing the same for me now," Tahcha said. "She's the one who pushed me to find out about getting a teaching certificate. I was welcomed with open arms at our res college. It was such a warm, wonderful meeting, Storm. I stood there wondering why I hadn't come back sooner. What was I thinking?"

"Maybe we needed this course correction to learn what's really important, Tahcha. That home really is where the heart and the spirit are located. As kids we heard that all the time from my dad, who would always mention it in our sweat lodges. He was right."

"I'm old enough now, Storm—and hopefully, wise enough—to know our elders can help us more than we ever realized."

"I need to ask you something," he said. "And this is scary for me."

"I'm an open book to you, Storm. I always was. So ask away."

Tahcha saw the turmoil in his eyes. Feeling him struggle, she waited patiently while he wrestled with whatever it was that was bothering him.

"What about you?" he asked at last. "Do you have a relationship at the moment? Someone you're involved with or interested in?"

It was an easy question for Tahcha to answer. She told him of her engagement to Dan and finished by saying, "I have no one in my life right now, Storm. To tell you the truth, I wasn't looking. I had my career and I loved what I was doing." Giving him a shy glance, she added, "And now I realize I was comparing every man I met to you. It was unconscious, but I knew why I never fell in love with anyone else. No man I met measured up to you, your stature or integrity."

"Oh." Storm was stunned. The tension he sensed between them was both exhilarating and freeing. She felt the same way he did, and yet, could he do this? Give his heart to her again?

"I just paid you a compliment, Storm."

Grinning sheepishly, he nodded. "Yeah, I got that. Thank you."

"So, where does that leave us now?" she asked.

At that moment, the phone rang. Groaning, Storm gave Tahcha an apologetic look and stood.

As her heart pounded with fear over what he might say, Tahcha forced herself to get busy. He was speaking in Lakota on the phone, probably to one of his patients, so she took the plates and silverware to the sink and rinsed them. By the time she'd cleaned up the table, Storm had hung up the phone.

"The weather last night has made it impossible for two elderly women on the res to chop wood for their stoves," he reported. "They need help or they'll freeze tonight. Want to come with me?"

"Of course. Let's go. We can talk later." Wood stoves needed to be fed around the clock. A foot of new snow could make it tough, if not impossible, for an older person to get outdoors, much less negotiate the icy conditions. It could mean the difference between keeping warm and freezing to death.

"Yes," Storm said, giving her a fond look, "we can talk later."

Without another word, they fell into seamless teamwork. They left the kitchen and dressed for the outdoors. For Tahcha, it felt wonderful to be spending the day with Storm once more, just as they had when they were younger.

Once he'd retrieved two axes and a wedge splitter, they climbed into his truck. They set off as the sun peeked through a break in the light gray clouds covering the sky.

Tahcha felt euphoric as she sat beside him. "We're together again, Storm."

He glanced at her as he turned onto the snow-covered highway. "Yeah. It feels good, doesn't it?"

Tahcha read the emotion burning in the depths of his eyes. Saw it in the expression of his chiseled features. Heard it in the vibrato of his low, growling tone. She allowed herself the pleasure of grazing his cheek with her fingers. Surprise and then heat built in Storm's gaze.

"When we're done helping the elders, I'm staying at your home tonight, Storm," she murmured. "At least I want to."

CHAPTER SEVEN

IT BEGAN TO SNOW in earnest as Storm pulled into the driveway of his ranch. He and Tahcha had spent the entire day going from one elder's home to another, making sure they had adequate wood for their stoves.

Tired, but feeling more alive than he could ever recall, Storm walked with Tahcha up to his front door. Her cheeks were flushed, her dark eyes glistening with anticipation. Once inside, they sat down on the small bench in the hallway and divested themselves of their boots, jackets, hats and gloves.

As he reached for his elk-skin moccasins nearby, she curled her fingers around his forearm.

"Hey," she whispered, meeting and holding his gaze, "let's go take a shower together, okay? I don't know about you, but I'm ready for one. Are you game?"

Tahcha gulped after making the brazen suggestion. What if she was moving too fast for Storm? Every cell in her body screamed for union with him, on every level. Holding his hooded gaze, she saw the gold in his eyes flare to life. The thin line of his mouth softened.

"Yeah, I'd like that. But are you sure?" Storm stared at her. "Tahcha, this isn't a one-night stand. If I make love with you, it's a forever thing. Do you understand that?" He grasped her hand.

Tahcha met his eyes, which burned with hungry desire. "I know that, Storm. The last time you kissed me was when I left the res." She managed a wobbly smile and touched her lips. "I was so madly in love with you that I never forgot it, or you."

Her words, spoken so softly and hesitantly, touched Storm. Tears glimmered in her eyes as he cupped her upturned face. "You are so brave. You carry the courage of a warrior in your heart, sweetgrass woman."

The beautiful endearment resonated in Tahcha's heart. Sweetgrass was a sacred herb that opened one's soul to the Great Spirit, to receive the gift of love and healing.

Storm's callused fingers slid across her jaw and tightened. How badly she wanted his mouth upon hers! "Kiss me," she urged, stretching upward.

Closing her eyes, she absorbed the feel of his strong lips on hers, his moist breath fanning her cheeks. As his fingers tunneled through her hair, she sensed he was holding back. Tahcha knew he wanted to crush her against him, be inside her. Wanting the same thing, she raised her arms and slid them around his powerful shoulders. Their mouths clung together.

Time ebbed and swirled like the flow of a snow-fed river in winter. As Storm's mouth cherished hers, she realized they were no longer shy teens giving one another longing glances or exploratory kisses during stolen moments. Now they could act upon the feelings buried for so long in their aching hearts. Moving her lips boldly across his, Tahcha pressed herself tightly against Storm's broad chest. As she did, she could feel his heart thundering like a drum beneath his shirt.

Storm groaned as their kiss grew heated. Tahcha's mouth was bold, searching and hungry, just like his. His body flared in response. Nothing had ever seemed so right, so beautiful and poignant as what they were sharing right now.

Dazed by the honey of her mouth, the clean scent of winter woven through the strands of her hair, Storm gradually eased away. Her lashes fluttered, and then he was drowning in the splendor of her burning gaze again. Storm found his heart opening like the first spring flowers after a long, hard winter.

"Come with me, sweetgrass woman."

"I'd love to," she whispered, and stroked his cheek.

Without a word, Storm led her to the small bathroom and turned on the shower. There wasn't much space, but there didn't need to be. He helped her pull off her sweater. Beneath it was a pink silk camisole. Tahcha did not wear a bra, and her nipples were pressed insistently against the soft material. Aching to touch her breasts, he fought for control. There was such love glistening in her eyes! His hands moved in concert with hers, divesting her of her jeans, socks, silky panties and finally, her camisole.

Tahcha stood naked and proud before Storm. His scorching gaze trailed across her body, making her respond like an animal in heat. There was no question he wanted her. In every way. She smiled brazenly and reached to unbutton his shirt, finding pleasure in removing the clothing from his masculine body, and discovering what was beneath.

Steam fogged the glass shower stall as they stood naked together. Storm opened the door and Tahcha stepped in. The space was roomy and comfortable, the moist heat curling around them like restless, hungry hands. When the door closed, Storm picked up a square of pale-green sage soap. Turning, he lathered it briskly between his hands, then spread the thick, fragrant suds across her shoulders, caressing her slender neck and arms.

Tahcha sighed and closed her eyes. There was such power in Storm's touch, and such reverence. She reached out and clasped his narrow hips, catching her breath when his sudsy hands roved across her collarbones to envelop her breasts.

When he rubbed his thumbs lazily across her hardened nipples, she felt heat explode between her thighs. An ache spiraled upward. Oh, how she wanted Storm! All of him. The warm water was like another pair of sensuous hands as he turned her into the flowing stream.

Once more he soaped up his palms and let them wander across her rib cage, abdomen and hips, finally cupping her rear. Storm pulled her against him and they melded like hot lightning caressing Mother Earth.

Tahcha opened her eyes and smiled up at him. She reached for the soap and began her own erotic assault, determined to let him know just how much she loved him. She spread the fragrant bubbles across his skin, evoking an appreciative growl in response.

His body became hard and insistent, pressing against her abdomen. Without words, Tahcha created more sage-scented lather and spread it across his chest, his taut torso, and finally, his maleness. The water of the shower pounded their shoulders, then flowed down their bodies in tingling rivulets.

Tahcha watched Storm's lean, muscular body tense as she glided her hands along his length in exploration. She didn't stop there. His lips drew away from his teeth, his eyes closed and his nostrils flared like those of mustang stallion. His scent was of the earth, and it was a perfume to her awakening senses. As Tahcha finished washing his strong male body, he opened his eyes. They blazed gold and burned with desire. She trembled in response.

"Who's more nervous here?" Storm teased huskily, running his fingers through her hair. The dripping strands covered her upper body like an ebony cloak.

"I think I am," Tahcha said, glad that he was sharing his vulnerability with her. She slid her hands up his chest and folded them behind his neck. "I want to make love to you right here, right now, Storm. I'm so hungry for you I'm shaking." Searching his face, she added, "But I'm also anxious that I won't please you, that you'll feel cheated…."

Whispering her name, Storm tugged her against him. Their bodies were slick and clean, and the scent of sage surrounded them. "Listen," he rasped against her ear, his hands once more capturing her buttocks. "I worry about the same thing. All I want to do is please you, Tahcha. I want to give you more than my body. I want to share my heart in every touch, every kiss I give to you, from this moment on."

As he lifted her upward, Tahcha laughed softly and eased herself against him. She tightened her arms around his neck, and pressed her face against his wet hair. "You can never hurt me, Storm. I see love—love shining like Father Sun—in your eyes. I did from the first moment we met again." She pressed a kiss to his forehead.

Storm supported her easily. Tahcha wrapped her legs around his narrow waist, the core of her throbbing with need for him as he gently lowered her. A low, animal-like growl of pleasure slipped from her lips when he entered her, and she clung to him, her head pressed against his skull. The water flowed around them as they held each other tightly.

The moment they were one, a flash of triumph, of joy, seared through her. She gripped him convulsively, then relaxed as he penetrated more deeply into her hot, awaiting body. Then he began to move.

The moments shredded like lightning across a dark and turbulent sky. With each slow thrust, Tahcha whimpered in satisfaction. Heat and excitement boiled within her as she relished his thickness, his hardness, until she was feverish with need.

When at last a white-hot explosion rocked her, Tahcha cried out in joy. She tipped her head back, unmindful of the water flowing across her face, shoulders and breasts. Caught in the ecstasy of orgasm, Tahcha felt Storm's mouth close around one of her nipples. He suckled her and she went rigid, bliss throbbing through her on every level. She was being loved, pleasured and cherished, all at once.

Groaning, Storm felt her release, and it triggered his own. His entire body became harder still, and then exploded in pleasure. Her inner muscles pulsed around him rhythmically, prolonging his response. The volcanic sensations melded into one another until Storm couldn't tell his body from hers, the warmth of the water from the caressing steam.

Feeling dizzy, Tahcha slumped in Storm's arms. He was trembling now, like a mountain being rocked by an earthquake. With a sigh, she allowed him to embrace her, support her. Her mind was spinning with rainbow colors, her body vibrating with life. And her heart was wide open, brimming over with love.

Eventually, Storm eased her from him and gently lowered her. Unwilling to leave his arms, she pressed herself against him, laughing softly. "My knees feel like jelly," she murmured, nuzzling his flesh.

"I'm shaking, too," he confided, pressing his lips to her glistening cheek. Strands of her dark hair teased his mouth, and he inhaled deeply, absorbing her into him.

Almost reverently he stroked his hand down her spine, memorizing the sensations. "You're like Mother Earth," he whispered against her ear. "Your body has hills, valleys, mountains and plains. I love moving my hands over you and exploring all these mysteries."

When Tahcha arched against him he felt a wave of fire shoot through him all over again.

Tahcha sighed contentedly and smiled up into his eyes, which were alight with love.

"How about we dry off and go to your bedroom." Tahcha whispered, "Let's hurry...."

Storm grinned in agreement and helped her out of the shower, drying her with a thick green towel. Every time he met her eyes he felt like the luckiest man in the world, seeing her expression. The soft parting of her well-kissed lips, the proud way her nipples thrust upward filled him with a secret delight.

She dried him off in turn, and when they emerged from the steamy bathroom, he scooped Tahcha into his arms and carried her down the hall.

Tahcha had not seen Storm's bedroom. When he nudged open the door with one foot and stepped inside, she caught her breath in surprise. The queen-size bed was covered with a quilt she instantly recognized.

Tahcha's mother had taught her to quilt when she was young. Many Lakota girls learned to do so, for it was an honored tradition among the women. Special quilts were made and given to men who went out on a vision quest. The one Tahcha saw on Storm's bed brought tears to her eyes.

As he deposited her gently upon it, she whispered, "This was the quilt my mom and I made for you that spring before your first vision quest." Tahcha ran her hand lovingly over the colorful wedding ring design. *Wedding rings.* What had her mother thought, so long ago? Had she foreseen her daughter and Storm falling in love? Perhaps marrying one day?

Storm settled Tahcha between the white sheets. Sliding in next to her, he pulled the covers up and then drew her against him. Tahcha lay facing him, her head on his arm, his other hand caressing her hip.

"I thought you might recognize this quilt," he told her quietly.

"It's so amazing," Tahcha whispered, nuzzling his jaw. "I had forgotten about it. My mom said you needed a special gift. We worked on it for six months. I always loved

sitting with her at night, sewing these squares into place...."
Her voice trailed off as Storm kissed her cheek, her parted
lips.

Lifting his head, he held her gaze. "This quilt has been
with me almost everywhere, sweetgrass woman. I took it
with me when we left the res. I had it stored when I went
to Afghanistan. When I came home, I sent for it, and spread
it across my hospital bed. It was the only bunk at Walter
Reed that looked homey, let me tell you! You have no idea
how many nights I lay there in pain, gripping this quilt. I'd
hold on to it, Tahcha, and remember our happy times
together." Storm smiled and kissed the tip of her nose. "I'd
swear it took away some of my pain, some of my home-
sickness, and the grief I felt over the loss of my parents. It
helped me keep my soul intact. It got me through so many
dark and agonizing times.

"And stupid me," he whispered. "Why didn't I realize
that it was you—your energy, and the love you had sewed
into this quilt as you made it with your mother—that was
helping me heal? Helping me to go on, and not give in to
depression after being wounded. You have no idea how
much you've been a part of my life, Tahcha."

His words started tears welling in her eyes again. "I had
no idea, Storm.... None."

Shaking his head, he brushed strands of hair from her
glowing skin. "I didn't, either. I finally put it all together
after you came home. And the more I thought about it, the
more I knew that I had always loved you, Tahcha. I never
stopped loving you."

Holding her glistening gaze, he added in an emotional

tone, "And I'll love you forever. What is in my heart for you has always been there. I was a fool to ignore it, but sometimes life has to teach us things the hard way. When you returned to the res, I knew the Great Spirit was giving me a second chance. But I was afraid, Tahcha. I was reeling from a bad divorce. I was projecting my experience with my ex-wife onto you, and that wasn't fair or right." With a grimace, Storm glanced across the room toward the partly opened door. "I had to settle my past within myself before I could come to you with an honest and open heart."

Tahcha saw the pain, the uncertainty in Storm's eyes. And yet golden hope glimmered there, too. Reaching up, she caressed his cheek. "I understand now, Storm. I understand everything. And it's all right. I made mistakes as well. I saw you in every man I met. And I never realized until recently how I was unconsciously comparing all of them to you. You have always been the love of my life. I was so blind…. And I was so shattered by my helicopter crash. I felt like a failure, a loser, I didn't think you'd respect me when you heard what had happened."

Giving her a tender look, Storm stroked her hair, her shoulder. "Great Spirit is giving both of us another chance together," he told her. "This morning, just before you arrived, a white owl flew in and landed on the fence post near where I was working. It looked at me, and I knew something special, something life altering, was about to happen. And then you drove over the hill." He gazed into her eyes. "You came back into my life."

Tahcha's brows arched in surprise. "And it was your white owl spirit guide that saved my life the day my copter crashed." She heaved a sigh. "Why didn't I realize that you had never really left me, Storm? Love can't be destroyed. It continued to live between us even though we went in different directions."

Storm caught her hand and pressed a kiss to it. "Listen to me, Tahcha, nothing is ever wasted. We needed that time apart. You're right—we never stopped loving one another, and on some level, that got us through the hardships we had to experience." Giving her hand another kiss before he released it, he added huskily, "And look at what we've been given now. Gifts earned by people don't come easily, without a lot of pain and suffering. I'm glad my spirit owl was there to save your life. To bring you back to me."

Snuggling into his arms, Tahcha held Storm tightly. Pressing a kiss to his neck, she whispered, "You want to know why I showed up here this morning?"

"Yes. What brought you back to me?"

She looked up and met his burning gaze. "Last night at Gram Willow's place, I opened up my small medicine bag, which your father gave me when I was a child."

"Yes, I remember. My dad told me when I was older and could understand, that you needed a special protection that he, as a medicine man, could give you. He often saw future events, and I'm sure that's why he gave it to you."

Tahcha nodded. "I sat on my bed in Gram's cabin and opened it up. Oh, I know you're not supposed to check what's inside a medicine bag, but something drove me to do so."

"What did you find?"

"There was only one item in it, Storm. A feather from a white owl…"

Stunned, Storm stared at her. "You're kidding me."

Tahcha shook her head. "No, I'm not. I've carried that medicine bag all my life. I always tied it to my waist belt or stuck it in a pocket of my flight uniform. I was never without it, Storm." She searched his wide eyes, which were filled with shock. "I believe your father saw that his owl spirit would one day be transferred to you, upon his death. That you would become a medicine man in his footsteps. And I believe he knew that I'd became a pilot, and that I could die in a fiery crash in Afghanistan. I believe he gifted me with a feather from his white owl spirit to keep me safe. To bring me back home to you...."

Storm was as awed by the blazing love in her eyes as he was by the magic of the world they lived in. "My father must have foreseen our lives, our separation, and you possibly dying before we had a chance to reunite. To love one another. To come full circle."

Nodding, Tahcha said, "Yes, I believe that, Storm. Your father saw the future. And he knew. He knew that if I died in that helicopter crash—and I should have—that we would never have a second chance with one another."

Storm drew a deep breath. "This...is incredible."

"It's beautiful. Haunting. Right."

Gazing at her, Storm said, "Nothing has ever felt so right to me. You belong at my side, Tahcha. I think we knew that as teens."

"The white owl spirit has been watching over both of us all this time," Tahcha whispered. "When I shared this with Gram Willow last night, she told me to go see you today. That you needed to know about the feather. She said it was a sign."

"Gram couldn't have been more right," Storm agreed. He squeezed Tahcha gently. "Share my blanket with me, sweetgrass woman." Lifting his hand, he smoothed it across the quilt that she and her mother had made for him so long ago. "Share my heart, this house and this bed with me."

Drowning in his golden gaze, Tahcha vowed, "From this day forward, my beloved. I'm never going to leave you again. Or this res. You hold my heart. This land cradles and feeds my spirit. That's all I'll ever need."

Storm cupped her face and kissed her deeply, with tender yearning. His heart pounding with a fierce love for this woman warrior, he whispered, "The white owl has been with us since we were born. And you and I will share a life together from this moment forward. I'll never want anyone but you, Tahcha. Ever."

* * * * *

Aunt Delia's Legacy

CARA SUMMERS

Cara Summers has written more than twenty-five books for Mills & Boon. Cara loves writing for Mills & Boon because she's been able to write so many different kinds of love stories – from Gothic thrillers to light romantic comedies. Cara lives in upstate New York – where the winters are long and snowy – and when she isn't creating new stories, she teaches in the writing programme at Syracuse University and flies frequently to Florida to visit her two grandchildren.

To my Mom and Dad – Janet and Andrew.
Thanks for the rich legacy you've left me.

PROLOGUE

SENSING THAT THE CURTAIN was about to fall on the final act of her life, Delia Waring ran down her checklist, as she did every night now, to make sure the stage was perfectly set. Her glance took in the portrait covering the wall safe, then moved to her bedside table. Everything was perfect except for the diamond necklace. Very carefully, she placed it in position and then nodded in satisfaction. Good to know that her days as a theater major in college hadn't been wasted.

Reaching for her brandy, she settled herself against the pillows and raised the glass in a little toast. "To a great opening night and a winning run." Then she took a sip and enjoyed the warmth that moved through her slowly.

She'd hatched her little plot almost a year ago, on that sunny fall day when the doctors had told her that her time was running out. She'd told no one, but according to their estimation, she should have been pushing up daffodils by last spring.

Delia laughed softly. She'd spent her whole life establishing a reputation for being unpredictable. Spring had come and gone, and she'd managed to live long enough to see one last January nor'easter whip up the coast and blanket the little town of Westhaven, Connecticut, in more than three feet of snow. She raised her glass again, this time toasting the snow that had arrived just in time for the Winterfest celebration.

Still, Delia knew that she couldn't beat the odds forever. Tonight's town meeting had exhausted her, and it had taken more out of her than usual to repeat her nightly ritual of setting the scene here in her bedroom. She took another sip of brandy. As someone had once said, "The end of every true story was death."

With a wry smile, Delia settled herself more comfortably against her pillows. Not that she was able to sleep much anymore. And she'd always figured that sleep was a waste of time when there was so much life to be enjoyed, anyway.

She'd certainly enjoyed hers—which hadn't always pleased her family. Her ultraconservative brother had often referred to her as a confounded free spirit. Delia supposed the title fit, and it had always amused her when her more tolerant nephew, Calvin, referred to her as his auntie Mame. She'd even gotten a chuckle out of the fact that her niece, Susan, had dubbed her the black sheep of the family.

In a way, she'd been that, too. Instead of marrying and settling down the way Calvin and Susan's father had, she'd chosen to become a bit of a nomad, traveling the world in search of adventure and love. She'd found both, more than once, and in her earlier days, she stirred up her fair share of scandals. There'd been that very handsome count with close ties to the royal family in…

With a sigh, Delia took another tiny sip of her brandy. All that had been years ago. More recently, she'd come back to her home in Westhaven, and in her own way she supposed she'd settled down—if becoming an activist against some greedy land developers who wanted to ruin the landscape of the town with an ugly strip mall counted. Then, at the age of eighty, she'd run for mayor and to her family's surprise and consternation, she'd won.

Now Susan no longer thought of her as a black sheep. Instead, Delia figured Susan and her son, Dougie, had her pegged as a royal pain in the ass. They not only owned the development company trying to build the strip mall just inside the town limits, but they'd also tried to persuade her to sell them her farmhouse and the surrounding land.

Not in her lifetime. Delia glanced around the room again. If her little plot went well, hopefully not in Susan's or Dougie's, either.

If there was one thing that Delia regretted, it might be the fact that she'd never had children. But at least she'd had a close relationship with her nephew Calvin and her great-niece Carly. Of all the Warings, Carly was the one she'd always had a sense of kinship with. Deep inside, Carly was a free spirit. But her great-niece had also inherited some of her father's and grandfather's more conservative genes. Delia respected that. More, she had to honor that.

Wasn't that why she'd interfered in Carly's life nine years ago? At eighteen, with her whole future ahead of her, Carly had been ready to run away with town bad boy Ren Maxwell. And Delia had put a stop to it.

Now that the time was right, she intended to interfere in Carly's and Ren's lives again. As part of her plan, she'd recently appointed Ren Maxwell as deputy mayor so that when her time ran out, he could take over in the mayor's position until he or someone else was officially elected. That part of her plan had gone very smoothly.

As far as Carly went, all Delia had to do was get her to return to Westhaven and put her in Ren's path for a little while. The fact that Carly hadn't set foot in Westhaven for nine years told Delia more than anything else that her niece still had feelings for Ren.

Delia felt her eyes drifting shut. The same feeling of exhaustion she'd felt earlier at the town meeting was creeping up on her again. She was just going to have to put her faith in the fact that Carly still had that free spirit she'd had nine years ago. And it was just too damn bad that Delia wouldn't be around to see how it all turned out....

CHAPTER ONE

STUFFING HER HANDS in the pockets of her peacoat, Carly Waring stood in the center of Westhaven Town Square and ordered the jittering nerves in her stomach to settle. They'd begun their little dance when her great-aunt Delia's attorney had phoned and requested her presence for the reading of her aunt's will. She would have refused to come today if Mr. Grady hadn't told her Aunt Delia had specifically requested her presence.

Carly was almost getting used to the little band of pain that tightened around her heart whenever she thought of her aunt. It was so hard to get her mind around the fact that she would never see her aunt Delia again. The family-only memorial service her father had arranged in New York City had been surreal. Coming here for the reading of the will was definitely a reality check. She had to face the fact that she would never see, never talk to Aunt Delia again.

Carly pressed her hand to her stomach. As a doctor who'd become skilled at pinpointing her patients' ills, she knew that the loss of her aunt wasn't the only cause of her jittering nerves. There were memories here in Westhaven that she'd run away from nine years ago, and they all centered on Ren Maxwell and the abortive affair she'd had with him that summer. Clearly, she was afraid that coming back here would stir those memories up.

And that simple diagnosis ticked her off. She was not a coward. A quick glance at her watch told her that she had fifteen minutes until her appointment at Mr. Grady's office. Time enough to face some of those memories down, she decided. Lifting her chin, she let her gaze sweep over the picture-postcard scene in front of her. Snowdrifts were piled high on either side of the paths that crisscrossed Westhaven's Town Square. The scenic space was bordered on one side by a canal and on the other by the foot of Main Street. And this was where her love affair with Ren Maxwell had begun and ended.

She shifted her gaze to the gazebo where she'd waited until nearly dawn for Ren to come to her on that long-ago night. He hadn't come. End of story.

There. That hadn't been so bad. Of course, it wasn't the memory of his betrayal that worried her. The heartbreak she'd suffered had eventually focused her and made her realize what she'd nearly given up to be with Ren. So she'd worked harder than ever to get through medical school and a double residency in internal medicine and pediatrics.

No, what worried her most were the memories of the beginning of her affair with Ren Maxwell. So they had to be dealt with. Drawing in a deep breath, Carly turned and strode down the path to the foot of Main Street where the Waring Bank building stood. It was right there that she'd first met Ren. She'd stepped off the curb, and he'd run into her—quite literally—on his motorcycle.

Even now, her memory of the accident was fuzzy. All she

could picture was his face bending over hers—those incredibly blue eyes, the dark hair that was never quite tame, the strong angled cheekbones. He'd reminded her then of some wickedly dark angel.

And his hands. She recalled exactly how strong they'd felt when they'd clasped hers to get her on her feet. He'd kept her hands in his even after he'd gotten her safely back on the curb. The accident had happened in the middle of the day. Carly knew that cars and people had streamed passed them, but she and Ren might have been alone on the planet.

He'd completely enchanted her. What she'd felt that day was what they wrote about in books, love at first sight. Each time they'd met that summer, her feelings had deepened, and they'd only grown stronger when she and Ren had become lovers.

Carly frowned. She couldn't deny the strength of what she'd felt for Ren Maxwell. Nor had she ever been able to come close to feeling that strongly about any other man. Which was perfectly fine with her. She never wanted to feel like that again. In a few months, when she finished her residencies at Mt. Sinai Hospital, she'd be joining her parents' practice on Park Avenue. She'd have the life she'd always wanted.

And if she ran into Ren Maxwell today? Carly frowned. She supposed there was a remote possibility that she would. Over the years, her aunt had mentioned Ren now and then, so she knew he was living in Westhaven and that he taught math in a nearby private school. He'd even been appointed deputy mayor.

For the life of her, she couldn't picture the Ren Maxwell she'd known in either of those roles. They seemed too…straitlaced and conservative for the slightly dangerous man he'd been at twenty. That younger man had been a risk taker, a truly free spirit—in short, everything that she hadn't been. She'd had plenty of time to think about why he'd been able to make such a complete fool of her, and she was pretty sure it was that he'd been so different from her. Clearly, that had been the fascination.

Well, she was older now, smarter now. Deliberately, she glanced back at the gazebo. Everything was different now. Then with a frown, she narrowed her eyes and spotted what she hadn't noticed before. There was a banner over the front of the gazebo proclaiming the start of Winterfest that very day.

Winterfest. The pain around her heart tightened so much that she rubbed her fist against it. Delia Waring had created the Winterfest celebration in her first year as mayor. Carly recalled hearing the pride in her aunt's voice as she'd related that over high tea at the Waldorf-Astoria where Delia had always stayed in New York.

One loud chime of a clock had Carly gathering her thoughts. It was one o'clock. Turning, she crossed the street. The clock on the Waring Bank building kept perfect time, and she just hated to be late. Still, she stopped dead in her tracks and stared when she spotted the sign in the window of the now vacant bank: Home of the new Delia Waring Clinic.

Aunt Delia had intended to build a clinic? She'd never once mentioned that. As Carly hurried on down Main Street in the direction of the Grady and Grady law firm, she wondered what other surprises her aunt might have in store for her.

REN MAXWELL PROPPED a shoulder against the bookcase in the offices of Grady and Grady and surveyed the room. If there was one thing that Delia Waring had loved to do it was to set up a scene, and this one had her name written all over it.

Directly in front of him, Rupert Grady, Esquire, sat behind his desk. With his lined face and slight, almost fragile stature, the man reminded Ren a bit of Yoda. Delia had once summed Grady up by saying, "He might be pushing eighty, but as an attorney, I'd pit him against anything coming out of law school these days."

To Rupert's right sat Delia's niece, Susan Waring Mansfield, and her son, Douglas Junior, who was called Dougie. Douglas Senior had to forego the little gathering because he was speaking at a conference in Boston. In his gut, Ren knew that there were going to be some fireworks when Delia's bequests were read. At any other time, he might have looked forward to them, but right now, Ren wished the older man would just read the damn will.

The clock on the Waring Bank building had chimed the one o'clock hour five minutes ago. Catching the older man's eye, Ren raised a quizzical eyebrow. What were they waiting for? Why not get started? He barely stopped himself from saying the words aloud.

Susan Waring Mansfield said them instead. "Isn't it time we got started, Mr. Grady?"

"In a moment. Would you like more coffee, Mrs. Mansfield?"

Tapping her fingers on the arm of her chair, Susan shook her head, but Dougie rose and refilled his cup. The young man was tall and blond like his mother and handsome in a preppy, movie star kind of way.

"Mr. Maxwell?" Rupert asked.

"No. Thanks." Ren had declined the offer of coffee the first time around. He'd had to cancel a precalculus class at St. Martin's Academy, the small very private school where, in addition to his teaching duties, he chaired the math department and coached ice hockey. If the reading of Delia's will didn't start soon, he'd have to cancel a second class. That would please his students enormously—until he posted the double homework assignment onto the class listserv.

Mr. Grady had insisted that he be present. Delia Waring's wishes had been very clear on that point, and because they were Delia's wishes, Ren had bowed to them. As he'd bowed to so many of her wishes in the past.

He was going to miss that soft throaty laugh of hers that could fill a room. And he was going to miss that mischievous gleam in her eye when she was about to hatch some new scheme. Delia Waring had been a woman of many talents, but she'd been a real genius when it came to manipulation. Dammit, he was going to miss *her.*

He was still mad as hell at her that she hadn't let anyone know she was dying. If only he'd known... What? In the days since Delia Waring had passed away, he'd gone over and over what he might have done for her if he'd known.

The only thing he'd come up with is that he might have refused the appointment as deputy mayor. She'd purposely persuaded him into the job, knowing that when she died, he'd be stuck as the acting mayor. The wily old fox.

Ren glanced at his watch. It was now almost ten past the hour.

"Look," Susan said, "who are we waiting for? Dougie and I are due back at the office."

"We're waiting for Dr. Waring," Rupert said.

Susan threw up her hands. "That could take forever. He could be dealing with an emergency at the hospital."

Rupert nodded. "Just a few more minutes."

It hadn't escaped Ren's attention that the Mansfields had been studiously ignoring him since they'd arrived. Ren assumed they would interpret his presence to mean that Delia had left something to him. Knowing Delia, she'd probably left him some little trinket just to piss them off.

There was little love lost between Delia and the Mansfields. According to Delia, Susan had never approved of her lifestyle, and Delia certainly hadn't won any points with her niece a year ago when she'd rallied the citizens of Westhaven to fight against Mansfield Ltd.'s plans to build a shopping mall just inside the town line. However, during the past year, Susan and Douglas Senior had been trying to mend fences, no doubt because they wanted to get their hands on the one hundred plus acres of land surrounding Delia's old farmhouse. Ren had a hunch that Delia had other plans for the land, but he didn't doubt for a minute that she might have led them on a bit. Delia Waring enjoyed making other people dance to her tunes.

Susan sat forward in her chair. "Why don't you call my brother and find out what's delaying him?"

"It's not your brother, Dr. Calvin Waring, that we're waiting for," Rupert said.

Susan frowned. "Who then?"

"Dr. Carly Waring."

Dammit, Ren thought. Why in hell hadn't he seen this coming?

Then the door opened. "Ah, here she is now," Rupert Grady said, smiling as he rose from his chair.

Ren was vaguely aware of greetings being exchanged. But he couldn't make sense out of them. He couldn't seem to do anything but stare at Carly. The one coherent thought that streamed through his mind was that she hadn't changed. It was as if nine years had simply melted away. Her ebony-colored hair still fell straight until it brushed her shoulders. A memory flashed into his mind of how that fall of hair had felt brushing along his skin. Her body was still slender as a reed. Another memory flashed and he recalled how that body had felt pressed to his.

With one sweep of his glance Ren took in the slim, gray pin-striped trousers and the bright red peacoat. The way she dressed hadn't changed, either. There was still that contrast between the conservative and the passionate.

Then she met his eyes, and in that freeze-framed moment, he felt the same instant connection he had nine years ago— that snap and sizzle in his system, as if two wires had suddenly come in contact to create an electrical current.

Carly was the one who broke eye contact and moved to take her seat next to her aunt Susan.

Damn. Ren scowled and fought back the urge to walk out of the office. This was not happening to him again. What he was feeling had to be some kind of intense déjà vu. But even as he told himself that, he could have sworn he heard Delia's soft throaty laugh filling the room.

CHAPTER TWO

REN. HE WAS HERE. It was the shock of it. That had to be why her heart was beating so fast. It couldn't be the flight of stairs she'd just climbed. She worked out four times a week. She did Pilates. She was a New Yorker, so she walked. She shouldn't be suddenly short of breath.

Breathe. Carly drew in air and let it out. But she didn't take her eyes off Ren Maxwell. He was regarding her in that steady, intense way that she remembered. There were other people in the room, but in that moment, she couldn't see them. How could she have forgotten how large he was—those broad shoulders, the narrow waist and hips? His face seemed leaner, his cheek bones sharper. And his mane of hair in that incredibly rich, mahogany shade. The reality of his presence made the way she'd remembered him in the park seem like a faded sepia photograph.

The one stray thought that slipped into her mind was that he still looked too dangerous to be a math teacher or a deputy mayor. In some other era, he would have led men into battle.

And he certainly didn't look happy to see her.

As the room began to spin, Carly ordered herself to breathe again. And move. Tearing her gaze away from Ren's helped, but she couldn't feel her legs as she got to a chair and sank into it.

Then she ruthlessly gathered her thoughts. There was absolutely no way that she was going to allow Ren Maxwell to tempt her off course again. What she'd just experienced was a momentary aberration. It had to be part of the general disorientation she'd felt ever since she'd learned of her aunt's passing. She was grieving for Aunt Delia. That had to be it.

In any case, she'd be on the train back to New York in a couple of hours, and Ren Maxwell would once more fade into a distant memory. End of story.

For the first time, Carly became aware that her aunt Susan and cousin Dougie were present. Her father and Susan had never been close. When the Mansfields had come to Aunt Delia's memorial service, it was the first time she'd seen them in ten years or more.

"Since we're all gathered now, I'll read the last will and testament of Delia Waring," Rupert Grady said.

Carly folded her hands in her lap and tried to concentrate on what Mr. Grady was saying.

"'To Linney Banks who has been my housekeeper for close to fifty years, I leave the sum of $100,000.'"

Of course her aunt would have provided for Linney. Carly made a mental note to stop by and see the housekeeper before she left town.

"'To my niece, Susan, and my great-nephew, Douglas Junior,'" Rupert Grady continued, "'I offer my sincerest wishes and prayers that you do not succeed in commercializing the town of Westhaven.'"

"What's that supposed to mean?" Dougie shot out of his chair.

Rupert cleared his throat. "If I might continue?"

"Of course," Susan said, placing a hand on her son's arm.

"'To my great-niece, Carly Waring, and to Ren Maxwell, who has been a true friend to me, I leave the rest of my estate, my money and investments, all my property in Westhaven, the house, everything in it and all my worldly goods. I know that you love the old house and the land as much as I do and that together you will make wise decisions.'"

For a moment, shocked silence stretched in the room. Carly heard Ren mutter something behind her as she swallowed hard. What in the world had her aunt done?

"That's it?" Dougie asked. "You're done?"

"Those are Delia's wishes." Rupert slipped off his glasses and folded his hands on the top of his desk.

Carly shot a look over her shoulder at Ren and saw a gleam of amusement in his eyes. It was enough to convince her that he hadn't known about this, either.

"There's been a mistake."

It was Dougie who spoke the words that were foremost in Carly's mind. But knowing her aunt, she was pretty sure it was wishful thinking.

"I can assure you it's no mistake," Rupert said.

Dougie jerked his head toward Ren. "He's not family. He can't…he shouldn't…"

"Delia can leave her land and money to anyone she likes, Dougie." Susan's voice was soft, but tight.

"Correct." Rupert nodded.

Dougie stepped forward and jabbed his index finger impatiently on the attorney's desk. "What about the diamond necklace? Great-Aunt Delia promised it to my mother. And we can prove it. She put it in writing."

For the first time, the attorney frowned. "She made no mention of the necklace specifically in the will. Legally, it would be included in all her worldly possessions and be shared equally between the two beneficiaries."

Carly's head was spinning. She knew the necklace they were talking about. Delia had worn it all the time, and it was worth a small fortune.

"We'll contest the will," Dougie said. "That necklace belongs to my mother."

Rupert cleared his throat. "Dr. Waring, Mr. Maxwell, if you'd be so kind as to step into my conference room and allow me a few moments with Mrs. Mansfield and her son?"

"Of course." Carly rose and moved toward the door. Ren reached with her for the doorknob, and for a moment his hand covered hers. His palm was still large, still hard. Heat arrowed through her, bringing back vivid memories of other times, other touches. Even after the contact was broken, she struggled not to think of those other times, those other touches.

Ordering herself to breathe didn't help because she drew in his scent—a mix of soap and something that was uniquely Ren. She would have recognized it anywhere.

As they moved down a narrow hall to where Rupert Grady's receptionist held another door open, Carly quickened her step. She had to think. The small conference room was lined with bookshelves and the carved oak table nearly filled the space. She circled it, putting it between herself and Ren, and this time when she breathed in, the scent was of lemon wax and old books. All right. Get it together, Carly.

So what if Ren Maxwell had the power to stir her up? She was no longer an impressionable girl of eighteen. She could and she would control the feelings that he could still arouse in her. And right now she and Ren Maxwell had much bigger problems to solve.

The will.

What had her aunt been thinking? Leaving everything to Ren and her didn't make sense. Frowning, she shoved her hair back and began to tap her foot. Aunt Delia never did anything without a purpose. And the one thing her aunt loved was stirring up a bit of drama. It occurred to her that the little scene she'd just witnessed in Mr. Grady's office would have pleased her aunt no end. The thought nearly made her smile.

But it wasn't really funny. With a shake of her head, she turned to face Ren. "Tell me you've got a plan to get us out of this mess."

"Not yet." Because the mix of amusement and annoyance in Carly's tone was the perfect match to what he was feeling, some of Ren's tension eased. With a smile he settled a hip on the conference table and watched as she slipped out of her coat.

The way she moved had always fascinated him. Her walk was always quick and purposeful, and there was a business-like precision in the way she neatly draped the coat over the back of a chair. She wore a silk blouse in a creamy color and gray trousers. There'd been less control a few seconds ago when she'd tossed her hair back and tapped her foot. It was the contrasts in her that had appealed to him right from the start.

And if he was smart, he wouldn't let himself be pulled in again. "I was hoping *you'd* save the day, Doc."

She studied him for a moment. In nine years, he hadn't forgotten those eyes. Right now they were the color of rich milk chocolate, but he'd seen them darken with temper—and with desire.

"Did you know she was going to do this?"

Ren reined in his thoughts and kept his gaze steady. "Nope."

Narrow-eyed, she regarded him for another few seconds before she nodded. "I didn't think so. Any idea why would she leave everything to you and me?"

He inclined his head toward the door. "You mean other than to annoy the hell out of Dougie and his mom?"

Her lips twitched. "Yes. It's not funny really. If all she wanted was to cause that little scene, why involve us?"

After his first shock, Ren had given it some thought. "Maybe we're the two she trusted to carry out her wishes."

"What wishes?"

"For starters, there's her vision for the town." Ren settled himself more comfortably on the table. "In her five years as mayor, your aunt was actively engaged in keeping strip malls, big-name warehouse stores and tacky housing developments out of Westhaven. Her goal was to preserve the small-town atmosphere that she's always valued and to protect the small business people who always suffer when the big chain stores move in. Susan Mansfield, her husband and son have been leading the fight against Delia. And there are townspeople who side with them, namely the ones who would profit from the quick sale of their land. So far, Delia's been winning."

Carly couldn't prevent a smile. "I'm not surprised. She always had a knack for getting her way."

"Yes, she did." And she could be ruthless in her tactics, Ren thought. His lips nearly twitched when he recalled that night nine years ago when she'd handcuffed him to a pipe in the kitchen of the gardener's cottage until he'd agreed to write Carly a note breaking things off between them.

Carly began to tap her foot again. "And you think she wants us to step into her shoes and take up the fight?"

"That certainly is one possibility," Ren said.

"Well, I can't do it. I don't have the time. I'm not sure that I even have the interest. Why would she think that I would care about what happens to Westhaven? I haven't even been here in nine years."

Precisely, Ren thought. But you're here now. And Delia knew what to do to get you here. He watched as the little frown line appeared on Carly's forehead. Then, with her hand on one hip, she began to pace. She'd always done that when she was trying to figure something out.

He'd had time during the reading of the will to study her a bit more, and his first impression had been wrong. She had changed. The girl he'd known nine years ago had been pretty. The woman pacing back and forth in front of him was beautiful. And more controlled. When he found his mind wandering to what it might be like to strip that control away, he refocused on the present.

"When I asked about her wishes, you said, 'for starters.' What did you mean by that?" Carly asked.

"Think about it. If she wanted to split her estate between us, she could have divided her assets, given you the house and me the money or vice versa."

"True. But she left everything to us jointly. So that we have to sort things out between us...."

Her eyes went dark with temper the moment it dawned on her.

"She must have *wanted* to throw us together."

"That's the way it looks to me, too, Doc."

"But why?"

He raised an eyebrow. "Why not?"

She met his eyes very steadily. "Because we've been there and tried that. It didn't work."

One of the things he'd always liked about her was that she was up front. Most of the time she said exactly what she thought. But her cool tone of dismissal grated on him.

"We come from different worlds—isn't that the way you described it in your note?" Carly asked.

Even now, nine years later, Ren didn't want to think about the note. It had been a cruel way to break things off. He'd argued with Delia for hours, wanting to tell Carly in person, but Delia had insisted he put it in writing and that he not see Carly again. She'd been right, of course. If he'd seen Carly again, he never would have been able to break things off. Even though intellectually, he'd agreed with everything that Delia had said on that long-ago night.

"We still come from different worlds," Carly continued. "Nine years hasn't changed that. My life is in New York. In a few months I'm joining my parents' practice. Your life is here. We each want different things." She glanced away then and he saw color rise in her cheeks. "I mean, even if we still felt the way we used to about each other, which we clearly don't…"

Was she trying to convince him or herself?

"We don't know if we could still feel that way about each other," Ren pointed out. "Maybe Delia wanted us to find out."

Carly's chin lifted. "Well then. We'll just have to avoid that little pitfall. It shouldn't be hard." She picked up her pea coat. "I'm taking the next train back to New York. I'll arrange for some official kind of paperwork so that you can handle everything on this end."

A knock on the door had them both turning to see Rupert Grady enter the room. "I'm terribly sorry about the uproar. I was expecting something like that. I warned Ms. Waring that the Mansfields would not be happy."

"Did you manage to settle them down?" Ren asked.

Rupert cleared his throat. "What I suggested was a compromise. Mrs. Mansfield is going to locate the letter from her aunt that proves Ms. Waring's intent to leave her the diamond necklace. If the letter does indeed exist, they would have a good chance of contesting the will successfully. At the very least, they could get the necklace. But that would take months, even years, and the estate would be all tied up in the meantime, and the two of you would be left in limbo. The tack that I took with the Mansfields and that

I'm suggesting to you is that you settle things amicably by giving them the necklace if they agree not to contest the will."

"And they agreed?" Carly asked.

"After I explained to them how long the proceedings might take."

"A bird in the hand," Ren murmured.

"Yes, indeed," Grady said.

Ren glanced at Carly. "What do you think?"

She shrugged. "It's your call."

He met Rupert's eyes. "We'll consider your advice and after we talk it over, we'll let you know."

The lawyer cleared his throat again. "In the meantime, young Mr. Mansfield wants the necklace to have it appraised. I told him that I could probably arrange that."

Ren glanced at Carly again, and when she shrugged, he said, "We'll agree to that."

Rupert beamed a smile at them. "Good. The sooner we settle this matter, the better for you. Ms. Waring was adamant about wanting everything to run smoothly." Then he pulled a set of keys out of his pocket and handed them to Ren. "I'll tell Mr. Mansfield to drop by the house in an hour. Shall we say three-thirty?"

"Fine," Ren said. Rupert held the door as he and Carly filed out of the room. It wasn't until they reached the street that Carly spoke the thought that was on his own mind.

"Run smoothly, my foot. Aunt Delia wanted to leave us in the middle of a mess."

"I'll second that."

She glanced at her watch. "Well, this is one time when

she isn't going to have it all her way. I'll have my family's lawyer draw up some papers that give you power to do whatever needs to be done. You can drop me at the train station on your way to the house."

He wondered if she realized just how much she sounded like her aunt in order-giving mode. The course of action she'd just mapped out would get them both off Delia's hook. He should put her on that train and let her go back to her own very different world in New York.

Later, he would wonder why he hadn't. Probably because of the duchess-to-serf tone she was using. She'd never used that particular tone when she was eighteen. Or perhaps, it was that she'd so quickly dismissed the idea of finding out if they could rekindle the feelings they'd had for each other nine years ago. Was that why he was so tempted to do just that?

Or was it simply the sight of her standing there in the winter sunlight in that bright red coat that made him smile slowly and say, "Hey. If you're going to dump this all in my lap, the least you can do is stick around until we can jointly hand over the necklace to Dougie. That way he's not so likely to accuse me of nipping it and replacing it with glass and paste."

Concern flooded her eyes. "Is he likely to do that?"

Ren shrugged. One thing hadn't changed. She was still ready to jump to his defense, it seemed. "He might. I may be the deputy mayor now, but to a lot of people, I'm still that bad Maxwell boy." Then because he had another card up his sleeve, he played it. "Linney would love to see you."

It took her only an instant to decide. "All right. I'll take the later train."

CHAPTER THREE

CARLY MENTALLY KICKED herself as Ren drove his little red sports car past the train station. What was she thinking? Staying here in Westhaven any longer than she had to was a mistake. If only he hadn't smiled at her in just that way…

There was still time. The two-thirty train hadn't left yet. She drummed her fingers on the armrest. Catching that train smacked of running away. And wasn't that exactly what she'd been doing for nine years? Plus, there was a part of her that wanted to stay in Westhaven—for just a while longer. Carly knew that side of her nature all right. Aunt Delia had called it her free spirit. It was the same part of her that had been fascinated with Ren Maxwell.

Dammit. He was the one who'd brought it up—what if they *could* still feel for each other what they'd felt nine years ago?

No. She was not going to go there. She recognized a Pandora's box when she saw one. She'd kept those feelings that Ren had stirred up in her locked away, and she wasn't about to release them now. The life she'd always wanted was waiting for her in New York, and just as soon as they handed the necklace over to Dougie Mansfield, she was going back to it. End of story.

Folding her hands in her lap, she glanced at Ren's profile.

What were the chances that she could feel about him what she'd felt at eighteen, anyway? They'd both changed too much.

The younger Ren had been charming, a risk taker. She could still recall that devilish glint in his eyes that first day when he'd dared her to let him take her back to Aunt Delia's on the back of his motorcycle. She hadn't been able to resist the challenge. Just as she evidently hadn't been able to stick to her plan to catch the two-thirty train.

Biting back a frown, she noted that the laugh lines around his eyes were still there; they'd just deepened. And he drove the fast car in the same relaxed and competent way that he'd always handled the motorcycle.

Maybe he hadn't changed so much after all. He'd been very laid-back in Rupert's office. But Ren had always been able to present that kind of a facade. Beneath it lay a simmering energy, the kind that a large predatory cat radiated even when it was lazily stretched out in the sun. That energy, that threat of potential danger, had played a large part in the attraction she'd had for him.

Don't even think about it, Carly. With grim determination, she turned her gaze to the road.

"Thanks for doing this for me," Ren said.

"No problem." Even as she said the words, Carly vowed to herself that she would not, could not let there be any problem between her and Ren.

"I have to make a quick call," he said, taking his cell phone out.

Carly kept her eyes on the road as she listened to Ren cancel his afternoon math class.

There was a grin in his voice as he spoke. "They'll be jumping up and down for joy. Make sure before you turn them loose that you remind them they have to add on the class work to the homework due on Monday."

As he pocketed his phone, Carly kept her gaze on the scenery. "This all looks so strange to me. I've never been here in the winter," she said.

"You've picked a good weekend to come," Ren said. "The Winterfest activities officially start tonight."

"Aunt Delia often spoke of them. She invited me down last year." Guilt twisted into a lump in her stomach. "I should have come. I didn't know that she had so little time left."

"None of us did," Ren said. "She didn't want anyone to know. In spite of the fact that he's officially retired, Doc Bradley over in Chesterfield was taking care of her. I called him first thing after Linney called me over to the house."

She stared at him. "You found her?"

"No. Linney found her. Since I was nearby in the gardener's cottage, Linney called me first, and I came right over. Delia died in her sleep. Doc Bradley said that it was a peaceful passing."

"She always seemed so alive to me."

"Yeah." Ren smiled. "When I brought her home from the town board meeting the night she died, she was talking about what she would wear to kick off the Winterfest activities."

For a moment, silence stretched between them. Then Carly asked, "What exactly are the activities?"

Ren shot her a grin. "Small-town type stuff. We have

skating races on the canal, sledding races on the hill near
the old elementary school, a snowman contest, a chili cook-
off. J. C. Nickols sells his special spiced apple cider, and
Mr. Carney sets up a tent and grills his famous hamburgers."

"Mr. Carney is still working?"

"He comes to the diner every morning, but it's his son
who's taken over running the place. That business has been
in the Carney family for over three generations now.
Nichols Pharmacy is run by its fourth generation. They're
two of the reasons that Delia has fought so hard to keep strip
malls outside the town limits."

"To protect the small businesses here in Westhaven."

"And to hold on to the feeling of community that this
place has enjoyed for so long. The whole town turns out for
the two-day Winterfest event. And we're inundated with
visitors from Chesterfield, Brantford and Shelton. Some of
my students from St. Martin's Academy will be playing in
the Sunday concert."

"You like teaching, don't you?"

He sent her a brief glance. "I wouldn't be doing it if I
didn't. How about you? Are you enjoying being a doctor?"

"Yes. I'm doing a final tour in pediatrics right now.
Joining my parents' practice will be a little different, but I'm
looking forward to it." At least she was hoping she would.
She had to, didn't she?

"How different?" Ren asked.

"They have their office on Park Avenue and their patients
are mostly very well-to-do and travel in the same social
circles as they do. Their specialty is internal medicine. I
doubt I'll be seeing many children."

"What happened to your dream of practicing family medicine and caring for people from the cradle to the grave?"

"I changed my mind." But had she? Wasn't her dream of practicing family medicine one of the reasons she had done the extra residency in pediatrics, against her parents' wishes?

When Ren turned onto a narrow road, Carly turned to him in surprise. "I thought we were going to my aunt's place."

"We are. You'll see it around the next curve."

Carly studied the land to her right. "I don't recognize it." The fields had always been green. She thought she recognized the old oak tree that stood in the center of the large field ahead of her, but without its leaves it looked skinny and naked. "There used to be flowers along the drive."

"There will be again in the spring. The storm last weekend dropped nearly three feet of snow. A lot of the shrubs and even a few of the hedges are buried."

She leaned back in her seat. It occurred to her that they'd been talking quite easily for the last few minutes. But then, Ren Maxwell had been the one person besides her Aunt Delia whom she'd been able to talk freely with about anything. Her parents had always been so busy—with their work and with each other. Plus, she'd never wanted to talk to them about anything that might cause them concern.

When they rounded the curve, the old farmhouse with its sloped roof and large wraparound porch came into view. "I almost don't recognize it," she said. "I always picture it in my mind surrounded with green lawns and the gardens. Aunt Delia still had her gardens, didn't she?"

"She hired a service to cut the lawns and trim the hedges. I helped her out with the rest. We put in a new rose arbor last spring."

"You helped with that?"

"Your aunt and I had an arrangement for years. I got to live in the gardener's cottage rent free and in return I provided slave labor for anything she wanted in the garden."

"She never mentioned that." But then there was a lot her aunt hadn't mentioned, Carly thought. The will being one of the biggies. The fact that she might be about to discover more surprises didn't bode well.

The moment Ren pulled to a stop, she got out of the car. A path had been shoveled, and snow was banked high on either side. Drifts rose nearly to the level of the porch. Minus the flower beds and pots of geraniums flanking the front door, the house looked bleak—as if it were in mourning. She paused at the bottom step, and that familiar band of pain tightened around her heart.

Stopping beside her, Ren asked, "What is it?"

"I...it's coming here. I'm still trying to get my mind around the fact that she's gone. The will and now this makes it more real."

"Yeah." His hand grasped hers, and for a moment they just stood there. Comfort. She hadn't expected it, certainly hadn't thought that she would find it with him. When it occurred to her that he, too, had suffered a loss, she gave his hand a squeeze.

Then the door burst open and Linney, her aunt's longtime housekeeper, stepped out onto the porch. "Miss Carly? I didn't know...didn't expect..."

Nine years hadn't changed her, Carly thought. She was still the same small, skinny woman in a black dress and a crisply ironed white apron. Her hair might have grayed some, but that beaming smile was as welcoming as it had always been. When the older woman took a halting step forward, Carly saw that she was more frail. So she hurried up the steps and took Linney into her arms. Her scent was exactly the same. Rosewater and starch. For the first time since she'd heard of her aunt's death, Carly felt tears fill her eyes and spill down her cheeks.

AS REN STOOD AT THE bottom of the steps, watching the scene unfold, he tried to deal with the emotions tumbling through him. He'd given in to impulse when he'd urged Carly to come to the house with him. He'd used Dougie-boy's antipathy toward him as a ruse, knowing that she would respond. The truth was he could handle Dougie Mansfield. But he'd wanted Carly to stay longer.

That had been a mistake. What he felt for her was not simple desire. It never had been. If Linney hadn't appeared at that moment, he would have turned Carly into his arms and he'd be holding her just as Linney was now. And would he have been able to stop with just holding her?

He certainly hadn't all those years ago when he'd nearly run her down with his motorcycle. Impulse is what had driven his actions that day, too. What he should have done was help her up off the pavement, dust her off and send her on her way. Instead, he'd walked her to the nearest park bench, fetched her a cold drink from Carney's Diner, and then he'd convinced her to let him give her a ride to her aunt's place on the back of his motorcycle.

It should have ended there. But once the door between their very different worlds had opened, neither one of them had been able to close it. He'd felt a connection with Carly that he'd never felt with another woman. And just where had it left him?

He was treading on some very dangerous ground here. As the son of an ex-con and a woman who'd made most of her money on her back, he'd been pretty much raised on dangerous territory. But Ren didn't like to make the same mistake twice. True he'd made something of himself. But Carly was a high-society doctor now, and he was a math teacher in a small private school.

So why in hell was he standing here thinking about opening up that door again?

His thoughts were interrupted by the two women. Linney pulled out of the embrace first, and Carly quickly scrubbed away her tears.

"Sorry," she said. "I didn't mean to fall apart. Aunt Delia wouldn't want us to cry."

Linney patted her shoulder. "Don't you worry a thing about it. I've been doing my share of crying. I figure Miss Delia will just have to put up with it." She shifted her gaze to Ren. "And what am I thinking keeping the two of you out in the cold. Mr. Ren, you come on in the house where it's warm."

Ren followed the two women into the wide foyer where Linney hustled them out of their coats.

"I'll put these away and I'll bring some hot tea into the parlor. You go along in and make yourself at home."

"Mr. Grady sent us here to pick up Aunt Delia's diamond necklace," Carly said. "Dougie Mansfield will be here in half an hour to pick it up."

Linney's smile faded at the mention of Dougie's name, but she said nothing.

"Do you know where my aunt kept her necklace?" Carly asked.

"I put it in the safe for her that night," Ren said. "When I brought Delia home, she said she was feeling tired and asked me to help her up the stairs." He glanced at Linney. "She didn't want to wake you. She'd asked me to see her up to her room a few times in the last couple of months."

"Linney, why don't you hold the tea until Dougie gets here?" Carly asked.

"Certainly." Linney turned, and they could hear her give a little sniff as she bustled away.

Carly met Ren's eyes. "She doesn't think much of my cousin."

Ren smiled. "You think?"

"Aside from a few moments at Aunt Delia's memorial service, I haven't seen him since he was a self-absorbed and fairly obnoxious teenager. What did he do?"

"Dougie and his mother have been frequent visitors lately."

"I thought you said that Mansfield Ltd. lost its bid to build their strip mall largely because my aunt opposed the plan. Weren't they upset with her?"

"They have other irons in the fire, and they evidently felt it was in their best interest to butter Delia up."

Carly frowned. "Did they bother her?"

His grin widened. "On the contrary, I think it amused her to listen to them and perhaps lead them on a bit."

She smiled at him then, and it occurred to Ren that it was the first full smile he'd teased out of her. He felt the same rush of emotions he'd felt just moments before when he'd taken her hand, and the desire to reach out to her was so strong that he barely controlled it.

For a moment neither of them spoke. Neither of them looked away. As the silence stretched, Ren found himself trapped between twin desires—to move forward, to run away. In the end it was Carly who broke the contact by starting toward the wide oak staircase, then pausing in the archway to the main parlor.

"This hasn't changed a bit."

Ren shifted his gaze purposefully toward the room. Sun streamed through windows framed in red-and-gold striped curtains. Light, intensified by the fallen snow, gleamed off highly polished maple floors and highlighted the rich colors in the scattered oriental rugs.

"It's still like a museum," she added.

That it was, Ren thought as he watched Carly weave her way between tables and overstuffed sofas until she reached one of the many display cases that contained artifacts from Delia's travels. In addition to the cases, armoires and curio cabinets lined the walls, and this was one of the least crowded of the rooms.

Carly made a slow tour, and Ren saw the play of emotions on her face. Once more he had to strap down on the urge to go to her and take her in his arms. Instead, he stood perfectly still as she ran a hand over an intricately embroidered throw and then picked up an ivory statue that captured a young couple in a passionate embrace.

"This whole place is a celebration of her life."

"Yes, it is," Ren said letting his gaze sweep the room. For the first time the enormity of the task that Delia had tossed in their laps was beginning to sink in. From the expression on Carly's face, he figured that she was realizing the same thing. For starters, what were they supposed to do with all of Delia's stuff?

"We should go up and get the necklace," he said. "Dougie will be here soon."

"Yes." She replaced the ivory statue on a dainty writing desk and followed him out of the room.

CARLY WAS CAREFUL to keep close to the railing as they walked together up the wide staircase. It would be best if she didn't come into even the most casual contact with Ren again. There'd been that moment when their eyes had met in the foyer. He'd been looking at her in that intent way of his that always made her feel as if he understood her in a way no one else ever had. She'd barely kept herself from going to him and asking him to simply hold her. Thank heavens she'd come to her senses.

Except it was her senses that were the problem. She couldn't trust them where Ren was concerned. She drew a deep breath as they reached the landing. She would just think about something else. Dougie, for instance. "You mentioned something about my cousin and my aunt Susan having other irons in the fire?"

"Delia's farmhouse sits on over one hundred acres of

land, and Mansfield Ltd. has plans for developing it. The way Delia explained it to me, the plans call for a residential community of single-family homes and condominiums that would provide country living and bring a great deal of tax revenue as well as consumers into Westhaven. At least that's how they portrayed it to your aunt."

"But she didn't buy it."

"The far side of your aunt's property lies along the highway that leads into Shelton. Delia learned that they intended to build their strip mall along that highway."

At the head of the stairs, Carly turned down the hall to her aunt's room. "Was she upset?"

"I think she was annoyed that they hadn't been honest with her. That may be why she didn't leave the diamond necklace to Susan in her will."

"A little payback. That would be so like her. So—" Carly paused in front of her aunt's bedroom door "—let's just get it and hand it over to my cousin." This time she was careful to let Ren open the door, and she moved quickly ahead of him into the room. Then she stopped short. If she hadn't been so intent on keeping her distance from Ren, she might have had time to prepare herself for the memories that swamped her.

The last time she'd been in this room had been the night Ren hadn't shown up at the gazebo. She hadn't returned to the farmhouse until nearly sunrise, and Delia had brought her up here. She couldn't drag her gaze away from the red leather box that still sat on Delia's nightstand. The folded piece of paper had been leaning against it. Delia had sat her down on the side of the bed and handed it to her. Even now,

Carly could recall the texture of the paper against her fingers, the sharpness of the fear balling hard and tight in her stomach.

The details of what had gone on after she'd read Ren's message were blurred. Vaguely, she recalled being held in her aunt's arms. Had she finally fallen asleep that way? The pain she was feeling right now wasn't blurred at all. Fisting her hands, she let the sharp sting ride through her in a wave.

"What's wrong, Doc?"

Panic sprinted through her, and it was all she could do not to turn and run from the room. "I can't stay here." Drawing in a deep breath, she turned to face him. "I know that I'm leaving you with a real mess. I'd forgotten how much she'd collected over the years. But I have to go back to New York tonight. I'll do some of the work. I can hire someone to come and appraise the contents of the house and arrange an estate sale. I'll even hire a real estate agent to put the place on the market. We can split the profits right down the middle. As far as the rest of the money goes…"

Her voice trailed off when she noticed the intent way he was looking at her.

"What are you so afraid of, Doc?"

Temper flared inside of her. He'd always been able to see more than she'd wanted him to. "I'm not afraid."

"Liar."

"Think what you like. The truth is I'm busy. I have a life in New York. You should probably hire your own accountant and an attorney to oversee how we split her other assets up."

"It's more complicated than that."

"No. It doesn't have to be. I trust you."

"I can't agree to sell."

She stared at him. "Why not?"

"I think Delia left us the house and the land because she trusted us to carry out her wishes. If we put the place on the market, the first offer will come from Mansfield Ltd. And you can bet that they'll top any other offers we might get. Delia would haunt me for the rest of my life if we let them develop this land."

Carly raised her hands and dropped them. "If we can't sell this place, what are we going to do with it?"

"We'll figure something out. I have great faith in your ability to come up with a solution."

"How can you—how can she expect me to do that when I have no idea what she wanted?"

"There's the sticking point. You might consider staying around long enough to find out."

He was right. She was afraid. And she was a liar. Carly could still see the red box in her peripheral vision, and panic fisted in her throat. When Ren moved toward her, it was all she could do not to take a quick step back.

"Why don't you tell me what's really bothering you, Doc?"

The temptation to do just that warred with fear. In the end what she said was, "Memories."

He frowned. "That's the truth but not the whole truth."

"Memories," she repeated, more firmly this time. She wasn't going to talk about that letter. She'd gotten over it. Put it behind her.

He held her gaze for one long moment before he turned

away. "I'll get the necklace, and we'll go down and have some of Linney's tea."

She nodded, drawing in another deep breath as he strode to the painting that covered her aunt's wall safe. It was good that she'd come up here, she decided. She needed to remember the pain her relationship with Ren had caused her in the past. It was a wise woman who didn't make the same mistake twice.

When Ren pushed the painting aside, Carly saw that the safe was already open. She watched him put his hand in and feel around.

"The necklace isn't here."

CHAPTER FOUR

"IT's NOT HERE?" Carly hurried toward him.

"See for yourself. The safe is empty."

"Then where is it?"

"That's the quarter-of-a-million dollar question." Ren faced her then. "Your aunt always wore it to the town meetings—she said it was her lucky necklace. Usually, on those nights, I'd drive her home and come in with her to rehash what had gone on. Then I'd help her up the stairs. Not that she admitted she needed any help. The last year she'd been getting a little frail, and I'd been urging her to put in an elevator. She wouldn't hear of it. Anyway, I normally locked the necklace in the safe for her before I left. It was part of our regular routine, and we followed it on that last night. Delia wasn't wearing the necklace when Linney brought me up here the next morning."

"Who knew the combination besides you?" Carly asked.

"Linney."

Carly frowned. "She wouldn't steal it."

"I agree." The woman had been with Delia forever.

"Then Aunt Delia must have changed her mind and taken it out of the safe after you left." She glanced around the room. "It's got to be here somewhere."

For ten minutes they searched the room in silence. Carly was grateful that Ren took the area around the bed, turning back the covers, checking the floor. She concentrated on the dressers and the vanity. At least this room wasn't as overflowing with furniture and knickknacks as the rooms on the first floor. She found a jewelry box, but the necklace wasn't in it.

Ren was opening the red leather box when she turned. Swallowing to ease the dryness in her throat, she said, "Anything?"

"Just some papers."

"Miss Carly."

They both turned to see Linney standing in the doorway.

"Mr. Douglas Junior is here."

"Linney," Carly said, "we couldn't find the necklace in the safe. Do you have any idea of where it might be?"

The older woman shook her head. "Miss Delia wasn't wearing it when I found her. She'd taken to wearing it a lot the last few months. Sometimes she wouldn't put it back in the safe. I'd find it lying around the house—once on a table in the parlor, another time in a blown-glass bowl in the library."

"True," Ren said. "Last month when I came to pick her up for the board meeting, she was searching every cabinet and looking under every cushion in the parlor."

Linney nodded in agreement. "I even found it in the pantry one night. She'd come down to make some hot chocolate for herself. I scolded her about her carelessness, but all she said was, 'Now, Linney, who would steal it?'"

"You haven't come across it since we found her?" Ren asked.

"No. I would have told you when you first mentioned it."

"Why don't you go back and tell Mr. Douglas Junior that we'll be right down," Carly said. "Serve him some tea."

The moment that Linney left, Carly moved to the door and closed it. Then she began to pace.

Ren studied her closely. At least that stricken look she'd had a few moments ago had disappeared from her face. He still wondered what memories had brought that lost expression into her eyes when she'd first entered the room. And he wished to hell that he could shrug off the feeling that he'd somehow caused it.

"Dougie's going to be upset," she said.

"Seems to me that you're upset too."

She shot him a look. "Of course I am. My cousin is ready to contest the will unless we produce the necklace and agree to give it to his mother."

Ren leaned a shoulder against the wall. "Do you think I stole it?"

"Of course not."

Ren couldn't name the feelings that swept through him at the simple conviction in her tone.

She pointed a finger at him. "But that's exactly what Dougie is going to think. And then he'll start blabbing that all over town."

He sent her a quick grin. "The mess Delia left us in just gets messier."

Heat flashed into her eyes. "This is serious. Aunt Delia wouldn't have wanted you hurt by this will of hers. What are the chances that someone could have gotten in here and stolen the necklace?"

Ren had been thinking about that very possibility. "The house has a pretty good security system. I talked Delia into installing it five years ago, and I turned on the alarm before I let myself out that night. Plus, the thief would have had to have known the combination to the safe."

She planted her hands on her hips. "So if it *was* stolen, any investigator worth his salt will see it as an inside job. And your fingerprints are going to be on that safe. Dougie will have a field day with that. Not to mention the sheriff if we report it missing."

"Maybe I should get myself a good defense attorney." He'd said it to tease a smile out of her. He got a scowl instead.

"I don't think we should let anyone know it's missing yet. Not until we know more. How about Linney's story that Delia had gotten into the habit of leaving it around the house?"

Ren considered. "She was sitting on the side of the bed fully dressed when I left her. She'd poured herself a brandy down in the parlor before we came up. I declined to join her because I had some math tests to correct."

Carly walked to the safe again. "Maybe she just wanted it near her. So she took it out and then…maybe she wanted another brandy or something to eat—or maybe she went to the library for a book. Then she comes back up here, discovers she doesn't have it, or even forgets that she took it with her. That would explain why the safe door was open."

"That doesn't explain why Linney hasn't come across it."

"She wasn't looking for it specifically. I'll help her search the place. It has to be here somewhere."

"I can help you tomorrow morning. But tonight I have to step into Delia's shoes and kick off Winterfest. We're starting at 5:30 p.m. I think you'll find that Linney is planning to be there. Pretty much everyone in town will show up for the festivities."

"Then I'll look for the necklace myself." She glanced at her watch. "With any luck at all, I'll still catch the last train back to the city."

Once again, Ren found himself stifling an urge to reach out to her. He didn't want her to leave. He wanted her here. And the more time he spent with her, the stronger that desire grew.

Impossible, he warned himself. "Let's go down and tell Dougie."

"Are you kidding? The last thing we're going to do is tell my cousin that the diamond necklace is missing. You'd better let me handle this."

FIFTEEN MINUTES LATER Ren had to admit that Carly was doing a marvelous job of handling her cousin. Of course, Ren could have handled the pompous young man himself. He didn't give a damn what kind of vicious rumors the Mansfields spread about him. The townspeople who were his friends wouldn't believe them. As for the others—well, he'd learned over the years not to pay very much attention to what they thought. In their minds he'd always be that no-good Maxwell boy.

"More tea, Dougie?" Carly offered.

"No, thanks."

From his vantage point at the window Ren could see that

his presence was annoying Dougie-boy no end. The guy had probably wanted a private conversation with Carly so that he could start pushing Mansfield Ltd.'s agenda for Delia's land.

"How long do you intend to stay in Westhaven, cousin?"

Carly sipped her tea. "I intended to catch the last train back to the city tonight, but I'm thinking of changing that plan. I'll have to rearrange my schedule at the hospital."

Dougie beamed a smile at her. "If you're staying over, I insist you have dinner with Mummy and me."

"She's already promised that if she stays, she'll come to Winterfest." The lie came out before Ren could stop it.

Dougie ignored him. "You can't seriously be thinking of going to that silly event. It's so…corny. Mummy and I know this little Italian place in Chesterton. It will give us a chance to catch up with each other."

"Aunt Delia loved Winterfest so much. She invited me down several times, but I refused." The smile she sent Dougie was sad. "I suppose it's guilt, but I want to go to this one," Carly said.

"Well." The word came on a huff of breath. "If I can't persuade you to come to dinner, perhaps you could join us for lunch tomorrow? Mummy will be so upset if you go back to the city without spending some time with us." He glanced at Ren for the first time since they'd joined him in the parlor. Then he shifted his gaze back to Carly. "For the last few months we've been discussing some ideas with Aunt Delia for the development of the land surrounding the house. Perhaps she mentioned them to you?"

Carly shook her head. "No."

Dougie inched forward in his chair. "Then it's really important that we fill you in on them. Delia was very interested in what we were proposing. Mummy and I want to bring you up to speed."

"Why don't I give you a call in the morning? Hopefully, my plans will be more definite by then."

"Well." He set his teacup and saucer on the table with a little snap.

Temper, temper, Ren thought as color rushed into Dougie's cheeks.

"In that case, I'll just take the necklace and be on my way."

"I'm afraid that won't be possible," Carly explained.

Dougie stared at her. "But that's what I came for. Mr. Grady said…you agreed—"

"I agreed that the necklace should be appraised. But I want to have that done before I turn it over to you. I spoke with my father and he agreed, so I've arranged to have it sent to the jeweler in New York that Aunt Delia always dealt with."

"I…well…."

"We'll probably have an answer by Monday."

Admiration and surprise streamed through Ren. Dr. Carly Waring could lie like a pro. Nine years ago she'd never have been able to pull this off. He wondered what other surprises she had up her sleeve.

Carly slipped an arm through Dougie's and urged him into the hallway, all the while assuring him that she would be in touch just as soon as she got her bearings and arranged her schedule.

When she came back into the room, Ren said, "The way you handled him reminded me of your aunt."

"Thanks."

Her cheeks turned pink at the compliment, and he was once more surprised at how much he wanted to go to her. The more time he spent with her, the longer he talked with her, the more he wanted to know if her taste was the same, if the texture of her skin was the same. If her hair still carried the scent of spring. As their gazes continued to hold, the urge to satisfy his curiosity grew stronger and stronger.

The only thing that kept him rooted to the spot was the very real fear inside of him that if he touched her even once, he might not be able to stop.

Once again it was Carly who broke the contact by moving to the tea cart and picking up her tea. "At least I've bought us some time."

Us. The word triggered emotions he couldn't name. "How much of what you said to Dougie-boy was the truth?"

Her brows rose. "Well, I'm certainly not getting the necklace appraised until we find it. Then I'll arrange to have it sent to the jeweler Aunt Delia used in the city."

"What about the rest? Do you really intend to rearrange your schedule and stay here for a while?"

"I can't leave until we find Aunt Delia's diamond necklace." She set down her cup. "If I'm lucky, I'll find it tonight. Then—we'll have to come to some decision about what to do with all of this."

"Come to Winterfest with me."

"That's not going to help us find the necklace."

"Since you've decided to stay to search for it, I want a chance to show you the town your aunt devoted so much time to. I'd like you to see it through her eyes and try to picture her dreams for it."

"I—"

"All I'm asking is that you multitask. We can search for the necklace together tomorrow." Ren knew what he was going to do even as he moved toward her. He also knew that he was playing with fire. But now that she'd decided to stay for a day or so, he was going to find out what they still had together. They both were.

"C'mon, Doc. Aren't you even a little bit curious about what your aunt wanted for the town?"

"I suppose." She sighed. "Yes."

"Good." He framed her face in his hands. "And you're curious about this, too. We both are."

"Wait." She pressed a hand to his chest.

She'd said the same word, used the same gesture the first time he'd kissed her. But she hadn't stopped him.

"I've already waited," Ren said, "I've thought of doing this ever since you walked into Rupert Grady's office this afternoon." He leaned down to brush his lips over hers. "Sooner or later we're going to have to find out what's still here…or what isn't."

"This is a mistake." But she made no movement to back away when he began to take her mouth slowly.

"Probably." But one worth making, he thought as he sampled desire and a passion that was barely restrained. When she moaned softly and her fingers curled into his shirt, he angled his head and took them both deeper. The sweetness that had haunted his dreams for years had grown darker, richer.

More. He struggled to take his time. He wanted to savor each separate reaction—the catch of her breath when he nipped on her bottom lip, the soft moan vibrating against his lips as he explored the soft skin at her throat. When she began to tremble, Ren felt his mind cloud. How could he have forgotten how responsive she was? How generous? She'd never once held anything back. Heat shot through him when she raised her hand to grip his shoulder.

Clamping down on the needs building inside of him, Ren stepped back carefully. Her eyes were misted, her mouth moist and swollen from his kiss. It cost him to drop his hands.

"Well," he managed.

When she had to shake her head a little to clear it, Ren nearly reached for her again.

"We shouldn't have done that."

"We did. Now we know, and we'll have to decide what to do next." Before she could reply, he leaned down and brushed a quick kiss against her lips. "I'll be back to pick you up at five," he said.

In the archway he paused and turned. "You're going to need something warm to wear. Try Charity Samuels's Boutique on Main Street. Delia went there all the time."

Then he strode out of the house before he made the decision for both of them.

CHAPTER FIVE

TWO HOURS INTO WINTERFEST the town square teemed with people. Chinese lanterns enhanced the light spilling from a full moon, and the air carried the scents of cinnamon, grilled hamburgers and coffee. Carly sipped the hot spiced cider she'd bought from J. C. Nickols's stand and savored a moment alone.

From the time she'd arrived and Ren had left her to carry out his master of ceremonies duties, a seemingly endless flow of people had come up to her, most offering their condolences on her aunt's passing. A few had asked outright what she was thinking of doing with her aunt's property. One of them, Arnold Deasy of Deasy Real Estate, had even offered his business card. Not only was Mr. Deasy interested in listing Delia's land, for which he could guarantee getting her top dollar, but he had also offered to get the Waring Bank Building off her hands. He'd actually inferred that her aunt's desire to build a clinic in Westhaven had been a silly pipe dream, encouraged by people who had a backward view of the progressive road that Westhaven should be taking.

Even if she and Ren did decide to sell her aunt's land, Carly had decided that Mr. Deasy was not getting the listing. She walked forward on the path that led to the canal. To her right a small hill had been fashioned out of the fallen snow, and children in a rainbow of snowsuit colors sped down it on small plastic sleds. Their bursts of laughter and gleeful squeals blended with the strains of "The Skater's Waltz." The music was being provided by a small band on the gazebo. On the canal behind them, skaters flowed to and fro. The whole scene reminded her of the little village that her mother carefully unpacked every year and placed under the Christmas tree.

Ren had been busy from the time they'd arrived. She'd been grateful for that. Right now he was pinning a yellow ribbon on the Third Best Snowman in Westhaven. A young man with a mile-wide smile was jumping up and down in delight, and a photographer from the *Westhaven Weekly Gazette* was busily capturing the event on film.

The master of ceremonies role fit Ren like a second skin. It wasn't that she was surprised by his ease of manner with the townspeople. She'd just never thought of him that way before.

Of course, she'd spent nine years determined not to think of him at all, hadn't she? And if he *had* slipped into her mind, she'd always pictured him as the young man he'd been that summer with the wicked grin and the reckless gleam in his eyes. Ren Maxwell had been her one devastating experience with sampling forbidden fruit, and it had been enough to keep her on the straight and narrow ever since.

When the photographer finished, Ren turned toward her, and for a moment their eyes met and held. Carly felt the familiar punch and sizzle of heat, the melting sensation that began in her stomach and spread until it liquefied her legs. And before she could prevent it, she was thinking of that kiss again. However much they'd both changed, the chemistry was the same. Maybe better. What would happen if he kissed her again? A sliver of panic raced up her spine. No. She still wasn't ready to deal with this. With him.

Ren hadn't brought up the kiss on the ride into town, and neither had she. Before that, she'd pushed it out of her mind, concentrating instead on calling her parents and re-arranging her schedule so that she could stay at least until Tuesday. Surely, they would find the necklace by then. After her phone calls she'd asked Linney for the keys to her aunt's car. *Her* car now, Carly reminded herself. She'd needed to drive into town to shop for the suitable clothes Ren had suggested. Toiletries weren't a problem since the guest bedroom was fully stocked with everything she could want, including a bottle of her favorite scent. It was almost as if Delia had prepared it especially for her.

In town, she'd taken Ren's suggestion and tried the boutique on Main Street. Not only had she liked Charity Samuels, who juggled raising two boys and running a business, but Carly had also been impressed with the se-lection and quality of the clothes. The sweater she'd chosen had been hand knit by a local woman, and the fur-lined boots more than matched the quality of anything she'd seen in New York. Since Charity had already known that she and Ren were the sole beneficiaries of her aunt's will, Carly figured so did everyone else in town.

"Carly?"

Turning, she spotted her aunt Susan striding along the path in her direction. Susan's blond hair was swept back from her face, and she wore a long fur coat that brushed the tops of her high-heeled boots. When Susan reached her, she leaned closer to air kiss the area near Carly's left cheek. "For a moment I wasn't sure that I would find you in this crowd."

"Dougie indicated that you weren't coming to Winterfest."

Susan glanced around. "Oh, I'm not. I can't imagine why Delia ever started this thing." She shifted her cool, blue eyes back to Carly. "Dougie's in the car over there by the Waring Bank. I thought I might be able to change your mind about joining us for dinner. Surely you've had enough of this."

"Actually, I haven't." Carly glanced down at her clothes. "And I'm not really dressed for the kind of restaurant that Dougie described."

Susan smiled, but Carly didn't miss the quick flicker of annoyance in her eyes before she spoke again. "In that case, I'll just give you this right now."

Carly took the piece of paper and unfolded it.

"I got it out of my safety deposit box this afternoon. I'm sorry for your cousin's outburst this morning. He's always so protective of me, and he knows the kind of sentimental value that I've always placed on that necklace. So of course he was shocked and angry when Delia didn't mention me in the will."

Carly began to read what her aunt had written.

"CONGRATULATIONS, Danny," Ren said.

"Yeah! Thanks!" Danny pulled his hand away, then

turned and waved the blue ribbon high in the air. "Hey, Mom! Look!"

Ren turned also, just in time to see Susan Mansfield hand Carly a folded piece of paper. The fact that Delia's niece was seeking Carly out at Winterfest, an event that she'd never before attended, meant that Susan wasn't happy with the way Dougie's meeting had gone with Carly earlier. He'd watched Susan Mansfield in action before, and her usual method was to hang back and let her husband or her son tackle the problem first. Dougie played the bad cop, Douglas Senior the good cop, and then Susan came in and closed the deal. Usually, she didn't take over the reins this soon.

He shifted his gaze to Carly. It had hit him hard just a few moments ago when their eyes had met just how much he enjoyed seeing her standing there in the middle of the town square—as if she belonged.

He wanted her to belong here, and he'd realized something else in the few hours since the official start of Winterfest. He wasn't going to let her get away this time, not without putting up a fight.

But what was his best strategy? Nine years ago he'd made his moves quickly. That was exactly what he wanted to do this time, too. He'd barely kept himself from asking Carly for more when he'd kissed her earlier. Hell, he wouldn't have had to ask. He'd tasted her surrender. But they were different people now. If they were going to have a chance this time, they needed to get to know the people they'd become.

Ren watched Carly open the letter in her hand, and

while she read it, he shifted his gaze to her aunt. What was Susan up to? That was the question on his mind as he moved toward them.

SUSAN BLEW ON HER HANDS and rubbed them together. "What you're reading is a copy of a letter Delia sent me shortly before I was married. As you can see, she lent me the necklace to wear on my wedding day. It's part of a long family tradition that the Waring women wear the Waring diamonds when they say their vows."

Carly read the words on the page.

My dearest niece, on your blessed day, please wear this as your something borrowed. Since I have no daughter, no doubt the necklace will be yours one day, and you will have the pleasure of passing it on to the next Waring bride.

"In addition to that," Susan said, "Delia told me on more than one occasion that the necklace would be mine one day. I've spoken with your father and he recalls being present on one of those occasions."

Carly handed the note back to her aunt. "You seem to have a very strong case."

For the first time Susan's smile warmed. "I want to get this matter settled as quickly as possible, and I don't want to be the cause of bad feelings between our two families."

Carly studied her aunt for a moment. As far as she knew, there had never been much feeling, kind or otherwise, between her parents and the Mansfields. They'd never been the sort of family that gathered for holidays.

"I'm disappointed you feel you have to send the necklace into the city for an appraisal. There's a perfectly good jeweler in Chesterton. Dougie should have offered to take you there. We could still do that."

"The necklace is gone," Carly said. "I thought that it would be better to use the jeweler that Aunt Delia did all her business with."

Annoyance flickered across Susan's face. "Will he have a report ready for you on Monday?"

"I'll call him first thing in the morning," Carly promised.

"Rupert Grady says he can meet with us on Monday morning at eleven to look at this letter. Will that work for you?"

Seeing no way out, Carly said, "That should be fine, but I can't speak for Ren."

"Ren?" With a frown, Susan shifted her gaze briefly. Following it, Carly saw that Ren was walking toward them. "Dougie and I would really prefer that you come alone to the meeting. This is a family matter."

Carly met Susan's eyes steadily. "As one of the two beneficiaries of the will, Ren has to be there. He'll have to be part of any agreement we come to about the necklace."

Reaching out, Susan gripped her arm. "There are things you should know about Ren Maxwell and your aunt."

Whatever else Susan might have said was prevented as something rolled into Carly from behind, causing her to lurch forward. Cider splashed out of her cup onto her aunt's fur coat.

"Oh!" Susan gasped, taking several quick steps back.

She might have tumbled into a nearby snowbank if Ren hadn't caught her arm and steadied her.

"You all right?" Ren asked.

"I'm fine. It's my coat." Susan pulled a tissue out of her bag and began to blot away the cider.

Seeing that her aunt was safe, Carly turned and looked down into the grinning face of a toddler.

"You all right?" Carly asked, pulling the little guy to his feet.

"Sorry about that." A breathless Charity Samuels scooped up the toddler. "This is my youngest, Tad. He got away from me." She turned to Susan. "I'm so sorry. I'll pay for the cleaning bill, Mrs. Mansfield."

"Not necessary." Susan's smile was a little frosty. "It's my fault. I'm really not dressed for this type of event. I just came to have a word with my niece." She met Carly's eyes. "I'll see you on Monday at eleven."

No one spoke until Susan was out of earshot. Then Charity said, "I've been hoping that she would drop into my shop one day. I think I've just blown any chance of that."

Carly put a hand on her arm. "Her loss. I love the things you carry in your shop."

"Thanks."

"Sled." Tad bounced up and down on his mother's arm. "Do it again. Do it again."

"That's my exit line." Over her shoulder, Charity beamed a smile at Ren. "Good choice on the first-prize snowman."

When Carly sent him a curious look, Ren said, "Her other son, Danny, won the blue ribbon." Then, after a pause, "What did Susan want?"

"Good question. She said she wanted to give me a chance to change my mind about dinner, but she also brought a copy of the note that my aunt sent her about the necklace."

"She wants this thing settled."

"Pronto." Carly met his eyes, then glanced away.

"What else did she want?"

"She doesn't want you at the meeting with Mr. Grady on Monday."

"And?"

She faced him. "She was about to tell me something about you and my aunt when I dumped the cider on her."

"Ah," Ren said. Susan was moving fast, which meant that he would have to move a little faster.

"I told her you had to be at the meeting." Carly glanced down at her watch. "I should go back to the house right now and begin the treasure hunt."

Taking her hand before she could turn away, Ren flashed her a quick smile. "Not before you participate in at least one Winterfest event. Delia always did."

Ren knew that the little line on her forehead signaled her inner debate. He could almost hear what she was thinking. It was already eight o'clock. A good time to start searching for the necklace. But there was another part of her that wanted to stay, and that part wasn't allowing her to pull her hand free of his.

"We're going to find it, Carly."

"What if we don't?"

"We will. C'mon, Doc. When was the last time you did something just for the fun of it?"

Carly glanced around. "I'll never fit on one of those sleds the kids are using."

"They're renting skates. You up to it?"

"You can skate?"

He grinned at her. "Sure. I even coach hockey on Sunday mornings at my school. You can lean on me."

"What makes you think I'd have to?" she said, leading the way down the bank to the canal.

Delight streamed through him at the glint of challenge that had appeared in her eyes. This was the Carly he'd tumbled into love with.

CHAPTER SIX

TWO HOURS LATER THEY were both laughing as Ren led her up the bank of the canal to the steps of the gazebo where they'd left their boots. The whole time she'd been on the ice, Carly hadn't let herself think of anything but the wind and the speed. She'd forgotten how much she used to enjoy skating. She'd also forgotten how easy Ren was to be around.

She tugged one skate off. "That was fun."

"You want to come Sunday morning to my school? I'd like my guys to see you do that double axle thing."

Surprised, she stopped unlacing her second skate to glance at him. "Sure. I suppose so."

"Good." He tugged on his boots and rose. "Hungry?"

"Starved." She reached for her boots.

"Don't move. I'll be right back."

She glanced to the line of food stands. "It looks like they're closing down."

He flashed a grin over his shoulder. "I'll try my charm on Mr. Carney."

Carly pulled on the fur-lined boots, wrapped her arms about her knees and stared out at the canal. She would have to get up early to look for the necklace, but she wasn't going to regret the two hours she'd spent skating with Ren. The time had been worth it just to see the surprised expression on his face when she'd dropped his arm and swung into a spin. And it had pleased her that she could still do a double axle.

Ren's question about when was the last time she'd done something just for fun had struck home. Medical school didn't leave time for much fun. Her back-to-back residencies in internal medicine and pediatrics had forced her to practically live at the hospital. As far as she could remember, the last time she'd just enjoyed herself was that summer nine years ago.

Overhead, the Chinese lanterns clicked off one by one. Soon, the only light left would be from the full moon. It had been full on that long ago night when she'd waited here for Ren.

Firmly, she pushed the memory away and ignored the sudden urge she had to get up and run. She was not going to leave Westhaven until she found the necklace and figured out what Delia wanted her to do with the land.

Carly turned even before she heard Ren's footsteps on the hardened snow and watched him stride toward her. She still hadn't decided what she was going to do about that kiss, either.

REN STRODE ALONG THE PATH. Getting the food had taken him longer than he'd planned. Mr. Carney had been about to close down when he got to the booth. Now Carly was all alone in the gazebo—just as she'd been that night when Ren hadn't shown up.

Was she remembering that? He quickened his pace.

When he finally reached the steps, he sat down and began unloading the paper bag.

"I got us cheeseburgers loaded. And here's a cup of chili fries we can share."

"Smells like heaven." Carly unwrapped her burger and Ren contented himself with watching the expression on her face as she bit into it and chewed. "Nobody makes them better."

"Agreed," he said as he took a bite of his own.

"I've been thinking," she said around her next mouthful.

Ren studied her as he reached for a fry. "What about?"

"I'm not sure if I should thank you for bringing me here tonight." She gestured at him with her burger. "You knew exactly what you were doing. In one fell swoop I've met all the people who will be most affected by whatever we decide to do with Aunt Delia's property."

"It complicates things, doesn't it?"

"A lot. And it isn't as if the whole thing isn't complicated enough already."

"You'll figure it out, Doc. Delia wouldn't have set this whole thing up if she hadn't had faith in you."

"If she were here right now, I'd have a few things to say to her."

"I'm with you there."

"Mr. Deasy wants to list the bank as well as the land and the house."

Ren gave a low whistle.

"He called the Waring Clinic a pipe dream. He stopped short of saying that Aunt Delia was suffering from dementia, but he came close."

"Your aunt was as sharp as a tack. I hosted a poker night last week for the town board members, and she went home the winner."

They reached for a fry together and their fingers brushed. For a moment they both went perfectly still. In the moonlight, her eyes were darker and her skin looked like delicate porcelain. Ren dropped his gaze to the base of her throat where a pulse fluttered wildly. He wanted his mouth right there. Right now.

Very carefully, he withdrew his hand, leaving the fry behind. Then he reached for his drink and took a long swallow. He had a plan, he reminded himself. And it didn't include making love to Carly—at least not yet.

"Why a math teacher?" Carly asked.

Grateful that she'd brought it up, Ren said, "My first semester in college I discovered I have a real talent with numbers. So I majored in accounting. The teaching thing I sort of fell into by luck."

As he spoke, he crumpled up the wrapper of his hamburger and watched Carly neatly fold hers. "They needed someone at St. Martin's Academy midterm, and Delia recommended me for the job. I found I liked it. Not that I've given up the accounting thing. In addition to what I make at the school, I make extra money during the tax season— enough to buy the gardener's cottage from Delia."

"You own the cottage?"

"I bought it four years ago. One of the things that your aunt Susan probably wanted to tell you is that I've been living off Delia all this time. That was true enough in the beginning."

"Exchanging gardening and odd jobs for rent hardly qualifies as living off my aunt."

"A lot of people wouldn't see it that way. Delia also lent me the money for my first semester of college. I paid her back every cent."

"You don't have to tell me all this."

"Yes, I do." He offered her the rest of the fries and when she shook her head, he put them back in the bag. "There's more. Aren't you at all curious about why I didn't come to meet you here in the gazebo that night?"

"No...I—" CARLY SHOVED herself up from the step and moved to the railing that ran around the gazebo. She wasn't going to run. She just needed a moment. "It was a long time ago. It has nothing to do with now."

"Delia handcuffed me to the pipes in the kitchen of the gardener's cottage."

Wide-eyed, she whirled to find he'd followed her. "She what?"

Ren's lips curved. "It was the only way she could keep me there. At first. She'd found out that we were seeing each other, and she'd somehow discovered that we were planning to run away. So while you were waiting all night here, your great-aunt and I were hammering out an agreement in the kitchen of the gardener's cottage."

"An agreement." Carly tried to picture it in her mind. But the image wouldn't form.

When he reached out to her, she backed away, battling hurt and anger.

"Carly—"

"Wait." She held up a hand. She could control her temper. She'd spent years learning to do that. Still, a red haze formed in front of her eyes as she tried to get her mind around it. "She talked you into dumping me."

He frowned. "No. She made me see reason. If we'd run away together, you never would have become a doctor. She made me see that. We were too young."

"You could have come to me in person instead of—what was it you said…oh, yes—hammering out an agreement."

"I fought her on that. But it was either write you a letter or nothing. She kept me handcuffed until you'd read the letter and left."

Carly pictured what she could recall of that night in her mind, reading the letter and crying herself to sleep in her aunt's arms. And all the while Ren had been handcuffed to a pipe? "What right did she have? What right?"

"She loved you Carly. I loved you."

"And the agreement the two of you…?"

"I had to promise not to follow you or contact you in any way until you were a doctor."

"Oh." The red haze thickened. "I see." To hell with controlling her temper. She used both hands to give him a shove that sent him back two steps. "That's just great. I sat here all night, my heart breaking. And all the while you and my great aunt plotted out my life."

When she tried to shove him again, he was ready for her, and it was like pushing into a brick wall.

"Answer this. Do you like your life, Doc?"

"Yes. Dammit," she shouted. Then she simply stared as he threw back his head and began to laugh. The rich sound of it filled the gazebo and had her anger fading.

"What's so funny?"

"I'd forgotten what a temper you had. And when you get riled up like this, you remind me so much of Delia."

She lifted her chin. "I'm not taking that as a compliment right now. What the two of you did wasn't right. I should have been told the truth."

His grin faded. "Maybe. Maybe that's why I'm telling you now. She loved you, Carly. She wanted you to fulfill your dream of going to medical school. Think about it. She did the right thing."

She drew in a deep breath. "Okay...her intentions were good." The she studied him for a minute. "Why did you tell me all this tonight?"

"Because I want there to be a clean slate between us. I'm sorry that I hurt you. But Delia was right. I would have hurt you more if we had run away together."

"Maybe."

"You might as well know something else. I think the will and the missing necklace are all part of her plan to throw us together again—maybe to make up for what she did that night."

Carly stared at him.

"I know what I want, Carly. The statute of limitations has run out on what I promised your aunt. I want you just as much as I wanted you nine years ago. And we're not kids anymore."

Her throat went dry at what she saw in his eyes. She

lifted her chin. "So I'm a doctor now, and you're going to make your move? Well, I like my life just the way it is."

Temper snapped again in his eyes. "Yeah. I can second that. I didn't come seeking you out."

When she moved to shove him this time, he gripped both of her hands in his.

"No, you didn't. Just like you didn't come to me that night."

"I'm here now." He dropped her hands, clamped his on her shoulders and jerked her against him. Then his mouth crushed hers.

She'd seen the intent in his eyes, so she'd had a moment to brace herself. But it didn't do any good. This was nothing like the kiss he'd given her in the parlor. That had been a tentative exploration. This was rough, enervating and irresistible. Response ripped out of her before she could stop it.

She was drowning in him—in his scent, in his dark, rich flavor. She didn't even think of trying to save herself. She couldn't think at all, not with her heart racing faster and faster in perfect rhythm with his. No one had ever made her feel this way. Only Ren. And all she wanted was more.

He released her just as abruptly as he'd grabbed her. When he stepped back, she gripped the railing behind her to steady herself.

His voice was rough when he spoke. "We're standing right where I was supposed to come for you that night. But that was then and this is now. We're starting over, Doc. Delia may have set the stage, but it's up to us how we play it out."

"Yes, it is. But don't you push me."

"I can give you some time. I promised myself that I would. But I'm not sure how much."

Carly said nothing. She couldn't argue with a thing he'd said.

"C'mon. I'll take you back to your aunt's house."

CHAPTER SEVEN

"MISS CARLY, YOU'VE BEEN working for six straight hours. You need to take a break."

Carly glanced up from the curio cabinet she'd been unloading to see Linney set a tea tray on a nearby table. They'd agreed to work separately. Linney was working her way through the dining room and butler's pantry. "What time is it?"

"Nearly three. You hardly touched that sandwich I fixed you for lunch, so I made some scones. You need something in your stomach."

Carly took the cup that Linney handed her, knowing that if she took a break Linney would, too. "Six hours and I'm only on my second room." She'd tackled the parlor when she'd woken up before dawn. Linney had brought her coffee and later a sandwich while she'd been plowing through one cabinet after another. But she'd come up empty-handed and moved on to Delia's sitting room.

"You'll find the necklace when you least expect to."

Carly sipped her tea. "Ren thinks that Aunt Delia hid the necklace on purpose—to force me to stay around."

Linney's lips twitched as she offered the plate of scones. "Wouldn't surprise me. These last few years she worked a lot to preserve this town. She'd want you to see that. Did you go to the clinic yet?"

"No." But she'd been thinking about it more than she was comfortable with. Why had Delia never said anything to her about it? "She could have asked me to come here while she was still alive and shown me everything herself."

Linney's brows shot up. "Would you have come?"

"Probably not."

Linney nodded. "This way she gets to pull the strings even though she's not around."

Carly frowned. "Yeah. But I'm not sure I want to be her puppet anymore."

Linney's lips curved upward as she shrugged. "You can always cut yourself loose."

Easier said than done. Carly took another sip of tea as she watched Linney move slowly out of the room. It had taken her a long time to fall asleep last night. She'd examined the problem—no, that was wrong. There were two problems. There was her aunt's vision for the town. And there was Ren. And while she might allow Delia to manipulate her with regard to the land, when it came to Ren she was going to make her own decision.

And where had he been all day? Not only hadn't he shown up to help her search, he hadn't even called. The anger she was feeling wasn't directed only at Ren. She was just as mad at herself for wanting him to be here. Dammit, she missed him. How was that possible? Until yesterday the man hadn't been a part of her life for nine years.

The loud noise at the French doors had her jumping and whirling just in time to see a second snowball smack into a pane. Hurrying over, she saw Ren standing ten feet away, tossing a snowball into the air and catching it. He wore a helmet with a visor that covered his eyes, but the grin was unmistakable. She opened the door.

"Time for a break, Doc."

She was ridiculously pleased to see him. But she fisted her hands on her hips. "Where have you been all day? I thought we were both supposed to search for the necklace."

He gestured to his right, and for the first time, she noticed the snowmobile—black with the same white stripe that decorated his jacket and pants. "Snowmobile races were held this morning."

Thinking about the hours she'd spent digging through cupboards and cabinets, she narrowed her eyes. "You raced?"

His grin widened. "My civic duty. A man has to do what a man has to do. Want to go for a ride?"

Those were the same words he'd used on that first day; only then he'd been talking about his motorcycle. Still, the idea of taking a fast ride over the snow held some appeal. It would give her a chance to clear her head.

The snowball caught her smack in the center of her chest. "Sorry."

He would be, she vowed as she turned and hurried back into the house.

REN HAD STAYED AWAY as long as he could. He'd only signed on to race at the last moment because he'd known that it would keep him occupied for most of the day. Then, he'd told himself, he was going to join his comrades at The Drake

Tavern for a beer. Instead, the snowmobile had come back here.

He needed to see her. It was as simple as that, and he'd stood there watching her pace back and forth in Delia's sitting room until the need had escalated into an ache.

He flicked a glance at the front door, and knowing the way her mind worked, he leaned down, scooped up more snow and began to build a small arsenal of missiles. She'd gotten into his system again just as she had nine years ago. He'd spent a long sleepless night thinking of what he'd said in the gazebo—that he hadn't sought her out. Delia had mentioned that she'd graduated from college and medical school in six years instead of the usual eight. He'd known that she was a doctor, and he'd done nothing. Out of fear. So he could understand what she was going through.

When she stepped out the front door, all muffled up in a red scarf, his heart took a little tumble.

And the snowball smacked into his chest. Dead center. He dodged the next one, swearing as he twisted to recover his balance. Her next throw caught the back of his helmet, and he felt snow slither down his neck.

Whirling, he noted she was pulling the snowballs out of a bag she had slung over her arm. The image of her on the back porch, arming herself in preparation for their battle had him grinning.

"Sneak," he shouted, sending one into the arm that held the bag.

"Whatever." She managed to hang on to the bag and send two more balls flying in quick succession. The second one hit him in the shoulder.

He scooped up two from his arsenal, then zigzagged his way toward her. When she landed one right on his visor, she began to laugh. Seeing his advantage, Ren went in low and took her down. He knew it was a bad move the instant they landed. Her body lay beneath his, each curve molding to his. Perfect fit.

It was a mistake to stay this way, even for a moment. But he couldn't move. Lifting a hand, he tugged off his helmet and tossed it aside. He rid himself of his glove next and traced a finger over her cheekbone. Gazing into her dark eyes, he saw himself—trapped. And he had no desire to run. There was something about her, had always been something about her that weakened him and destroyed his control. Without any help from his brain, his mouth lowered to hers. Her lips were cool, but they instantly began to warm beneath his. Oh yes. This was everything he wanted.

HE'D NEVER KISSED HER this way before. Oh, he knew how to be a gentle lover, but there was a sweetness, a tenderness here that was…different. She was used to the heat that they always made between them; this time it was a warmth spreading through her like a river.

As he nipped at her bottom lip and gently took them both deeper, her hands went limp. She was sliding down to a place where it was hard to breathe. A mist clouded her mind, and she could feel herself giving, yielding everything she was to him.

When he lifted his head, she nearly cried out. He didn't speak. Instead, he merely studied her in that intent way he had, and she saw the question in his eyes. If he asked her now, she'd go with him to the gardener's cottage and they'd finish what they'd started. But he was leaving it up to her. A sliver of panic raced up her spine. He'd promised her time to make a decision, but she feared it had already been made.

For a few moments, the silence hummed between them. Then Ren broke it. "Up for that ride?"

Her brows knit. "On the snowmobile?"

"Yeah." A smile flickered briefly at the corners of his mouth before he dropped a kiss on her nose and eased himself off of her. "I can give you a little more time before we take that other ride together."

CARLY DONNED THE HELMET he handed her and settled herself behind him on the snowmobile. She understood that he'd given her a reprieve. But her gratitude was tempered by the fact that he'd conjured a vivid image of their making love together. It didn't help one bit that she had to wrap her arms around him and mold herself to his body to keep her balance as he punched up the speed and sent them flying over the snow.

Think about something else, she ordered herself. But she was hard-pressed to get a coherent thought into her mind with that muscled back pressed against her. She shouldn't even be here. But it was difficult to complain with the wind on her face and late afternoon sun slanting over the snow. She was even enjoying the vibrations of the speeding engine beneath her.

"Hang on." They crested a hill and went flying.

The laugh escaped before she could prevent it. "Again," she yelled.

He obliged her.

After that she lost track of both the time and the direction. Ren didn't stick to the roads all the time, so she was surprised when she saw the outskirts of Westhaven come into view. Did he have some duty to fulfill?

The town square was filled with people. From the looks of it a chili cook-off was in full swing. That must be it. He was going to feed her. But he bypassed the square and instead parked in front of the Waring Bank building.

The light dawned. This was where they'd been headed all along. She wiggled off the snowmobile before he did and dragged off her helmet. "I told you not to push me."

He took off his own helmet and met her eyes squarely. "Tell me you haven't been curious about this place since you first got to town. Yet you haven't come here."

"I had it on my list."

"Well, let's check it off. You need to see this if you're going to understand all of what Delia wanted for the town."

When he opened the front door, she followed him in.

He flipped a switch and a bare light bulb went on overhead. Sawhorses and drop cloths littered the large room. Lumber and drywall were stacked in piles along the glass windows that faced the street.

"Don't be put off by the mess," said a voice from behind them. "It's a work in progress."

Carly turned to see a tiny redhead with a baby propped on her hip, moving toward her, hand extended.

"I'm Gayle Jensen. I was over helping my husband—he's in the chili cook-off—and I saw you come in here. I followed you."

Carly nodded.

Gayle beamed a smile. "And that doesn't tell you a thing, does it? Harley, my husband, says I talk a lot without getting to the point." Pausing, she drew in a breath and let it out. "I'm a nurse practitioner. I took a leave from my job in the city when Billy here came along. Even while I was expecting, your aunt talked to me about her plans for the clinic. She thought I might be interested in working here. And I am. So I thought if you have questions, I might be able to answer them."

"Did my aunt have any ideas about finding a doctor?"

For the first time the bright smile on Gayle's face dimmed a bit. "I saw Mr. Deasy talking to you last night. He thinks that it will be impossible to attract a doctor in a small town like this. Some others agree with him."

"Mr. Deasy is right. I can't think of any young doctor just getting into practice coming to a town like this. Not when they have so many more lucrative possibilities."

"Your aunt would agree with you. That's why she approached me. Her plan was to try to get a doctor to commute here once a week, and I would handle the clinic in between. We'd hire staff and a couple more nurses."

"I see." This time when Carly let her gaze sweep the space, she saw more than she had before. It could be done, she thought. A doctor could commute here once a week and still be part of a practice elsewhere. She could do it and still work with her parents. For just a moment she let herself imagine it. Being in a place like this would give her the opportunity to pursue a dream that she'd always had, practicing family medicine.

"Delia even had an idea of including a birthing center and offering the services of midwives," Gayle said.

"I see," Carly repeated and suddenly she did. Anger bubbled up. The only people she'd ever confided her dream to were Ren and her aunt. Delia was at it again—pulling those damn strings.

"Are there any more questions that I can answer, Dr. Waring?"

Carly tamped down on her feelings before she turned to face Gayle. "No, but thank you for coming over."

"Thank *you* for listening. There are a lot of people in town who supported Delia about the clinic."

Carly waited until Gayle was out of the building before she turned to Ren. "Aunt Delia's trying to manipulate me again."

He moved to her and ran his hands up and down her arms. "Delia set the stage, Doc. It's up to you how you play it."

"She doesn't play fair."

He threw back his head and laughed. "Why should that change simply because she's no longer with us?" Then he put a companionable arm around her shoulders. "C'mon. Let's go sample some of that chili before we head back."

CHAPTER EIGHT

THE HOUSE WAS DARK when Carly let herself in. She'd called Linney earlier to tell her not to wait up, and now she was glad that she had. The moonlight pouring in through the glass panels in the front door allowed her to see the time on the grandfather clock. Nearly eleven.

Carly started up the stairs. Not only had she sampled the chili, but somehow she'd also managed to let herself be persuaded into filling in for one of the judges who'd come down with the flu.

The night before she'd been an observer at Winterfest, but tonight she'd felt as if she were truly a part of the Westhaven community. The only similar feeling she'd ever felt in New York was at Mt. Sinai Hospital. No chili cook-offs there.

The best part of the whole evening was that she'd been able to put everything out of her mind for a while—Delia's clinic, the missing diamond necklace and even what she was going to do about Ren. Now it was all coming back.

With a frown Carly paused at the top of the stairs. She still hadn't found the necklace, and the task was beginning to seem Herculean. Then there was the clinic. As much as she hadn't wanted to think about it, the image of what it might be like was planted firmly in her mind.

Last, but not least, there was Ren. She'd barely seen him all evening. Once she'd shouldered her judging duties, he'd faded into the background. She'd caught a glimpse of him now and then, chatting with this person or that one. But it was only because she'd actually been looking for him. When he'd dropped her off, she'd expected him to escort her up the porch steps. If he had, she might have invited him in. But all he'd said was, "Good night, Doc."

He hadn't even made a move to kiss her good-night. She should be happy about that. Fisting her hands, she turned and strode down the hall. Clearly, he was backing off. She should be feeling happy about that, too.

So why did she feel so miserable?

Carly opened the door and strode halfway across the floor before she realized that she was in her aunt's room instead of her own. Nerves twisted in her stomach as she fought the urge to turn and leave. Instead, she moved to the bedside table and turned on the Tiffany lamp. Then she let her gaze slowly sweep the room.

She'd avoided coming in here since yesterday when she and Ren had found the safe door open and the necklace missing. The room looked exactly as it had when they'd left to join Dougie in the front parlor. For that matter, it looked exactly as it had in the wee hours of that morning nine years ago when her aunt had brought her up here and handed her Ren's letter.

A fresh wave of anger sliced through her as she glanced at the red leather box Ren's letter had rested against. Perhaps this was exactly where she needed to be if she was going to decide what to do about Ren. Lost in thought, she paced to the window. Moonlight spilled across the land, glistening off the snow and sending long shadows across the path that led to the gardener's cottage. Though the two-story structure was nearly hidden behind a tall elm, she could see that the only light was coming from the first floor. Probably from the kitchen.

Carly could hardly miss the irony of the situation. Here they were—nine years later—in much the same places they'd been that night. Ren wasn't handcuffed to a pipe, and she wasn't huddled in her aunt's arms crying. But they still came from different worlds. Nine years ago their difference hadn't mattered to her. When had she turned into such a coward?

Turning, she strode toward the door. They were older now, wiser. Weren't they smart enough to find ways to make those worlds intersect?

REN PUSHED THROUGH the front door of the cottage, tossed his gloves on a bench in the small foyer and strode into the kitchen. Dammit! Running a frustrated hand through his hair, he filled a glass of water at the sink and drained it. She didn't want to be pushed, so he'd backed off.

Why in hell was he so sure that he was handling everything wrong? And why had fear formed a cold hard ball in his stomach?

Lifting his head, Ren stared at his image in the pane of glass over the sink. "Because you've fallen for her again."

On some level he'd known the jig was up when she'd walked into Rupert Grady's office. His heart had taken that long, slow tumble just as it had when he'd taken her hand to help her up off the asphalt. Any doubts he might have had were erased this afternoon when he'd kissed her. While she'd been lying beneath him in the snow, he'd looked into her eyes and felt parts of himself slipping away.

She'd looked so right in the Waring Bank building. As Gayle Jensen had been talking to her, an image of Carly standing there in a white coat, a stethoscope hooked around her neck, had filled his mind. Watching her pin the yellow third place ribbon on Harley Jensen's jacket had been the clincher. Couldn't she see how easily, how perfectly she would fit into life here in Westhaven?

But what if that wasn't what she wanted? The fear inside of him turned icy. Ren began to pace in the small kitchen. "Good going, Ace," he muttered. Before Carly had come back, he'd liked his life just fine. It was a good town, and he liked his job at the school. He'd even convinced himself that he liked being single—preferred it, in fact.

Now, thanks to Delia, that life wasn't going to be enough for him anymore. If she were here right now, he'd have a few choice words for her. He shot a look at the pipe where she'd handcuffed him all those years ago. If he'd been free of those restraints, he'd have gone to Carly then. Rubbing his hands over his face, he wondered how he'd become such a coward. Maybe it was time to take a lesson from the boy he'd been at twenty. To hell with what he'd promised Carly and promised himself.

THE MOMENT SHE STEPPED around the bend in the path, she saw him striding toward her. The thrill was brutal and had her breaking into a run. When she reached him, he lifted her off her feet and kissed her hard. They were both a little breathless when he released her mouth. Then she was in his arms and he was carrying her back towards the cottage.

"Looks like we were thinking the same thing," she said.

He gave a short laugh. "Doc, I haven't been thinking of anything else since you walked into Rupert Grady's office." He pushed through the cottage door, kicked it shut behind him.

"We'll have to talk," she said.

"Yeah." He murmured the word against her mouth, then nipped her bottom lip. "Later."

"'Kay." She was on her feet, her back against the wall while they struggled with clothes, tossing their jackets aside.

"It was easier in the summer," he muttered.

She yanked his belt free, tugged at the snap on his jeans. "Maybe we don't have to take off all of our clothes."

"Yeah." He trapped her hands in his to still them. "I think we do." His eyes were steady on hers as he gripped her hips, and she scooted up to wrap her legs around him. Then he started down the short hallway. "I want you naked in my bed."

The words, the intent way he looked at her while he said them gave her another brutal thrill. She tried to draw his mouth to hers, and when he turned, she satisfied herself by pressing her lips to his throat. She wanted to devour him. "I don't know why it took me so long to decide, why I waited so long for this."

"We're on the same page there, Doc." He kicked the bedroom door open, and when she was once more on her feet, she found herself trapped between the bedpost and his body.

"We were always in such a hurry before. This time we'll try slow and easy for a change."

"Really?"

"Really." His eyes never left hers as he slid his hands beneath her sweater and pulled it over her head. She watched as his eyes dropped to the bra she wore beneath it and absorbed his quick intake of breath.

He ran a finger over the sheer peach colored lace, then down slowly to circle her nipple. "Your taste in lingerie has changed, Doc."

"You're the one who suggested I shop at Charity Samuels's Boutique."

"It makes it hard to stick to the plan."

"Your plan, not mine." Her heart was pounding so hard that she wondered whether she could be heard above the noise.

He met her eyes then. "Do the panties match?"

She lifted her chin. "Who says I'm wearing any?"

"Doc." The word came out on a moan. Then drawing in a deep breath, he leaned his forehead against hers. "I want to go slow. You're making it hard."

"I want to make it impossible." She wrapped her arms around him and toppled them both onto the bed. For one moment, she lay trapped beneath him as he kissed her throat. Then he moved slowly downward until she felt the moist heat of his mouth through the thin silk of her bra. The weakening pleasure spread quickly until her muscles went lax and she sighed his name.

He rolled and flipped her over onto her stomach. "Let's try this." He drew her trousers down over her hips and away. Then he said nothing, did nothing for three full beats. His voice was hoarse when he finally spoke. "Nice thong." Heat flooded through her as he ran a finger down the thin strip of silk to where it disappeared between her legs. Keeping his finger right there, he pressed his mouth to her neck and began to work his way down her spine.

Carly's mind clouded. His lips lingered, seemingly fascinated with the little hollow at the base of her spine, then he slipped his finger beneath the thong and into her.

"Ren. Please."

"Please what? Tell me what you want."

"You."

When he turned her slowly over, she wanted to reach for him, but she grew even weaker as he tasted her lips, her breasts and began a slow journey down her stomach. When he dipped just the tip of his tongue into her navel, she arched upward. Finally, he pressed a hand against her heat, torturing them both until he once more slipped a finger into her. Heat spiked through her as she dug her nails into his shoulders and arched upward.

Ren caught her cry with his mouth and feasted on hers as she rode out the climax. He was steeped in her now, that heady fragrance, that tart, sweet taste. But it wasn't nearly enough; he needed more. Using his hand alone, he drove her to a second climax. Then strapping down on his control, he drew away to deal with his jeans and the condom.

She reached for him, wrapping her hand around him

and guiding him to her. Pleasure sharp and hot pierced through him as he filled her, as she surrounded him.

He linked their hands, kept his eyes steady on hers as he began to move. As they began to move together. Her eyes darkened, her pulse quickened, and still he struggled to keep the rhythm slow, savoring each rise and fall. Only when he felt her clutch around him did he cover her mouth with his. Then he let himself soar and fall with her.

CHAPTER NINE

CARLY STOOD, HANDS ON HIPS, and turning slowly, surveyed the chaos she'd created. The library was the largest room on the first floor of the house, and it had taken her three hours to empty the cupboards beneath the bookshelves.

She'd had high hopes for the library. It made sense that if Delia had been having trouble sleeping, she might have come here to find a book. Running a hand through her hair, she stared at the variety of stuff that now littered the floor. Among other things, she'd unearthed her aunt's entire music collection that ranged from 78 and 33 RPM recordings to CDs. Aunt Delia even owned an iPod device.

The only thing to do now was to search behind each and every one of the books. After pressing fingers to her temples where a nagging little headache throbbed, Carly moved to one of the stained-glassed windows and stared out at the snow.

Ren was at Winterfest. Today was family day. There would be bobsled races on the hill near the water tower and the closing ceremonies were scheduled for 5:00 p.m. He'd asked her to come with him, but after spending the morning watching him coach ice hockey at St. Martin's Academy, she'd explained that she had to continue the search. They only had today and tonight left to find the necklace.

Since there was no room on the floor, Carly stifled the urge she had to pace. Her desire to find her aunt's diamonds was only part of the reason why she was here and Ren was at Winterfest. She'd stayed behind because they hadn't talked yet, and in spite of what they'd shared during the night, doubt and fear had begun to creep in again.

Pressing her forehead against the coolness of the pane, she closed her eyes and willed the headache away. They'd talk tonight, she told herself. It was just that they hadn't had time yet. During the night they hadn't been able to get enough of each other, and in the morning they hadn't even had time for coffee before they'd left for Ren's school.

Still, she couldn't help wondering what they'd say when they did talk. Had anything really changed between them? She let out the sigh that she'd been holding in all day. For her everything had changed. She could still picture in her mind the way he'd looked at her as they'd made love during the night.

There were other images, too. She saw him squatting down low on his skates, his hands resting on his knees, as he spoke earnestly to the members of his hockey team. She also recalled the way he'd put a comforting hand on the goalie's shoulder right after the young man had let the puck get through. If she hadn't already fallen in love with him all over again, her heart would have taken the tumble right then and there.

He was good with kids. He understood them. After practice, he'd taken her on a quick tour of the school, and she'd seen for the first time how right he'd looked standing there at the front of his classroom. That's what they'd talked about on the ride home—how lucky they both were that they'd each found a career they really loved.

But there'd been no mention of what they were going to do next. Carly let out a little huff of breath. Nine years ago they'd spent hours and hours planning out a life together. If she was being a coward about it, so was he.

A knock on the door caught her attention. Ren?

But it was Linney who poked her head into the room. "Miss Carly, Mr. and Mrs. Mansfield and Mr. Douglas Junior are here to speak with you. I showed them into the front parlor."

Whatever they wanted, it wouldn't be good. Carly glanced at her watch. It was only three. Ren wouldn't be here until after five, so she'd have to face them alone.

"Should I bring tea?" Linney asked.

Carly nodded as she threaded her way to the door. "Yes. And some of those little sandwiches if it's not too much trouble."

Once in the hallway, she dragged her hands through her hair in an effort to straighten it. Still, when she walked into the parlor, the pristine picture that the Mansfields presented made her feel like a bit of a ragamuffin.

With Susan seated in a wingback chair, Douglas Senior behind her and Dougie to her right, they might have been posing for a portrait. As her uncle moved toward her and enveloped her in a hug, she was once more impressed with what a handsome man he was. Except for the graying of his hair at the temples, he never seemed to age.

"Carly." Susan spoke softly, her voice was all concern. "Whatever have you been doing?"

"Trying to clean out the library," Carly said, taking the chair opposite her aunt Susan's.

Dougie frowned. "You shouldn't be doing that. We can give you the name of a reputable company that handles estate sales. They'd be happy to go through everything for you. You wouldn't want to throw away anything valuable."

"Dougie, I'm sure we can trust Carly not to toss out anything valuable."

It took only that one mild rebuke from Susan to have her cousin clamping his mouth shut, and Carly didn't have to fake a smile. "To what do I owe the pleasure of this visit? I thought that we were scheduled to meet tomorrow in Mr. Grady's office."

"We came to find out about the necklace," Susan said.

Carly raised her brows. "I won't have any news—"

"My dear, your little charade is over." Susan waved a dismissive hand. "I called your father yesterday and he reminded me of the name of the jeweler Aunt Delia always used—Chadwick on Park Avenue. Since Aaron Chadwick sits on several boards with Douglas, I was able to contact him at home. He claims you haven't contacted him yet, that to his knowledge you haven't special-messengered him anything."

Nerves knotted in Carly's stomach.

"We want to know where the necklace is," Dougie said. "And why you've been lying to us about it."

"Dougie." This time Susan's voice was sharp.

Carly drew in a deep breath. "I'll be sending the necklace to Mr. Chadwick just as soon as I locate it."

"Locate it?" Susan and Dougie spoke in unison as Linney wheeled a tea tray into the room.

Glad to have something to do with her hands, Carly reached for the teapot and began to pour. "It's nothing to worry about. When Ren and I checked the safe on Friday afternoon, the necklace wasn't there. Linney claims Aunt Delia had developed a bad habit of leaving it lying around the house."

Susan frowned. "But you haven't found it yet?"

"It's only a matter of time…. Cream or sugar, Uncle Douglas?" Carly didn't miss the look her aunt and uncle exchanged before Susan spoke again.

"This is exactly what we were worried about."

"It's Ren Maxwell," Dougie fumed. "He's taken it. He probably lifted it years ago and replaced it with a fake."

Carly willed her hand to be steady as she passed a cup to her uncle and filled a second one for her aunt. "I'd be very careful what you say about Ren Maxwell, cousin. You could be sued for slander."

"He'd have to produce the real necklace first," Dougie countered.

Carly set down the teapot. "Why are you so bound and determined to accuse Ren Maxwell of stealing that necklace? You have absolutely no proof."

"On the contrary," Susan said. "We have a pattern of behavior that we believe you should be aware of."

"What pattern of behavior?"

"Now, now." Her uncle moved toward her and took one of her hands. "We don't want to upset you, but when Sue discovered that you hadn't sent the necklace as you'd claimed you had…well, we were worried. We know how Ren Maxwell works."

Carly pulled her hand away and met her aunt's eyes steadily. "What pattern of behavior?"

"Ren Maxwell had a very close relationship with your great-aunt for a long time, and let's just say that the...connection between them has benefited him very well."

"Just what are you saying, Aunt Susan?"

"What do you think she's saying? He's a Maxwell," Dougie said. "Everything he is today is because Aunt Delia either paved the way with money or pulled in some favors. He's used her and now he's using you."

"That's not true."

"What is true," Susan said, "is that nine years ago your aunt paid Ren Maxwell off to keep you from making a terrible mistake."

Something inside of Carly went very cold. "How do you know about that?"

"This is a small town," Susan said. "We believe Aunt Delia did the right thing. The problem is that Ren Maxwell didn't just take the money and run. He saw a chance to make even more money. Why else has he hung around all these years?"

"Now it's certainly paid off for him," Dougie added. "He's influenced her to leave half her estate to him, and he's the acting mayor."

Carly struggled to control her temper.

"That's why we came today," Susan continued. "We don't want you to make the same mistake you made when you were eighteen."

"I don't intend to make a mistake."

"He has a way about him." Susan raised a hand and

dropped it. "Look at the position he's put you in. You've lied to your family about that necklace in order to protect him, haven't you?"

"No, I—"

"It's all right. We don't blame you," her uncle said. "He was your first love. And he has a certain charm."

"Charm?" Dougie snorted the word, then subsided when his mother shot him a look.

"Your uncle is right," Susan said. "We just wanted to warn you. Ren Maxwell has had Delia in his pocket for years. There's no better proof of that than her stubborn refusal to let us help her develop her land. She stood to make a fortune. Ren Maxwell has blocked every effort we made to convince her that the future of Westhaven depends on development. Young people will move out. The town will eventually stagnate and die. I'm sure he's told you that Delia wanted to preserve tradition."

"Yes, he has, but—"

"Of course he has," Douglas Senior murmured. "That way he continues to be the big fish in a small pond. Imagine—a Maxwell as mayor. But he needs you on his side, my dear."

"All he's done is try to let me see Westhaven the way my aunt saw it," Carly replied.

Susan leaned forward. "You of all people ought to know how persuasive he is. You nearly gave up your whole medical career because of him. And he's working on you again. We know where you spent last night."

Carly's eyes narrowed. "You were watching me?"

Her uncle patted her shoulder. "We're worried about you."

Carly rose. "I'd like you to leave."

"Fine," Susan said. "We'll leave, but just remember this. Ren Maxwell took money over you once. And he'll do it again. So if you can't produce the necklace by tomorrow morning, we will go forward with contesting the will. Think about it. We're hoping that you'll join us."

Carly didn't move until she heard the front door close behind them. Then she turned to find Linney standing in the hallway with a worried frown on her face.

"I couldn't help overhearing," she said. "Those things they said about Mr. Ren—they're not true."

Carly moved to the older woman. "I know they're not true. But if we can't find the necklace, they can cause trouble for Ren."

"I've looked everywhere," Linney said.

Fisting her hands on her hips, Carly began to pace. "You know, Ren thinks that Aunt Delia hid the necklace on purpose to keep me here. If that's true, she must have been hiding it every night. She couldn't have known which night would be her last." Carly started up the stairs. "While you clear away the tea things, I'm going to look around her room one more time."

REN GLANCED AT HIS WATCH for the fifth time in as many minutes. There were three more bobsled races to go and then the closing ceremonies. He'd been restless and on edge ever since he'd left Carly at the house.

He missed her. It was as simple as that. And he wasn't sure how that had happened. He'd lived without her for nine years, and now after only a few days of having her back in his life, he felt alone when she wasn't with him.

Time. He'd convinced himself that he had to give her some. They needed to get to know one another again, didn't they? He glanced at his watch again. So why was he so convinced that time was running out on him?

"Those hands on your watch aren't going to go any faster just because you're checking them more often," Harley Jensen commented.

"Yeah. I noticed that."

"Gotta be somewhere?"

"Yeah," Ren said. "I think I do."

"Women. They can sure complicate your life."

When Ren shot him a look, Harley shrugged. "My wife says the way you were looking at Carly Waring in the clinic yesterday, you're sunk."

"Maybe." Who was he kidding, Ren thought. He'd been sunk since the first time he'd laid eyes on her.

"I can handle the last three races," Harley continued. "It doesn't take a lot of judgment to decide who crosses the finish line first."

"There's still the closing ceremonies." Ren glanced around the crowd. "I think I'll ask Rupert Grady to do that. As an old friend of Delia's, he'd probably like to stand in."

"Good luck," Harley said.

"Yeah." Ren had a feeling he was going to need it.

CHAPTER TEN

CARLY SAT ON THE EDGE of Delia Waring's bed and tried to put herself in her aunt's mind. The will had only been step one in making sure that Ren's path and hers would cross again. In order for the plan to work, Delia had to make sure that she and Ren would have to spend some time together.

What better way to accomplish that than to hide the necklace and make sure that suspicion would fall on Ren? Well, it had certainly worked. Carly had changed her plans and stayed on in Westhaven with the sole purpose of protecting him. Her aunt knew her very well.

Rising, she walked to the safe, mimed taking the necklace out. If Delia had been feeling weaker than she'd been letting on, the town meeting would have exhausted her. Would she have had the strength to go downstairs?

Plus, if Delia *had* set the scene up every night, then the hiding place had to be close at hand. Carly moved back to the bed. But it couldn't be an obvious place if Delia was indeed using the necklace to buy some time. If she and Ren had discovered the diamonds on Friday afternoon, the whole setup would have been for nothing. So where would her aunt have stashed the diamonds?

Carly's gaze settled on the red leather box. So many of her memories of that long ago night surrounded that box. She could still see Ren's letter propped against it, her aunt picking it up and handing it to her. And when she'd thrown the letter on the floor in fury and denial, she could see her aunt picking it up, folding it, and tucking it into the box.

When they'd searched the bedroom on Friday, she'd let Ren handle the bedside table. He'd said that there were papers inside of it. Had her aunt been banking on the fact that she'd want to avoid searching it for herself?

Carly reached for the box and opened it. There was a folded paper, but even before she lifted it out, she saw the sparkle of diamonds beneath one of its edges. Oh, Aunt Delia, she thought. Then blinking away tears, she unfolded the letter and began to read.

My dearest Carly,
Now that you are reading this, I can finally forgive myself for the pain that I caused you all those years ago…

SHE WAS SITTING THERE on the bed when Ren entered the room. The late afternoon sunlight played off the diamond necklace that she held in one hand, and he noted the letter she held in the other. When he noticed the tear marks on her face, panic bubbled inside of him.

"You found it," he said.

"Yes." She met his eyes and hers narrowed as she studied him. "You had to have seen it when you opened the box on Friday. The letter didn't quite conceal it."

He stuffed his hands in his pockets. "Maybe. Yeah. I saw the sparkle."

Her eyes narrowed even farther. "And yet you let me worry, you let me spend hours searching this museum. Why?"

"When I saw it, all I could think of was that you'd turn it over to Dougie and leave." When she said nothing, he continued. "Well, am I right? Isn't that what you would have done?"

"Probably."

He couldn't read her. Why the hell couldn't he read her? "I didn't want you to leave. I wanted to buy us some time."

"Time for what?"

Her calm, almost disinterested tone had his panic spiking. Pulling a hand out of his pocket, he dragged it through his hair. "I wanted you to see the town the way your aunt saw it. I wanted time for us to get to know one another again. I wanted you to see me as I am and not the boy I was at twenty."

Slowly, she rose from the bed. "Well, I'd say you accomplished your mission. Now what?"

This time it was pure fear that shot through him. Closing the distance between them, he gripped her shoulders. "Linney told me that the Mansfields were here. Just what did they tell you?"

"In a nutshell they told me that you weren't interested in me, that you were only interested in money, and that if I believed you, I'd be repeating the same mistake that I'd made nine years ago."

He gave her shoulders a little shake. "It wasn't a mistake

then. *We* weren't a mistake. Our timing was just off. Otherwise, why would Delia have gone to all these lengths to bring us together again?"

"Ren, I—"

"No." Dropping his hands, he stepped back from her. "Give me a minute here. I should have said all this earlier. I had to bite my tongue on the ride to the school this morning, then again on the way back. But I thought you needed time. I thought I needed time. I don't. I know what I want, Doc."

SEEING WHAT WAS ON his face, in his eyes, suddenly Carly did, too. And all the nerves, the worries that had been plaguing her all day suddenly settled. But she wanted the words first. "And that would be?"

"You. I want you in my life. Friday, when I first saw you, I didn't think I did. There were reasons that I never went after you in New York. I thought there was too much history between us, that the same things that made it impossible for us to be together before still existed. But I was wrong."

He took her arms again and hauled her up on her toes. "If you think you can get rid of me by going back to New York, it won't be that easy. I'll follow you this time. I can teach school there just as easily as I can do it here."

He dropped her then but held her gaze.

"What about Delia's plans for Westhaven?"

"To hell with them! She can't have everything her way."

The fury, no, more than that—the determination in his eyes—sent her heart soaring. "Ren—"

"No, I'm not done. You wanted to talk and I'm still

talking. I said I want you in my life, but that's not enough. I want more than I did at twenty. I love you and I want to build a life with you. And if you think—"

"Same goes."

"What?"

"I love you and I want to build a life with you." She laughed as she moved toward him. "*I'm* going to so enjoy describing the look on your face when I tell our grandchildren about this." Then she placed her hands on his cheeks and drew his mouth down to hers.

"THAT WENT WELL." Carly tucked her hand into Ren's as they stepped out of Rupert Grady's office the next morning. "I don't think that the Mansfields will be contesting the will."

"I agree. Delia was smart not to leave the necklace directly to Susan in her will."

"Delia said in the letter that she wanted us to be able to use it as a bargaining chip. She was banking on the fact that if we agreed to give Susan the diamonds, Susan might not want to risk the chance of losing them if she contested the will."

"A bird in the hand," Ren said.

"Exactly. Aunt Delia had a knack for reading people very well."

"Including us."

"That, too." To her surprise Carly realized that Ren wasn't walking toward where he'd parked in front of the Waring Bank building. Instead, he was drawing her along the path to the gazebo in the park. There were a few workmen on ladders, tearing down the banners advertising Winterfest.

"You know, I'm going to enjoy telling our grandchildren about the look on Dougie's face when you announced we were engaged."

She smiled at him. Her heart swelled whenever she thought about the fact that she and Ren were going to have a future together.

"It's the second time you told him a bald-faced lie, Doc."

"What do you mean?" Carly asked.

"We're not officially engaged. Not until my ring is on your finger."

Carly simply stared as he pulled a small box out of his pocket. "When did you get that?" Her eyes flew to his face. "There wasn't time."

Opening the box, he pulled out a ring. "I bought this nine years ago, Doc. I intended to give it to you when we met here at the gazebo that night."

Carly couldn't speak for a moment. The diamond was small, but to her eyes it sparkled even brighter than her Aunt Delia's necklace. "You kept it—all these years?"

"Yeah." He slipped it on her finger. "We'll go shopping, find you something bigger."

"No. This one is perfect. You're perfect."

And standing in the wintery morning sunshine, she could see a whole future in Ren's eyes. As his mouth met hers, Carly was sure for an instant that she heard her Aunt Delia's soft throaty laughter.

* * * * *

Caught by Surprise

LAURA MARIE ALTOM

After college, bestselling, award-winning author **Laura Marie Altom** did a brief stint as an interior designer before becoming a stay-at-home mum to boy/girl twins. Always an avid romance reader, she knew it was time to try her hand at writing when she found herself re-plotting the soaps. Laura loves hearing from readers at either PO Box 2074, Tulsa, OK 74101, USA or e-mail through www.lauramariealtom.com.

For Margaret Daley – an amazing writer
and even better friend.
Thanks for putting up with me!
I'd be lost without you!

CHAPTER ONE

TABITHA SUMMERWELL was on top of the world.

Poised at the peak of Mt. Victoria, just outside her hometown of Snowflake, Colorado, she raised her ski goggles, releasing a long-held exhale while surveying the view.

She'd come a long way to this moment, when all of Columbine Valley spread dreamily before her, glistening like her white sequined prom dress in the bright, February sun.

Prom.

How much in her life had changed since then, and yet how much sadly, remained the same. Funny, too, how it'd been the gown she'd worn on her date with Brodie that had brought renewed hope, rather than her wedding dress. Though she'd never recapture the girlish anticipation she used to hold for her future, with the divorce from David behind her, she no longer dreaded each upcoming day.

For now, that was enough. She had the rest of her life to work out nagging details.

"Good to have you back, Tabs!" Ray Smith waved as he sailed by in a flash of his red-and-black ski patrol uniform.

"I'm not *back!*" she shouted after him. "Just visiting!" Either he hadn't heard or didn't care, since he was already schussing down the double black diamond run. Hard to believe the guy voted class clown had now been charged with safekeeping the tourists, who were the town's life-blood.

When Kelsey and Britt—her best friends since fourth grade—gifted her with the Valentine's Day trip to Snow-flake, she'd at first thought it a joke. It had been over a decade since any of them had set foot in the town. Why would she want to return now?

For great skiing, they'd told her.

And if I happen to run into you-know-who? she'd asked.

They'd explained that the likelihood of running into Brodie—now Doctor Brodie—had been about as nonexis-tent as a reunion with her cheating ex. In other words, it would never happen. A fact for which she was glad, as this long weekend was to be devoted to relaxing. Seeing her high school flame would be more in line with jabbing a ski pole through her heart.

"Hey! It's the Tabbinator!" Jake Grimshaw hollered over his shoulder with his teen students close on his heels. "Ray said you were back!"

"I'm not—" By the time she'd uttered her partial response, the former town ski bum, who now coached the Snowflake High ski team, led his charges down the mountain.

Grinning, Tabitha shook her head. Tilted her face back, drinking in the sun. Crisp, conifer-laced air.

Returning to the mountain she'd so loved as a kid and teen had been a good call. With the benefit of hindsight, this was the last place she'd been deeply, truly happy. Granted, it was also the first place where her life had gone horribly wrong, but for the purpose of the next few days, she'd solely focus on good times.

Squaring her shoulders, she drew down her goggles, cutting out the sun's glare on fresh powder. All around her, folks were having fun. Families and couples and hotshot teens. Seeing how she couldn't remember the last time she'd actually enjoyed herself, Tabitha vowed that from here on out, as miserable as the past few years had been, that was how good the next would be.

She'd start by tackling this legendarily tough run.

She hadn't skied in a while, but everyone said it was like sex—once you learned the basics, you never forgot. Well, once upon a time, she'd been a great skier. As for the last time she'd had mind-blowing sex…

Despite the morning's frigid temperature, the criminally handsome face flashing before her mind's eye scorched her cheeks.

Crazy—that's what thinking of Brodie was, and to stop herself from any additional treks down memory lane, she pushed up and over the run's edge, taking the mountain at breakneck speed. Devil's Tears hadn't earned its name by being a bunny hill, but a wicked-steep, narrow trail snaking through aspens and firs. For fun, boulders jutted at lethal angles, forcing skiers to perform gravity-defying jumps or crash into granite too steep to be softened by a snow cushion.

"Watch it!" called an overzealous snowboarder. "Old folks should stay off the mountain!"

Tabitha was too focused on her form to devise an appropriately witty comeback. Teeth gritted, thigh muscles screaming, she held tight when her skis chattered across an icy patch.

Maybe she should've started on an easier run. She didn't remember this being so hard.

"On your right!" a masculine voice called. She didn't dare look up to see more of a fellow skier than a peripheral glance of royal blue.

Man, oh man, what had she gotten herself into?

Faster and faster she flew until soaring firs became green blurs.

She tried slowing by carving, but when even that didn't help on the iciest spots beneath the trees, she resorted to snowplowing. And when that didn't work?

Tabitha screeched before falling, falling, then blacking out.

"WHAT ARE YOU doing here?"

"Nice to see you, too," Dr. Brodie Kimball said to Gladys, his office manager and occasional nurse.

From her desk in the clinic that was starting to look more like her doily-covered living room than a medical office, she glared past hot-pink sequined reading glasses that'd slid to the tip of her nose. "You're supposed to be out finding a date for Valentine's Day. That's why Marcy and I cleared your schedule."

Marcy was his full-time nurse and, along with Gladys, a 24/7 pain in his behind. The two had been blessed with great marriages and were constantly foisting their match-making skills on anyone dumb enough to let them. He'd fallen into that category more than a few times and had always regretted it.

"Where is your partner in crime?" he asked, sifting through the office mail.

"Skiing with her kids. They have the day off for parent/teacher conferences. While she's there, she's scouting single female tourists you might find appealing."

He sighed, slapping the mail on the brown laminate patient check-in counter. "You guys have got to knock it off. For the last time, I appreciate the fact that you think I'm lonely and want to help, but I'm good. Great." Planting a kiss to Gladys's tight grey curls, he added, "Now, if you need anything, I'll be in my office, playing catch-up with patient files."

Right. After suffering through five more minutes of reasons why he needed a Valentine's Day sweetheart, Brodie finally escaped to the clinic's last remaining manly refuge. While the rest of the place was cutesy with lace curtains, floral upholstered furniture and pinkish walls covered in vintage Rockwell prints that Gladys had decided he collected, Brodie's office was just as he liked.

Big oak desk free of clutter. Big picture window with nothing on it to block the gorgeous mountain view.

Best of all, four white walls bare of anything save for the one poster he'd carried with him for well over a dozen years. The shiny black background was crinkled, but the white block letters were still easy to read:

Success is the Best Revenge.

Every chance they got, Gladys and Marcy tried redecorating, a large part of their efforts going toward losing the poster. They'd told him the slogan was unfitting for a man of his community stature. They'd said he should have family portraits on his walls. Diplomas or hunting trophies—anything but the tattered print.

Thing is, those words meant more to him—had done more for him—than any person ever had. Except for maybe the girl—now woman—who'd given him the poster. At the time Tabitha "Tabby" Summerwell had meant for him to succeed in crushing his personal demons. Or, in other words, the folks around their small town who'd never believed he'd amount to anything more than a two-bit thug.

Never would he have thought that the person he'd most want revenge on was Tabby, herself. She'd hurt him. No, *annihilated* might be a more fitting way to put what she'd done to him. Even years later he couldn't get past it. There were times when he'd even wondered if maybe his marriage failing was because of what Tabby had done.

The way she'd gotten under his skin, making all women pale compared to his memory of her.

Then there were other times—obviously, much saner times—when he knew the best course of action would be ripping the poster from the wall, then running it through the office shredder. Once and for all banishing the girl and her unsolicited advice from his heart.

A knock sounded on his office door. "Doc?"

"Yeah, Gladys?" Not for the first time Brodie wished for an intercom.

The older woman burst through the door. "Marcy just called from the ski lodge, and not only will you not believe who she ran into, but what happened to her."

Sighing, Brodie shook his head. The last time Gladys

rushed into his lair bearing such *exciting* news, it had been a set-up for a seriously awful blind date.

"Well?" she asked, hands on her ample hips as if put out by his lack of enthusiasm. "Aren't you the least bit interested in who it is Marcy ran into?"

"Nope." He reached for a patient file in need of updating.

"What if I told you this special someone is a woman?"

He case her a *back-off* glare. "Then I most especially wouldn't be interested."

"And if I told you the woman is none other than Tabitha Summerwell? And that she probably broke her leg, and that you're the only man for miles around who can fix it?"

Tabby? Here? On his mountain?

A cold/hot sweat crept up Brodie's chest. This was a joke, right? A bad one. Because if it wasn't, the only possible way he knew to deal with the situation was by taking early retirement!

CHAPTER TWO

"Brodie, I..." From the second he'd walked into the cramped lodge infirmary, Tabitha hadn't been able to catch her breath. Tall, dark and handsome didn't begin to do the man justice.

"Somehow, in ski boots, you managed a distal ankle fracture. In time, it'll heal nicely enough, but you won't be using the rest of your weekend's lift tickets."

"That's all you have to say to me?"

Snatching her X-rays out from in front of the light box, Brodie asked, "You have questions? We've already been over your pain meds. My nurse will be right in to apply your cast. As for the bill, we've got your insurance information, so—"

"Stop."

Save for a muscle ticking in his whisker-stubbled jaw, he froze.

"Please, Brodie. You have to know this is every bit as awkward for me as it is for you. Had I known you were not only the town doctor, but on call for the lodge, I never would've come."

"Now that you do know, maybe it'd be best for you to leave."

She sighed. "Does it really have to be like this?" Eyeing

the bottle of pain meds he'd given her, she added, "Believe it or not, I look back on the time we shared with great fondness. You meant the world to me, Brodie, and I—"

"If you have any questions, my phone numbers are on your follow-up sheet. Don't hesitate to call should your pain worsen or you develop a high fever."

"Please, Brodie, don't—" He was halfway out the door when without thinking, she hopped off the exam table to stop him. Bad idea, seeing how her injured right ankle screamed. "Ouch!" she yelped, adding a pitiful moan.

Now he was the one sighing, as he scooped her into his arms and set her right back atop the table. "That was a dumb move."

"You think I don't know that?" she said, shooting him her most scathing look. Her eyes stung from the pain shooting through her entire leg and from even worse, the smarting of Brodie's unexpected coldness toward her. So he wouldn't see her cry, she glanced out the window at the now gray day.

"Look, Tabitha, there's really not—"

"You used to call me Tabby."

"I used to do a lot of things, but I grew up. I assumed you had, as well."

"What's that supposed to mean?"

"Just that from the moment I knew I'd be treating you, I've tried to be professional, keeping our past out of your current situation, but—"

"Boy, is it getting dark out there." The plump, perpetually smiling nurse who'd introduced herself as Marcy bustled through the door, arms laden with what Tabitha assumed were cast-making supplies. Though Tabitha's parents and two older brothers were doctors, as well as her ex-husband, she'd wanted nothing to do with the profession. Too much time away from family. Too much heartache when things went wrong. "I just heard from Lauren, at the front desk, that we're in for a monster storm. As soon as I'm done with your cast, I'm headed down the mountain before I'm stuck up here with my kids for the next three days. Doc, you'd best do the same."

Tabitha was grateful that the woman happily busied herself with her task, apparently oblivious to the tension between her patient and her boss.

"Now that you mention it," Brodie said, never breaking Tabitha's gaze, "after checking on Mr. Talbot, I'll—"

"He still hugging the throne?" Marcy asked.

"Not as of this morning. Those suppositories seemed to do the trick."

"Good," the nurse said. "His wife was worried."

"Mom!" a little girl's voice called from the infirmary's sterile beige waiting room. "Joey ate a checker!"

"Is he still breathing, or turning blue?" Turning to Tabitha, Marcy said, "Sorry. I didn't expect to be working today, so my babies are with me."

"He's breathing, and he bit me."

"Joey—corner!"

"But—" a boy's voice complained.

"Now!"

"Yeah, well, like I was saying," Brodie interjected, apparently used to the ruckus, "after I check on Mr. Talbot, I'm out of here, too. Ms. Summerwell, call if you need anything."

Call if you need anything, Tabitha said mocking his voice in her head. Oh, she needed something, all right. To kick the man in his too-perfect derriere! Who did he think he was, insulting her like that? Back in high school, she'd been voted Homecoming Queen, Prom Queen and Most Likely to Break a Boy's Heart—not the other way around!

Though fat lot of good all those titles did her now.

Fighting the knot of pain and frustration lurking at the back of her throat, for the second time that day, Tabitha vowed to put Brodie Kimball out of her mind. A task that, considering the pile of pain meds she'd been given, should be easy enough to do. Getting him out of her heart, however, she suspected may be a bit more of a challenge.

BRODIE GROANED.

Why? Why did Tabitha Summerwell have to be stretched out in front of the Western-themed lodge's great room's crackling fire instead of the one she could've enjoyed in the privacy of her suite? And while he was lamenting his lousy string of luck, why had Mr. and Mrs. Talbot turned chatty right before the onset of a major blizzard? By the time he'd called to check in on a few of his patients who could potentially be affected by the storm, snow was falling so hard, he couldn't even find his green Range Rover, let alone maneuver it down the treacherous mountain road.

He'd just turned to hide out in the infirmary when from behind him, Tabitha asked, "Trying to avoid me?"

"Nope. Just thought of something I need to do."

"Other than me?" She winked and grinned.

Despite his best intentions not to, Brodie made the

mistake of catching her big brown gaze. Her eyes had always fascinated him. Not a good thing, considering how for a time, the memory of those eyes had haunted him. Now? He hoped himself immune. "Again, Tabitha, I wasn't trying to avoid you."

"I know. I'm just a tad loopy on that pain medicine you gave me, and was teasing. Sit down," she said, with her free hand, patting the thick cushion beside her. In her other hand, she held one of the lodge's blue mugs.

"Do you really think that's a good idea?"

"Unless you failed to tell me that in addition to a broken leg, I also have some wildly contagious disease."

Oh—she was contagious, all right, but not in the way she'd meant. The years had been kind to her both in face and figure. She still wore her hair long and blond and her complexion was creamy as ever. At a height of 5'5", she had curves in all the right places and not a love handle in sight.

"Please, sit with me," she urged, voice throaty, full lips unwittingly pouty. "I'm bored. Lonely."

"Then maybe the best place for you in your current, admittedly *loopy*, condition would be bed."

"I tried, but I'm not tired. Besides, no one else I've seen here at the lodge is as gorgeous as you."

He cleared his throat. "I'm flattered, but—"

"Seriously, Brodie, you've grown into a fine-looking man. I'm amazed you're not married. Glad, really." Her expression clouded. "You're not, are you? Married?"

"No."

"Whew."

"Tabitha, how about letting me help you to your room?

You need rest." Not to mention tape for the mouth temporarily out of her control.

"I already told you, I'm not sleepy. Please, Brodie. Talk to me."

"All right," he said, partially because he didn't want her alone in this drugged state, but mostly out of sheer morbid curiosity as to what she might say next. "But only a few minutes."

For midafternoon, the cavernous space was empty save for the two of them and a couple of oblivious teens playing handheld video games in front of a big screen TV.

While there was plenty of room on the couch beside Tabitha's feet, Brodie chose the armchair alongside her. "So? How have you been?"

"In a word—lousy." She laughed, sipped at the contents of the mug, around which she was warming her hands.

"I'm sorry. Breaking your ankle on a ski trip is a bad cliché to find yourself saddled with."

"This—" she wagged her hot-pink cast "—is the least of my worries."

"Oh?" Eyebrows raised, he said, "Last I'd heard, you were in Denver, living happily ever after with a filthy rich cardiologist."

"He was rich all right—in women."

"He cheated on you?"

"Another cliché I've fallen victim to. She was his favorite nurse—at least I hope she was his fave, seeing how he got her pregnant."

"Sorry."

She snorted. "Me, too." Taking another sip of what he

now saw was cocoa, she set the mug a little too sharply on the side table, causing the contents to spill on her hand. She licked off the chocolaty drink.

Brodie swallowed hard and shifted in his seat.

Did she have to be so damned seductive performing such a simple task?

"On second thought," she said, "I'm not sorry. Out of respect for David, we had good times, but I never gave myself wholly to him."

Why? Brodie wondered.

"In retrospect, I'm thinking it was you I've always loved."

"All right," Brodie said, pushing to his feet. "Now, I know it's time for you to hit the sack."

"I'm serious," she said, placing her pale hand on his forearm. Though he knew it to be a medical impossibility, he felt as if her mere touch had singed a hole through his sweater. "Breaking up with you was the worst mistake of my life—and trust me, I've made some doozies."

Never taking his eyes off of her, Brodie slowly lowered himself back into his chair. "W-what did you just say?"

"*Doozies.* It's a fun word, don'cha think?"

"Dammit, Tabby," he said, voice low, "knock it off. It may not be manly to admit, but you hurt me—bad. It's in seriously poor taste for you to now joke about something that…" *Even now, I'm not sure I'll ever be over.*

"I'm not joking," she said, expression back to a wounded pout. "I really do love the word *doozies* and I love *you.*"

CHAPTER THREE

HOW MANY NIGHTS had this woman kept him awake, wondering what the hell he'd done to drive her away and now all of the sudden she was announcing her undying devotion?

No way was this happening.

"Okay, Miss Chatty," Brodie abruptly said, sitting up in the chair. "Time for a nice, long nap."

"You wanna know why I broke up with you?" She took his hand, drew his fingers to her mouth, kissing each tip.

Did he want to know?

That's all he'd ever wanted for as long as he could remember. What the two of them shared had been amazing. Her love had made him want more than the no-count life he'd been barreling toward. And then, just as suddenly as she'd given that love, she'd snatched it away. Without reason. With barely any words. One day she'd loved him, indulged in fantasies of what their adult lives together would be like. The next, she'd told him it was over. She never wanted to talk to him again.

"Yes," he ground from between clenched teeth. "I want to know."

Squeezing his fingers, she said, "It's ridiculously simple,

really. Not that that made it easier to bear, but here goes…Mom and Dad found out we were sleeping together, then—"

"How? We were careful."

A strangled half laugh escaped her. "Parents have methods. Anyway, they found out. Felt like you'd abused their trust. They told me either I could break up with you, or they'd call the sheriff. Have you arrested for statutory rape."

"What?"

"See? When you think about it, my choice was simple."

Brodie snatched his hand free. Doubled over, elbows on his knees, the heat from the fireplace threatened to bring up the microwave burrito he'd had for lunch.

"You hurt them, Brodie. My parents thought you hung the moon. They thought of you as some fabulous makeover project. You know, as this scruffy dog they'd saved who'd turned around and bit them when they'd least expected it."

"I hurt *them?* Good lord, woman, what do you think all of you did to me?"

"The only reason I'm telling you all of this is because I felt I owed you an apology. Not only for walking away from you without a word, but for allowing my parents to frighten me into dictating who I should and shouldn't love."

"So essentially, you're saying you broke up with me to save me?"

Unshed tears pooled in her eyes, telling him that no matter how much her speech made him want to retch, she believed her actions had been noble. It didn't matter that as a street-smart kid, he knew he could've somehow gotten out of the bogus charges. It didn't matter how many times he'd told himself he hated her and how many times he'd held her responsible for his marriage breaking up. Because compared to her, no other woman had ever made him feel even half as complete. Nothing mattered other than stopping Tabitha's tears.

Easing off of his chair, Brodie knelt beside her, smoothing fallen hair back from her eyes. "You're making it hard to hate you."

"I don't blame you for hating me. There have been times I've hated myself for not having been stronger. But looking back on it, I did what I thought was best."

"After graduation, once you'd turned eighteen, why didn't you call me?"

"And say what? We were both dating other people. You wouldn't even look at me, let alone talk to me."

She was right. Back then, he'd been so hell-bent on proving to himself and the world that he was over her, that no matter what she'd have said, it wouldn't have mattered.

And now? Now he felt exhausted. Empty. Like her words were too little, too late.

"What're you thinking?" she asked, nibbling her lower lip.

Sitting back, he laughed and shook his head. "Truthfully, it's been a long day. My mind's pretty much fried. Thank you, though, for telling me the truth. Of all the scenarios I'd run in my head, having your folks sic the law on me never came up."

"Yes, well…" She held out her arms for a hug, and he met her halfway. Holding her again felt so damned good.

But their time had come and gone. They were different people. Moreover, what if what they'd shared hadn't been all that special? But had time and the pressures of everyday life made their brief fling seem more—bigger—than it'd actually been?

Releasing her, Brodie asked, "How's your ankle?"

"Good." Grinning, she said, "Obviously, so is the medicine you gave me."

"Ready for that nap?"

She nodded.

Helping her hobble to her room, immersed in her sophisticated, intoxicating scent, Brodie summoned everything in him to remind himself that despite her drug-induced admission of love, nothing between them had changed.

Tabby was still—and would *always*—be the girl who'd pulverized his heart. All the apologies in the world couldn't erase the shadowy pain he'd never been able to let go. All the love in the world couldn't bring back the shattered innocence and trust and anticipation he'd once had for his future—*their* future.

Because Tabby was physically hurt, he'd care for her. After all, his professional oath bound him to that. As for anything else? Like allowing himself to feel anything for her other than polite detachment?

Never going to happen.

THE NEXT MORNING Tabitha woke to throbbing pain in her ankle and embarrassment crushing her chest. Hands cradling her forehead, she prayed she really hadn't spilled the secret to Brodie that she was afraid she had.

I love you.

She groaned.

Outside snow obliterated the view, cocooning her in a cold, whitewashed world nothing like yesterday's sun-sparkled wonderland. Despite the room's cozy, rough-hewn pine log furnishings, rock fireplace and upholstery and carpeting done in warm shades of cranberry and copper, she was freezing.

She tugged the covers up to her neck, but it didn't help. But then what would when the cold numbing her came from the inside out?

She hadn't been completely honest with Brodie last night. Even on pain pills, she'd recognized that he'd been so upset that she couldn't tell him about the baby—*their* baby. To this day, guilt for not having told him consumed her, even thought she hadn't even known she was pregnant until that horrible night when grief sliced through her abdomen and she'd miscarried.

The emergency room doctor—a family friend—had diagnosed her. The look of disappointment in her parents' eyes had been too much to bear. As much as she'd loved Brodie, her sense of family allegiance wasn't something she could've let go.

Hugging herself, Tabitha remembered the shame she'd felt. Worse yet, the overwhelming loneliness of having lost the tiny baby she and Brodie's love had created. Truth be known, it'd been easier breaking up with him than it would've been telling him the truth. That her parents had been right in that she and Brodie had been too young for sex. For the level of intimacy it'd bred.

Given all that, why did she still love him?

She could hear the icy wind howl, the force of it causing the historic lodge's paned windows to shudder. Was Brodie still here? Was he forced into spending the night by the ferocity of the storm?

Part of her desperately wanted to see Brodie again. Another part was mortified by her admissions and never wanted to see him again. Had it been pain medicine he'd prescribed or truth serum? Had her girlfriends secretly schemed for she and Brodie to meet up again, or had it been fate? Obviously, they couldn't have known she'd end up needing his services, but had they known he served as the lodge's on-call physician and hoped for an accidental meeting?

Too keyed up to sleep, she hobbled out of bed and hopped to the bathroom. Marcy had shown her how to wrap her cast so she could shower, so Tabitha did that, then dressed in a comfy burgundy velour jogging suit and forced her hair into pigtails. After which she was too tired to mess with makeup and again ready for bed, but she was also hungry.

Figuring by the time she'd placed a room service order and had it delivered that she could have already eaten her fill of the sumptuous breakfast buffet, she grabbed her crutches, tucked her room's card key into her back pocket and opened the door. Only seconds later to wish she hadn't!

CHAPTER FOUR

"HEY. I WAS JUST COMING to check on you." Brodie stepped off the elevator and spotted his patient hobbling toward him on her crutches.

His patient.

No matter how adorably mussed she looked this morning with her long, blond hair in uneven pigtails and a refreshing lack of makeup, Tabitha was his patient—that's all she'd ever be. He appreciated finally learning the truth, but it didn't change his own truth. The fact that this woman and her parents had left one hell of a scar on his soul. If they were so ticked with him for sleeping with their daughter, why couldn't they have at least treated him like a man and told him to his face?

"How's the ankle?" he asked.

"Not as painful as my bruised ego."

She remembered everything she'd said?

She glanced down, then up. "Sorry. I must've come across as a major head case."

"No harm done. Besides, after all you've been through lately, with your divorce, and now this—" he gestured to her cast "—that pretty much entitles you to one or two free meltdowns."

"You're sweet."

"And you must be hungry. Come on," he said, easing alongside her, offering himself as her crutch.

Touching her was a mistake. As was drinking in her expensive floral scent. It wasn't so much a heavy perfume, but an overall hint of orange blossoms and jasmine. Maybe the smell came from soap or lotion? Pricey shampoo? Whatever its origin, the fragrance was sophisticated. Told of a world he'd once wanted more than anything to belong to. Now, however, he'd made peace with his own.

Back at the elevator, Brodie pressed the Down button.

Tabitha smiled up at him, but exhaustion shaded her eyes.

"Tired?" he asked.

She nodded.

Had she still been his, he'd have encouraged her to rest her head on his shoulder. Or, for that matter, he'd have scooped her into his arms, then carried her to bed. No messing around, just resting. "Want me to help you back to your room? Order you something from room service?"

She shook her head. "I thought about it, but figured it'd be just as easy to trek downstairs."

"Sure."

The elevator dinged, opening with a soft swish of the doors.

Brodie helped her on, and while Tabby held the car's pine rail instead of him, she graced him with another winced smile.

"You in pain?" he asked.

She nodded.

"Why haven't you taken any medicine?"

"Truth? Last night was a disaster. I'm not usually like that. You know, spilling my guts to a stranger."

"I'm hardly a stranger, Tab." And the notion that despite her outpouring of love, that's how she viewed him, touched a nerve.

"You know what I mean."

"You should take your medicine. Stay in your room, if you feel the need, but don't needlessly suffer."

"I'm hardly suffering," she said with a dramatic roll of her eyes.

"Don't pull that with me."

"What?"

The elevator jolted to a stop on the first floor, momentarily pausing the conversation while he helped Tabitha out and an elderly couple stepped in.

"You know what I mean," he said once they were again alone, this time in a red-carpeted, hunting trophy–lined hall. "The eye thing. You used to do it every time I told you to put on a jacket, or eat more of your lunch so you wouldn't be hungry all afternoon."

She did it again. "You were my boyfriend, not my father."

"True. But seeing how you never listened to your father, either, I felt it was my duty to step in."

"And now?" she asked in front of the restaurant's open double doors. "Seeing that I'm a good girl and taking my medicine again falls under the category of duty?"

Scowling, he sighed. "As your current doctor, yes."

"Okay, that accounts for why you're bugging me now, but why'd you do it back then, Brodie?"

The maitre d' approached. "Table for two?"

"Yes," Tabitha said.

"No," Brodie said.

"Where are you going?" she asked. "I thought you were eating with me?"

"I lost my appetite."

"Stop it," she hissed under her breath. "You always were a bear when you didn't get your way. I remember the time you—"

"Pardon—" the maitre d' wagged red, leather-bound menus "—but will there be one of you for breakfast or two?"

"One," Brodie said.

"Two," Tabby countered. For him only, she whispered, voice warm and husky in his left ear, "If you don't eat with me, not only will I *not* take my medicine, but I'll tell everyone you're such a horrible doctor that you never even prescribed pain meds. Instead, you told me to 'suck it up.'"

Now Brodie was rolling his eyes—and smiling. He knew full well she'd never do such a thing, and the mere suggestion made him want to laugh. Which, in turn, made him want to be with her all the more.

"Two," he said to the scowling maitre d'.

"THAT WAS SCRUMPTIOUS," Tabitha said, pushing away her empty breakfast plate. She and Brodie had compromised on the pain pills, and she'd taken one instead of the recommended two. The pain wasn't completely dulled, but then neither was her mind!

Though the world was still white beyond the towering

paned window they'd been seated alongside, the lodge's dining room was balmy with a fire crackling in the river rock hearth. Helping warm her was a third cup of mint tea. As for her incredibly pleasant dining companion, she had to admit to feeling a bit of warmth for Brodie, too.

"The food was good," Brodie said. "This place makes the best French toast in town."

"What about Aunt Mable's? Remember how we used to skip first period French and hide in the corner booth there, sharing an order with extra powdered sugar?"

"Didn't you hear?"

"What?"

"It burned down. Last summer. Electrical fire."

"Oh, no. Aunt Mable wasn't hurt, was she?"

"No, but she used the insurance money to buy a beach condo in South Carolina. Said she was tired of 'smellin' like bacon' and wanted to be closer to her grandkids."

Laughing, Tabitha said, "That sounds like her." What a treat it was, sharing memories—even if in this case, the site of one of her favorite places was no more. She ought to have taken it as a sign. One urging her to remember she and Brodie were also no longer a couple. But her pleasantly full tummy and the room's heat combined with his strikingly handsome all-grown-up features made for a potentially explosive situation where her feelings for him were concerned. Being holed up with him had bred a sense of intimacy. Despite the room's other diners, she felt as if they were alone, which emboldened her to ask, "Earlier, when you were reminding me how you used to have to nag me into eating or wearing a coat, and I asked why you'd done it, you never answered."

"Nope." He sipped at his coffee.

"Why?"

"Why, what?" His sexy smile told her he knew full well what she was getting at. It also told her he wasn't about to spill his secrets as easily as she had hers—most of them, anyway.

The granddaddy of them all, she still held safely locked inside.

"You know *what,* you big creep."

"Yep." He took another sip.

"I think it's because you loved me every bit as much as I loved you. You wanted to protect me. And for that, I should've been grateful instead of snarky."

"Yep." He was at it again with his grinning.

"David never did that."

"What? Look after you? That's a shame, seeing how obviously, judging by your busted ankle, you still need an awful lot of adult supervision."

She tossed her yellow cloth napkin at him.

"Double creep."

"Hey," he said laughing, and easily dodging her weapon, catching it midair, only to set it on the table between them. "Watch it. I'm the only doctor for miles around. You hurt me, and who's going to help when you suffer your next accident?"

"Who said there's going to be another?"

"If my memory serves me correctly, when you're involved—fate." Sadly, he was right. She had always tended to be accident prone. Especially with him, as she'd been so busy appreciating his chiseled face, that more often than not, she'd forgotten to look where she was going and tripped over curbs or chairs, or whatever else had happened to be blocking her way.

"Touché."

She joined him in laughing, and the sharing felt so good. Like coming home. Only she wasn't home, but stuck in a ski lodge with a man she only *used* to love, right? Despite the previous night's ramblings, in the light of day, she realized she didn't even know him anymore, so how could she love him?

"If you don't mind my asking," he said, setting down his mug. "What happened between you and your husband? Aside from his affair. I mean, things couldn't have been that great between you if he was stepping out."

"True," she said with a sigh. "I could be kind and leave it at just saying we grew apart, but I didn't like the man David had become. I seriously didn't like who I had become as his wife."

"Care to elaborate?"

"I don't know. It's hard enough for me to understand, let alone explain. I guess lots of little things went wrong. I quit my advertising job to go into full-time volunteering."

"What's wrong with that? Sounds noble."

"Oh, sure. Except it wasn't initially my idea, but David's. He wanted to be considered for chief of staff. He felt it might be helpful if the nominating committee saw what an asset I was."

"Did you ever tell him you felt used?"

She shrugged. "For a while I felt like I really was doing good. But then it felt shallow. Like the politicking between all these society women was coming before whatever *cause du jour.*"

"What would you rather have been doing?"

Raising my own babies, rather than holding infants others had given up.

The painful admission was too great to voice aloud. Same as the fact that she suspected a large part of why David had left her was because of her inability to carry a child to term. She'd been to a dozen specialists, all of whom had reached the same conclusion: there was nothing medically wrong with her. When the timing was right, she would be able to have children. Too bad for her, the *right* time for her husband had been when his nurse carried his child, rather than his wife.

"Tabby?"

Hearing Brodie call her by her old pet name was her undoing. How long had it been since anyone had cared about how she'd thought or felt? For most of her adult life, her main concern had been supporting her husband. His career, his whims, his financial empire. But she was tired of all of that. This weekend was about looking after herself. And at the moment there could be no greater balm than the concern in Brodie's blue eyes.

"What did you want to do with your life?"

"I don't know…" She covered her lie with a half-hearted laugh. "The usual. Have my own career, I suppose."

"What if I told you I don't believe you?"

CHAPTER FIVE

BRODIE HADN'T MEANT to actually voice the question, but now that he had, he really did want to know. "Whatever happened to you wanting to be a teacher? When you worked part-time after school at the church's daycare, you were great with kids."

"Thanks," she said, glancing away from him and toward the driving snow. Her expression was that of a lost child. Was she emotionally lost? Would she have even known?

"No, I mean it," he insisted. "I thought you wanted to teach fourth grade, because the kids were big enough to talk intelligently, but not so big as to be scary."

"You remember me saying that?"

"I remember lots of things," he said softly, swallowing hard. With everything in him, he wanted to reach for her hands, brush the soft tops of them with the rough pads of his thumbs. He wanted to taste her—no, devour her—but all he really did was look away, forcing a deep breath.

"What else?" She leaned forward, completely engaged, completely engaging.

"What I think back on the most was this—our ability to talk for hours and never get bored."

"I enjoyed that part of our relationship, too." She cast him a surprisingly shy smile. Why shy? he wondered. Because all of a sudden she'd realized how much she'd enjoyed what they'd shared? Not that she hadn't already known, but maybe not to the extent that their romance was still so fresh in her mind.

The waitress refilled Tabby's hot water and Brodie's coffee.

While Tabitha dangled her tea bag in her mug, then added lemon and sugar, she glanced outside only to face a wall of white. She had to regroup. Gather her thoughts. Remind herself that she and Brodie had once had their chance, but now it was gone.

Beyond the thin glass, wind howled.

Inside, her heart suffered a more quiet, yet equally intense storm.

She asked, "You mentioned last night that you weren't married, but surely, in all this time, there's been someone important in your life?"

"There was. I'm divorced now." He traced the lip of his mug. "Jenna and I were in med school together, but after completing our residencies, we drifted apart."

"Why?"

Pressing his lips tight, he appeared to carefully consider his answer. She liked that about him. That he didn't have a canned, ready-to-serve speech like so many of her divorced friends. "I think we were drawn together because of the pressures of school. We were each other's island in the storm. But once the storm ended, and our lives finally settled down, there was nothing left. We'd thrived in chaos."

There was that word again. *Storm.*

Was it fate that both of them had weathered their own personal storms only to end up together again during a blizzard?

"I'm sorry," she said.

"For what?"

"That things didn't work out. I know that one day having a family of your own meant a lot to you. It probably still does." *Knowing that, losing your baby—our baby—hurt all the worse even though my parents felt I should've been relieved.*

"Yes, in fact, I—" His cell rang, making him grimace, while he reached into his jeans pockets. "Sorry."

"It's okay," she said, studying the dinner menu's wine list while he took his call.

"Important?" she asked once he flipped the small phone shut.

"Very. Remember Kelly Stevens?"

"Sure. She graduated the year after us, right?"

He nodded, already pushing to his feet. "I hate to eat and run, but she's going into labor—a month early. I've gotta borrow the lodge's Sno-Cat, then get to town ASAP."

"In this weather? Will it be safe?"

"Probably not, but what else can I do?"

"Good point," she said. "Which is why I'm going with you."

"What?" He left thirty dollars on the table to pay for their breakfasts.

"You heard me," she said, reaching for her crutches to push onto her feet. "I love babies. Plus, this'll give me a chance to see you in action."

"Tabby…" He groaned. "The trip itself is dangerous. You're on crutches. How are you supposed to maneuver around to help me? Then, once we get to Kelly's, there's no guarantee her labor will go well."

"Yes, it will," she said, reaching for Brodie's hand and giving his fingers a squeeze. "You're too stubborn to let it go any other way."

"COME ON, KELLY, PUSH!" Brodie urged. As luck would have it, the woman's husband was stuck in Aspen, where he worked at City Hall as the tax collector. "Kelly, I see her head. Come on, honey. Just one more."

"I can't!" the woman cried, thrashing her head.

"Sure you can," Tabby crooned, holding Kelly's hand. "Just think how awesome it's going to be when you finally hold your baby in your arms."

Teeth gritted, Kelly nodded. "O-okay. I—I think I can."

"Of course you can," Tabby said, smoothing hair from Kelly's sweating forehead.

Kelly fiercely nodded, then let loose with a scream.

Seconds later, her baby released her own wail.

Brodie had been worried about the infant's lung development, but judging by the wee thing's volume, she was breathing just fine.

Brodie placed the infant on her mom's tummy. "You did great, honey. Derrick's going to be proud," he told Kelly.

"She's healthy then?"

"Perfect."

"She really is beautiful," Tabby said, tears shining in her eyes.

You're the beautiful one. While helping babies enter the world was always a thrill for Brodie, something about Tabitha's awed expression made this delivery especially dear.

"What're you going to name her?" Tabby asked.

"Penelope—Penny for short. After Derrick's grand-mother."

"That's sweet," Tabby said.

"Thank you both for getting here through the storm," Kelly said, gently kissing the crown of her baby's head. "I don't know what I would've done here by myself."

"Probably been fine, but I'm glad it didn't come to that," Brodie said. "Now, how about letting me cut the cord, then Tabby and I will get this cutie cleaned up while you get some rest. Marcy should be here any minute to help you."

"She didn't have to come all this way in the snow."

"Sure I did," Marcy said, brushing melting flakes from her red beanie. "Clyde and Pete let me in." Clyde and Pete were eighty-year-old brothers and Kelly's closest neigh-bors. They were downstairs, presumably brewing the tar they called coffee while keeping Derrick posted on his wife's progress. "Well? I see I can report good news."

"The best," Kelly said. "Does Clyde still have Derrick on the phone?"

"Yep. I guess sometime between agony and excruciat-ing pain, you told him you never wanted to talk to him again," Marcy said.

"I did?" Grinning, Kelly shook her head. "It was pretty rough there for a while."

"I wouldn't sweat it," Marcy said. "Let me help you get more comfortable, then you can smooth things over with your man."

IN A BUTTERFLY-THEMED hall bathroom, watching while Brodie tenderly ran a damp washcloth over the newborn's pink limbs, Tabitha tried desperately not to burst into tears. She'd wanted a baby for so long.

Would her dream ever come true?

"You all right?" Brodie asked.

Not trusting herself to speak, she nodded. Faintly smiled. "Thanks for coming."

"It was no big deal."

"Seriously," he said, running the orange cloth between teeny toes. "I couldn't have done that without you."

"Of course you could've."

"All right, let me rephrase. I wouldn't have wanted to. Kelly needed you, and I'm glad you were here."

"It was my pleasure," she said, praying he never knew just to what an extent she'd enjoyed the long day—now night. Not the part where their old schoolmate had been in pain. Just the miraculous part at the end where a cherubic baby girl had been born of Derrick and Kelly's love.

"Want to hold her?" he asked after making quick work of diapering the baby, slipping on a pink cotton shirt and swaddling her in a fuzzy pink blanket.

"I'd love to," she said, forcing down the knot in her throat. Never had she felt more alive than when volunteering with newborns. Something about them was all at once warming and intriguing. The blank slates of their lives.

Brodie passed the angelic child into Tabitha's arms, and she clung to her, trying to hide her own incalculable pain. Not the dull ache in her ankle, which she could easily bear. It was inside where it hurt most.

"She is awfully cute," Brodie said, stroking Penny's cheek with his fingertip. "Some kids pop out with pointy heads. You're lucky you got a good one for your first time seeing the show."

Smiling and shaking her head, Tabitha said, "Consider yourself lucky I need both hands to hold this baby, and steady myself against this counter, otherwise, you'd be in big trouble."

OH, BRODIE WAS IN trouble all right, he thought an hour later, remembering Tabby's teasing, but it had nothing to do with ugly babies. His landed more in the realm of dealing with a gorgeous woman.

"You cheated!" Tabitha hollered to Pete above the sax wailing on a Dave Matthews Band CD Marcy had put on. Brodie suspected Tabitha had let Pete win their third game of backgammon, seeing how he'd never played before tonight.

While Kelly and the baby were upstairs sleeping, seemingly everyone else on the street had stopped by for an impromptu party.

Tabitha was popular not only with Pete, but with other guests as well, since she'd whipped up a delicious buffet out of the meager contents of Kelly's pantry and fridge.

"Hey!" Ray said, a beer in one hand, slapping Brodie on his back with his other. "Good to see Tabby back, isn't it? Even if she did suffer a nasty fall."

"Yeah," Brodie said, captivated by her habit of nibbling her lower lip while rolling the dice. "She said you all were great about getting her off the mountain in a hurry."

Ray shrugged. "Last time I checked, that was my job."

"Well, nice job."

"Thanks." He chugged his beer. "Any chance of you two hooking up?"

"Nah," Brodie said without a moment's thought.

"That was fast. Suspiciously fast, if you ask me."

Ray nodded toward the table where she sat. The jacket of her warm-up suit was open at her neck, allowing for a full-on view of her elegant throat. Brodie used to nuzzle her there. It'd driven her wild. She'd giggled and laughed, shrieking for him not to give her a hickey—not that he ever would have, but it'd been fun teasing her all the same.

"Seeing how well old Pete's getting along with her, you might ought to officially toss your hat in her ring. That is, if you still have a thing for her."

"I don't."

Ray winked before downing more beer. "That why you've been staring at her all night?"

CHAPTER SIX

"DID YOU HAVE FUN?"

Tabitha glanced up from a two-day-old *Snowflake Daily Sentinel* to find Brodie bare-chested, his hair damp from a shower. Flannel pj's covered his long legs. "I did have a great time tonight. You?"

"Sure." He sat opposite her on a brown leather love seat. "I'm tired now, though. It's been a long day."

It had. While there were no longer whiteout conditions, outside Brodie's snug A-frame house snow still fell hard. It'd been a mutual decision that to take the two-hour trek to the lodge would have been foolhardy in the dark. She would sleep on his sofa, then he'd run her up the mountain in the morning.

"When do you think Derrick will make it back?" she asked.

"We should wake to sun in the morning, so hopefully by tomorrow night, he'll be home."

Home. Tabitha wasn't sure she even had one anymore. She had a house, but seeing how it was only her living there, it didn't feel all that inviting—not that the six-bedroom modern monstrosity she'd shared with David ever had.

Brodie's A-frame had a soaring living room ceiling with a wall of windows she assumed would look out on an amazing alpine view, once the storm subsided. The place was small—just the open area they were now in, which also housed the kitchen, then there was a small bathroom and a bedroom Brodie had turned into a home office. His room was the loft crowning a steep flight of stairs—the reason why she was sleeping on the sofa. She had been touched, though, that he'd thought to offer to give up his bed to her.

"This is nice," she said, nodding to the fire crackling in the stone hearth. She'd stretched out on a sofa that matched his love seat, her legs covered by a thick, earthy-colored afghan he said had been crocheted for him by the same neighbor who was babysitting his dog. "I like your decorating."

He laughed. "These sofas were Marcy's idea. She said as the whole region's doctor, I couldn't be sitting on the same furniture I bought at her yard sale when I first came to town."

"I agree. Here you have this amazing house, and yet you aren't even a little inspired to fill it with wonderful things?" The other furnishings she'd seen, while nice enough, were a hodgepodge of styles ranging from fifties-era postmodern side tables to funky seventies-era lamps to current-day, assemble-it-yourself bookshelves.

"Inspiration's a funny thing. Maybe I'm just not inspired by *stuff.*"

"Then, what?"

Chuckling, he pushed himself up from the sofa. "That, my dear, was a loaded question. Want hot chocolate?" he asked, walking to the kitchen area.

"Yes please."

While Brodie bumbled about the kitchen, Tabitha stared out the windows at the snow. With only one lamp on and the glowing fire for light, gumball-sized flakes were plain enough to see. She had been out in the snow less than an hour earlier and knew it was the perfect consistency for building a snowman. Something Brodie long ago told her he had never done.

She asked, "Did you ever get to build that snowman you always wanted?"

"In a manner of speaking. My frat house was real big on having the biggest, baddest snow creatures on campus—though they weren't always kid friendly."

"That's terrible."

"That's frat guys for you." He handed her a steaming mug topped with marshmallows, then reclaimed his former seat. "I figure once I have a few kids of my own, I'll focus my snow-building skills on more traditional items such as snow people and forts."

"You do want them, then?"

"What? Kids? Sure—doesn't everyone?"

While she couldn't speak for all on the planet, Tabitha didn't just *want* kids, but craved them. After three miscarriages—each with seemingly no medical explanation—she'd all but given up hope.

"Tabby?"

She squeezed her stinging eyes shut.

Kelly's baby was perfect. Tiny and pink and lovely. Smelling of baby powder and lotion.

What must Kelly be feeling now? Tucked into the comfy bed she shared with her loving husband, cradling their child in her arms, perhaps even breast-feeding her. The longing Tabitha felt to experience all of that was biting and sharp.

It was late and she was tired.

Tired of the ache in her ankle, weary of the ache in her heart, stemming from losing three babies she'd so desperately wanted.

Tears fell swiftly and silently and wouldn't stop.

"Tabby?" Instantly at her side, pulling her cheek against his solid chest. "Honey, what's wrong?"

She'd wanted to go to him after her first miscarriage, wanted to grieve with him. She should've told Brodie the whole truth the other night. She'd been close, but—

"Hey," he said, tugging lightly on her hair and tipping her head back. "If your ankle's hurting that bad, take medicine. I promise, as tired as you must be, you'll be out before anymore secrets spill."

His smile was so dear and familiar and yet untouchable.

He was hers—had always been hers in a long-buried part of herself. But after hearing the secret she'd kept from him for so long, would he even want to look at her? Let alone hold her in his arms?

"Honey, please…I can't help if you won't tell me what's wrong."

"T-tonight, I w-was so jealous of Kelly. I want a husband who really loves me. I want a baby. Not just one, but a half-dozen. I w-want—"

"Shh…" Brodie stroked her hair. "You'll have all of that. It just takes time."

She thrashed her head against him. "No. I can't. I lost David's babies and yours and—"

"What?"

"B-Brodie—that's why my parents were so furious with you. I was pregnant. But I lost our child. I wanted so badly to tell you, but Mom and Dad—they threatened to send you to jail. I loved you. I couldn't have hurt you like that after all you'd already been through."

His expression cold, impossible to read, he eased away from her, sitting back on his heels. "You were pregnant? With my child? Yet you didn't even have the decency—the respect for me, for what we'd shared—to tell me? *Ever?*"

"I'm sorry! I was protecting you. You have to understand."

"Oh," he said with a bitter laugh, "I understand all right. I understand that if you were able to keep something that important from me, then everything we've ever shared must've been a lie."

CHAPTER SEVEN

"DON'T GO," TABITHA pleaded, following him with her eyes as he went upstairs. "Please, Brodie, let me explain."

When he didn't even slow his steps, she lurched up from the sofa, instinctively standing on both feet, only to fall.

She yelped in pain, and then Brodie was there, helping her back onto the sofa. But that was the extent of it.

"Stay there," he said. "I need time—space—to think."

"O-okay," she said with a sniffle, again, watching him go.

More than anything, Tabitha wished she could make him understand. Understand why she hadn't found a way to get around her parents and share her loss—their loss—with him back in high school. But how could she, when to this day, she didn't fully get it? There'd been a dozen ways she could've gotten word to him. Through notes and friends. But could the real truth have been that, while yes, she was heartsick over losing their baby, another part of her had been relieved? Had she never told him, or anyone else outside her immediate family, because she'd been secretly ashamed of what she and Brodie had done? And now, because of that shame, she was terrified God wouldn't entrust her with another child?

Upstairs, Brodie paced.

Fumed.

Silently mourned.

What the hell was he supposed to do with this information? How did he process such a thing? Here, all of his adult life, all he'd ever wanted was to start the family he'd never had, only to now find out he'd once been so close.

True, but had he been capable of supporting a child his junior year in high school? Let alone a wife? And he would've insisted Tabby marry him. No way would he abandon her the way his father had abandoned him and his mom and his brother.

Trudging down the stairs, he said in the dying fire's eerie orange gloom, "You awake?"

"Uh-huh."

"Good. We need to talk." He tossed a couple logs on the glowing coals, then sat on the coffee table and faced the source of his consternation.

As she sat up, he propped a few throw pillows behind her back. The pillows were lumpy and ugly. Gifts from Marcy's artistically challenged kids, which made him love them all the more.

"Okay," he finally said, struggling to find the right words. "I get the fact that you were trying to protect me. I see where this would have been a huge family scandal. I see why your parents and brothers never even so much as looked at me again. What I don't get is how no one thought I deserved to know. Dammit, Tabby," he said, reaching for her hands and holding on for dear life, "I should've been there, helping you through physical and emotional pain. Moreover, I should've taken my fair share of the blame."

She nodded.

"I loved you. I would have done anything for you."

She nodded.

"If only you'd given me the chance, I would've helped."

She nodded again, then started crying.

He pulled her into his arms, at the same time shedding his own pain. Truth be told, he'd halfway suspected the reason behind her parents' sudden hatred of him, but figured if Tabby had been pregnant, he would have known. There would have been a sign. Morning sickness or weird cravings. Now he knew that some women never experienced any of the stereotypical tendencies accompanying pregnancy. But back then, all he'd had to go on were gut instincts. Obviously, those hadn't served him well.

"I'm sorry I snapped at you," he finally said, letting her go. "You know after Mom died, and I was on my own with Nathan, I had a rough time of it."

"How is your brother?"

"Wish I knew. I haven't heard from him since my college graduation."

"I'm sorry."

"Yeah. Me, too." The brother, seven years Brodie's senior, who'd raised him from the age of ten, hadn't been much of a role model. From him, Brodie had learned to party hard and hit a beer can with a .22 from a good fifty yards. Everything else he'd learned from Tabby and her family. Both her parents were doctors. They'd been the ones to instill in him the drive to go farther with his dreams than bartending or working at the local auto mechanic's. Not that those weren't respectable professions, just that Marcus and Deanne Summerwell had told Brodie he could do more. He'd believed them. For the magical year he and Tabitha had dated, they'd become his family. The fact that at the first sign of trouble they'd thrown him to the proverbial wolves didn't sit well. Had never sat well.

"I'll bet he was proud of you—Nathan."

Brodie shrugged. It didn't matter. He was proud of himself, and seeing how all he'd ever really had in this world was himself, that would have to do.

"I'm tired," she said. "Rest with me."

Beyond the living room's wall of windows, the sky had cleared. The moon was nearly full, and its light reflected off the snow. Backlit by the ethereal glow, Tabby had never looked more beautiful. Knowing what he knew now, he'd never been more wary of losing himself to her all over again.

It'd be so easy. Tell himself all was forgiven, and they could start anew. But he'd already suffered their break-up and a broken marriage. No matter how badly he wanted a family, could his heart withstand another round of pain?

"Please…" she said. Her voice struck him as small and lonely and maybe even a little scared. And because he felt all of that, too, he scooped her into his arms and carried her up the stairs.

He needed sleep. Blessed sleep. And with so much currently on his mind, the only way he knew to drift into unconsciousness was by holding the source of his trouble in his arms.

BRODIE SANG in the shower.

Drenched in sunshine streaming through the loft's peaked windows, Tabitha fought the knot in her throat. Hugging the pillow beside her, she pretended it was him, loving the way it still smelled of him. Of his citrus aftershave and soap and an intangible manly something that had always turned her on.

Right at this moment, what was he thinking? Would he ever fully forgive her for guarding a secret that never should've been kept?

He'd held her through the night, making her feel safe and wanted and so very alive, but despite his outward tenderness, she'd sensed him holding back. She hadn't a clue what today held in store.

"Hey. You're up," he said a few minutes later, emerging from the bathroom wearing buttonfly jeans and nothing else. Her mouth went dry. Was it wrong of her to so badly want to skim her hands along his powerful chest? "Get some good rest?"

"Uh-huh," she said, covering a yawn. "Best I've had in a while. Must be true that truth's good for the soul."

When the smile he cast didn't come close to reaching his eyes, her stomach sank.

He ducked into a walk-in closet. "Hungry?"

"Starving."

"The polite thing would be serving you breakfast in bed, but seeing how that would consist of a Pop-Tart, how about we jump in the Sno-Cat and head out across the frozen tundra for a bite to eat?"

"DR. KIMBALL?" A doe-eyed little girl asked later that morning in Brodie's clinic. After stilted breakfast conversation at Waffle Hut, he'd planned on getting Tabby back to her suite at the ski lodge, but so far, since the phone had been ringing off the hook with snow-related injuries ranging from mild frostbite to a heart attack brought on by too much shoveling, he hadn't had much luck.

Making matters worse, since Marcy had stayed home tending her youngest child, who'd come down with the sniffles, Tabby had agreed to step in as his nurse whenever possible. He should be grateful, but considering how much was still left to be said between them, what he really felt was more in the range of a stomachache.

Tabby sat in a wheelchair alongside him, holding Mindy Jacob's chart. The girl's mother sat in the cramped exam room's chair.

"Yes, ma'am?" Brodie said, inspecting the girl's left ear and finding that, just as her mom had diagnosed, Mindy suffered from a pretty bad ear infection.

"I think I have dog jaw, too."

"Dog jaw?" he asked, wrinkling his nose. "I don't think I've ever heard of that. Have you, *Nurse* Tabby?"

"Is it something you catch from too much time spent playing with puppies?" Tabby asked with an admirably straight face.

"Maybe so," Brodie said, inspecting the girl's left, then right jaw, but, just as he'd expected, finding nothing abnormal, "but I—"

"Ruff, ruff!" Mindy said, pretending to bite him, then bursting into a giggling fit. "See, Dr. Kimball? I have *dog* jaw!"

"You're a ferocious little pooch," Brodie teased, embarrassed to admit the kid had caught him off guard. Hand to his chest, he complained, "My heart's still beating too fast."

"Mindy, that was naughty," her mother scolded. "Say sorry." Dark circles under Mrs. Jacob's eyes attested to the fact she wasn't in the mood for nonsense.

"There's no need for that," Brodie said. "No harm done." Especially, when truthfully, he'd been damned glad for the distraction from his thoughts of what'd transpired between him and Tabby the previous night.

"All the same. After you agree to see her for free and all, she should respect you more."

"Really, it's not a big deal," Brodie said, for whatever reason, wishing the woman hadn't mentioned the fact that he wasn't charging her daughter a fee. He wrote an anti-biotic prescription, gave the mom instructions to give her daughter two tablets a day, then escorted them to the waiting room where they clamored back into their coats, hats and gloves.

After seeing eight more patients of varying ailments and ages, Brodie finally got a rest. He wheeled Tabby into the sun-flooded back office, then grabbed her a snack from Marcy's secret stash of chips, candy bars and pops.

"Mmm…" Tabby said after her first bite of a Snickers candy bar. She'd already had a Kit Kat and an Almond Joy.

"Marcy's going to be mad at you for eating all of her good stuff."

"Me?"

Her adorable, all-innocent expression was so cute he couldn't help but grin. "I'm not the one who's downed eighteen candy bars."

"Three," she rebutted. "And sorry, but I'm hungry. My new boss doesn't give time off for lunch."

"Whoa." Brodie glanced at his watch, surprised to find it already after two. "Sorry."

"You should be," she teased. "I'll have to report you to the nurses' labor union."

"Yeah," he said with a snort. "Just try it. Then I'll report you for being unprofessional—laughing when our patient faked the dreaded dog jaw disease."

Tabby laughed. "You should've seen your face. Priceless."

"I'll give you priceless…." Brodie had meant to deliver a fake slug to her shoulder, but then her smile had faded, and she'd licked her lips, leaving them full and wet and inviting. "You need kissing."

"Uh-huh," she said along with a faint mew, using his shirt as leverage to draw herself out of her wheelchair and into kissing range.

Before Brodie had time to weigh the ramifications of once again kissing Tabitha Summerwell, he was doing it.

CHAPTER EIGHT

"Wow," Brodie said, head spinning from the emotions winging through him. How many times had he dreamt of again holding Tabby in his arms? "That was, um, nice."

"Just nice?" she asked with a playful growl.

"Okay," he admitted, toying with the zipper of her jogging suit, "but the only reason it was really more in the range of fantastic is probably because I haven't kissed anyone in a while."

"So what you're essentially saying is that if you weren't hard up for affection, my kisses would be just so-so?"

"Right." Only he assumed by the wicked-sexy grin tugging the corners of her mouth that the jig was up. She knew full well to what extent her kiss had rocked him. How? He hoped because she'd experienced a quake or two, as well.

Though, while in the shower that morning, he'd vowed to keep his distance, after all the woman had carried his child and hadn't even had the consideration to tell him, now he wasn't so sure. The issue didn't seem quite so cut-and-dried. Sure, she hadn't told him, but for what she believed to be good reason.

But was that his logical side talking in his head or his raging libido?

The clinic's phone rang.

"Damn," he said. "Think it could be a wrong number?"

No such luck. But at least the additional work took his mind off Tabby and her crazy-kissable lips.

BY THE TIME BRODIE got her home it was dark.

He supposed if he were politically correct about the situation, he should've thought of the house as his alone and not shared. But for the moment, anyway, with Tabby humming in the big water-jet bathtub—by doctor's orders, keeping her cast raised onto the side—she seemed to feel at home.

The roads were now clear, and Ray had stopped by the clinic with a couple of other guys to put the Sno-Cat on a trailer and haul it back to the lodge. Since Brodie had left his keys with his friend, they'd also brought his Rover. Ray had asked Tabby if she'd wanted a ride, but she'd thanked him and said Brodie still needed her at the clinic.

Part of Brodie felt badly because he could've easily handled the rare Sunday afternoon's load on his own—but he hadn't wanted to. Being around Tabby again was intoxicating. He loved not only her kisses, but also her sense of humor and way of putting his patients at ease. Whenever he was around her, it somehow didn't matter that he'd never felt more ill at ease. She'd hurt him to an unthinkable degree. He'd consciously never fall for her again. Trouble was, his traitorous, wanting body hadn't yet gotten the message.

"You okay in there?" he asked at the closed bathroom door. His golden retriever, Goldie, wagged her tail by his side.

"Fabulous!" she hollered. "This feels amazing."

"You're not getting your cast wet, are you?"

"And risk getting my doctor mad?"

Eyes closed, he visualized her sassy expression. Then his mind's eye turned to visions of another kind. Tabby, stretched out under the suds. Certain portions of her anatomy peeking through, torturing him to the point that he adjusted his fly.

"I, um, put your clothes in the dryer. Feel free to wear my robe if you're ready to get out before then." *Or to call on me if you need help with the soap.*

"Great! Thanks!"

Brodie supposed he should've stayed inside on the off chance Tabby needed help getting out of the tub, but the part of him who hadn't been with a woman in a few months couldn't take it.

Instead, he put on hiking boots, then he and Goldie trudged outside to shovel Mrs. Neilson's drive. Although, even in her seventies, there were days she seemed to have more energy than him, he didn't want her overdoing it, and risk a broken hip.

By the time he'd finished up there and shared a bowl of her homemade beef stew with his dog, he felt reasonably sure Tabby would be out of the tub, meaning he'd be relatively safe from fantasies of her anything-but-clinical form.

"You decent?" he asked at the top of the loft stairs over the applause of *Wheel of Fortune*.

"Yep. Where've you been?"

He found Tabby stretched across the foot of his bed, wearing his robe, holding his TV remote.

Goldie leapt up to join her.

"Hey, sweetie," she crooned, hugging the dog before switching to a cooking show, then decorating show, then basketball, then turning off the TV. "I'm glad you're home. There's nothing on."

"So…what? You want me to entertain you?"

"Might be nice."

"Maybe later," he said with a bearish groan, collapsing onto the bed beside her. "Now I'm too tired."

Goldie licked his nose.

"I saw you and your best girl, here, out shoveling your neighbor's drive. That was sweet."

Ha! If only Tabby knew the true reason as to why he'd needed to work off excess energy. "It was no big deal."

"I'm sure it was to whoever lives there."

He shrugged.

"Scoot over," she demanded.

"Why?"

"You look like you could use a backrub, and they happen to fall under my realm of expertise."

"This is heaven," he said a few minutes later, once she'd stradled him, then commenced with her special brand of most pleasurable torture with the dog watching on. "But isn't it hurting your ankle?"

"A little, but it's nothing I can't take."

"You should stop," he said, "I don't want you hurting at all. Plus, I don't want myself hurting when you leave."

"Quit being so bossy," she said, pushing him down when he tried getting up. "Just once, let yourself be pampered instead of the other way around."

"What do you mean?"

"I mean that ever since I've gotten here, I've been watching you take care of others. Be it me, neighbors, your dog or patients you treat for free on a Sunday afternoon, Brodie, you're always taking care of someone. Just once, can't you relax and let me take care of you?"

The notion seemed surreal. In his line of business, Brodie was used to hard work and long hours. It kept him grounded. The one time he'd let up, his marriage had fallen apart, almost as if their grueling workload had been the only thing he and his wife had ever truly shared. So now to have Tabby urge him to relax rang warning bells.

"Your shoulders are in knots. When's the last time you had a professional massage?"

He laughed into his pillow. "Try never."

"That's terrible."

"No, Tabby. That's the real world. I'll bet ninety percent of my patients have never been to a spa."

"You don't have to go to a fancy spa. I'm just saying that—"

"Let me up." Partially rolling, he grabbed her about her hips, gently easing her over and off of him. "I don't have time for this." Moreover, he refused to fall for her again—even if he only allowed himself to indulge in just her many physical charms.

"How can you not have time? We have the whole night if we want."

He got off the bed and pulled off his shirt, then he said, "I'm going to grab a quick shower then fix us something to eat. Want me to get your clothes from the dryer first?"

"I can manage," she said with a pout.

"I don't want you manuevering the stairs on your own. Let me carry you."

"Have you always been this controlling?"

"Controlling? I merely offered to get your jogging suit and delicates, so I can get my robe back."

"If you want your stupid robe so bad," she said, hobbling up from the bed, "here—have it."

She dropped the damned thing, then stood there in the center of Brodie's bedroom, perfectly naked, perfectly balanced on her good leg.

Mouth dry, torturing himself by averting his gaze in a gentlemanly manner, he grabbed an afghan from the foot of the bed, then wrapped Tabby in it. "Mind telling me what this stunt was really about?"

She nibbled her lower lip.

"Tabby?"

"All my life, I've been surrounded by powerful, take-charge men. Just once, I'd like to be in charge."

"Of getting laundry from the dryer?"

She shot him a scathing look. "That's not what I meant, and you know it."

"I know," he said, drawing her into his arms, kissing the top of her head. "I'm sorry if I came across as trying to control you, but, honey, believe me, that's the last thing I want to do."

She nodded against him.

"In fact, I think the best thing you could do for yourself after this weekend is take time to figure out what *you* want to do with the rest of your life. Not what your parents or friends think best, but what you truly want to do." *And if that means she's back in Denver full-time? Or Dallas or LA, would I be okay with that?* Brodie wanted to believe himself immune to Tabby's many charms, but he wasn't a fool. Despite having told himself just the opposite, truthfully, having her back in his life was nothing short of a miracle. What he had to drum into his thick head was that her being there—in his home, in his arms—was short term.

"You're right," she said. "But that's easier said than done, seeing how most days, even I don't know what I want to do."

"For a start," he said, "would it be all right if I carry you back to bed, so you can rest your ankle?"

SITTING UP IN BRODIE'S comfy bed, mounds of pillows behind her, Goldie beside her, stomach full from the simple, yet satisfying meal of tomato soup and a grilled cheese sandwich that Brodie had just prepared for her, Tabitha couldn't have been more physically content. Brodie softly snored beside her, while on TV, one of her favorite cable reality shows aired.

On the surface, life couldn't have been better.

So why was her brain going a mile a minute?

Why was she torn over the fact that one part of her wanted nothing more than to spend night after night just like this—engaging in a deliciously mundane routine with Brodie. While another part of her knew that would be taking the easy way out of her emotional issues. Brodie was right in that she needed to get on with what she wanted to do in life. Seeing how having a baby was out, that meant digging deeper. Finding the root cause of her discontent.

And if that meant giving up Brodie again?

The thought was too painful to bear.

Brodie groaned, then snagged her around her waist. "What's got you looking so serious?"

"Baggage."

"Whether to buy Louis Vuitton or Coach for your next cruise?"

She smacked him. "Not only was that a condescending remark, but how do you even know those brands? You're a yard sale kind of guy."

"My ex was big into that kind of stuff."

"Ah. That explains the Hermès tie I saw in your closet."

He reddened. "Busted. But back to your baggage, want to talk?"

Shaking her head, snuggling against his chest, she said, "I'd rather cuddle."

Savoring what little time we have left.

CHAPTER NINE

"YOU TWO LOOK AWFULLY CUTE together," Gladys said while Brodie was in his office, studying a patient file.

He glanced up, "What are you talking about?"

"Don't play coy with me," she said, helping herself to one of his two guest chairs. "If you ask me—"

"Which I didn't."

"—fate brought you back together. Mark my words, Tabitha Summerwell's back in Snowflake to stay. Look at her out there." Gladys gestured toward the sight Brodie had been trying to avoid. Tabby, in her wheelchair, making paper airplanes for the sick Peterson twins. The eight-year-old boys' smiles looked to be better medicine than any Brodie could provide. "That girl's wasting her life, planning all those fancy schmancy charity balls or working in advertising when she could be making a real difference working with kids."

Sighing, Brodie asked, "You finished? If so, I should see my next patient."

"Marcy and I both think you'll be making a big mistake if you let this one get away. She's changed, Brodie. Not at all the self-centered girl she was when she left town."

"Did the two of you ever stop to consider the fact that

I'm a grown man. Perfectly capable of finding my own woman?"

Gladys's answer to his question was a guffaw.

Throughout the day Brodie couldn't shake his growing apprehension. The battle raging inside him over whether or not to pursue a serious relationship with Tabby had grown from the moment he'd seen her again. Just as they had the first time they'd met—in algebra class a lifetime ago—they clicked.

On the surface they did seem ideal, but what happened if they took their blossoming friendship to another level? What happened should his old demons where she was concerned resurface? What if she again took it upon herself to keep the truth from him in a misguided attempt to shield him from pain? How would he live with that? Knowing she didn't trust him enough to share of herself one hundred percent? That she didn't trust him to be strong enough that together they could weather any storm?

Then there was the unresolved issue of her parents and brothers. For all he knew, they still despised him. One thing crucial to him in a future wife was that she share his love of family and community. True, he may not be surrounded by blood relations, but Gladys and Marcy and Ray and so many more people in town had grown to mean more to him than his own absentee brother ever had.

After closing the clinic, then getting Tabby and her cast settled in the passenger side of his Rover, Brodie headed up the mountain, rather than across town toward his home.

"Where are we going?" Tabby asked.

"The lodge. I figure you've probably had about all you can handle of my boring company."

"I've loved spending time with you," she said, her expression laced with concern. "Are you sure it isn't you who is ready to be rid of me?"

He turned on the radio. A slow, sad country song felt about right.

"Brodie? Have I done something to offend you?"

"Nope," he said, veering onto the long, narrow road leading to the lodge. "Guess I just don't feel comfortable playing house. You being fresh from a divorce, and all, I don't want you getting hurt." *Most of all, I don't want me getting hurt, when you realize you're bored stiff with my small-town way of life.* Worse yet, if she grew tired of him personally. He'd already lost her once. How would he survive losing her again?

Angling to face him, she placed her hand on his thigh, infusing him with heat. "That's sweet of you to care about me, but shouldn't I be the judge of how I feel?"

"It's not that simple," he said, hardening his jaw, wishing he could so easily harden his heart. "You've as much as admitted you don't have a clue where your life's headed. Sure, I'd love for you to stay on at my house indefinitely, but what's that going to do for either of us? We're too old to be shacking up, Tabby. There has to be something more." *Something reciprocal, like the love I'm so damned afraid I feel for you. Have* always *felt for you.*

"Sure," she said, easing her hand from his thigh, her voice barely registering above the engine's uphill roar.

"Then you agree?"

"To what?"

"That we should cool things off."

Staring out the window, she said, "Relax, Brodie. I wasn't even aware we had a *thing*. I thought we were just two old friends, hanging out."

Ouch. But then what had he expected? Hell, what he'd hoped for had been for her to fight—for him. For them. What had she done instead? Basically she'd agreed with him that they had no future as a couple.

The rest of the trip he wished he could say was made in companionable silence, but tension was palpable in the SUV's overheated air.

Upon reaching the lodge, Brodie parked in front of the main entrance, then hopped out to help Tabby with her crutches. "Wait for me in the lobby," he said. "I'll walk you to your suite."

"That's not necessary," she said.

"I know. But can't I do it because I want to?"

"I'd rather you didn't. I'm not anyone's obligation."

He raked his fingers through his hair. "Did I say you were?"

"It's implied. Obviously, I overstayed my welcome at your house, but you're too darned polite to ever come right out and say it."

"Tabby, I—"

"Stop, Brodie. Just stop." Her smile didn't come close to reaching her eyes. "I've enjoyed this time getting to know you again, but it's been a vacation *friendship*—nothing more. No need to feel guilty or like you didn't show me a good enough time. I'm a big girl. Fully capable of entertaining myself until I leave Wednesday morning."

"Mind if I stop by to see you off?"

"That'd be fine."

A tour bus pulled up behind him and honked.

"Guess I'd better get going," he said.

"Bye." Hands on her crutches, she wagged her fingers. The cold reddened her cheeks. She looked lovely in the fading sun, the mountain in all its glory, towering behind her, making her seem incredibly fragile in its strength.

Suddenly, like Tabby was his own personal Valentine's Day treat, Brodie had to have more. "Oh, um, hey—before I forget, you doing anything for Valentine's Day? The lodge restaurant puts on a big spread. All the steak, lobster, champagne and chocolate you can eat for $29.95."

The tour bus driver again laid on his horn.

"Tabby? Please? Have Valentine's Day dinner with me?" *Give me something more to remember you by than the unreadable darkness in your eyes.*

"Hey, buddy!" the bus driver hollered out his window. "Mind moving it along? I'm on a schedule."

"Yes," Tabby finally answered. "I'd love to have dinner with you."

"Great!" Brodie called, already heading around to the driver's side of his Rover. "I'll make reservations for eight."

Even though Brodie knew seeing Tabby again would only be putting off the inevitable, he didn't care. Maybe he was a glutton for punishment. Maybe Gladys's and Marcy's nagging for him to go on a real date had finally sunk in. Whatever the reasoning behind his asking Tabby to join him, he was thrilled she'd accepted.

But also, sick over how deeply he cared.

"YOU WHAT?" TABITHA'S best friend, Kelsey, asked over the phone. In the background, her toddler, Zack, happily plunked on his toy piano. It was cute, but made hearing his mommy a challenge. "How could you spend two nights with the man, then tell him you didn't want to see him again?"

"I didn't exactly say it in so many words," Tabitha said, putting the final touches on her makeup. "I hinted at it to see what he'd say. You know, hoping he'd make the first move, as to where he wants things to go. I mean, the least he could do is fight for me."

Kelsey sighed. "Have Britt and I taught you nothing? *You* have to fight for what *you* want. The question you have to ask yourself is, do you want Brodie back in your life?"

"Of course…" Tabitha stepped back from the mirror to admire the view. The red-sequined minidress her friends talked her into tossing into her suitcase at the last minute had come in handy, after all. As an added benefit, the garment fit like a sleek candy shell she dared Brodie to resist. "But what if I only want him as a way of putting off everything I have to do back in Denver?" *What if the only reason he wants to see me tonight is to in some warped way prove to himself that he's better off letting me go?*

"Zack, stop! Mommy's trying to talk!" The piano plunking that'd reached a feverish crescendo abruptly ended. "Sorry. Okay, back to the topic at hand, the only thing you have to do is be happy. All those decisions you *think* you have to make about whether or not to sell the house or get a job, or even find a whole new career, all of that can be indefinitely postponed for love."

"That's just it. How do I even know if what I'm feeling is love or vacation sizzle?"

Snorting, Kelsey said, "The two of you have slept together in his big bed for two nights now, and you still haven't had sex. Angel, that's not just love, but marriage. I should know."

A knock sounded on the door.

"He's here. I have to go," Tabitha said, hoping, *praying,* her hypothesis as to why Brodie had asked her out was wrong.

"All right, have fun. Think of us poor schmucks stuck at home while you're out partying the night away."

"I will. Bye."

Tabitha hung up the phone, then forced a deep breath—not an easy feat considering the dress's fit. "Okay, Brodie Kimball," she whispered under her breath. "Ready or not, here I come…."

CHAPTER TEN

"HAVE I TOLD YOU how amazing you look?" Brodie asked Tabby on the dance floor, swaying her—nearly carrying her—in time to Elvis's "Love Me Tender".

"Only about ten times. You'd better quit, or you'll give me a big head."

"Your head looks just about right from here," he teased.

"In that case," she said with a flirty flutter of her eyelashes, "tell me more about my ravishing beauty."

Groaning, he cinched her tighter. "I've created a monster."

"At least I'm a pretty monster. I could have speckled skin and green teeth."

"Touché."

Brodie had never seen the lodge decked out in quite such high style. It had always been the swankiest place in town, but management had outdone themselves by hiring a great band and creating a fantasyland in red, silver and pink. Everywhere he looked were roses and champagne fountains and hundreds of floating balloons. As impressive as all of that was, though, the woman he held was the night's best eye candy.

"Remember junior prom?" she asked, nuzzling his neck just above the collar of his starched white shirt.

"I'll never forget."

They'd left the high school gym early. Pretending to be married, they'd checked into a motel in a neighboring town. The plan had been to eat pizza and hang out, but it's funny how when you're a horny teen, alone with a gorgeous girl in a motel room, plans have a way of changing. Tabby's parents believed she was spending the night with her girlfriends. His brother Nathan couldn't have cared less whether or not Brodie had ever come home.

At first, they'd stuck to the plan. Laughing and wrestling on the bed. Watching a little TV. Downing pizza and chips and too much soda.

Then TV got boring, and kissing got hot. It wasn't too long before they were unwrapping each other like the candy bars he'd bought out of the motel's vending machine for dessert.

Making love sort of happened. Neither had thought to bring protection. Neither had been smart enough to even care. They'd both been virgins, and while the first time wasn't all that great, the second and third times steadily got better.

"Think that was the night you got pregnant?" he asked.

"Looking back on it, yes. Every time after that, we used a condom."

"We were wrong to sneak off like that. I was wrong to ask that of you, and I'm sorry."

"It's ancient history," she said. "Let's just enjoy tonight."

"I'm thoroughly enjoying tonight, but you have to know that in retrospect, I don't blame your parents for hating me."

"They don't hate you," she said, snuggling against his

chest, flooding him with warmth and well-being he had no right to feel.

"If I had a daughter some punk kid from the wrong side of town got pregnant, I'd hate him."

She said nothing.

He glanced down to find her eyes shining with unshed tears.

"What's wrong?"

"Nothing I can identify."

"Want to try?" he asked, nudging his finger beneath her chin, hoping she'd meet his gaze.

"I don't know…I guess thinking about our one and only prom night made me melancholy. Sometimes I feel consumed by regrets, anger, sadness, embarrassment, shame…"

"That's a lot of baggage to carry around. You'd have been better off going with the Louis Vuitton." He kissed her forehead, hating that he was still so torn over their broken past that he'd turned to jokes as a way to mask his pain.

"Hah. Brodie, I'm serious."

"So am I." About avoiding any additional pain. "Why is such a gorgeous, talented creature so burdened?"

The band wrapped up their latest song; then the lead singer announced they'd be taking a fifteen-minute break.

Brodie headed to their table with Tabby heavily leaning on his arm. "If I knew what was bugging me, I wouldn't be burdened, now would I?"

Pulling out her chair, he said, "How about we take it from the top? Dissecting each little thing?"

"You don't have to do this, Brodie."

"What if I want to?" *What if I have to?*

"Okay," she took a deep breath. "I've got regrets for the way I handled things between us. Or, rather didn't. I should've found a way to tell you the whole truth. It was cowardly of me not to."

"True. But you were a kid." *I need to forgive you, if for no other reason than to exorcise you once and for all from my heart.* "Next." He poured her more champagne from the bottle chilling in their table's ice bucket.

"All right, I'm angry about a lot of things. Why didn't you try harder to keep me? Why didn't you go all knight in shining armor and bust down the castle walls?"

He nearly choked on his latest sip of bubbly. "You're kidding, right? Considering the fact that I was barely seventeen and flat broke with hardly any family and you were Little Miss Everything, how was I supposed to have *rescued* you?"

"Realistically, you weren't, but that's always the way I fantasized it."

"And now? Fresh off your divorce and drifting, is that how you see me now? As some prince you want to save you?"

"No." Sipping her champagne, her eyes welled more. "I just—I hate the way things ended so badly between us. There was no big fight, no growing apart—there was nothing. One day we were secretly making love. The next, I wasn't even allowed to talk to you. You seemed to accept it so coolly. Like losing me didn't faze you, when it destroyed me."

"You'd have never known it by looking at you."

A harsh laugh escaped her. "I was pretending to be

happy, when inside I was falling apart. My whole life I've been flailing. One minute our love was there, and the next— *poof.* It was gone like fog."

No, it wasn't, Brodie longed to say. It was still every bit a part of him—she was as much a part of him—as she'd ever been.

"There were times near the end of my marriage when I wondered was I somehow flawed? Was that why David left me? Was there something else wrong with me aside from the fact that I'd never been able to give him a child?"

"Get this through your head," Brodie said, grasping Tabby's hands. "You're an amazing woman. Any guy would be lucky to have you as his wife." *Especially me.* But if he felt that way, why couldn't he tell her? Why the compulsion to hold back? Ignoring his own questions, he asked, "Tell me more about your miscarriages. What was your ultimate diagnosis?"

"I've had tens of thousands of dollars' worth of tests only to find there's no medical reason why I haven't managed to carry a baby to term."

"I see where that would be tough. Anyone ever tell you maybe you've been trying too hard?"

"My friends, Kelsey and Britt—remember them?"

"How could I forget? They made my life hell."

"How so?" She traced the diamond pattern on her crystal champagne flute.

"Because every time I so much as even thought about getting close to you, they were there."

"I've never told them the truth, either. Other than that my parents found out we were sleeping together, and made us break up."

"Did they blame me?"

"Not at all. In fact, they saw the whole thing as quite romantic. Romeo and Juliet, forbidden love… They were constantly after me to secretly contact you, but I was too afraid of what my parents might do."

"And now?"

She scrunched her nose. "What do you mean?"

"Now do you even care what your parents think?"

"No. I've hardly even spoken with them since Christmas. They're ticked about the divorce."

"They don't blame you for David's indiscretions, do they?"

"No. They just felt I should forgive and forget. But how could I do that when he didn't want me?"

He leaned in close, kissing her fingers. "Wanna know a secret?"

"What?" She licked her lips.

"I very much want you."

CHAPTER ELEVEN

"I'M SORRY," HE SAID. "Did I really just say that cornball line out loud?"

"Afraid so." And her heart hadn't stopped pounding since. All night—truthfully, ever since first seeing him again—she'd felt the same.

Wincing, he asked, "What's that look mean?"

"What look?" Panic seized her. Could he tell how she truly felt? That she knew the smart thing would be to walk away and head back to Denver in the morning. But knowing all that didn't change her yearning to make love to him just one more time.

"The one where your cheeks are flushed, you refuse to meet my gaze and you keep nibbling your lower lip."

"Oh, that look…" The laugh that escaped her sounded more like a strangled chicken than a *femme fatale*.

"Tell me what you're feeling," he urged, stroking the tops of her hands with his thumbs.

Her heart thundered.

How did she begin to tell him that she wanted to make love without coming off like a total slut? On the other hand, what did it matter, seeing how they were no longer in high school, but both consenting adults.

"Tabby?"

"I want you, too, okay? There. I said it. Now what? Do we run upstairs and make hot, sweaty, Valentine's Day love?"

"Hot, sweaty, Valentine's Day love?" He raised his eyebrows. "Um, as intriguing as that sounds, I had something different in mind."

She gulped.

The gaze he'd fixed on her was intense. Hungry. But at the same time vulnerable. Never had he been more handsome. Never had she wanted him more. But they'd been down this road before, and nothing save for heartache and a few moments of mind-numbing pleasure had come of their unions.

Ah, but surely even a few seconds of numbness would be preferable to the gnawing ache stemming from knowing that after tonight Brodie had no interest in again being part of her life.

Breath hitched, caressing his hands, she asked, "What did you have in mind?"

Ten minutes later in her suite, Brodie was well on his way to showing her, rather than telling her the finer points of his plan.

With the door shut and locked behind them, he'd scooped her into his arms and eased her onto the king-size bed. He kissed her dizzy. Then, when he straightened and seemed to be leaving, he pressed his finger to her lips to stop her protests. "I'll be right back," he said. He began building a fire in the cold stone hearth. "I've always wanted to see you—all of you—by firelight, and I figure this may be my only shot."

Why? she wanted to ask.

If only he'd make room for her in his life, she'd be all too willing to give herself to him again and again. But then Brodie being the gentleman that he was, he realized she was in no way emotionally ready to forge another relationship so soon after her divorce. And if he were truly a gentleman, would he make love to her without a commitment?

"There," he said, stepping back to admire his handiwork, holding out his palms to warm them beside the flames. "Part one of my fantasy is underway."

He flicked off the room's only other light, a desktop lamp, dowsing them in dancing golden shadows. Staring into the hearth, his profile was so sure and strong and handsome, the mere sight of him transported her in time to when she hadn't a care other than him. Talking with him, kissing him, making love with him.

When she'd been with Brodie, everything else faded away, leaving them in their own universe built for two.

He joined her on the bed, only he perched on the edge as if not sure he wanted to join her all the way. Skimming her hair back from her face, his palm was still warm from the fire, and she closed her eyes, leaning into his touch.

I love you, she thought. And she did. She so very much did.

GAZING AT THE WOMAN he loved but would never entirely have, Brodie was overcome by sadness. He'd wanted tonight to be magical—and it would—but it would also be bittersweet.

He nuzzled Tabby's neck, and she groaned, arching it for

him, just as she always had. How was it that after all this
time, he remembered every nuance of her body? Yet they
remained virtual strangers in every other way?

"How do I get this thing off?" he asked, slipping his
finger under one of her dress's delicate red straps. "Is there
a zipper?"

She shook her head, casting him a Mona Lisa smile.
"You'll have to peel it off. But first…" She slipped his black
suit coat over his shoulders and arms, then tossed it to the
floor.

"Hey," he said, teasing, pressing steamy kisses along
her collarbone. "Do you have any idea how long it took the
dry cleaner to iron that?"

"Nope," she said, making swift work of removing his tie,
"and I really don't care."

"Yeah, me neither…" He planted a leisurely kiss to her
mouth.

She nimbly undid the buttons of his starched white shirt,
and when his chest was bared, she skimmed her hands over
his pecs. Eyes closed, when she sat up in bed, he succumbed
to the sweet torture of her raining dozens of kisses over his
chest.

What was it about Tabby that'd always made his body
sing? Was it a purely hedonistic, chemical connection? Or
something more?

After all this time, did he still love her heart and soul? If
so, where did that leave him? It may not be the most manly
thing to admit, but he couldn't stand the pain of losing her
again. Meaning he must willingly send her away. She had to
be free to grow into the woman she was destined to become.

As for him… He'd always have tonight.

As if unwrapping her gift to him, he slowly peeled her dress off. She wore no bra, and her panties were a lacy red scrap.

"I like these," he said, fingering the flimsy string sides. "But they're going to have to go." The stitching easily gave, baring her further still.

"Those were expensive."

"Mmm…" he moaned. "I'll buy you another pair."

When he finally entered her and she cried out with pleasure, he covered her mouth with his own, drinking her in, memorizing the sight of her, the feel, the taste, the tantalizing mewing sound.

I love you, he thought over and over with each thrust, pretending she said the same with her body, though she may never say it with words.

"THANKS, GLADYS," Brodie said into his cell phone the next morning, already slipping on his boxers, then pants. "I'll be right in." Leaning over the bed, he kissed Tabby's bare shoulder where it peeked out from beneath the sheets and down-filled comforter.

"Mmm…" She rolled over, stealing his breath with her sleep-sexy smile. "Good morning. Why aren't you still in bed?"

"Duty calls," he said, kissing her lips. "Terry Moore— he's Becky Priztcik and Raleigh Moore's kid, remember them? From our graduating class? Anyway, the ten-year-old decided to go sledding before school. Slammed into a metal fence post. Gladys met the family at the clinic and says she doesn't think he broke ribs or punctured a lung, but he is pretty banged up."

"Then, of course, you have to go." Her return kiss destroyed him. For the first time in his professional life, he wished he'd chosen to be anything other than Snowflake's only doctor.

"Your flight to Denver's at ten, right?"

She nodded.

"With my regular patient load, and now this, I can't see you off."

"I know," she said, rising in bed to wrap his waist in a hug. "My ex, brothers and both of my parents are doctors, remember? I didn't expect you to wave as I boarded the plane."

What did *you expect?* It was on the tip of his tongue to ask, but he didn't. As she'd pointed out, Tabby was a big girl. Judging by the heat between them last night, if she wanted something, she'd ask. Obviously, this was the end of the road where she was concerned.

"Call when you get home?" he asked, releasing her to put on his shirt and jacket.

"I will."

Snatching his keys and wallet, he said, "I hate leaving like this. I wanted to at least buy you breakfast."

"I'm fine," she assured him. "Go. Duty calls."

But I selfishly want you to be my duty, as well, he thought.

"Brodie, go to that sweet little boy. I promise I'll phone when I've landed safely."

What then?

"Sure," he said with a sharp nod. "So then this is it?"

"I—I guess." She wouldn't meet his gaze. Instead, she stared out the picture window at the dirty-snow colored sky. "I mean, we're both busy. Live in different worlds."

"Right. Well…" He jiggled his keys. "It was great seeing you again."

"You, too." Had he only imagined it, or were her eyes shiny, and had she swallowed hard? Like fighting back tears?

He hated being a jerk, but if she was on the verge of crying…good. So was he. She'd hurt him bad in the past, and now she was at it again. Why? Why couldn't she make a stand, and for once do what she wanted in regard to him, instead of what she apparently still thought others wanted?

Get it through your thick skull, man. What she wants is a clean break from you.

"Miss? Everything all right?"

In the one-room airport, Tabitha looked up to see an old friend. Alice Baer, dressed in the regional airline's crisp red uniform. "Yes, thank you. I'm—"

"Tabby? Is that really you? I heard you were back, but—"

"I'm not back," Tabitha said with a sniffle, blotting her eyes with a tissue.

"That's not what I heard." The strawberry blonde helped herself to the seat beside Tabitha's. "Town gossip says you and Brodie are together again, and that last night, over an insanely romantic dinner at the lodge, he proposed. Well? Let me see the ring. He's quite a catch."

"Sorry," Tabitha said, "but there's no ring or proposal."

"What? Why?" Her old friend appeared genuinely crest-fallen. "Me and some of the other girls from our class are already planning a surprise engagement party." Hand clamped over her mouth, she said, "Oops. Guess I blew it, huh?"

Tabitha couldn't help but laugh. "Really, it's okay. Especially since there's no need to even have a party."

"You two were together last night, weren't you?"

Nodding, Tabitha said, "We had a wonderful time, but…" She shrugged. "Guess it just wasn't our time—if you know what I mean."

"But you all used to be so cute together. Everyone's always wondered what went wrong."

Me, too, Alice. Me, too.

Sadly, though, the fact that Brodie hadn't so much as wanted to exchange e-mail addresses with her shouldn't have come as a shock. She'd hurt him badly by not telling him about having lost their baby all those years ago. She'd deepened the wound by not immediately coming clean with him Friday night. No wonder he hadn't asked to see her again. Sure, she'd been fun to reunite with for a night, but as for anything more than that? Ha! He was a smart guy and knew better than to get himself mixed up with a basket case.

"You going to be all right?" Alice asked with a kindly pat to her forearm.

Truthfully, I don't know.

CHAPTER TWELVE

Six months later
Omni Medical Convention, Las Vegas

"YOU DIRTY ROTTEN, scum-sucking son of a…"

Bam!

Brodie had barely recovered from the left to his jaw, when the ambush attacker delivered a stunning right.

Adrenaline surging, fists at the ready, Brodie glanced up at his assailant, only to find the guy looked familiar.

Hotel security arrived in the form of a pair of uniformed guards, both of whom Brodie outweighed by fifty pounds.

"Drop your fists and step away from the victim," the taller of the two guards said.

"He had it coming," Brody's attacker said. "This toad knocked up my sister *twice,* without even so much as apologizing."

"Craig?" Brodie mumbled, rubbing his jaw. *"Tabby's brother?"*

"Don't you dare even speak her name."

"Look, man," the shorter guard said, "I don't blame you for giving the guy what he's got coming, but you can't do it in here."

"I'm done." Craig's fists were still clenched, but he'd backed away.

Having spent the afternoon bored out of his mind at suture technique sessions for which he already had the skills, he found this encounter with Craig a little surreal. "How about you let me buy you a beer, and I'll tell you my side of the story."

"What story? Judging by the size of Tab's stomach, you did a lot more than set her busted ankle during that supposed ski trip of hers."

What?

"In fact, the only thing I want to hear from you, Kimball, is what you plan on doing to help my sister along."

"Plan on doing? I didn't even know she was pregnant—either time."

"Likely story."

"Story, hell." Brodie bristled. "It's the truth."

"Whatever."

"Look." The tall guard interjected. "We've got to get back to our rounds. You all aren't going to start swinging again, are you?"

"No," Craig said.

Brodie wasn't making any promises.

How many peaches short of a bushel was the woman he loved, when here she was carrying his child for a second time, and she didn't even see fit to tell him? He'd started so many times to try tracking her down, but hadn't. Instead waiting for her to send some sort of sign that she'd tackled whatever demons haunted her and was ready to start a new life—with him. And, yet, all the while—

"I asked you a question, Kimball. What are you going to do?"

"Do?" Brodie asked with a sarcastic laugh. "What I should've done years ago—marry her."

"BRODIE?" TABITHA RUBBED sleep from her eyes, flicking on the porch light. "It's barely six in the morning. What are you doing here? How did you even find me?"

"The better question is, when were you planning on telling me about this?" Sinking to his knees right there on her remote mountain cottage's front porch, he hugged her, cradling his cheek against her belly's bulge.

Tears came fast and hot.

The moment was like a dream. How many nights had she lain awake wishing Brodie were here? However, she hadn't wanted to be a burden in his wonderful life until she figured out what to do with hers. But then she'd discovered her pregnancy, and, suddenly, there'd been no more questions, only steely determination to carry their precious child through to term.

"Why, Tabby?" he asked, voice hoarse. Was he crying, too? "Why didn't you tell me? I'd have been here. Helping. Buying pickles or ice cream or whatever—"

"Gummi Bears," she said with a teary, sniffling laugh. "I can't get enough. And I was going to tell you, but I've been so afraid."

"Of what?" he asked, gazing up at her with a look of such undeniable love that she was left doubting her own actions.

"Losing the baby. Having you hate me."

"I could never hate you. I love you."

"Then why didn't you ask me to stay with you?"

"Because you yourself said you needed to go. Get your head on straight. Walking out your door was the hardest thing I've ever done—other than losing you the first time. But this time," he said, rising to his full, glorious height, "you're not going anywhere without me." From his rumpled dark trousers, he pulled a robin's egg–blue box; then he popped open the lid to reveal a square-cut diamond solitaire sparkling in the porch light's glow. "Marry me. *Now*."

She nodded.

"No more secrets."

She nodded. "I love you. I'm sorry."

Slipping the ring on her finger, Brodie said, "I love you, too. I'm sorry I didn't just make the first move six months ago."

"It wouldn't have mattered. I didn't want to be a burden to you."

"A burden?" He laughed. "What do you think carrying around all this angst inside concerning you has been?"

"I'm sorry."

"Dammit, Tabby, stop apologizing and let's get on with our lives."

She grinned.

"What about that is remotely funny?"

"Nothing," she said with another smile, gazing at the sun rising over Denver's twinkling lights.

"Didn't you just promise no more secrets?"

"Yes, but—"

"Tell me."

"Okay. It's just that every time I ran into someone in

Snowflake, they'd assume I was *back,* and I'd have to tell them I wasn't. Only now, once we're married," she said, admiring her ring, "I will be back. For good."

"Woman," he said after a light growl, tugging her into his arms. "You wear me out."

"Just wait till the baby comes. Then you'll really be tired."

"That," he said with a gentle kiss to her forehead, "is an exhaustion I've waited my whole life to share."

* * * * *

Star Light,
Star Bright

ANNE STUART

Anne Stuart has written over sixty novels in her more than twenty-five years as a writer. She has won many major awards, including three RITA® Awards from the Romance Writers of America, as well as their Lifetime Achievement Award. When she's not writing or travelling around the country speaking to writers groups, she can be found at home in northern Vermont with her husband and two children.

For BK and Mort – Romex rules!

CHAPTER ONE

First Week of Advent

It was snowing again. Angela McKenna navigated the icy roads with her usual panic, driving her old Jeep at a snail's pace. At least it had all-wheel drive. But even that wonderful invention wasn't foolproof when it came to ice. This was her second winter spent on the shores of Lake Champlain, and she would have thought she'd have gotten used to the driving by now. After all, she could navigate the heart of Chicago, the insanity of New York, the freeways of L.A. without breaking a sweat. But let a few flakes of snow start drifting out of the Vermont skies and she was swamped with a tightly controlled terror. It was a good thing she didn't have to go anywhere for work—she would have been hopeless. Except, maybe that would have forced her to learn how to drive in the snowy vicinity of Crescent Cove without courting a heart attack.

She usually avoided going out entirely when the weather was bad, but right now she was driving home from Burlington Airport after spending Thanksgiving with her parents in Chicago, and the sooner she got back the better. It was only going to keep on snowing.

They'd put the holiday decorations up in the middle of town while she'd been gone. Reindeer danced from every streetlight, and the big tree at the end of the main street was ablaze with lights. Wreaths were on every one of the white clapboard houses she passed. Just after four and already growing dark, the sidewalks of Crescent Cove were empty.

She had to get home and off these snowy roads, she thought as she made her way through town with single-minded concentration, past the stores and restaurants, heading north, breathing deeply as she listened to the New Age holiday music on her car's CD player, when for some reason she hit the right turn signal. She took the turn, half in a daze. In all the time she'd spent in Crescent Cove she'd never gone down this particular narrow road, never even noticed its existence, and why she'd do so in the middle of a raging blizzard made no sense at all. Nevertheless, that was exactly what she had done.

Well, it wasn't actually a raging blizzard—more a flurry or two. And maybe she'd just been daydreaming—forgetting where she was, and taken the wrong turn. It would be easy enough to stop and head back the way she'd come. She'd never been gifted geographically, and if she kept going in a strange direction, God knows where she'd end up. Her safest bet was to turn around.

The street was packed with the early snow, and she pulled into a driveway beside a small store, then backed out again. Not into the street, but into a parking spot just outside the tiny shop.

Crescent Cove was too small a place, especially in the winter, for Angie not to have known every single side street, every shop, every restaurant. Nevertheless, this tiny shop was entirely new to her, and the warm light spilled out onto the sidewalk.

On impulse she turned off the car and climbed out. She never could resist a mystery, and the appearance of a new street, a new store, was unimaginable. Of course the street wasn't new—that would be impossible. She just hadn't seen it before—the snow made everything look different.

And once she could read the faded gilt sign over the front door she breathed a sigh of relief. Christmas Candles by Mrs. Claus, it read. The very cuteness of it should have been cloying, but Angie was in a generous mood. No wonder she'd missed it—it was a seasonal business. No one would be buying Christmas candles in the busy summer.

The snow was falling gently on her shoulders, and she realized she should return to the car and get her butt safely home, but something kept her rooted to the sidewalk. After all, she'd decided this would be the Christmas she would go all out, and it was important to support local businesses. Buy Vermont First, they said, and she opened the old oak door, listening to the silvery laughter of bells as she stepped inside.

She was expecting to be assaulted by artificial perfumes, but instead the place smelled warm and delightful, like Christmas cookies. Candles of various shapes and sizes were arranged on a number of tables, decorated with festive tablecloths and sweet-smelling greenery, and Angie felt a surge of happiness that hadn't been there in a long, long time. Christmas always did that to her.

"Merry Christmas, dearie." The woman seemed to materialize out of the shadows, and Angie would have laughed, except it seemed so right. The owner of the shop had dressed the part—rosy cheeks, wire-rimmed glasses, a red-velvet mob cap atop her soft white hair.

"Merry Christmas," Angie replied automatically. "I don't really know why I'm here…"

"You're here for a Christmas candle," the woman said in a comfortable voice.

"Well, I suppose I am," Angie admitted. "I just hadn't realized…"

"We seldom do," the so-called Mrs. Claus said. "I've got just the one for you, Angie."

Angie was startled. "How did you know who I was?"

"This is a very small town in the winter, dearie. Everyone knows everyone."

Angie was about to point out that Mrs. Claus was a complete stranger to her, but she was polite enough to keep quiet. Besides, it wasn't strictly true. There was a familiarity about the old lady that was unmistakable.

"I'm not sure what I'm looking for. Whether I want some kind of Christmas scent or—the candles are unscented," she said suddenly, just realizing it.

"No, they're not. They only release their fragrance when they're lit. And I promise you, there's nothing artificial about the scent. If you smell cinnamon and apples, then that's what's in the candle."

"Well, maybe a nice big red pillar," Angie said, always a sucker for cinnamon and apples.

"No, dearie. I'll get yours." The woman disappeared into the back of the store with a swirl of her red velvet skirts, then reappeared holding a wide, slightly conical shaped candle. It was deep gold, with Florentine scrolling around the top and bottom, and a line of angels dancing. It was a work of art, undeniably beautiful, and not in Angie's budget. If she had any money to spare it was earmarked for presents, not her own pleasure.

"I don't think I can afford it," she said.

"Oh, you don't have to pay for it," the woman said. "It's already been taken care of. You notice there are three angels dancing on the side of the candle? One is for Christmas past, one for Christmas present and one for all the Christmases of the future. It will last just until Christmas morning, and when the candle burns down completely everything you need will be yours."

Angie would have objected, but the old woman put the pillar in her hand. It felt heavy, warm and oddly comforting. "But who…?"

"Does it matter? Think of it as a gift from Santa Claus. Or are you going to tell me you don't believe in him?"

She had been about to say that very thing but something stopped her. Certain things were meant to be accepted, not scrutinized, and she accepted the gift as she accepted the existence of Santa Claus. Unlikely, but very nice anyway.

"I guess I'll have to find out on my own," she said.

The woman calling herself Mrs. Claus smiled sweetly. "I guess you will, dearie. In the end, we all have to find out on our own."

Not until Angie was halfway down the town road to Black's Point did the oddness of the encounter hit her. The candle sat on the seat beside her, the rich colors glowing in the darkness. If all her wishes were going to come true when the candle burned down, then she'd better plan to burn it night and day. The old woman said it would last until Christmas Day, but Angie doubted it would make it halfway through Advent, the four weeks before Christmas. Still, it was a lovely thing, and its very presence in the car seemed almost a blessing, to ward off the danger of the snowy roads.

At least they'd gotten around to plowing Black's Point Road. Since she was the only inhabitant out there during the winter, and since the town road crew knew perfectly well that she didn't have to get out to a job, her road was low priority. She'd spent four days last winter trapped there, about to run out of canned soup, when her best friend, Patsy, had raised holy hell and gotten them to plow her out.

Had Patsy arranged for the candle? Unlikely—she and Ethan were saving every penny for their new baby, and besides, Patsy was a weaver. She made her own presents.

Angie was in luck this time—the plows had been through recently, and she only slid a little as she took the sharp turn left onto the narrow road. The snow was tapering off—typical that once she was safely home the driving would suddenly become safe once more. Maybe fate was trying to tell her she shouldn't have run away to Vermont when her marriage failed. Well, she had no intention of listening to such an arbitrary judgment. She'd had to rethink her entire life in the wake of Jeffrey's behavior, and she wasn't about to let a little thing like snow stop her from living the life she wanted. And there was no place in the world, not even the house she grew up in outside of

Chicago, that felt like home the way Crescent Cove did. She was never sure why—it simply was.

She pulled into her narrow driveway. They'd kept plowing past her house for some reason—usually they just turned around in her driveway and headed back into town. Must be someone new on the road crew who didn't know the rules, she thought. There was no one else to plow.

Still, it would make walking easier. She no longer played tennis or racquetball, and even though she now lived in Vermont, she'd decided that downhill skiing was vastly overrated. Particularly when you were skiing alone.

But walking in the silent woods that surrounded Crescent Cove was good for the body and soothing for the soul. She'd worked out all sorts of problems while she walked, and when the snow got really deep she even resorted to high-tech snowshoes. The weather wasn't that bad yet, though Vermont had had more than its share of snow already. And it wasn't even winter yet. Technically.

Weather-wise, winter in Vermont began around November 15. They'd already had two nights of below-zero temperatures, and caterpillars and the *Farmer's Almanac* had predicted a long, cold season.

The house was icy when she unlocked the door. She kept the heat down to sixty-two degrees most of the time, and augmented it with a cast-iron wood-fired stove. She shivered, closing the door behind her and flipping on the lights. Maybe she'd indulge in cranking the heat up, just until she had time to get changed and start a fire. Or maybe she wouldn't, and then her money would last her just a bit longer.

That was the problem with having married a lawyer, she thought, kicking off her soaked shoes and walking on the icy floors to the old farmhouse kitchen. Not only had she spent her marriage in a lifestyle well above what she was accustomed to, but her divorce settlement had been minuscule. It was her fault—she'd wanted to end her relationship with her philandering husband as quickly and neatly as possible, and land values in Crescent Cove had skyrocketed. The monetary value of the old farmhouse was impressive to any judge. The only problem was, she had no intention of selling the place, and it was the only thing she'd come away with from the failed marriage, while Jeffrey had kept the house, the car and most of their joint property.

She could always try to get a real job, but assistant professors of English literature were not in high demand, even with a number of colleges and universities nearby. And somehow the very thought of academia sent chills down her spine, colder than the Vermont winters. She wasn't in the mood for politics, students, or the Dead White Guys that made up most college curricula. The full professors got the fun stuff—the assistants were left with the same old crap. If she had to teach Charles Dickens one more time she would scream. Well, maybe not if she was teaching *A Christmas Carol.* But then, she'd always been a total sucker for Christmas.

No, she liked what she was doing just fine. Even loved it. She'd always loved to bake, and providing pies and breads and other goods to the local businesses kept her busy and brought her some peace of mind. Sister Krissie's

Bar and Grill, Mort's Diner, even BK's Grocery provided enough standing orders that she stayed reasonably solvent.

The smell of the farmhouse welcomed her like an old friend. The place had been empty for years—Jeffrey's parents had acquired it as an investment and then forgotten all about it. Why they couldn't have bought her own family's house when finances had forced its sale was another question. Instead, the *über*-wealthy Jacksons had bought it and bulldozed it to make room for another tennis court, wiping out generations of love and memories. Typical of the new breed of summer people, she thought. Wipe out memories and traditions in favor of ostentation. The Jacksons had only been the first of the professional invaders. Their company, Worldcomp, made so much money that no one could figure out what they were doing in a quiet little seasonal community like Crescent Cove.

Except to tear down her family's home, she thought grumpily. And bring Brody Jackson into her life, someone she could have well done without.

She put the candle down on the scrubbed kitchen table and set to work. It didn't take her long to get a new fire going, and the heat began spreading through the kitchen. She lit the candle, and the scent was amazing. It smelled like cinnamon, and delicious enough to make her stomach rumble. She closed off most of the place in the winter—surviving nicely on the first floor with a bedroom, a bathroom and the parlor along with the huge old kitchen. In the summer she threw open the upstairs and invited everyone to visit, but the winters were hers, and she welcomed that season's approach with a sense of relief.

While the room was heating, she quickly put on some warmer clothes—jeans and a sweater and thick wool socks. She didn't bother with her indulgent silk long johns—those she kept for subzero weather. Today was comfortably in the upper twenties, according to her outside thermometer. A nice, brisk afternoon.

Five trips later, everything was in from the back of the car. One suitcase of her own, and four more that she'd borrowed from her mother. The first one was filled with Christmas presents from Marshall Fields. The other three were packed with family Christmas ornaments that her mother had finally decided to hand over.

Angie could never understand why her mother had held on to them for so long. Her academic parents had downsized when Angie had married, moving into a small apartment that overlooked Lake Michigan, and from then on they'd only had a tabletop tree, with no room for many of Angie's favorite ornaments or the Christmas tree house, an ornate tree stand made by her father's great-uncle Otto early in the last century. For some reason her parents had preferred to keep things in storage rather than let her have them, which was unusual, because her parents tended to dote on their only child.

Her marriage had ended Christmas Eve, and she'd spent the next few weeks huddled in a hotel room, not in the mood to celebrate a damn thing. By the next Christmas she'd been divorced for nine months and living in the farmhouse in Crescent Cove, and Jeffrey's new wife had just given birth. To Angie's surprise her mother had called, offering to ship the Christmas decorations east to her, but she'd politely declined, planning to spend the holiday alone in her farmhouse with nary a decoration or a Christmas carol to keep her company.

Big mistake, she'd realized. Fortunately, her old friend Patsy and her husband were living in town, and they'd dragged her out of her morose isolation and into the warmth of their large family holiday that had included Patsy's mother and her new husband, Patsy's father and his new wife, Ethan's father and his new wife, and Ethan's mother, newly widowed, plus five brothers and sisters and their spouses, countless children and even the ninety-year-old matriarch of the family, known to all as Aunt Ginny.

It had been impossible to stay depressed in such chaos. Impossible not to feel the faint, tentative rebirth of the Christmas spirit. And now that another year had passed, she was once more ready to celebrate the holidays with a vengeance.

She'd been half tempted to go right out and find the perfect tree the moment she'd come home from Chicago. A great many people in Crescent Cove put up their trees the day after Thanksgiving and took them down the day after Christmas. Since Angie had every intention of leaving her tree up until Twelfth Night, she decided it might not be smart to cut one so early, and besides, her mother was shipping the Christmas tree house stand to her. Time enough to find a tree when that arrived.

But she wasn't going to wait any longer to get the smell of pine in her house. She needed to make an outdoor wreath, an Advent wreath, a kissing ball and anything else she could think of, anything to start the season off properly.

She grabbed the clippers from the jumbled junk drawer, put on her felt-lined Sorrels, her down jacket, her turtle fur hat and her leather work gloves and headed out into the gathering New England dusk.

She knew just where she was going. The trees down by the edge of the lake were thick and cluttered—she could easily trim a boatload of branches off them and it would only help them flourish.

Tucking the clippers in one pocket and her flashlight in another, she headed down the freshly plowed road, toward the lake, with the vast, comforting silence of the Vermont winter all around her.

A little too silent. There were still the occasional bears around, and fisher cats were downright nasty, so she began humming, then started singing. Loudly. "Good King Wenceslas" was an excellent song for tromping through the snow, and she'd always had a good strong voice. Patsy had talked her into joining the church choir for the Christmas season, and Angie had rediscovered the joy of singing. And on this deserted spit of land she could sing as loud as she wanted and no one was around to hear.

The edge of the lake was covered with a rime of ice, but beyond the crusty sheet it lay dark and cold and mysterious. She'd skirted the opulent Jackson compound, moving past the snow-covered tennis court that had once been her front porch, and ended up by the lake, where their rickety dock had jutted out into the water. She hadn't been down here since last spring—she did her best to avoid the flatlanders who spent their summers on Black's Point, particularly the robber baron Jacksons, who'd only been coming to Crescent Cove for the past twenty years. Rank newcomers compared with most of the summer population, whose grandparents and great-grandparents had settled in the cottages along the shore more than eighty years ago.

But things were changing, and she had to accept it. In the 1930s, Crescent Cove had been the summer colony of Ivy League professors, a few ministers and the occasional grudgingly accepted lawyer. Now the academics could no longer support the taxes and upkeep on second homes, and the very wealthy had moved in, buying up land and houses, and in the Jacksons' case, tearing down existing buildings to make more room for their extravagant and totally inappropriate taste.

She shook her head and began cutting branches, letting them fall into a neat pile on the snow, as she switched songs to "Silver Bells." She was so intent on what she was doing, so lost in her glorious solitude on the deserted tip of Black's Point, that she didn't hear anyone approaching.

"You're trespassing."

She let out a shriek, the clippers went flying, and she spun around in the snow, her heart pounding. "You scared me!" she said, breathless, too rattled to be polite.

"You're trespassing," he said again, patiently. She couldn't see him clearly in the gathering darkness, only a general outline. It was no one she recognized, and she knew most of the caretakers in town. He was tall, lean, young and not a local. There was something vaguely familiar about him, something about his voice, but she couldn't quite pin it down.

"I'm the only one living out on the point during the

winter, and no one's going to mind if I take a few branches to make some Christmas decorations."

"You'll be sorry."

"Is that a threat?" A wiser woman would have been nervous, but her instincts told her that she wasn't really in any kind of danger. Then again, those infallible instincts had told her Jeffrey was her soul mate, and look how that had turned out.

"Not a threat," the man said in a calm voice. "You're cutting cat spruce. You put that up in your house and it'll smell like a litter box."

"Damn," she said, staring down at the pile at her feet. She'd forgotten about cat spruce, and it was too cold to notice the pungent smell. She glanced up at the stranger again. She couldn't see his face, and pulling out her flashlight and blinding him with it wasn't very polite. She knew that voice, somewhere far in the back of her memory, and it was driving her crazy.

"Listen," she said. "I don't know who you are or what business it is of yours, but I really don't think the Jacksons will mind if I pilfer some evergreen branches from the land that used to belong to my family. They may be greedy robber barons, but a little thing like this isn't going to matter to them—they won't even be aware that I've done it. Most of them haven't been up here for several years, so they're unlikely to notice. By summer everything will have grown back, and no harm done. Except—" she looked around her "—I lost my clippers when you startled me."

"Greedy robber barons? That's a new one." His laugh was without humor. "And believe me, they'll know."

She did believe him. Because it finally hit her who he was. She didn't need to see his face—she was only surprised she hadn't realized right off.

"You're Brody Jackson," she said flatly.

"Yes." He didn't bother asking her who she was—it probably wasn't worth his attention, but she persevered anyway.

"I'm Angie McKenna. I live in the old Martin farm down the road. You probably don't remember me, but we used to hang out together when we were kids. A century and a half ago."

"Did we?" His voice was noncommittal. He'd forgotten her, of course. Why should he remember? Brody Jackson had been the golden boy all his life—beautiful, smart, athletic and charming, adored by all the girls, both summer and year-rounders, admired by the boys. For all that she'd been his next-door neighbor, after the first summer they hadn't had anything to do with each other. She was just one of a gaggle of girls at the Crescent Cove Harbor Club, and while she'd always been acutely aware of him, it was little wonder she'd passed beneath his radar. Except for two occasions, and she wasn't going to think about that.

"What are you doing here? I didn't realize your place was winterized."

"I can manage," he said. "And why are you here? Where's Jeffrey? I thought the two of you were America's sweethearts." His voice was faintly ironic—something new. And then she realized with a start that he knew exactly who she was.

"We're divorced. I've been living here for a couple of years."

"Another illusion shattered," he said. "I suppose I would have known that if we'd used the house in the past couple of years."

"I…"

"I'm not really in the mood to catch up on old times," he said. "You better go home."

The flat, weary tone in his voice made that clear, though it told her little else. Except that he didn't sound like the golden boy he once had been.

But she wasn't about to argue. She bent to scoop up the branches, cat spruce and all. "I'll just clean these up."

"Leave them."

No way she could argue with that, either. All she could do was aim for a dignified retreat. "Well, I'm, er, sorry I bothered you."

He said nothing, and she shrugged. She wasn't quite sure how to end the conversation. *See you around* was a possibility, but he'd probably come back with *not if I see you first.*

"Goodbye, then," she said. "Merry Christmas."

"Isn't it a little early for that?"

"It's never too early for Christmas," Angie said. "Sorry I bothered you."

"You already said that. Go home, Angel."

There was nothing she could do but leave, aware that his eyes were on her as she made her way through the snow to the plowed road. When she got there, she turned back to try a pleasant wave, but he'd disappeared.

"Hell and damnation," she muttered, tromping back down the road. Brody Jackson was the last person she needed around here, especially if he'd gotten mean in his old age, and he certainly behaved as if he had. At least he wouldn't stay long—there was nothing in the town of Crescent Cove for the likes of Brody Jackson.

Her house was toasty when she went back in. She kicked off her snowy boots, put another log in the stove and began to make herself some dinner. Not until she was falling asleep several hours later did she remember what he'd called her.

IF BRODY JACKSON STILL had a sense of humor he would have laughed. Angel McKenna had thought he wouldn't remember her. He remembered everything about her—her unflinching gaze, the freckles across her nose, the husky voice that he'd always found such a turn-on. Of course, as a teenager he'd found everything a turn-on. But in particular, Angel McKenna.

She didn't look that much different. She must be thirty now, and she wore her brown hair long, to her shoulders. Her eyes were the same rich brown that could have the most unnerving effect on a boy. And a man. And her slightly breathless voice was as familiar as if it were yesterday that he'd last spoken to her.

But that wasn't the case. It had been years, and he still hadn't quite gotten over her.

It wasn't arrogance to know that he could have had any girl he wanted in Crescent Cove. Any girl but Angel, who never went anywhere without Jeffrey Hastings by her side. They would have been prom queen and king, he thought cynically. Childhood sweethearts, teenage steadies, the perfect marriage that had been preordained by the Fates.

A marriage that had shattered. He wondered why.

It wasn't important. He hadn't come back to Crescent Cove to relive old times; he'd come to lick his wounds and keep a low profile. Softhearted people would say he'd come to heal. More realistic ones would argue he'd come to hide.

In fact, the house on Black's Point was one of the few things he had left, after the government got through with him. The penthouse apartment in New York, the house in Tahoe, the condo in Hawaii were all gone. As well as the cars, the money and any shred of reputation he might have once had.

And his brothers.

They'd wanted him to join them. They'd siphoned off enough of the money from Worldcomp to keep them very comfortable for the rest of their lives, while thousands of people had lost their life savings, pension plans had gone bankrupt and the very name of their company was becoming synonymous with corporate greed and treachery.

But he'd stayed. As only a junior partner, he stayed to face the music. Once his brothers had left the country he had no more allegiance to anything but the truth, ugly as it was. The Jackson brothers had ripped off hundreds of millions of dollars, covering up that the company was in desperate financial trouble, and they'd departed before it had all blown up in their faces. Leaving Brody behind with his inconvenient conscience.

They'd finished with him in Washington. He'd testified, answered questions, unearthed hidden records—and lost almost everything. He had the house in Vermont, an old Saab, ten thousand dollars and a law degree that he'd never used. And never would, given his reputation.

It was irrelevant that he hadn't known what his brothers were doing. That was no excuse—it had happened on his watch and he counted it as his responsibility, while his brothers enjoyed life in the Cayman Islands.

He kicked the branches that Angel had cut. She certainly didn't have much of an eye; these trees were sparse and spindly. He picked up the pair of clippers that had gone flying when he'd startled her and shoved them in his pocket. He'd have to find some way to return them, and the smart thing to do would be to avoid seeing her again.

He could pretend that he hadn't known she was in Crescent Cove when he'd made up his mind where he'd go, but he'd never been very good at lying to himself. He'd known she was here—the *Crescent Cove Chronicle* kept a busy social page for such a tiny town—and her presence had been a dangerous lure he couldn't resist.

He needed to resist it now, now that he'd come face-to-face with her. He hadn't realized she'd had such an effect on him. Even with Jeff Hastings out of her life, she was still unfinished business, and he'd be wise to keep her that way, at least until he had a better idea of what he was going to do with his shattered life.

At this point there was no room for Angel McKenna, no matter how much he wanted there to be. He'd thought maybe they could have a few laughs for old times' sake. But he was surprised to find his feelings for Angel were just too powerful. He needed to be smart for once and keep his distance.

Life was complicated enough.

CHAPTER TWO

Second Week in Advent

Angie slid into the booth at Mort's Diner, dumping her mountain of packages onto the seat beside her before she could meet Patsy's amused gaze from across the table. "Been shopping?" Patsy inquired in a dulcet tone.

"It's Christmas. What can I say?" Angie reached for one of Patsy's French fries.

"Weren't you the person who just last year said she was never going to celebrate Christmas again? It was all Ethan and I could do to drag you over to our house for Christmas dinner. You didn't even have a tree, for heaven's sake. And now you've gone all holly-jolly on me. What's the change?"

Before she had a chance to speak, Mort herself set a mug of coffee down in front of her. "Pie's almost gone," she said. "You gonna get back to work?"

"I'll bring you a delivery by this afternoon," Angie said, feeling guilty. There were four pies sitting on the counter in the old farmhouse, just a part of Mort's most recent order. She'd been halfway to Burlington before she'd remembered them, and she'd almost turned back, but they were talking about snow tomorrow, and she didn't dare wait any longer.

Mort departed in a dignified huff, shuffling in the run-down slippers she habitually wore in the old-fashioned diner, and Angie took a deep sip of her coffee, shuddering. "There are times when I would kill for a latte. This stuff could strip the enamel off your teeth."

"You could have had one in Burlington," Patsy said. "As a matter of fact, that's one of the best things about this miserable pregnancy—I can no longer tolerate the battery acid Mort calls coffee. If Junior ever decides to pop out I might just never go back."

Angie eyed her friend's huge belly, which was pushing against the table in the small booth. "She'll come when she's ready," Angie said, deliberately keeping up their ongoing battle. Patsy insisted her baby was a boy; she'd been so exhausted from morning sickness and so uncomfortable and unwieldy later on that she'd decided only a male could be oppressing her. Her husband had received this bitter pronouncement with his usual calm good humor. It was almost impossible to ruffle Ethan, and he had kept his volatile wife on a relatively even keel during most of her difficult, long-sought-for pregnancy.

But Angie had decided it had to be a girl, and she was hearing nothing else. Mort was running a pool on sex, weight and birth date, and so far most of the town was siding with Angie's pronouncement.

"There are things more important than lattes," Angie said.

"Name one."

"This!" Angie grabbed a brightly colored bag, opened it and whipped out a tiny red scrap of fabric. It looked as if it might fit a doll, but the red embroidery on the lacy collar said "Baby's First Christmas."

Patsy accepted the gift with feigned displeasure. "Junior's not going to like being in drag for his first Christmas."

"Any child you raise is going to be completely broadminded about such things," Angie said. "Besides, he's going to be a girl."

"Humph," said Patsy, clearly not in the mood for fighting. "What else did you buy?"

"Lots of things."

"Like what?"

Angie took a deep breath. "Christmas napkins, Christmas glasses, soda pop with Santa on the can, Christmas pasta, Christmas paper plates, Christmas candy, Christmas towels. I even got enough fabric to make a Christmas shower curtain."

"Good God," Patsy said weakly.

"Plus, I got a baby's first Christmas tree ornament, a baby's first Christmas bib, a baby's first Christmas picture frame, even a pair of miniature red overalls on the rare chance that I'm wrong about your incipient offspring."

"You've gone crazy," Patsy said flatly. "Next thing you'll tell me is that you bought Christmas toilet paper."

"No. Christmas paper towels, and a Christmas toilet seat, but no toilet paper. Why, do you have some?"

"If I had such a revolting possession you can rest assured I'd give it to you immediately," Patsy said with a shudder. "As it is, I'm too busy being pregnant to think about Christmas. Ethan's already brought home the tree, and it'll be up to him to decorate. I never wanted this baby in the first place."

"Of course you didn't," Angie said in a soothing voice. "And all those trips into Burlington, all those painful procedures were what…? An excuse for a girl's day out with me?"

"Exactly," Patsy said, casting an accusing glance, daring her to disagree. "I want the last piece of pie."

"Of course you do," Angie said. She looked at the counter. "What's with all the flatlanders?" There were more than half a dozen strangers there, choking on Mort's coffee, talking in low voices among themselves.

"What do you think? The media have arrived. They think Brody Jackson is here."

Angie blinked. "Really? Why would they care?"

"Don't you read the newspapers, Angie? Worldcomp has gone bankrupt, and he and his smarmy older brothers hid the financial details until they could get their own money out of it. They've bankrupted hundreds of thousands of people. It's even worse than Enron."

"I gave up newspapers when I moved here," she said. "I had no idea. Why are they looking for him?"

"He's one of the most notorious men in America. His brothers skipped the country and are out of reach, but Brody stayed."

"Why?"

Patsy shrugged. "You remember Brody. Always the handsome prince. He's probably just living up to his self-image of nobility."

"You are so cynical," Angie said, taking another sip of coffee and shivering.

"Maybe he thought by coming clean he'd get off easy.

He handed everything over to the special commission—all the records, everything like that. In return he didn't have to go to jail. Things won't go so well for his sleazy brothers if they ever set foot back in this country." She finished the milk shake with a noisy slurp. "As for Brody, he lost everything. Absolutely everything. The press love stories about how the mighty have fallen, and he used to get a lot of press, he and that model wife of his."

"He's married?"

"No, she divorced him before any of this came out."

"That's a shame," Angie said, wondering why she was feeling sudden relief.

"So," Patsy said, "are you going to warn him?"

Angie jerked her head up. "What do you mean?"

"I know he's here, Angie. Everyone does. You can't keep secrets in a town this size, though as far as I'm aware he hasn't left Black's Point since he arrived. You're the only one out that road. There's no way you wouldn't have seen him."

"He wants to be left alone."

"I understand that. And none of us will help these vultures. But it won't take long for them to find out where the Jackson place is. It's a matter of town record. Hell, if they went to BK's Grocery they could even buy a map of the area with everyone's house marked on it."

"I've got to go." Angie couldn't shove the table back any farther against Junior, but she slid out, grabbing her packages. "Tell Mort I'll be back with the pies in a few hours."

"Where are you off to? Or need I ask? You're going to warn him, aren't you? You always had a soft spot for Brody."

"I never had a soft spot for anyone but Jeffrey since I was a kid and you know it," she said stoutly. "I just happen to hate seeing anyone hounded."

"Sure you do," Patsy said with a smug smile. "Say hi for me, will you?"

The men at the counter watched her as she headed toward the door, and she forced herself to slow down, not scramble desperately. It was none of her business. If Brody and his older brothers had ripped off thousands of people— no, hundreds of thousands, Patsy had said—then he deserved everything that happened to him.

But she had a natural aversion to the tabloid press in all its various guises. Besides, she had to get home anyway, she reminded herself with a fair amount of righteousness. She had to make two more pies to go with the ones she'd already finished. And she found she was in sudden, dire need of a little exercise. A short walk down toward the lake would be just the thing.

There were still no tire tracks on Black's Point Road except her own. The town had plowed down to the Jackson compound, but so far she hadn't seen anyone else drive past her house. No sign of Brody Jackson at all.

Well, that wasn't strictly true. There'd been a sign, all right. The morning after her arrival back in Crescent Cove she'd found a huge pile of freshly cut evergreen branches on her porch, with her missing clippers on the railing. No note, but then, there was no doubt where they'd come from. She'd scooped them up and inhaled the fragrance. Not a cat spruce among them.

The whole house had smelled like Christmas ever since.

He'd brought her more than she'd needed—she'd made the Advent wreath, setting the Christmas candle in the middle of it, a wreath for the front door, a wreath for the fence at the end of the driveway, and if she'd been able to figure out how to do it she would have made a wreath for the front of her Jeep. She made a kissing ball to hang in her living room—not that anyone would be kissing her in the near or even distant future, but she'd always liked them. She made boughs for her mantel and the arched doorway into the parlor, and she had still had enough greenery left to make one more wreath and kissing ball. The wreath would be a simple thank-you to her invisible neighbor, and the kissing ball would be for... Maybe sour old Mort might appreciate one in the diner. Anything was possible.

She jumped out of the car, leaving her purchases piled in the back seat, and grabbed the extra wreath off the front porch. She hadn't planned to deliver it in broad daylight—after all, he'd dropped his unexpected gift off when she'd been asleep. It would be easier if she didn't have to see him at all, but with the media hot on his trail she figured she owed him that much, if for nothing more than old times' sake, which he'd forgotten long ago.

She'd planned to walk down to the Jackson place, but at the last minute she got in the car again and drove the quarter mile down the road to his driveway. She pulled her car across the front of it, effectively blocking access, and climbed out, then headed down the narrow, snow-covered path to the house.

There was no sign of him, no sign of a car, but the snow on the front deck was freshly shoveled, and she knew he

was still there. For a moment she almost chickened out—
he was hardly her responsibility, and sooner or later he'd
have to face what he'd done.

But then, Patsy was right. She'd always had an irrational
soft spot for Brody Jackson, even though she and Jeffrey
had been practically joined at the hip. For the sake of that
long-ago, almost indecipherable feeling, she owed him this
much.

She didn't even have to knock on the door. She was
halfway across the snow-packed deck when the glass door
opened and Brody stood there, a mug of coffee in one hand,
an unreadable expression on his face.

It was the first real look she'd gotten—when she'd run
into him a few nights earlier he'd been nothing more than
a huge, dark figure. In the light of day he was startling.

He was the same man, yet entirely different. His shaggy,
bleached-blond hair was now a definite brown, and didn't
seem to have been cut in months. His eyes were still blue,
but they were shadowed now, and his face was lean, drawn.
He'd had the most remarkable mouth—smiling, lush, ridiculously kissable.

She should know—she'd kissed him. Twice.

But that mouth was drawn in a thin line. His blue eyes
were expressionless and he only opened the door a crack.
Enough for her to see the faded jeans on his long legs, the
bare feet, the old flannel shirt with several buttons missing.

Oh, he was still gorgeous—there was no question about
that. Bad luck and bad behavior couldn't change that much,
and the scruffy stubble and shaggy dark hair only made him
appear more real.

"Why are you here?" he greeted her in a wary, unwelcoming voice. "And what's that?"

For a moment she forgot why she was there. He was still distracting, even in his current downbeat state. "I made you a Christmas wreath. You were so nice to bring me all that greenery that I wanted to thank you."

"I brought you the greenery so you wouldn't come traipsing around my house," he said. "And I'm not in the mood to celebrate Christmas."

"Tough," she said. There was a cast-iron hook beside the door, one that held a hanging plant in the summer, and she dumped the wreath over it, against the house. "I've got more than enough Christmas spirit to spare. But that's not why I'm here."

"I assume you'll tell me sooner or later."

The cynical, world-weary tone was so unlike that of the Brody Jackson she'd once known that she was momentarily silenced. But only momentarily.

"There are camera crews in town, searching for you. I saw at least half a dozen of them in Mort's Diner, as well as trucks from CNN, Fox and a couple of the networks."

Brody's response was swift and obscene. "Why aren't they here yet?"

"They don't know where you are."

"And you didn't tell them? Why?"

She considered it for a moment. "I'm not really sure. It's not as if we've ever been particular friends. I guess I don't like people being hounded. Or maybe I just don't want a bunch of people crawling around Black's Point."

"I think you're too late." They could both hear the sound of the trucks and cars, noisy in the winter stillness, as they left the main highway and started down the narrow road.

"Not necessarily. I don't give up easily."

"And you're implying I do?" Brody said.

She didn't answer that. "Where's your car?"

"We have a garage, remember?"

"Then go back in the house and stay put. I'll get rid of them."

His expression was dubious. "You think you'll be able to accomplish something the best lawyers in the country couldn't? They're like barracudas—they won't be satisfied till they tear the flesh from my bones."

"Very melodramatic," she said, her voice brisk. "They're only trying to make a living. I just don't want them doing it in my backyard."

"And you imagine you can stop them?"

"Watch me." She thought twice. "I mean, don't watch me. Get back in the house and don't come out until they're gone."

"Fine with me, but I don't need you fighting my battles."

She wrinkled her nose. "It's my battle. I came here for peace and quiet, not *60 Minutes*."

"Actually, I don't rate that high. I usually land on some tabloid show on Fox."

"How the mighty have fallen."

"Do you have a reason for disliking me? Apart from my charming behavior last week? I'd been drinking."

"How reassuring," she said sweetly. "If I have to choose between a drunk and the paparazzi I'm not sure—"

"I'm not a drunk."

The vehicles were drawing closer. "Go back inside, then, and I'll get rid of them."

For a moment it seemed as if he might argue, but he simply nodded and disappeared into the house, closing the door behind him.

She'd reached her car before the first truck pulled up, and she leaned against the back of it, arms folded across her chest, effectively blocking access to the driveway.

"Can I help you?" She used the tone that had always been effective on frat-boy athletes who thought they could coast through English lit, and the reporter who was approaching her hesitated. Probably a frat boy in his youth, Angie decided dispassionately.

The others with him were busy unloading the van, but she wasn't about to move, and there was no other way they could get down to the lake. The early snows were thigh-high in some places, the other driveways weren't plowed and the trees grew so thickly that anyone venturing down there would probably end up walking around in circles. It was a nice thought, but she couldn't take a chance on their stumbling across the Jackson compound.

"Rex Hamilton, Fox news," he said with a showy smile, and Angie kept a deliberately stony face. Brody had known exactly who his stalkers were likely to be. "We're looking for Brody Jackson…"

"I'm sure you are, but he's not here."

"Come on, miss. We know he is. He flew into Burlington eight days ago and he hasn't flown out. Passenger lists are simple enough to trace."

"I'm sure they are. He was here for one night, picked up a few things and then left. Driving, not flying."

Rex Hamilton didn't appear convinced. "Where was he headed?"

"I have no idea, and I don't care. Probably someplace warmer."

"That's easy enough to do," the man said, shivering. "Randy, set up a shot of this nice young lady and we'll go from there."

"You'll go nowhere but back into your van and on the road again."

"Do you know who I am?" the man demanded, affronted.

"You told me. Rex Harrison."

"Hamilton!" he snapped.

"Of course you are," she said in a soothing voice. "But you're not filming me, and you're going to get back in your truck and drive away. This land is private property, and posted against hunters, trappers and trespassers. I'm sure you fit in at least one of those categories."

Hamilton waved the cameraman off, fixing a disgruntled stare at her. "You the new girlfriend?" he asked.

She had to laugh. "Not likely."

"Because he goes through women like water. He's used and dumped supermodels and A-list actresses in the blink of an eye."

"Not really in his league," she drawled.

Hamilton tilted his head to one side. "Oh, I'm not sure about that."

"I am. Go away. If you're as good a reporter as you seem to believe you are it won't take you long to pick up his trail."

"Why are you defending the man? He and those brothers of his ripped off thousands of people."

"Then why isn't he in jail?"

"Because he can afford the best lawyers."

"Then why have his brothers left the country? Can't they afford the same lawyers?"

"You seem to know an awful lot about the case for an innocent bystander."

"Actually, I know very little. But as a gesture of goodwill I'll tell you what he was driving, and maybe you'll be able to track him down. He was in a Ford Explorer, dark blue or green, headed south."

"I don't suppose you have his license plate number."

"I don't even know which state issued it. All I can tell you is he drove out of here last week and I haven't seen him since. And as I'm the only person living out here in the winter, I'd know."

"And you are…?"

"Extremely tired of talking to you. Go away or I'll call the police."

"On what? Cell phones don't work in this godforsaken place."

"Where do you come from, Mr. Hamilton? New York City?"

"L.A. Why?"

"And you call this place godforsaken? Go back to the City of Angels, Mr. Hamilton. Or go chasing after Brody Jackson—I really don't care. Just go."

During their conversation three more vehicles had pulled up, blocking the narrow road. There was no place for them to turn around, and they were going to have a hell of a time backing out. Rex Hamilton looked at her for a moment longer, then shook his head in defeat. "We'll find him. I promise you that. He can't rip off the American public and get away with it."

"I don't care whether you find him or not. I just don't want you finding him here." Not the best choice of words, because Hamilton gave her one last, assessing stare.

Apparently, her innocent, self-righteous demeanor convinced him. She half expected him to make like The Terminator and say *I'll be back,* but he spared her.

By the time the last truck had headed south on Route 100 Angie was freezing. Two of the vehicles had gone into a ditch, and the film crews had shown a surprising spirit of cooperation in helping push each other out. By the end they were wet, tired, cold and frustrated, and it was evident that nothing short of a prearranged interview would get them back out there. Crescent Cove in the winter wasn't made for the faint of heart. She leaned against the hood of her car, listening to the sounds of the trucks as they faded into the distance, letting the peace of the snow surround her.

"How'd you manage that?"

She turned, startled. Of course the snow muffled everything, but she still thought some preternatural instinct might have warned her.

"I told them you were gone. It took some convincing, but they finally believed me. And you were supposed to stay put until I gave you the all-clear."

"I was curious. Maybe I should hire you as my bodyguard. You accomplished what few others have managed."

"I'm not interested in your body." That came out all wrong, and she could have kicked herself.

"No, I'm sure you're not," he said. "More's the pity."

She jerked her head around to stare at him. "What did you say?"

"You heard me." He walked past her to the end of the driveway, peering down the road. "You think they'll be back?"

"I doubt it. Once you get that badly stuck in the snow it pretty much ruins things." She could get a good look at him with his back turned to her. He was thinner than she remembered—instead of the buff golden boy she'd once been uneasily aware of, he was now wiry, almost tough, wearing rough winter clothes that had seen better days, and his unbleached hair was too long.

She'd had a crush on him—she might as well admit it. She and Jeffrey had gone together practically since childhood, and she'd never really noticed anyone else, believing in their fantasy of soul mates, but she'd noticed Brody. Who could miss him, with his easy charm and effortless grace? He'd dated just about every age-appropriate, halfway-decent-looking female in the summer population, except for her, of course.

And out of the blue, she suddenly remembered Ariel Bartlett.

Fate hadn't been kind to Ariel. She'd been plump, plain and hardworking, and had come from a family who'd farmed in Crescent Cove since the early 1800s. Her mother had given her that particularly unsuitable name, and she'd made her way through life, seemingly stolid and unimagina-

tive, working as a waitress for Mort's Diner, working as a
checkout girl at BK's Grocery, working at the Crescent
Cove Harbor Club during the summers, while the teenage
children of the vacationers played. She'd had a huge, em-
barrassingly obvious crush on Brody, and they'd all found
it vastly amusing. Jeffrey in particular had taken to calling
her Brody's pet cow, and he'd told Angie she was being a
stick-in-the-mud when she'd tried to silence him.

Not that it would have done much good. Everyone
thought her calf-eyed devotion was a riot. Everyone except
Brody.

He'd never said a thing when people teased him, and
he'd been unfailingly kind to Ariel. And at the Founder's
Day dance, which always signaled the end of the summer,
he'd brought her as his date, treating her with exquisite
sweetness, much to Jeffrey's amusement.

That should have tipped Angie off to the fact that her
intended was a snake, but she'd been too busy living up to
expectations. And trying to ignore the fact that some tiny
part of her, for the first time in her life, wanted to be Ariel
Bartlett.

"Why'd you do it?"

Brody turned to look at her. "Do what? Steal billions of
dollars from the unwitting?"

For a moment she was distracted. "Did you? Really?"

He shrugged. "I was a major executive at Worldcomp,
and I should have known what was happening. I'm responsible."

"But you didn't do it, did you? Those slimy older
brothers of yours did."

"Why would you care?"

"Actually, I don't. I was asking you about something else."

He didn't move. "I'm waiting."

"Why did you bring Ariel Bartlett to the Founder's Day dance?"

She'd manage to surprise him, but he recovered quickly enough. "Maybe I thought she deserved to have a night where she wasn't waiting on a bunch of spoiled kids who laughed at her. Or maybe I knew she had a crush on me and I decided to be condescending enough to give her the thrill of a lifetime. Why do you ask?"

"I don't know. I just thought of her."

"You'll be glad to hear she's a very successful chef in Philadelphia. She's happily married with two children."

"I know that. This is a small town, remember. Have you kept in touch with her?"

He sighed. "What the hell does it matter to you, Angel?"

She'd forgotten he'd called her Angel. The only one who ever had, it had been both mocking and oddly affectionate back in those days. "It doesn't."

"Good. Thank you for your noble rescue of the fallen knight. I owe you."

"You don't sound very happy about it. If you care to, you can repay your debt right now and we'll call it even."

"What do you want, Angel?" He sounded wary.

"A Christmas tree." It came out of the blue, and it wasn't until she'd said it that she realized that was exactly what she wanted. A Christmas tree from the place where she'd spent her summers a lifetime ago. When she'd first fallen in love.

"There are fifty million trees on this spit of land," he drawled. "What are you asking me for?"

"I want a special one. It's near your tennis court. I planted it the year before we sold the house—I thought it was going to be there for my grandchildren. But instead my parents sold the house and it somehow escaped the bull-dozer when you leveled the place. I'd like it."

"Show me."

It was tough going through the deep snow, especially with Angie breaking trail, but now that the idea had come to her she wasn't about to let go easily. If she'd had to walk barefoot in the snow to get her tree, she'd do it.

She circled the tennis courts, heading down toward the lake, ignoring the stab of pain that always hit her. She used to spend hours sitting on the porch, staring out at the lake, eating gingerbread, drinking grape juice, playing canasta with her friends. She'd probably miss it for the rest of her life.

The blue spruce stood there, where she'd planted it so many years ago. Now tall, thick, beautifully shaped, it was her last tie to this land that had once been in her family for generations. It was time to sever it.

Brody had come up beside her. "Too big," he said, looking up at it. "Unless you have cathedral ceilings, which I doubt. I suppose you could top it."

"Top it?"

He glanced at her. "I thought you'd been living here for a while. 'Topping' means using the upper part of it for your tree. You could maybe use half the tree that way."

"Never mind. It was a stupid idea."

"There are lots of other trees around. Take your pick."

She shook her head. "Forget it. I'll just buy one when I get around to it. I don't need my main tree until Christmas Eve, anyway."

"Your main tree? How many Christmas trees do you have?"

She mentally counted. "Six. No, seven. One medium-size one in the kitchen, two small ones in the living room, one in the bathroom, one in the bedroom and two on the porch."

"You're crazy."

"I guess I am. And I guess you'll still have to owe me," she added with a certain amount of satisfaction. "I've got some baking to do. Let me know if you need rescuing again."

She half expected him to growl. After all, she was baiting him.

But to her amazement he smiled, a slow, reluctant grin that brought the memory of Brody Jackson back full force. "Yes, ma'am," he said.

HE WATCHED HER as she walked away. Angel McKenna was still a force to be reckoned with, as he'd always known. He wasn't surprised she'd managed to run off the news crews. She'd always been ridiculously subservient to Jeffrey Hastings, but when he wasn't around she'd been her own woman, vibrant, strong, enticing. Even when she was fourteen years old and he'd kissed her on her front porch, the summer Jeff's parents took their kids to Europe instead of Vermont.

It hadn't been much of a kiss, but then, they'd both been pretty young. And for all the innocence of it, it had lingered in his mind for years. Until he'd kissed her again—the biggest mistake of his life.

No, the biggest mistake of his life was trusting his older brothers with their elastic sense of morality. Second biggest was marrying Estelle when she had the intellect of a toaster and the warmth of a walk-in cooler. But she'd been decorative, understanding and inventive in bed. At the time it seemed enough.

Kissing Angel McKenna hadn't been a mistake. He just should have kissed her a hell of a lot more, and not given a damn about Jeff Hastings. Since in the end it didn't look as if Jeff had given a damn about Angel.

How could he have cheated on her, left her? Then again, Jeff had always been a dog-in-the-manger type. He wanted what everyone else had, and the more he suspected Brody's attraction to Angel the tighter he'd held on. Jeff would have done better with a party favor like Brody's ex-wife Estelle—he'd always been attracted to shiny objects. Angel was too deep, too multifaceted for a man like him.

And for a man like Brody. He'd been made for models and female tennis pros and debutantes. Not for women like Angela McKenna.

Except that there were no women like Angela McKenna. And he was old enough to know that and stop denying the truth. That all he ever really wanted in this life was the girl next door. And that was the one thing that was always out of his reach.

CHAPTER THREE

Third Week in Advent

At least there were no storms predicted for the next few days. Angie watched the local weather with all the intensity of a Greek sibyl trying to read the future, and while she trusted no one, she had a small margin of faith in channel three.

The back of her Jeep smelled heavenly, even after she'd dropped off thirteen pies, six tortes, two carrot cakes and one wicked concoction known only as Chocolate Suicide, and with each delivery she'd brought dozens of cookies. Her oven was on constantly, adding a nice dollop of heat to her drafty old farmhouse, and the smells of sugar and spice were divine. Almost as divine as the Christmas candle.

Angie had been unable to figure it out. It burned steadily, every night, but there were no drips—the flame glowed straight and true, and the fragrances were unbelievable, ever changing. One day it was bayberry, another pumpkin spice, then another day where it smelled just like cranberries. She'd given up trying to guess how the woman calling herself Mrs. Claus had done it—she simply enjoyed it.

She'd spent the afternoon with Patsy, drinking decent coffee while Patsy grumbled over her milk shakes, sorting through baby clothes, arguing about names. "This kid better not be born on Christmas Day," Patsy warned, taking a break and collapsing into the oversize rocking chair Ethan had found for her. "Nothing worse than having a birthday and Christmas all at once—you get shafted. Besides, I don't want to spend Christmas in the hospital."

"I thought you were planning on a home birth?"

"I am. But you and Ethan and everyone under the sun keep telling me I'm nuts," Patsy said. "The doctors say I'm strong as an ox, the midwives around here are the best in the country, and I think you're all fussing for nothing. This time I don't think I'll be my usual obedient self."

Angie laughed. "The day you're obedient is the day I learn to drive in snow."

"You drive in snow."

"Not if I can help it." She sat on the floor, folding the cloth diapers Patsy had insisted on. "I just wish I'd been able to get you a candle like mine. It's the most amazing thing. It smells like something different and wonderful every day, and the glow seems to fill the entire house. I wanted to buy one for everyone and I can't find her shop."

"Are you talking about that stupid candle shop again? I told you, there's no such place in Crescent Cove and never has been," Patsy said, putting a hand on her rounded stomach as Junior delivered a particularly powerful kick. "You must have been dreaming."

"You can't dream a candle into existence," Angie protested.

"Yes, but you brought back hoards of Christmas things when you went home for Thanksgiving, and you've gone out every clear day this month and brought back even more. Admit it—your back seat is filled with more stuff, isn't it?"

"Just a couple of new Christmas CDs," she said defensively.

"And…?"

"A Christmas sweater, green and red yarn to knit a scarf, a musical globe, a couple of Christmas mystery novels, cereal with red marshmallow stars and green marshmallow trees and—"

"Spare me," Patsy said. "At least they don't make Christmas diapers."

"They do! They're disposable, and, yes, they're against your environmental conscience, but I thought when you travel they might come in handy."

"Oh, God," Patsy said weakly. "Anyway, you probably picked up that candle in one of your insane shopping forays and just forgot where you bought it. And then you had some crazy dream about a shop run by Mrs. Santa Claus on some nonexistent street, and you don't remember where you really picked it up. Which is a shame, because it sounds cool, and I'd love to have one."

"I didn't dream it."

"Suit yourself. Are you staying for dinner? After all, you brought it. If you don't stay I'll worry that you don't trust your own cooking."

Angie looked out at the darkening afternoon. "As long as you promise it won't snow."

"Wuss," Patsy said genially.

Four hours later she regretted her decision. Channel

three had betrayed her, and a few lazy flakes were swirling down under the moonlit sky. Angie crept along the bare pavement, clutching the steering wheel. *There's nothing to fear,* she told herself. *It can't turn into a blizzard until you get home—there isn't time.*

Though of course at the pace she was driving, she might not be home until midnight. She pressed her foot a little harder on the gas pedal, cautiously, and the Jeep moved with a bit more vigor. She had the heat on full blast, and the car still smelled like a bakery. She only slid a bit when she turned into her driveway and came to a solid stop against the snowbank.

The lights were on, and smoke was pouring out of the chimney. She never left that many lights on, and the fire should have died down by now. For a moment she considered putting the car in reverse and getting the hell out of there.

And then the snow started again, and she knew perfectly well that home was the safest place to be. Besides, if she'd imagined Mrs. Claus's Candle Shop, then she might very well have imagined she'd turned off the lights when she left.

She grabbed an armful of packages from the back of the car, trudged up the front steps onto the porch and opened the door. Then dropped the packages as she saw him.

"What do you think you're doing?" she demanded.

Brody looked up from his spot on the floor. The perfectly shaped Christmas tree towered over him, albeit at an odd angle, and he'd managed to assemble Uncle Otto's Christmas tree house, but the actual mechanics of it seemed to be providing more than its share of frustrations.

"What do you think I'm doing? Repaying my debt. And you might want to close the door before you freeze us both."

She kicked the door shut behind her, leaving her packages where they'd fallen. "By breaking and entering?"

"You don't lock your house, Angel. And you asked for a tree. I brought you one. Sorry it couldn't be the one you planted, but I have a certain affection for that one, and besides, it was too big. This, however, is perfect. If I can just get it to stand straight."

It *was* a perfect tree. "It needs two people," she said, stripping off her down jacket and gloves and kicking off her boots. "You hold it while I tighten the screws."

"I'm already down here. You hold it."

There was no way to avoid coming close to him—managing the Christmas tree required proximity. She kept as far away as she could, focusing straight ahead as she reached through the thick branches to grasp the tree trunk. The Christmas candle sat where it always did, in the middle of the table, shedding its golden glow, and she felt some of her tension begin to drain.

"I don't know why you need so many trees," he muttered, practically beneath her skirts if she'd been wearing any. Fortunately, she had on jeans, but his head was uncomfortably close. "Most people get by with one, and it's usually artificial."

"I'm not most people."

"And you should never leave the house with a candle burning," he said, looking up at her. "I don't care how safe you think it is, a cat could knock it over. We've even been known to have the occasional earthquake."

"Highly unlikely. I don't have a cat at the moment, and for that matter I didn't leave the candle burning. I'm not a complete idiot."

"It was burning when I got here," he said. "And anyone who marries Jeffrey Hastings qualifies as at least a partial idiot. You can let go now."

She released the resiny trunk and stepped back. The tree stayed where it was, straight and true. "What have you got against Jeffrey?"

He scooted back from the tree, making no effort to rise. "Same thing I've always had," he said. "I would have thought you'd learned your lesson."

"Our divorce was very civilized. And just because our marriage didn't work out doesn't mean he's a monster."

"No, not a monster. Just a total pig's butt. Always has been, always will be." He rose, in one fluid movement, reminding her with sudden, disturbing clarity how tall he was. "Don't tell me you're still in love with him. You spent half your life thinking he was God's gift. I would have thought you'd learned better by now."

"I'm not still in love with him. Though I don't know what business it is of yours."

"Don't you?" he said, his face enigmatic. "Where are your lights?"

"I beg your pardon?"

"Your lights. I'll put the lights on the tree before I go. I'm taller than you are, and I can reach higher. Unless you want to kick me out."

She wasn't sure what she wanted. Having him there was bringing back all sorts of memories, disturbing ones, confusing ones. But if he left she'd be alone with those thoughts and regrets.

She swallowed her protest. "That would be very kind of you," she said. "They're in the trunk under the table. Can I get you something to drink? Maybe some eggnog?"

"You don't have eggnog. I already searched your refrigerator. And why do you have light beer? You don't need it."

She let that pass. "I can make eggnog," she said.

He'd been rummaging through the trunk of Christmas lights, but he raised his head up at that, his dark hair falling into his face, and she found she wanted to push that hair away from his eyes. What the hell was wrong with her?

"How do you make eggnog? I thought it came from the grocery store."

"You use milk and whipping cream and raw eggs and brandy."

"Raw eggs? You're trying to kill me."

"I get the eggs from the Gebbie farm. They aren't carrying any disease."

"I think I'd prefer to go straight to the brandy."

"I can do that. I don't suppose you're hungry. I could probably make you something."

He grinned. "Don't sound so pained. If you really don't want me here just tell me."

She wanted him there. That was the danger. The Christmas candle cast a warm, romantic glow to the room, and he was reminding her of things better left in the past. At least she had the dubious relief of knowing he'd forgotten that night entirely.

"I want you here." She could have bit her tongue. It was

his fault; he'd backed her into saying it, and it had come out all wrong. "That is, I don't mind."

"Don't spoil it, Angel. No one's wanted me around for a long time."

"I find that hard to believe," she said, managing to put a touch of asperity into her voice.

His smile was almost devilish. "Why, Angel. I do believe you don't hate me after all."

"Of course I don't hate you. I never have."

"Not according to your former husband."

"You discussed me with Jeffrey? When?"

"Relax. It was a long time ago. He didn't like the idea of anyone sniffing around you, particularly me. He was just warning me off."

"Don't be silly. I know that the two of you never got along for some reason, but it had absolutely nothing to do with me."

There was real amusement in his laugh. "Believe that if you want to."

"And no one was 'sniffing around' me, as you so elegantly put it. I was hardly a bitch in heat."

"More's the pity," he murmured. "What do you put on the top of the tree? A star or an angel?"

"What do you think?"

"Bring me the angel," he said.

The tree really was beautiful. And for some odd reason, she felt totally comfortable to be decorating it with Brody Jackson. He handled the antique glass balls with exquisite care, the ones that her mother would never let Jeffrey touch. He laughed at the string of nun lights, and he didn't laugh at one of her kindergarten attempts that her mother had refused to part with—a string of spools painted gold. The Christmas candle shone brightly, and she found herself loosening up, like a cat after a long nap. She sighed, a tired, happy sound, feeling better than she had for some time.

He turned to look at her. The tree was finished, the brandy was drunk, the candle light sparkled off the glass ornaments. "I suppose I'd better be going."

"Yes," she said, because she couldn't say anything else.

He reached for his old barn jacket and shrugged into it. He seemed a million miles away from the elegant executive who'd supposedly swindled thousands, he seemed a million miles away from the golden boy of summer she'd had a secret crush on. He seemed like a stranger, and the other part of herself.

And she must have had too much brandy. "Do you have a flashlight?"

"It's a full moon. I can find my way home." He had started toward the door, when suddenly she spoke.

"Would you tell me something, Brody?"

He stopped, turning. "Anything," he said simply, and she believed him.

"Do you even remember the Founder's Day dance?"

"The one I took Ariel Bartlett to? I thought we already talked about that."

"No. The last one. Ten years ago."

She examined his blank gaze and knew, as she'd expected, that he didn't remember a thing about it. A few short minutes out on the deck at the Harbor Club that had shaken her to her core, and he'd been too drunk to even recall them.

"Not in particular," he said. "Should I?"

He seemed so innocent that she had to believe him. "No," she said. "It was just the last time we saw each other before this winter. Jeffrey had left early for college and we danced. I think it was the only time."

"Did we?" He shook his head. "Sorry. Did anything interesting happen?"

"No," she said. "We danced, you were drunk, you made a pass and I fended you off. I just wanted to make sure there were no hard feelings." It was sort of the truth. If one had a very broad definition where truth was concerned.

"Really? Funny that I wouldn't remember. What did we dance to?"

"I have no idea. It was some old-fogey dance band the club had hired, and I don't think they played anything written before nineteen-fifty. It must have been some old standard."

"I suppose so. You still haven't told me why you're asking."

She gave herself a tiny shake. "Just curious, I guess."

"Okay," he said slowly, sounding doubtful. "Lock the door behind me, Angel."

"Why? We're perfectly safe out here."

"Do it for my peace of mind."

"All right." She followed him to the door, holding it as he stepped out into the wintery night. He went down the front steps, then stopped.

"Lock the door," he said again.

"Yes, sir." She started to close it.

"And Angel…"

"Yes?"

"It was 'Night and Day.'"

He was gone before she could say another word.

SHE STILL DIDN'T know how she'd happened to find herself in his arms. She'd gotten along with almost everyone, but there'd always been tension between Jeffrey and Brody. For the first time in years she was there alone—Jeffrey had left early for college. She'd known Brody for most of her life, been to dozens of the same parties, yet she couldn't recall ever dancing with him. And suddenly she was in his arms.

"I'm very drunk," he'd told her with great deliberateness as they moved through the music.

"Maybe we should sit this out."

He shook his head. "This is my only chance. While the cat's away the mice will play."

She didn't bother arguing with him. He might be very drunk, but he could still manage to keep upright on the dance floor, holding her against him, not too tight, not too loose. "I hope you're not planning to drive home," she said severely.

"I'm hoping you'll take me home with you."

"You really are drunk, aren't you, Brody?"

"Very," he said. He'd managed to steer her over toward the French doors.

"Maybe you should get some fresh air," she suggested. He had a strong body, warm, lean, and he was taller than Jeffrey. And there was nothing wrong with a harmless little crush—everyone in Crescent Cove went through one sooner or later. It didn't mean that she didn't consider Jeffrey her soul mate and her future. It just meant she was human, and Brody Jackson had the most beautiful mouth she'd ever seen. And always had.

"Good idea," he said, steering her out onto the deck that hung out over the lake. They were alone out there—the night was cool, and a light mist was falling, and if anything would sober him up that would. But he didn't let go of her, and she didn't try to move away. He pulled her a little closer, so that she fit perfectly against his body, and she felt a huge knot of tension begin to dissolve in a pool of heat that the cool mist had no effect on.

Her face was tucked against his shoulder, her arms were around his waist and they were barely moving. She was suddenly, unaccountably happy. "You're not really going to marry that pig's butt, are you?" he whispered in her ear.

"Marry who?" she asked, moving her head to look up at him, smiling.

Big mistake. He kissed her then. He had to be drunk to kiss her like that, but she'd already known that he was, and she'd been playing with fire, coming out there with him. It was a shock of a kiss—openmouthed, hungry, and the biggest shock of all was that she kissed him back. And kept kissing him, as he pushed her into a dark corner where no one could see them. His hands touched her, his mouth promised her, and all she wanted to do was shut out the voices and the guilt and lose herself in Brody Jackson.

But they weren't inner voices; they were real ones, moving closer, and reality came rushing back. She pushed away from him, stumbling in her high heels, and she couldn't even bring herself to look at him. She'd run, down the steps to the street, and kept going until she reached her car.

It had taken her ten minutes to stop shaking. Fifteen minutes to pull herself together and start the car. Twenty minutes to realize he wasn't chasing after her.

"You okay?" It was Patsy's boyfriend, Ethan, peering into the car with a worried expression on his face. "Patsy sent me to check on you."

"I'm fine," she said briskly. "I'm just going home. I'm driving to Chicago tomorrow and I need to get a good night's sleep."

"He was drunk, Angie. He didn't know what he was doing. I doubt he even realized it was you, and he sure as hell isn't going to remember anything tomorrow. Are you sure he didn't hurt you?"

It had been too much to hope that no one had noticed. At least Ethan was trustworthy. "Of course not. I was just…surprised. Where is he now?"

"Passed out. I'm taking him back home and dumping him there, let him sleep it off. As long as I'm certain you're okay."

"Fine. I'm sure he had no idea what he was doing."

"None at all. You positive you don't want me to drive you home? He'll be out for hours."

She shook her head. "I'm fine, Ethan. Thank you." And she drove off before he could see the tears on her face.

"Is SHE OKAY?" Brody had been waiting, just out of sight.

Ethan looked at him severely. "All you did was kiss her, right? It's not likely to destroy her life. Just how did you manage to get that drunk that fast? If Jeff had been here you wouldn't have gotten within ten feet of her."

"Exactly," Brody said, turning his face up to the cooling mist. "What did she say?"

"She's leaving first thing in the morning. With any luck she'll forget this ever happened."

"Most likely," he said in an even voice. "Thanks, Ethan."

"Just how much have you been drinking?"

Brody gave him a calm, clear-eyed smile. "I'm just about to start."

ANGIE PUSHED the door shut and locked it in a daze. Everything she had believed to be true had just shifted, and she was on very shaky ground. He remembered. He knew. Those hurried, hungry kisses in the rain weren't some forgotten fantasy, fueled by drunkenness on his part and sheer insanity on hers. He remembered, he knew, just as she did.

She still wasn't quite sure what that meant. For him, or for her.

It was after eleven. The living room was lit only with the glow from the angel candle and the lights from the Christmas tree, and it was much too late to call anyone. Except that it was three hours earlier in L.A., and even if it had been three hours later she would have still made the phone call.

Jeffrey sounded the same—slightly self-important, oozing charm. How she ever could have believed in him so completely was still a source of embarrassment, but she'd had two years to come to her senses, and regret was a waste of time.

"What went on between you and Brody Jackson?" she said abruptly.

"And Merry Christmas to you, too, darling," Jeff said. "How lovely to hear your voice."

Angie sighed. Jeffrey would answer her questions in his own time, and the sooner she got through the formalities the sooner he'd be willing to talk. "Lovely to hear your voice, too. Merry Christmas, Happy New Year, how's Margaret, how's the baby, how's work, what went on between you and Brody Jackson?"

"Still my impetuous Angie. I thought age would have cured you of that," he chided. "Why are you asking me about that now? Brody Jackson has been out of our lives for years. He just missed being in jail by the skin of his teeth, and with luck he'll follow his brothers into exile and no one in Crescent Cove will ever have to see him again."

"He may be out of your life, but he's not out of mine," Angie said. "He's moved back up here, and I want you to tell me why the two of you never got along."

Jeffrey's lazy chuckle would have fooled anyone who hadn't been married to him. "Has he been putting the moves on you? Poor Brody—I would have thought he'd let go of that old rivalry. I've certainly moved past it."

"What rivalry? I know you two hated each other, but I never understood why."

"Jealousy," Jeff said. "He wanted what he couldn't have. It had nothing to do with you—he just wanted to score points off me."

"Why?"

"I have no idea. All I can say is he did his best to beat me at everything—tennis, sailing, golf. The one thing he couldn't beat me at was you, and it drove him crazy."

"Jeff, he wasn't out to beat you. He was just naturally good at all those things. Ridiculously so—he beat everyone. I don't think it was anything personal."

"Trust me, it was personal. You just happened to get in the way. Don't let him get near you, Angie. He probably thinks you're fair game since our divorce, and I wouldn't put it past him to try to score just for old times' sake, but he'd just be using you."

"My mother liked him."

There was a moment's silence at the other end of the phone. "What's that got to do with anything?"

"My mother didn't like you."

"And I blame her for the problems in our marriage," he said in a self-righteous voice.

"You blame my mother for you having a series of affairs? Somehow the connection escapes me."

"You're hurt and bitter. I understand, Angie, and I wish I could change the way things worked out."

"I'm not hurt and I'm not bitter, Jeffrey," she said patiently. "I just want to know what—"

"You were the one thing he couldn't beat me at, Angie. It's that simple. If you have any sense at all you'll keep away from him."

"I don't think I've ever been known for my good sense, Jeffrey," she said softly. And she hung up the phone.

CHAPTER FOUR

Fourth Week of Advent

Brody kept his distance, but it didn't do Angela much good. The beautiful tree in the middle of her living room was inexplicably entwined with the presence of Brody Jackson. Her first instinct, after that troubling phone call with Jeffrey, was to march straight over to Brody's house and demand an explanation.

But it was dark, cold and snowing. And she wasn't sure she could handle an explanation right then.

It was really very simple, she decided. Some kind of midlife crisis as she was approaching thirty. She'd had a crush on Brody, one she'd never been able to admit to or even fantasize about, and it had stayed buried deep inside her. And without the restraining influence of Jeffrey, without anything to do on the long, lonely nights, it was flowering like a crocus after an endless winter. And she couldn't quite bring herself to squash it down again.

It hadn't been the only time he'd kissed her, of course. If it had been, it probably wouldn't have seemed so earth-shaking. But that night on the deck of the Crescent Cove

Harbor Club had simply been the culmination of something that had started five years earlier.

The Jacksons were newcomers to Crescent Cove, part of the new breed of summer people. The town was evolving—it had been a farming town for more than a hundred years before the first Princeton professor and his family arrived on the shores of Lake Champlain.

But taxes were rising, professors could no longer afford to take the entire summer off and wives worked, as well, and slowly but surely the big old cedar-shingled cottages along the lake were being sold in rapidly escalating bidding wars.

No one was particularly thrilled to see an industrialist like Walker Jackson move in, but he and his wife had been friendly and unpretentious, and their three young sons had blended in quite nicely. And fourteen-year-old Angela had been admittedly fascinated by her new neighbors, in particular the youngest son.

He'd been beautiful even back then—hair bleached by the sun, a tanned body, a dazzling smile. But that first summer he'd been lonely, spending his time out on the lake on his laser sailboat. When he wasn't spending time with Angela.

There'd been nothing romantic about it at all. She was fourteen; he was a year older. Jeffrey's family was in Europe for that summer, and for the first time Angela was at loose ends, free to do exactly as she chose. And then there was Brody. She'd read enough books, seen enough movies to feel the first forbidden burgeoning of romantic longing, but she wasn't ready to do anything about it. Jeffrey would be back, and Brody was nothing more than an increasingly close friend. They could talk about anything and everything—Brody's bullying older brothers and Angela's life as an only child. The stupidity of their relatively decent parents, how they wanted to live in Crescent Cove year-round as soon as they were old enough to do so.

The Founder's Day dance at the end of the summer had been a disaster. It should have warned her to avoid all such occasions in the future. It was the first dance she'd been to apart from the Wednesday-evening square dances, but the boys she'd known all her life weren't ready to cross the dance floor and actually ask a girl to dance. The best that could be hoped for was a sullen stride through the crowd, a silent appearance in front of the chosen victim and then off to dance with suitable grimness.

Brody didn't even go that far. He stayed in the corner with a group of boys, not even looking at her. It would have been miserable, except that most of her friends were lined up like ducks in a row, with no one wanting to pick them off.

By the time they announced the last song she was ready to cry, but she'd been experimenting with makeup and she thought it would run. So she lifted her head high as the kitschy sound of an Air Supply song filled the room, and then she rose and crossed the endless dance floor to stand in front of Brody.

He'd seen her coming, and he'd tried to ignore her. But they'd been best friends, and she wanted her first dance, the last dance of the summer, to be with him. She plastered a hopeful smile on her face. "Would you dance with me, Brody?"

She'd forced him to look at her. He was surrounded by

his peers, all watching, waiting to see what he would do. She should have known it was a matter of teenage male pride and expected nothing less, but when he shook his head and turned back to his friends it crushed her.

She'd walked away, that same, endless walk, with remarkable dignity for a girl just turned fourteen. She'd walked out of the room, out of the building, and the two miles home on the moonlit path along the lake, wiping the tears and the makeup away from her face.

Her house was dark when she got there—her parents had gone to bed early. The Jackson house was still a blaze of lights, and she'd moved liked a shadow along the path. By that time tears and makeup and shoes were gone, and she wanted nothing more than to go curl up in bed.

She moved up her wide front steps quietly, reaching for the screen door, when she saw him in the darkness. He was there on the green wicker sofa where they'd spent hours talking, laughing, doing crossword puzzles or just sitting in a comfortable silence. There was nothing comfortable about the silence now.

He'd taken off his tie and jacket, and he looked as miserable as she felt. Her first instinct was to ignore him, go straight into the house and slam the door behind her. Her second was to demand what he was doing there.

She did neither. She went over to the creaky old sofa and sat down, curling up in her corner, wrapping her arms around her knees as she waited for him to say something.

He didn't say a word.

It was her first kiss, and it was a powerhouse. In itself it wasn't astonishing—just the soft pressure of his lips against hers. And then on her tearstained eyelids, and on her cheek, and on her lips again. He'd been good even back then, a natural, and it was no wonder she'd been ready to put her arms around him. But then the porch light went on, and he drew back as if bitten.

Her father stood there, rumpled hair, clueless. "Don't you think you ought to come to bed now, Angie? We've got a long drive tomorrow."

"I can sleep in the car." She didn't want to leave Brody. She wanted more kisses from his beautiful mouth.

"I should go," Brody said, starting to stand up. He had his jacket with him, and he held it in front of him. "Good night, Professor McKenna. Have a good winter. Goodbye, Angel."

It had been the first time he'd called her that. And then he'd gone, taking the front steps two at a time, disappearing into the moonlit night.

By next summer Jeffrey had returned, Brody had discovered he was irresistible to almost the entire female population of Crescent Cove and those chaste, almost dreamlike kisses had been forgotten. By Brody, at least.

But every time Angie sat on the green wicker sofa she remembered. And she spent a very large part of her summers curled up there with a book, trying not to think about anyone at all.

Oddly enough, she'd never kissed Jeffrey on the sofa. They'd necked on the steps, on the dock, in the boathouse, at the Harbor Club and just about everywhere else during their endless teenage years, but for some reason she'd never let him kiss her on the green wicker couch.

She never did find out what happened to the furniture after her parents sold the house and the Jacksons had it bull-dozed. Probably gave it to Goodwill—most summer cottages were furnished with shabby hand-me-downs and secondhand furniture to begin with, and there'd been nothing of any particular grace or beauty. And she wouldn't have wanted the couch, really. She couldn't imagine it on Jeffrey's mother's freshly painted porch; the woman probably would have insisted on painting it a baby-blue if she'd allowed it there at all. Angie decided she would rather have it gone, over with, part of her long-lost childhood.

Of course she was thinking about it now. Brody had invaded her life, her thoughts, just as he had so many years ago. She could remember the faded cabbage roses on the cushions, the stain from the grape juice she'd spilled when she'd beaten Brody at canasta, the faintly musty smell as she devoured romances and ate homemade cookies.

Cookies. She surveyed the kitchen, the sheets of parchment paper covering every available surface, with Christmas cookies on each one. She'd finally run out of eggs and room, and she needed to give cookies away before she could bake some more. And she desperately needed to bake—it was what grounded her and kept her sane.

The snow was falling lightly, two days before Christmas Eve, and she'd already given cookies to everyone she'd ever met. She knew she wasn't going to be getting into her car in such suicidal weather, and she knew the one person she hadn't given cookies to yet was in walking distance. And he probably had eggs.

A simple, neighborly gesture, she told herself. So they

had a confusing history together. They were both grown-ups, and that was in the distant past. She should go to show him she was entirely unaffected by it, and a friendly visit with a tin box of Christmas cookies would be just the excuse. If he wasn't there, even better. She would have made the gesture without having to actually talk to him and pretend it didn't matter. She blew out the Christmas candle, extinguishing its warm glow, and headed out into the night.

She walked past the snow-shrouded tennis court and the tree she'd planted so long ago. Funny that they hadn't bull-dozed that when they'd wiped out everything else. She circled the house, only to discover where her Christmas tree had come from. He'd taken one of the three carefully land-scaped balsams from the side of the driveway. His gardener would kill him.

The deck was freshly shoveled and his truck was in the driveway, but there was no sign of him. She could always hope he'd gone for a long hike. The wreath she'd made for him was still there on the side of the house, and smoke was curling out of the chimney. She couldn't see him when she peered through the French doors, and her knock was delib-erately soft. If he was meant to hear her, he would; other-wise, she could just leave the cookies and head back to the safety of her house.

She should have known fate wouldn't make it easy on her. Before she could knock one more time the door opened and he stood there, barefoot and bare chested.

"Here," she said, shoving the cookies at him. "Merry Christmas."

He stared at her for a long, endless moment. She finally

got a good look at the inside of his house—he'd brought a bed downstairs by the wood stove, the fancy kitchen was a mess and every surface was covered with books and newspapers. It was far too cozy, and she had to get out of there, fast.

He took the cookies, but he caught her wrist at the same time, and before she realized it he'd drawn her into the warm house, kicking the door shut behind them. "It's about time," he said, setting the cookies down on a nearby table. "Merry Christmas, Angel." And he pulled her into his arms, against his hard, lean body, and kissed her.

It was as if she'd been holding her breath, waiting for this, for the past ten years. Since the last time he'd kissed her. His skin was smooth, warm beneath the open flannel shirt, and his mouth was just as practiced as ever. He didn't give her time to speak, and she didn't want to. She just wanted to kiss him, touch him, let his hands strip the heavy coat from her shoulders and drop it onto the floor.

The house was dark with the oncoming shadows of early evening, and he hadn't turned on the lights. Maybe what happened in the dark stayed in the dark, she thought, as he gently moved her back, almost as if they were dancing again, until she came up against a piece of furniture.

He barely had to nudge her—she sank onto the sofa, still clinging to him, and he followed her down onto the cushions, his long hair falling over them both as he blotted out the light, and she closed her eyes, letting herself drift in the wonderful sensations. The smell of wood smoke and whatever soap he used, the feel of his hot skin against her hands, his hard lean body on top of hers, the taste of him, rich and dark and intoxicating. The muffled sound of the sofa as it creaked beneath their bodies, the distant sound of a phone ringing as he began unbuttoning her blouse.

He hesitated a moment, his hand stilled, and she put her hands over his wrist. "Don't stop," she whispered.

He smiled, a slow, sweet smile. "I wasn't going to," he said. "This has been too long coming." And he was reaching for the zipper of her jeans, when the answering machine clicked on and her ex-husband's smug voice filled the room.

She froze. "You haven't answered my phone calls, Brody. Too busy trying to steal my wife?"

She put her hands up and pushed, and Brody immediately released her, rolling off her to the side of the old sofa.

"It's a waste of time. I had her first and nothing can change that. I was her first and her best, and you'll just be an afterthought."

Angela got to her feet, fastening her jeans with shaking hands, buttoning her blouse crookedly. Brody lay on his side on the sofa, an unreadable expression on his face.

But Jeffrey wasn't finished with his long-distance monologue. "The only reason you might be able to get her in bed is that I warned her about you, and she's still so hung up on me that she'll do anything she can think of to pay me back. I didn't want to hurt her, but she didn't believe that, and hell hath no fury and all that jazz. Don't be fooled—she doesn't really want you. She just wants to get back at me."

Brody rose slowly, lazily, stretching as he ambled toward the telephone. Jeffrey's voice was getting edgier now, almost desperate. "I know you're there, Brody. It's a waste of time trying to avoid me. Sooner or later you'll have to face the truth. The only reason you want her is you never could have her, and you're a man who hates to lose. And all she wants is revenge. Brody—"

Brody picked up the phone, then set it down again, breaking the connection.

"Poisonous little son of a bitch, isn't he?" he said mildly, disconnecting the various cords from the telephone and the back of the answering machine. "He's been calling me for days now. You'd think he'd be ready to let go of you, now that he's got a new family, but he always was a dog-in-the-manger type. He may not want you anymore, but he doesn't want anyone else to have you. Particularly not me." He leaned against the counter. "But then that brings us to the question of you and your motives. Any truth to what he says?" He seemed barely interested. "Is that why you're here? For revenge against the man who dumped you?"

The room had been so hot, so cozy, the wood heat filling the high-ceilinged room. Now it was as cold as if he'd left the door open to the winter air. She turned her head to make certain it was shut, staring out into the darkness, but of course it was closed. It was only the ice in the pit of her stomach.

"Look at it this way," she said in a deceptively calm voice. "You finally got what you wanted, even if Jeffrey's phone call came at the wrong time. Consider me had. You've beaten Jeffrey. There is now no woman in Crescent Cove who wouldn't sleep with you."

"There are any number of women in Crescent Cove who don't want to sleep with me," he said. "Most of them, as a matter of fact."

"All of them," she said, picking up her coat and pulling it around her.

"Don't leave."

She paused by the door. "Why not?"

She would have taken something, anything. But he simply shrugged, and in the end there was nothing she could do but walk back out into the snowy night.

And in the distance she heard a crashing sound.

SHE SLIPPED on the icy road, sprawling in the snow, and the hard slap of the cold against her face was a salutary force. She scrambled to her feet again and ran the rest of the way, calling herself all sorts of names beneath her breath. What the hell did she think she was doing? All he'd had to do was touch her and she'd been ready to strip off her clothes and do anything he wanted. She'd done just what Jeffrey had warned her against, fallen into his bed without a second thought, and it had only been the phone call that had saved her from turning her life into a disaster zone.

Except that it hadn't been his bed. She'd been aware of very little but the man who was touching, kissing her. In retrospect, she knew what had felt strange, wrong but right, familiar yet strange.

He had the old wicker sofa from her front porch.

She couldn't figure out why. Most of the furniture in the place had been broken-down junk, and the green sofa had been sagging badly, the wicker split and cracked. There'd been a few real Stickley pieces in the living room—the Jacksons should have saved those, not a worthless piece of porch furniture.

But it hadn't been the Jacksons. It had been Brody. She knew that as surely as she knew her own name.

And that was about all she knew at that point. She'd run, the moment she'd had a chance, letting Jeffrey do what he was so good at. Making her doubt everything.

Why had Brody kissed her, why had he saved the ratty old sofa, why had he done any of the unfathomable things he had over the years?

It didn't matter. If Jeffrey was right, then Brody had accomplished what he'd set out to accomplish.

Then again, why was she trusting Jeffrey at all? He said he'd been her first and her best. Oh, God, she certainly hoped not.

The house should have been dark when she opened the door. She'd left when it was still light, and she hadn't expected to be that long. She'd blown out the Christmas candle, but she hadn't bothered to turn on any lights.

But the Christmas candle sat in the middle of the kitchen table, the flame straight and true, filling the room with a warm, comforting light.

She stared at it. She remembered she'd blown it out—she was always very careful about such things, especially since Brody had warned her. She looked around her, wondering whether she ought to be nervous, whether someone had broken into her house while she'd been gone.

But no one had been there—she was certain of it. The place would feel different if there'd been an intruder. And no one would have come in, lit the Christmas candle and then left.

There was no question that the candle was unique—it

burned forever with hardly any change in size, it didn't drip and the ever-shifting scents were a delight to the soul. Maybe the wick was made of some special substance that kept a dull glow, ready to flare back into life again when you thought you'd blown it out, like trick matches. Like childhood crushes. She needed to be more careful in the future.

She plugged in the lights on the Christmas tree, the extra glow filling the room. The woodstove was still going strong, and for the time being she didn't need to do anything but curl up on the sofa and pretend nothing had happened.

This was not turning out to be the Christmas she'd been determined to have. There were too many unsettled memories, too many voiceless longings.

And the time for denial was gone. Those longings all had to do with Brody Jackson.

CHAPTER FIVE

Christmas

He shouldn't have thrown his answering machine against the wall, Brody thought, but it had made such a satisfying crunch. Almost as good as if he'd slammed it into Jeffrey Hasting's smug face.

He'd said the wrong thing, of course. Once Jeffrey had begun to spew his nastiness, once she'd stiffened beneath him, pulling away, he'd known he'd lost her.

The question was, had he ever had her? Maybe Jeffrey was right—she was simply the one who got away. Except that despite Angel's flattering opinion of his irresistibility, there'd been any number of women who'd gotten away, including the first girl he'd had sex with, who'd dumped him for a football player; including his exquisitely beautiful, exquisitely shallow ex-wife and any number in between. He'd had his heart broken and he'd washed the pain away with a bottle of Scotch and emerged bloody but unbowed.

But he'd never gotten over Angel McKenna.

He was an idiot. He wasn't going to be fifteen again, stealing a kiss on a moonlit porch. He wasn't going to be twenty again, pretending to be drunk so that he could kiss her in the rain.

And he didn't want to be. He'd made countless mistakes in his life, lost just about everything, but in the end it had made him a halfway decent man.

And in the end, he still wanted Angel McKenna, and probably would until the day he died.

He ought to just get the hell out of there. Coming back had been a mistake, though his options hadn't been many.

But he had discovered that the perfect couple of Crescent Cove's summer population had split, and that Angela had moved up into a house on Black's Point. And invitations to stay with sympathetic friends in Hawaii, Aspen and Santa Fe had paled next to the chance to see Angel again.

To his shock, he still felt the same. No, scratch that. Not the same. When he was a teenager he'd mainly been interested in getting into her pants. What he was feeling now was stronger, deeper, surer. He wanted her on every level—as a friend, a lover, a sparring partner and anything else that came to mind. He wanted her, needed her, and he had the crazy hope that she felt the same.

He grabbed his coat and headed out the door. It was pitch-black—no moon that night, and snow was in the air. By the time he reached Angela's farmhouse he'd managed to build up a full head of steam, and his knock on the door was closer to a pounding.

He half expected her to ignore it, which wasn't an option, but after a moment the door opened and she stood there, looking small and wan, and some of his righteous anger vanished.

"What do you want?" she asked.

"We've got unfinished business," he said abruptly. Not the best thing to say—she immediately folded her arms across her chest in an instinctive defensive posture. "Not that," he said, irritated. "Though God knows that's been hanging fire for too damn long."

She didn't say anything. Behind her he could see a soft glow emanating from the living room, and the scent of bayberry mixed with the smell of Christmas cookies hanging in the air. Who would have thought Christmas cookies could be erotic? But then, that was his constant state of mind when he was around her.

After a moment she moved out of the doorway, holding it open for him. "All right," she said. She kept well out of his way when he walked into the room, which was probably a good thing. He might have forgotten his noble resolve and kissed her again, and as long as Jeffrey Hastings didn't call they'd finish what they started. But he'd rushed it. Just because he hadn't been able to stop thinking about her for the past ten years didn't mean she'd spared him a thought. He had to take his time. Give her time.

He closed the door behind him to keep the winter air out, but he didn't take his coat off. She looked as if she'd been crying, and a pang of guilt hit him. Angela wasn't the kind of woman who cried easily—she never had been. The question was, was she crying over her lost husband or him?

"I think we need to start over. From the beginning again," he said. "The history gets too confusing, particularly with your ex-husband's little tricks."

"Start what?"

"Start us."

"I don't think that would be a good idea," she said carefully.

"Maybe not, but I don't tend to give up easily. I want to set a few things straight. The only reason I hated Jeffrey was that he had you. Oh, and the fact that he's a total moral vacuum. There's no rivalry between us. There's only you."

He couldn't read the expression on her face, but he persevered. "I'll tell you what, Angel. I'll leave you alone for now. Give you time to think about it. About whether you're over Jeffrey…"

"Over Jeffrey?" Her laugh was genuine. "I got over Jeffrey a couple of years before I caught him cheating. The worst thing about it was that I was relieved when I caught him and had an excuse to leave. One can't break up a perfect couple with no excuse."

He took a deep breath. "Okay. Then what's the problem?"

"I don't want to be another in your long line of summer conquests."

"Oh, for Pete's sake! In case you hadn't noticed, it's winter. The time for conquests is over. I'm in love with you."

He should have regretted blurting it out like that, particularly given the look on her face, but he couldn't.

"Go away," she said in a cold voice.

"For almost fifteen years, Angel. Since the first time I saw you, curled up on that green wicker sofa, crying over *Little Women.* You were my best friend, the first girl I kissed, and I want you to be the last girl I kiss. It's embarrassing, unlikely, and from the expression on your face I can guess that it's entirely unwelcome, but the fact is, I'm in love with you, and all the distractions in the world can't seem to shake it."

"You're lying," she said, but her voice was doubtful.

"If it makes you feel better you can believe that. You can spend the rest of your life missing Jeffrey."

"I don't give a damn about Jeffrey!" she said. "But I'm not about to trust your highly improbable declaration of love."

"Of course you're not," he said soothingly. "So we'll take it slow. Just promise me one thing. That you won't run. You'll keep an open mind, and we can see what happens."

"You don't love me."

"Just forget I ever said that," he said. "I promise I won't say it again. At least, not until I think you're ready to hear it."

"You don't love me," she said stubbornly, and she sounded close to tears. A very good sign, he thought. If she didn't care about him then his stupid-ass declaration wouldn't bother her so much.

He didn't bother arguing. "I'm going to leave this up to you," he said. "The ball's in your court, Angel. You make the next move. But I'll be ready when you are."

She bit her lip, and for a moment he thought she might be wavering. He took a step closer, just in case. But she took a step back, and he accepted the inevitable. For now.

"Don't take too long, Angel," he said. "And don't forget to blow out the candle when you go to bed. It's a fire hazard."

"I'll be fine."

She would, unfortunately. She didn't need or want him half as much as he needed her. But maybe that would change. It had to.

SHE WAS OUT of her mind, Angela thought. Totally and completely out of her mind. Brody Jackson wanted her, and he said it had nothing to do with Jeffrey. He even thought he was in love with her, though she had her doubts about that. But there was no doubt at all that he wanted her.

Almost as much as she wanted him. Which was the danger—she didn't want to risk that kind of cataclysmic relationship.

She needed time, she thought. He was right about that. He was right about a lot of things. He had no idea she'd spent seventh grade writing "Mrs. Brody Jackson, Mrs. Angel Jackson, Mr. and Mrs. Jackson" in her math notebook.

He didn't know just how pathetic she was when it came to him, and she knew she was going to have to tell him. Sooner or later. Preferably later. It was the night before Christmas Eve, her baking was done, her presents were wrapped, and maybe the safest thing would be to see if she could get a last-minute flight to Hawaii to have Christmas with her vacationing parents.

It would mean she wouldn't have to do anything about Brody for at least a week. She could just put him out of her mind, concentrate on the season.

And pigs could fly. Besides, Hawaii was no place to celebrate Christmas—Vermont was made for the season.

And if she made it through the night without going to him she was going to be amazed.

Did she believe him? Was she willing to risk it? There didn't seem to be any choice in the matter. Sometimes fate handed you a gift so powerful that you were afraid to grab it.

She went to the door, looking out the frosty pane of glass into the cold night air. It was a clear night, not a stray snowflake in sight. Nothing to keep her from going out, maybe discovering if he really meant what he said.

Her boots were already on when the phone rang, and she grabbed it, breathless, certain it was Brody.

"Get your ass over here," Patsy snarled. "I'm in labor, damn it."

And Brody would have to wait.

IF ANGELA HADN'T BEEN so exhausted she would have been highly amused. Patsy's manner of dealing with labor was to cuss everything and everybody, and even her husband's steady demeanor began to fray a little. Angela had had nine months of trying to talk Patsy out of a home delivery, but Patsy had strong opinions about everything, and Merline Kittredge was the best midwife in the Champlain Valley; plus, unbeknownst to the soon-to-be mother, the rescue squad was standing by, ready to whisk her off to Burlington at the first sign of trouble.

But there was no trouble at all. Harriet Patricia made her appearance after four and a half hours of very efficient labor, and she came out yelling almost as loud as her mother. Even Patsy was silenced by the sight of her perfect, healthy daughter.

"You're crying," Angela said.

"Am not," Patsy insisted, staring down in wonder at the tiny creature she'd just managed to deliver. "It just hurt."

"Pain's over, and you didn't cry during labor. You just cursed," Angela pointed out.

"Don't bother me. Can't you see I'm bonding like any good mother?"

"And I'm taking you to the hospital," Ethan announced. "You got to have your blissful crunchy granola back-to-nature home birth, and everything's fine, but we're going to check the two of you out and then we'll be right back. It won't take more than a couple of hours. Assuming the storm lets up."

"S-s-storm?" Angela stammered.

"Yup. A Christmas Eve nor'easter. They're figuring twelve to eighteen inches of snow, maybe more, with high winds and maybe even some freezing rain. If I were you I'd stay right here until we get back. We've got an extra bedroom."

"You think she'd drive in this stuff?" Patsy emerged from her rapturous examination of her infant for a brief moment. "She's the all-time wuss of the universe. Besides, she doesn't have to be anywhere. Her family's in Hawaii and there's no one else who matters. Is there?" She looked her calmly in the eyes.

"I should have never told you anything," Angela muttered.

"What the hell are you talking about?" Ethan demanded.

"Angie's in love."

"I am not!"

"With who?" Ethan asked, clearly bewildered.

"The same person she's been in love with since we were kids. Brody Jackson. The problem is, the only way she's going to get to him is through a blizzard, and she barely drives on cloudy days. And here it is, Christmas Eve, and there's never been a better time to admit it and be with him."

"Go to the hospital and get checked out," Angela snapped. "I'll be here when you get back."

Patsy smiled a catlike smile. "Sure you will."

They went off in the ambulance, driving slowly, the red lights flashing. They disappeared into the swirling snow almost immediately, and Angela closed the door behind them, leaning her forehead against the cold window.

Spending Christmas Eve with Patsy and Ethan and the brand-new baby was a perfect way to celebrate. It was safe and warm here, and people loved her, and there wasn't any risk of getting her heart broken, or driving off a cliff, or...

It was Christmas Eve, and she was too much of a Christmas slut to ignore it. She shoved her feet into her boots, pulled her coat around her and stepped out onto the porch. The icy snow whipped against her face like a cold slap, and the wind was howling down the main street, obliterating the lights and the town Christmas decorations. She walked down the steps, through the thick snow—they'd had almost a foot of snow since she'd first come to help Patsy, and it wasn't about to let up any time soon from the looks of things. The snow was mixing with pellets of ice, the kind that would probably cover every available surface and send her sliding into the lake. If she tried to drive in this stuff she'd die. It was that simple.

She managed to open one of the car doors, letting snow

fall onto the seat, and grab the snow brush. She started at the front, moving around the car, brushing off the thick, wet stuff, and by the time she reached the windshield again another inch had piled up. She was going to die.

Maybe the car wouldn't start. She climbed behind the wheel, knocking the snow off her boots before closing the door, and turned the key. The damn thing started like a charm.

She took a deep breath. "You can do this," she said. "All you have to do is drive very, very slowly. You can do this."

Unfortunately, no one was listening, especially not her subconscious. She shoved the car into gear, put the four-wheel-drive in low, flicked on the lights and began to inch forward.

She could barely see five feet ahead of her. Visibility was slightly easier with the lights on dim, and when she tested the brakes she only slid for a moment before the reassuring chunk-chunk sound of the antilock brake system kicked in. She had her seat belt on, and she was clutching the steering wheel so hard her fingers were growing numb. She turned on the radio—there were nothing but Christmas carols playing on Christmas Eve and she figured that might help her to breathe. Or at the very least she'd die in a state of grace.

"'Sleep in heavenly peace,'" she sang under her breath, an octave lower than the thundering choir on the radio. They didn't sound as if they knew much about heavenly peace or sleeping, but at least she could sing all the verses, and it *was* a holy night, a silent night, no sound penetrating the thick blanket of snow.

She missed the turn onto Black's Point Road. Well, not actually missed it—she just failed to put the brakes on in time and went sliding past it, off into the ditch at the side of the road.

"Near enough," she muttered, turning off the engine and the lights, leaving the keys where they were. If someone wanted to steal the car they were welcome to it. After tonight she might never drive again.

Except that her hands weren't shaking, and she no longer had that sick feeling of panic deep inside her belly. It was almost a sense of elation.

She was afraid she might get lost in the snow—on foot the visibility was even worse, the snow lashing at her eyes in the inky darkness. Her sense of time, of direction, was shot to hell. What usually took her five minutes to drive had taken her close to forty-five minutes. Her house wasn't far from the main road, but with her luck she'd stumble right past it and into the lake.

She hadn't left any lights on, not even her Christmas tree, but the faint glow was unmistakable. She knew what it was, and that it would lead her safely back home, and she no longer even thought to question it. When she stumbled in her front door the Christmas candle sat in the darkness, its warm glow filling the space.

If she had even half a brain at all she'd strip off her frozen clothes, build up the stove and get into bed. But she hadn't risked life and limb out on the roads because she had sense, or because she wanted to sleep alone. She picked up the candle and started back out into the stormy night.

The snow should have dowsed the flame. The wind

should have blown it out. But it stayed, straight and true, leading her through the snow-filled woods to Brody Jackson.

The house was dark as she climbed up onto the front deck. He hadn't shoveled since the latest storm had begun, and she had a sudden awful feeling. He hadn't said he was going to be there for Christmas, had he? And she'd pretty much told him she didn't trust him and never would. Why would she think he'd be there that night?

It was too late now. The candle had led her there, through the storm, and this was where she was meant to be.

She pushed the door open, and the wind blew drifts of snow onto the floor. She shoved it shut behind her, then turned to look at the room.

He was lying in the bed by the woodstove, sound asleep. The covers were at his waist, exposing the long, beautiful back that she still remembered.

It would have helped if he'd woken up, said something, but he slept on, the rat. She set the candle down on the table. The only other light in the room came from the small white lights on the Christmas tree he'd brought in. There were no ornaments on it, but it was surprisingly beautiful.

She was soaking, weighted down with melting snow, and she'd come this far. And only good things can happen on Christmas Eve, right?

She pulled off her jacket and boots and left them by the woodstove. Her jeans were soaked halfway up her thighs, and they were cold, clammy and uncomfortable, when she took them off. She was shivering, but she stripped off her turtleneck and her sweater, too.

Colder still. She needed covers and a warm body. She peeled off her wool socks, but at the last minute couldn't bring herself to remove her bra and panties. She tiptoed over to the bed, but he slept on. She picked up the covers and slid underneath them, close to him but not quite touching, holding her breath to see if he'd wake up.

He needed a shave. His long hair fell over his face, his mouth had a stubborn, sexy look even in sleep, and she put her head down on the pillow, feeling suddenly, unaccountably peaceful. She should be nervous, climbing into bed with a man when she wasn't sure she was welcome, but she felt very calm. Safe. Home.

"It took you long enough." He didn't open his eyes, but reached out his arm and pulled her up against his warm, muscled body. "Your feet are cold."

"Everything about me is cold," she said with a little shiver.

"Not for long."

It wasn't perfect. Sex wasn't meant to be perfect, graceful, elegant. But it was gloriously right. His hands knew just how to touch her, how hard, how gentle, how long. He did things with his mouth that she hadn't even imagined, and when he pushed inside her she climaxed immediately, unable to help herself.

He held her tightly as the spasms racked her body, an unending shimmer of delight, and when they finally slowed he whispered in her ear, "Hey, I'm not that good."

She cupped his face with her hands and smiled up at him dizzily. "But I am," she said with a mischievous smile. And she wrapped her legs around him, pulling him in deeper.

The night was too short, yet endless. They made love, slept, made love again, ate Christmas cookies and drank eggnog, then made love once more, and the light from the Christmas candle spread a soft, magical glow around the cavernous room.

When she awoke it was near daylight and she was sprawled across his body in a haze of total well-being. She could tell by the change in his breathing that he was awake, too, and when he spoke she lifted her head to see him.

"What the hell is this?" he said, holding up her discarded underwear. "Are there Christmas trees on your bra?"

She smiled at him. "Of course."

He groaned. "Oh, God. You're going to make me wear Christmas boxers next year, aren't you?"

"Absolutely." She put her head back down on his warm chest, closing her eyes as he stroked her shoulder. The early light of dawn had filled the room with a warm glow, almost like the candle. And then she opened her eyes, to see if it was still burning.

It was gone. The candleholder was still there, but the candle had burned to nothingness, not even a trace of wax left behind. Only the faint scent of cinnamon and cranberry lingered to remind her.

She closed her eyes again, letting out a deep, satisfied smile. "Merry Christmas, Brody," she whispered.

He put his hand under her chin, tilting her face up to his. "Merry Christmas, Angel," he said. "And a happy new life."

* * * * *

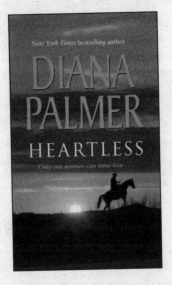

THE O'CONNELLS DYNASTY

Passion and seduction guaranteed!

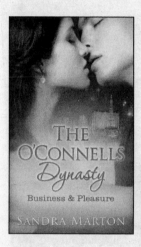
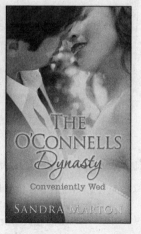

millsandboon.co.uk Community

Join Us!

The Community is the perfect place to meet and chat to kindred spirits who love books and reading as much as you do, but it's also the place to:

- Get the inside scoop from authors about their latest books
- Learn how to write a romance book with advice from our editors
- Help us to continue publishing the best in women's fiction
- Share your thoughts on the books we publish
- Befriend other users

Forums: Interact with each other as well as authors, editors and a whole host of other users worldwide.

Blogs: Every registered community member has their own blog to tell the world what they're up to and what's on their mind.

Book Challenge: We're aiming to read 5,000 books and have joined forces with The Reading Agency in our inaugural Book Challenge.

Profile Page: Showcase yourself and keep a record of your recent community activity.

Social Networking: We've added buttons at the end of every post to share via digg, Facebook, Google, Yahoo, technorati and de.licio.us.

www.millsandboon.co.uk

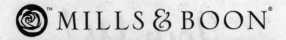